THE FILBERT RIDGE MIRACLE

THE FILBERT RIDGE MIRACLE

a novel

TAMELIA ADAY

WordCrafts

The Filbert Ridge Miracle
Copyright © 2024
Tamelia Aday

ISBN: 978-1-962218-07-8

Cover concept and design by Jonathan Grisham for Grisham Designs.

Published by WordCrafts Press
Cody, Wyoming 82414
www.wordcrafts.net

To my husband, Jon.

I

May 1, 1977

Alex McMillan raised the dead when she was seven years old. Patrick, her dad and pastor of The Lord is My Shepherd church, blamed the incident on her favorite baby board book, *The Story of Lazarus.*

The criticism zeroed in on Patrick's sermons and that he allowed Alex to sit in the adult services. Many members voiced their concerns following the event, saying if she attended children's church, she'd be learning about Noah's Ark and not performing miracles in the parking lot. "Messing with the order of things. There's a time to live and a time to die, and God should decide," as one elder put it. Patrick cleared his throat and pointed out what he thought should be obvious to them all, "and God raised Winston, so according to God, it wasn't Winston's time to die."

Where would the fallout land on this one? The McMillans suffered verbal abuse, never-ending gossip, and the occasional death threat due to misunderstandings related to doctrine.

Patrick knew, without divine discernment, that bringing Winston Brooks back to life would prove to be a poor PR move for his family, yet he quoted, "Blessed are the persecuted, for theirs is the kingdom of heaven." Days like these drove him to check his calendar, filled with pictures of beautiful palm trees and beaches. He looked for prophetic insight. Something that told him he'd be somewhere better soon. That Jesus was coming. But the sun rose and set again and again, and Patrick still remained with all the other Christians trying to be Jesus to the world. He looked to the sky, and in his mind he stood on an endless field of grass, all alone, the size of an ant. Where were the ones that believed in the power of God? Seeing Winston rise off the cement, like he'd been laying there for pleasure, made Patrick's blood pressure accelerate. With a glance, he knew the hearts of those closest to Winston. A lot of inheritance still on hold. No one attempted CPR, and Patrick wasn't sure if anyone called for an ambulance, but a child prayed, and heaven met earth.

Africa boasted of God-movements like this. Stories were told of people coming back to life and immediately wanting a cola. But here, in a tiny USA town, these kinds of miracles didn't occur, and the problems and the possibilities of what might happen already circled his thoughts. No one would appreciate the meanest man in town returning from the dead. Winston himself said he went straight to hell and was pulled out from demon claws when the little girl's voice penetrated the sulfuric air, exerting the force that saved him from infernal depths.

Despite suspicions of the townspeople, no one could deny that Winston went from being the twin of Scrooge to being the most generous man alive. His wife, who wasn't happy when she saw him come back to life, changed her tune. Within weeks she appeared ten years younger once realizing her mean old husband truly died and had been replaced with a gentle, loving, God-fearing man. It was hard for the common soul to grasp, but dying had scared the hell right out of Winston.

The sermon spoke of loving your neighbor—nothing that predicted an after-service resurrection. Before his death, Winston Brooks left during the fifth stanza of "Amazing Grace" as though flames licked at his ankles. The rest of the congregation filtered out to the parking lot at a more respectable time, standing about, chatting in the warm sunshine.

Patrick had Alex by the hand when the shouts pierced the air. They rounded a corner, and Winston's voice thundered to his wife from across the parking lot like a clap to call the reaper, "Hurry up!" Then he clutched his chest and toppled over nearly missing Vern, the oldest man in church. Silence descended, everyone stunned, as Winston crashed to the ground. Mrs. Brooks teetered across the pavement in her tall aqua heels, screaming at him to wake up.

Alex turned, jerking away from Patrick, and headed in the direction of the commotion.

"Alex!" He lost sight of her as she became engulfed in the massive entourage going toward Winston. Frantic, he pushed his way through the crowd, trying to catch a glimpse of his daughter. This would not happen to him again.

"Call an ambulance! He's not breathing!" a voice cried out above the murmuring. Yet, no one ran to the church building to use a phone. Patrick's legs wouldn't let him, not without Alex. Where was she? He called her name again, scanning the crowd, and then as his glance swept downward, he saw the blond curls brushing Winston's cheek, as she knelt beside him.

†††

Alex pushed forward, then sat next to Mr. Brooks, touching him with her small hand. She prayed in an unfamiliar language.

"What's she doing?" Mrs. Brooks screeched. "Get away from him!"

"Hey, get that kid outta here," someone else shouted.

"Whose child is that?"

"Preacher's daughter, the kooky one."

Alex heard her dad calling her name, his voice edged with panic like he fought his way through a wind tunnel. If only he could make her invisible. She pretended to be hidden by a mist and opened her eyes at the sky and pleaded for a cloud cover, heavy rainfall, or a supernatural fog. The sun lit up the pavement. No storm in sight. The shouts drifted away, the staring faces pushed back by a large hand, leaving her alone with Winston, and Jesus.

"Grab her!"

"I can't get closer!"

"I can't either. I keep bumping into something."

"Angels, they're everywhere!"

"Oh, for Pete's sake, Rebecca, you are always seeing those angels! Someone needs to get that little girl away from him. She's in the way!" Martin pushed himself forward, only to go flying back. "What was that?" He glared over at Gary. "You shoved me?"

"What are you talking about? I didn't touch you!"

Alex lifted her head to the sky. The scent of lilacs demanded life as a swift breeze rained bits of lavender onto the concrete. The chaos swirled around her, but she took the hand of Jesus and stood over Winston. "Winston, get up!" Not many heard the command, but everyone did take notice when the old man sat up, wide-eyed and dazed like a newborn baby.

Opening her eyes, silence mingled with the wind. People stared. The mist disintegrated—exposing her. A scream broke through the quiet, and a woman fainted. Alex turned and caught Mrs. Brooks frowning.

Winston stood to his feet, raised his arms high and let out a whoop. His pale face looked down, his blue eyes resembled rainbows, and she tore her glance away when he found hers. He went onto his knees and took her shoulders. "They were grabbing at me, they—they had claws and the most hideous faces, it was—I saw hell."

She tried to pull back from him, his touch sharp, from his long, yellow-colored nails. "Daddy!" she screamed. A whoosh of reality, like a punch in the gut went through her, as though she'd been in heaven and then rushed back to earth with no time to acclimate.

"Alex," Patrick appeared beside her. "Let go, Winston."

Mr. Brooks' hand fell away, and his head lifted to the sky. He looked back at Alex. "I won't ever forget this." A tear escaped, his smile radiant as he lifted his voice in song. The crowd stared. No one had ever heard Winston sing before. After a brief hesitation, some joined Winston in worship, while others ran to their cars and peeled out of the lot. A woman rolled down her window as she passed Patrick and Alex, her red lips curled in disgust as she uttered the word, "Witchcraft." Joe Brooks, Winston's son who owned a tavern, the Dockerbogger, stood across the parking lot, his arms folded, watching them. His eyes held hers from the distance. She looked away, gripped her daddy's hand tighter as they went back inside the church.

†††

Patrick could imagine the next step—meeting and talking it to death. He winced at the expression. Yes, they would decide that Winston hadn't really died. But then, he had seen hell. "C'mon, pumpkin, let's get Mom and the others." He held her tiny hand and wandered back inside to find Rose, who was often detained by either the curious or the needy. His body still trembled from losing sight of Alex in the parking lot. They ran into Robert first.

"What was that?" The fifteen-year-old scowled, looking from Alex to Patrick.

"That was a dead-raising, son."

"Who raised the dead?" His eyes held his sister's with suspicion.

"Jesus did," Alex piped up.

"Oh, no, please tell me Dad, she didn't do this."

"You heard your sister. Jesus did."

"Man, you know what they will do with a resurrection in the parking lot? And by her? Dad, they won't spare her just because she's a little girl."

"What'd Alex do?" Susan asked, skipping to her brother. Her black ponytails highlighted with pink ribbons made her blue eyes pop. She looked at her sister.

"She raised the dead," Robert said with a scowl.

"What?" Susan frowned. "Can she do that?"

"Jesus did," Alex said.

"Wow, that's cool."

"It's not cool, Susan, it's one more thing that makes us freaks. And of all the people to do it, it had to be her."

"Enough." Patrick found his voice. Tears pooled in Alex's eyes.

"Robert, you're a big bully." Susan glared at him as she stooped to Alex's level. "Who'd you raise from the dead, Allie?"

"Jesus told me to. It was Mr. Brooks."

"What? Mr. Brooks?"

Robert lifted his brow. "Great, it's worse than I thought."

"Robert! Let it go," Patrick warned. "Your sister did what Jesus told her to do."

"Right, can't argue with Jesus."

Rose came and stood beside her son. "What's going on here?"

The whole story spilled out again, and a whopper of a headache formed in the back of Patrick's skull.

Rose looked pleased. "Wow, I wish I would have seen that. How could I have missed such a thing?" She hugged Alex. "Good job, sweetie. Aren't we blessed, Patrick? I mean, this is the work of God! Revival is coming!"

"Uh, not to burst your bubble, but not everyone sees it in the same light," Patrick said.

"And let those who will, laugh and scorn—I shall not be silent; nor shall I hide the sign and wonders which the Lord has shown me," Rose quoted St. Patrick with ease, then bent down and spoke to Alex. "Remember, sweetie, Jesus used your childlike faith. You don't doubt it for a minute. We are going home to celebrate."

"Celebrate?" Robert mumbled. "More like picking our last meal before we are thrown to the wolves. Everyone will talk about us again."

"Robert, dear, they've never stopped, so let's enjoy ourselves." Rose smiled and lifted her face toward the sun.

"How are we going to celebrate, Mommy?" Alex asked.

"Strawberry pie, I made it last night. They weren't the sweetest, being from the store and all, but sugar covers a multitude of sins. In another month, we'll have fresh ones from the garden."

"Mm, yummy." Alex was all smiles now. Patrick breathed a sigh of relief. At least half the family was happy. He couldn't shake the fear that his resignation would be the next big event. The church board told Patrick upon hiring him that they didn't want any of his Pentecostal background taking over the services, and he informed them he would preach as the Holy Spirit led. They muttered among themselves about this unconventional method for a few minutes, then shook his hand, "No holy rolling and we'll be fine." Appropriate preachers must be hard to come by.

"I usually don't roll, sir," Patrick had said, not sure what else to comment on, since he didn't serve a religion, but a living God, and ultimately God was his boss.

That's how it started. He preached in a small town and to a congregation that feared the reality of the Holy Spirit. According to the majority, he'd married an eccentric woman, had misbehaved children, and played worship music. In order to preach his sermons, he tuned out everyone's opinions, and in doing so his own family suffered because he didn't notice the backlash Rose and the children endured until the damage was done. For Patrick, it appeared to be all lose-lose, until he got to the pearly gates.

Once back outside, herding the family into the car, he looked toward the sky. Yes, his spirit man was seated in heavenly places with Christ, and for a brief moment, Patrick closed his eyes and imagined his body and soul there as well.

"Patrick. Patrick?" Rose's voice broke through his attempt at transporting upward. He opened his eyes and took in the empty parking lot. A brief thought flitted across his mind—had they entered a new era? Unoccupied pews, or people wearing vacant stares. Patrick shook off the image. Word traveled fast in Filbert Ridge, then the opposite vision—and not with any less trepidation—a church full of show-seekers. The realization hit him like a blow to the stomach. He flinched.

"Are you all right, honey?" Rose's blue eyes, nearly transparent in the cold sunlight, jerked him back to reality.

He smiled. "Yes, can't wait for strawberry pie." He kissed Alex's forehead and then shut her car door, taking his place behind the wheel.

Driving home, he focused on his breathing and gathering spiritual strength. Every ounce needed to be accessed to endure the future. His thoughts strayed to the past; his grip on the steering wheel tightened. Had it been almost ten years already? He stepped on the gas, traveling faster through the tree-lined highway. The pain they endured—him, Rose, and Robert, might come crashing back, adding more victims, most likely Alex. People would talk, and just like when Stephen disappeared, it wouldn't be nice. In this case, there should be joy for Winston. But hadn't the power of God always brought controversy?

Beside him, Rose stared out her passenger window, searching the woods as she always did. He prayed silently, *Where, God, is our miracle?*

II

The next couple of weeks proved awkward in the pulpit. Distractions bounced from one pew to another with people checking out Winston for signs of relapse. Patrick wished he could close his eyes while delivering the sermon. Alex still sat right in front of him, which he preferred, despite the continued complaints. A wave of new enthusiasm hit some of the members, while a distinct displeasure skipped about, giving itself away on the faces staring at him.

†††

"I've invited them to dinner tonight," Rose twirled her dark hair into a knot. Patrick came behind her and nuzzled her neck. She leaned back into him, letting him hold her. He watched her in the mirror.

"I'm afraid to ask, but whom are we inviting?"

"The ladies."

Patrick quirked an eyebrow at her. "Aw, that explains it. Your lack of embellishment can only mean one thing, which brings my next question—why are you torturing yourself?"

"Well, I like to stay one step ahead of them, you know? And since the dead-raising they've been buzzing again, so to speak."

"What about the kids?"

"Susan will cover the other two's faux pas."

Patrick grinned. "You have great confidence in your plan."

"After I feed our guests, maybe they will calm down again. Or at least realize a little resurrection is nothing to get all worked up about." She went back to fixing a stray hair.

9

"I won't say my first thoughts on that one. Just remember, I love you." He turned her from the mirror and kissed her. The ladies, indeed. They were the equivalent to magpies.

He needed to be somewhere else for a moment and went into the bathroom and locked the door. Leaning against the counter, he crossed his arms and looked at the ceiling. "So, God, I'm going to need supernatural strength to make it through this one." He paused. "And please help my wife not be devastated when the old battleaxes do what they always do after she showers them with hospitality."

Patrick put his hand on the knob, stopped a moment, "And God, forgive me for calling them battleaxes." He left the refuge of the bathroom. Rose had him beat on not having any resentments. She also never lost hope, constantly expecting this time to be different, thinking the best of those around her, always waiting for outcomes Patrick had long since considered impossible. He took a deep breath and resolved, "It's show time!"

"Family meeting," Patrick spoke through the door of Robert's room. He found Alex reading a book, and Susan came into the living room.

"Dinner guests tonight," he told the three pairs of expectant eyes.

"Really? Like the last two weeks haven't been enough?" Robert threw a glance simmered with emotions in Alex's direction. "Dad, this is a bad idea. Remember when—"

"Robert, please, let's focus on tonight. Your mother has gone to the store to get something special to make. This dinner gathering—she needs to do this. She is attempting to smooth things over."

"Smooth things over? Since when? People talk, and the party lines only make it worse."

"Listen, just try. Robert, no glaring. Alex, no staring."

"Wait, what do you mean?" Alex asked.

"You stare at people, and it freaks them out," Susan said.

"It's 'cause they feel guilty. They assume you can see into their soul, and now, since the dead-raising, they are really afraid of you," Robert said.

"They are not afraid of Alex. She's a little girl," Patrick started.

"Once again, you haven't heard what's going on. You don't know what people say," Robert continued his rant.

"I have to keep my head clear, otherwise I can't stand in front of them and give a sermon. I'd be too busy wondering if they are saying stuff I don't want to hear."

"Hello, Dad, they are."

Patrick stared at his son. When had this happened? This way of speaking, so . . . belligerent? He sighed. "It's for your mother, okay? Susan, distract the guests from bad behavior."

Susan smiled big, and Patrick's heart sank. Teenage years flashed before him. She was only nine now, but she'd be beautiful. What had he gotten himself into? Why hadn't he remained single instead of being responsible for—he looked at each one—this brood. He'd already lost one of them. His head spun.

"Daddy, are you okay?" Alex tugged his hand.

"Sure, Pumpkin." Innocent blue eyes met his, and he asked for forgiveness again. After all, he was blessed with a beautiful, wonderful, albeit high-maintenance family. They needed him—surely he could rise to the occasion. He pushed his previous thought back into the place where experiences, events, and embarrassments lie dormant. Can't change the past. "All right then," he forced a smile, "let's do it!"

Robert rolled his eyes and went back in his room, slamming the door.

"C'mon, Alex, let's find pretty dresses to wear." Susan skipped through the hallway, her sister following.

Patrick stood alone in the living room, and for a moment he saw the floor, as the sea of glass in Revelation, shatter beneath him, and he fell—shards like diamonds flew through the house. Then silence.

Rose walked in, humming, with arms full of groceries, interrupting his vision of the living room being attacked. Patrick went to the door to help her. "Thank you," she glanced at him. "You're pale, dear. Are you sick?" Her brows furrowed in concern.

"I'm fine. So, what are we having for dinner?"

She set a bag on the kitchen counter. "I'm playing it safe with a lasagna, salad, garlic bread, and a dessert to die for," she giggled. "I guess I shouldn't use that phrase. It could *raise* some problems."

"I'm glad you can laugh at this mess." Patrick followed her and unloaded the groceries.

"Now, dear, we are pioneers of a new future. The church is going to change. Soon, we will be in a new building—the timing couldn't be better. I've seen it in my dreams. The power of God is going to flow, and he's using a young generation. People will attend church to commune with God, to worship Him, to spend time with Him—not just sit and listen to some sermon."

"Thank you, you've given me great job security."

She flashed a smile. "There's nothing wrong with the sermon, Sweetie. I'm saying the resurrection in the parking lot was not just a physical one. It marked the land the church stands on, representing the unsaved that will rise and call Him Lord. I've been waiting for this—the moment of change. New life is upon us. We will get what we lost. He'll come back."

Patrick's stomach twisted. She delivered her prophecy, but what was tacked onto the end made him doubt the rest. How many times would he have to endure this? "You mean Jesus, right? Of course, He'll come back. It's what we all wait for, to be—"

"No, I mean, of course, but I'm talking about Stephen. Goodness' sakes, you act like you've forgotten—"

"Rose." Her name came out sharper than he intended, and she flinched away from him. "Darling, of course I think of him every day, but it's been almost ten years." Would it be less cruel to hit her with a dose of reality? Robert was right. He may be a sullen teenager with a big chip on his shoulder, but this dinner party wasn't a good idea.

"Cancel dinner."

"What? I can't now."

"You can."

"But, why?"

Why? So she wouldn't disappear for hours every evening. So he wouldn't hear stories of her wandering the cemeteries because she longed to be closer to the dead than the living after some dinner party that didn't change how people perceived her? Her mania would be out of control and depression would claim her like a demonic force. He shuddered. He couldn't take it. Not again.

"He's not coming home. I'm sorry, but it's been too long." How had he let her delude herself all these years? It'd been easier than facing this.

She stared at him. "You're wrong." And then turned away to set out the food.

"Rose."

She set a salad bowl down with a thud. "We had a prophetic word from someone who didn't know us. You were there. They didn't know about Stephen. News coverage wasn't enough; posters weren't enough. There are people on the other side of the state who didn't even hear about it. How can you be so hopeless?"

"How? Because I've waited every day for him to come back, and he doesn't. Because I've seen enough prophetic words never come to pass. People aren't always hearing from God like they think they are. He'd be twelve years old, Rose. Missing children don't appear after ten years." His voice had risen, and he now faced the pain in her eyes mixed with anger that flashed fire. He hoped the children hadn't heard, because he vowed to never speak of Stephen in their presence. *Back off, Patrick.* What was he doing? Trying to destroy her before the dinner guests arrived?

She blinked back tears. "Twelve," she whispered.

Patrick pulled her close, letting her cling to him. A long moment passed. "Please, Patrick, I can't cancel dinner."

He buried his face in her hair and breathed in the floral scent. "I know, I don't want . . ." to hurt her? Well, he took care of that already. Now and ten years ago.

They would target her with their sword-like tongues, wagging about her eccentricities. He watched as she cooked; "Patrick, no weapon formed against us will prosper." She glanced at him with a smile.

He smiled back, but the niggling of doubt brushed his mind, as soft as the light stroke of a paintbrush, barely perceptible. He swallowed. "Is there something you want help with?"

"No, go relax before they come." She shooed him away with her hand. "Makes me nervous, you standing here, watching. I might burn dinner."

Patrick turned away, going back into the living room. He sat in his recliner. Some TV to forget why he'd let her talk him into staying in this town. Getting back up, he turned the channels, flipping the dial—*click, click, click*—then settled for the news.

Most families would have fled, gone somewhere new, but not the McMillans. They stayed to endure hell. Rumors of what was wrong with Rose burned the phone lines like a forest fire—from split personality, psychopathic behavior, to actual demonic possession swirled around them. But she was just a heartbroken mother. Couldn't he have talked her into a nice house on the beach? Surely, the ocean could compete with a lush green forest. But she always hoped Stephen would come back, and how could he ever find them if they left? The kid had been almost two and a half, and barely verbal. Not much chance of finding them anyway, but Patrick couldn't be cruel to Rose.

Stephen had been making good progress at the time of his disappearance—a few words, more eye contact, as though his soul had returned, bit by bit. Another miracle for the McMillan's and then the unthinkable happened. He vanished, without clues or a trail. They waited for him to come back, each day lingered—hours stretching like a late evening shadow, and now, after waiting year after year, another dead raising in the church parking lot seemed more likely.

Patrick's faith couldn't match Rose's. He was realistic. Despite prophets and promising prayers, his disbelief caught and carried him, like a blue helium balloon that went up and eventually became one with the sky, no longer able to be seen. When the one-year mark without Stephen went by, hope let go, deserting him. Rose hung on. But the missing child made her less whole—a puzzle missing its last piece. Patrick knew the dinner parties let her forget her pain, however brief, but nothing good came of having company. Time with *friends* sparked trouble, like a match set for arson.

†††

Meredith, Claudia, and Vivian, well-dressed with a hint of various perfumes, arrived together. Being twenty years older than Patrick and Rose, they often acted as disapproving parents. Patrick opened the door, letting them parade inside, and a scent of chocolate drifted through the entryway. Meredith and Vivian had salon fresh perms, except Meredith's had a mind of its own, going all directions, in a vibrant shade of red, while Vivian's appeared sophisticated and tame. Claudia kept her short, sleek bob all polished and silver, and her makeup in perfect place.

"Good evening, Pastor." Vivian came inside.

"Patrick." Claudia brushed by him.

"Rose insisted we bring nothing, but I couldn't. I brought brownies. I know the children love them—hope she won't care."

"Not at all, Meredith. She's in the kitchen." Patrick pointed toward the right. He glanced in the hallway, and spotted Robert glaring at them.

The evening progressed without event. Susan took up being the life of the party, bringing out compliments from the women. "Such a beautiful, witty girl," Vivian said. "My goodness, Rose, you teach this girl to cook as well as you and she'll be a catch for a nice young man someday."

Patrick cleared his throat. "Way off in the future, however."

Meredith cackled. "Oh, just like a father. None of them want to see their little girl snatched up, but it happens."

An odd silence fell around the table. Robert's expression turned to ice, and Alex watched them, with a strange expression on her face.

Claudia cleared her throat. "Yes, flawless manners that girl has." She pointed to Alex. "You could learn a lot from your older sister."

Alex said nothing, but kept staring above their heads. The women gave each other a look—one that would sear the phone lines later in the evening.

"The girl is in la-la land, if you ask me," Vivian chimed in, nodding toward Alex.

"No one asked," Robert said, taking his last bite of lasagna. Everyone stared at him.

"Well," Rose let out a small laugh, "I think it's time for dessert. Meredith brought some lovely brownies."

"I'm having strawberry pie," Robert said.

"Me too," Alex smiled at her brother.

"Brownies are great!" Susan said, a bit too quickly, but the women laughed, breaking some of the discomfort.

Patrick took a deep breath. *Disaster averted, for now.* "I think I'll have both." *Seemed the safe decision to make.*

"I have vanilla ice cream for anyone who would like," Rose said, sounding extra cheery.

"Let me help you, Rose." Meredith stood and went to the counter to help portion the desserts.

"Goodness, child, what are you staring at?" Vivian snapped her eyes on Alex.

Alex jumped, leaning toward Robert. "Black shadows, hanging over you, all of you."

Vivian laughed, filling the room with barbs of warning. "Such an imagination you have."

"It's not—"

"Alex sees things all the time. It's no biggie," Susan said.

Patrick could no longer taste his dessert.

"I think she should go to the doctor," Claudia took a sip of her water. "No dessert for me, Rose, dear." She turned back to Alex.

"You realize, it's not normal to see things. Really, Patrick, why don't you get the child checked out?"

"She's fine, more astute than the rest of us," Patrick said, taking another bite of strawberry pie.

"Astute? That's what you call it?" Claudia clucked her tongue and shook her head. "She needs some manners. It's not okay to say whatever you think, or whatever you *see*."

Alex frowned. "Mrs. Vivian asked me. I've always been told it's rude to not answer adults, unless you are by yourself and you don't know them."

Patrick hid a smile by taking an extra big bite of ice cream, paying for it by having a coughing fit.

"Goodness, Patrick, you needn't inhale the dessert." Rose gave him a pat on the back.

He took a swig of water, hoping he made them forget about Alex. The choking had been a bonus, buying more time.

"Oh, she's the smart one," Claudia said, ignoring Patrick's interruption. "Resembles you, Rose. She has secrets behind her eyes."

"First you say she blurts out everything she's thinking, and now you're saying she has secrets? Which is it?" Robert asked.

"Oh, Alex is only seven. She can't have secrets yet," Susan said. "Miss Merry, these brownies are wonderful, especially with the ice cream on top." She flashed an enormous smile in Meredith's direction.

All eyes turned toward Susan, and some of the tension left the table. "Why thank you, dear. It's as simple as can be. I bet you could make them all by yourself."

"I'd like to try."

"It's pretty easy. Comes in a box," Robert said.

"Robert, Miss Merry's are homemade. I know she makes nothing from a box. Pure cocoa in these," Susan took a big bite.

Patrick stopped eating for a minute and stared at Susan. "How do you know anything about how Meredith cooks?"

"The Girl Scouts go over to her house, Dad. We help her with the yard, and she gives us dessert and sometimes teaches us cooking."

Unlike Alex, Patrick knew why dark shadows hovered over these women. "I didn't realize." He stared at Meredith.

"Yes, well, the girls are helpful."

"Do you go to Mrs. Vivian's too?" He steeled his gaze across the table, watching Vivian pick at her dessert.

"Oh, no, Daddy, just Merry's. That's a good idea. We should—"

"No, you shouldn't."

"Patrick." Rose's tone warned him.

A pain started in his chest. *Just play nice for a few more minutes.* He forced a smile. "The dessert is wonderful."

Rose smiled back, relief in her eyes.

"Yes, Rose, you've outdone yourself, as usual. It's been too long since we have enjoyed your family. I take it, Alex, that you will be joining us in the children's class on Sunday?" Claudia asked.

Alex shook her head.

"You know, Patrick, you might have her join the children. I mean, after the most recent disruption, and you know, her seeing things—"

"Alex prefers the adult services. As far as disruption, I'm not sure what you mean?"

"The parking lot incident, of course. People shouldn't be hearing that going on."

"What are you referring to?"

"The tongues. She shouldn't be speaking in tongues. Others might get the wrong idea. Don't think the board isn't discussing it. Joe Brooks is especially upset with the way things were handled that day."

Patrick paused. "I suppose he'd prefer his father to have been carried off on a stretcher with his head covered. And Joe Brooks is not a board member."

"Paul does it. In I Corinthians 14:18," Alex piped in, ignoring the *Joe* comment.

"See, she misunderstands. The grown-up service is too big for her."

"On the contrary, Claudia, it's actually too serious for some of the adults."

Silence followed, while Claudia turned tomato red. "Your sermons are hardly too intellectual that we don't comprehend them."

"Oh, no, they're not difficult at all. Claudia, it's a matter of being in tune with the Holy Spirit. He reveals to you beyond anything I say. I'm not important, but He is. Children are often more open to His bidding than adults." Patrick drank a big gulp of water, comfortable in his topic, until he saw the look Rose seared him with. What? Had he said something so terrible? He paused, trying to neutralize whatever offense he created, then grinned. "The adults could attend the children's services." He glanced Rose's way, who rolled her eyes at him.

"Like topsy-turvy day!" Meredith laughed, but the comment appeared to have earned negative points from her two companions.

And so, the evening sputtered to an end, and they all went out the door, giving thanks to Rose. Claudia gave Patrick one last admonishment, "The board will review the incident further."

"Thank you, ladies." Patrick shut the door as their feet left the threshold.

"Okay, everyone, shake off the negativity." He shook himself to be free of whatever they brought in and left there. Alex and Susan joined him with enthusiastic giggles.

"Where's your mother?" He looked around.

"She left through the back door," Robert said, and spun back into his room.

Patrick froze. "Susan, please take Alex and play a game with her or read a book."

"Daddy?" Alex's eyes filled with tears. "Did I do something wrong?"

"Of course not, Sweetie. Go play with Susan for awhile, all right?"

She followed her sister to their room, dragging her feet.

Blast those women! Patrick gripped the back of his chair, not sure he could endure another one of his wife's breakdowns. Why did he let her have these parties? The stories spun around them, and he kept preaching, as though the whispers gathered no strength. He ignored the incoming storm.

Patrick looked out the window. Rose stood in the distance, at the edge of the yard, facing the darkness of the trees, her white dress flowing in the wind. Patrick's dread lifted. She hadn't left. He grabbed her coat and went outside to coax her back in, away from the memories of the woods.

III

October 7, 1967

The festival in Filbert Ridge, Oregon, came early, and many wondered if they had followed the usual tradition of celebrating the hazelnut harvest on the second Saturday of October, perhaps lives would have gone in a different direction—but instead families and town history changed forever because that was the day Stephen McMillan disappeared.

It was October 7, 1967, and the town committee had decided an earlier festival would mean better weather—a tad warmer, and more people would come and spend the day replenishing the council's slush fund. They threw in some new events, like the hokey pokey—*fun for all ages*—but drew the line at Meredith's idea of speed knitting for the sedentary crowd. The weather ended up being a tolerable sixty-four degrees and the wind nearly non-existent. Not a day where you'd expect anything unusual to happen.

Patrick should have recognized the voice of the Holy Spirit and obeyed the call to golf. He had an overwhelming pull toward the greens that morning but had promised to take the boys to the festival. Six-year-old Robert couldn't wait to get his face painted like a cat, and bring home a balloon. Stephen, at two, did not have any prior memory of the festival, but he always wanted to ride in a car, and this desire was as fierce as Robert's wish for fun. Gathering the boys and their jackets and Stephen's sippy cup, Patrick set off to the filbert orchard, a short drive from their home.

Corn dogs, chili dogs, hamburgers, and caramel apples had their own stands, but the most decorated table advertised the filbert. Plain or paired with chocolate—it had versatility. The boys, however, veered toward the swirls of cotton candy. Stephen smiled at the floating colored sugar and some of the tension eased off Patrick's shoulders as he followed them.

Children ran loose through the orchard, but Patrick hung onto Stephen's hand to keep track of the boy who was prone to escaping. His arm grew weary of being pulled at full length between Stephen's two favorite things, the woods, and the make-shift parking lot. He picked him up, but struggled to hold the whining, squirming toddler.

"Let the boy run a little," Vern commented, shuffling past. "Look around, he'll be fine." Patrick nodded, avoiding a reply. Turning, he ran into another couple who stopped on the other side of him. "Where's Rose?" The woman asked as they stared at Stephen who resembled a cat that did not want to be held.

"She's a little tired." The answer was short and safe. Rose avoided the festival every year.

"Oh, I imagine so. Pregnancy can wear you out. When is she due?"

Patrick tried to recall the woman's name. They were new to the congregation, and he fumbled for it, but Stephen got antsy to continue moving. "February."

"Be here before you know it. Hank and I have been trying for a while." The silence that followed demanded divine direction, and Patrick faltered for something to say. Hank's response saved him. "All in God's timing." Possibly seeing a toddler in action made the man less enthusiastic.

"Children are a blessing," Patrick smiled, putting down Stephen who immediately pulled on his arm, yanking him away while the couple stared after them.

"Dad!" Robert stopped and pointed near his feet. A Garter snake slithered by in the grass. Patrick welcomed this distraction and let go of Stephen's hand, having the boy stand next to him to watch, while Robert took to poking a stick at the creature. Patrick straightened, letting his arms dangle at his sides, and then rubbed his shoulder. In the distance, a couple argued near the vineyard display. Gary and Caroline. He'd counseled them many times. He turned his attention back to Robert. His older son deserved some of his time and these days often got overlooked because Stephen had grown to be a handful. The quick break refreshed him from the constant tugging. Caroline's shouting made him glance back. She pushed her finger into Gary's chest, and he batted it away, swearing at her.

Robert laughed, and Patrick shifted his eyes back to the entertainment with the snake. "Look!" It slithered onto its next destination, and barely missed someone's shoe. Patrick chuckled and reached for Stephen's hand.

Except he was gone.

Patrick's eyes swept over the distance, then took in a closer range. Nothing. Well, he couldn't have gone far. Patrick turned to gaze in the other direction. A mop of blonde hair caught his eye and relief flooded through him. He took a hurried step. The child turned, and Patrick stumbled back. It wasn't his son.

Patrick's breathing came faster. He called for Stephen. His mind clicked like a slide show with those times Stephen would explore and wander off without looking back, Rose chasing after...

Patrick's throat tightened. He shouted his son's name, but his voice staggered across the playing children and meandering adults, blending with the soft breeze and laughter.

A commotion came from the wine tasting table. Through the distance, Patrick saw Gary lifting his glass and declaring the end of his marriage to Caroline. "A toast to my second bachelorhood."

"Here, here!" Joe Brooks gave a cheer as his eyes followed Caroline, who walked away.

"Yeah, Joe. You especially will benefit from our break-up," Gary said, no need of a microphone, his voice carrying between the separation of Patrick and the field that stood between them.

"You're the one making a big announcement." Joe pulled out a flask and took a swig, as Patrick got closer. "I'm not the only one who cares," he grinned in the distance.

Patrick could hear the cheers followed by antagonistic voices. Gary again. He saw Caroline in tears going toward the cars, but had to pretend he didn't see her, because the only thing that mattered was finding Stephen. He continued dragging Robert, who was crying, through the crowd. Joe's laughter filled the space between him and the wine tasting tent. No sign of his little boy anywhere. He needed access to the loudspeaker and fast.

Approaching the table of wine glasses, all set in a row, the music for the hokey pokey came on full gusto, drowning out Patrick's shout to wait. Truman announced the event and the masses followed the tune to join the fun which would end with the bunny hop. Gary and Joe were no longer there—only Vivian and Meredith talking about some crazy out-of-towner, who had tasted everything offered, from wine to chocolate hazelnuts, before running back into the woods.

"You might want to check on Rose, Patrick," Vivian said when she saw him. "I believe he's been living outside, you know how that sometimes happens—hippies living off the land and smoking dope." She looked closer at him. "What on earth is the matter?"

Patrick barely heard her. "Vivian, I need the loudspeaker. I've lost Stephen." Everything took too long—her sentences about the woods, his telling her the need of the microphone. A clock ticked with his every breath—Stephen becoming a speck too far to reach.

It was then that the woman noticed Robert and frowned. "Here? You lost him at the festival?" Her tone indicated he was crazy for bringing the child, but this gave Rose a break. Some cotton candy, face painting, and a pony ride were favorites of any two-year-old, weren't they? "Let's go to Truman. Make an announcement." She liked to take charge. Meredith gave him a panicked glance, and his heart rushed with fresh fear.

Caroline's red van sprayed gravel, and the tires roared onto the road, as Vivian had the music stopped. The squeal of the loudspeaker came on, and Truman announced the need to search for a missing boy. Patrick picked up his son, who had thrown himself on the ground, protesting against taking one more step. Ignoring Meredith's offer to watch Robert, he headed toward the woods. The last thing he needed was two missing boys.

Patrick stepped into the trees calling Stephen, shouting over and over again, as though repeating his name would make him appear. But Stephen didn't come. Robert, exhausted, his face red and eyes swollen with tears, wanted to go home.

Home.

Patrick didn't know how he was going to tell Rose. His prayers went up into the cloudy sky, and crashed down onto his heart.

IV

May 16, 1977

The traffic to Portland was a slow drain of sludge, but Patrick's thoughts rambled as though someone was in there dialing radio stations. He hadn't talked to the detective in charge of Stephen's case for some time. Receiving a phone call to meet the investigator for coffee made his pulse race as he sat in the morning commute. Howard had told him to come alone—that bringing Rose wasn't necessary, her intensity making coffee hour draining instead of stimulating. Patrick and Howard needed their moments of sipping java to be calm, like a gathering of sanity, before going over the insane reality of a child missing for almost ten years. He gripped the steering wheel tighter as a car cut him off and raced ahead. Everyone was in a hurry.

Exciting news would require both him and Rose to be present. This particular request of Howard's made Patrick think he wanted to discuss something besides Stephen—golf, children, or his marriage. Maybe he needed pastoral advice.

Patrick's thoughts jumped from one idea to another, never finding a place to rest, like popcorn in a popper. What were those things called—synapses of the brain? Well, he was no Einstein, so he wasn't sure why God made his thought life extra jumpy. *Right, Patrick. Blame God.* Then there was Alex. She was a bright one. Slamming on the brakes, he jolted forward. *Traffic is a bugger.* He heard the English accent, and he flipped on the radio to quench other random thoughts, arriving at Howard's office without further incident.

†††

Howard Trent leaned back in his chair with his feet up, and a mug sat next to him that read, "Golf is my second wife."

"So I'm right," Patrick sat across from him. "In need of marriage counseling?"

Howard let out a laugh, took his feet off the desk, and poured coffee for Patrick. "You like it? Delores found it for my birthday. She's a generous woman to share, don't you think?"

"If her only competition is a set of clubs, she has it pretty good, I guess." Patrick took a sip, his eyes taking in the stack of newspapers on the desk.

"You don't want to see these yet." Howard nodded toward the cup. "Drink up."

"That bad, huh?"

Howard shrugged. "Depends on your perspective." He reached beside him and shoved a box in front of Patrick. "Donut?"

"Uh, no."

"Guess you got enough baked goods. It's a miracle you stay thin, considering Rose's skills."

"Yeah, well, you know, I'm in the business of miracles."

"Ha! Which brings me to the topic of today." Howard's white teeth flashed against his cocoa skin. "Might as well read it." He placed the newspaper in front of Patrick.

The Lord is My Shepherd church conquers the 'shadow of death' in the parking lot on May 1. The doer of the deed is seven-year-old Alexandria McMillan, daughter of Pastor Patrick McMillan. Some say it's as fake as a tabloid, others proclaim it to be the work of the devil. Rose McMillan, Alexandria's mother, has

*quoted Saint Patrick, who was accused of
raising 39 people from the dead himself.
"It's a move of God," she said. "A new
beginning. An open heaven."*

Patrick tossed the newspaper aside, and Howard handed him another. "Accused? Is it a crime to raise the dead?" He went on to read the next headline:

*Winston Brooks of Filbert Ridge,
Oregon, sees hell and lives to tell
about it.*

He regarded Howard. "You find this amusing, don't you?" He saw the smirk that could only be detected by the slight upturn of one side of the investigator's mouth.

"This could be a good thing." Howard handed him the next paper.

*Filbert Ridge, where people disappear
and come back to life. Will the lost be
found?*

Patrick wasn't sure what Howard was getting at, but the next headline made his stomach roll.

*Stephen McMillan missing, since Oct.
7, 1967. This town and family are back
in the headlines. "Attention seeking,"
Beulah Chains of 'Stuff and More' claims.
"Was there ever a Stephen McMillan? I
tell you, half of us don't even remember
him."*

"What?" Patrick read in disbelief.

"And this." Howard pointed at another caption:

Filbert Ridge: fact or fiction?

"Who is Beulah Chains? What's Stuff and More?"

"Someone in Portland. It's a store with ... stuff." Howard grinned.

Patrick rolled his eyes, tossing the last paper on the desk.

"The way I see it," Howard started, "is that this brings people back to Stephen. We might get some leads. I've got phone calls already."

Patrick fingered the stack of papers.

Howard continued. "So far, they aren't helpful calls, but this is getting the case noticed again, and people, like Beulah, good press or bad, make it happen. Now's the time to get pictures out—updated drawings, and put it on the news again. Teresa can work on a more current sketch to help generate attention. A photo of Robert, one of you, and one of Rose—all at the age of twelve is what we need. We can do blending. He favors you, and Robert favors Rose, but the planes of the face with some study can give us a good drawing."

"How could it be possible?" Patrick couldn't let himself believe and didn't know how Rose did it. To keep expecting. Could he survive to hope that hard and have it explode into nothing?

"This is your subtle way of asking me if I believe he's out there. Alive," Howard said. "Not my job. I keep hunting for answers. I should warn you, the freak factor is high here."

"Pretty used to it."

"The good news is, any kind of news, especially freaky news, will get you noticed."

"Right." Past experiences of stories leaking out describing the McMillans as odd got them attention, yes. Helpful? Not really. He would have to debrief Rose, and now he wished she had come to wade through all this herself. He couldn't describe this meeting the way a woman would want him to. Every detail. Patrick already separated the unimportant from the facts. Beulah had fallen to the wayside.

"Great plug for the church, too, huh?" Howard folded a page, showing him the ad.

The Lord is My Shepherd Church: come join us! Sunday worship service at 11:00. Possible miracles in the parking lot following.

Patrick groaned. "Why the delay? I had two weeks of fairly normal services. Some new faces. Nothing overwhelming."

"It takes time for small town excitement to spread to the actual town. I believe you have a mole, so to speak. Someone spread the word. Perhaps the board you always refer to? After all, it is good publicity."

"The board specifically told me they didn't want any of this stuff."

"Yeah, but what if they realize it brings attention? Puts your church on the map. Maybe they changed their tune."

"What about Alex? How do I protect her from this?" Was he sacrificing one child in a possibility, as small as a particle of air, that he'd find the other?

"If the girl can raise the dead, she can handle some attention. No need for her to see the articles. She doesn't read yet, does she? Don't watch the news." Howard fingered the papers. "Otherwise, I don't know. Keep her close by." He grimaced. "Sorry, man. I'm just saying—"

Patrick held up his palm. "I know. She's seven, she's never far. Unfortunately, she reads everything. I'll do my best, though." And he had to do better than in the past.

V

Rose took out the day's goodies. Cinnamon rolls, muffins, cookies, and cupcakes lined up to be decorated, yet her mood was anything but sweet. These days her job at Tilly's Bakery left her on her own more often than not. Oh sure, she put on a good facade, but the past two weeks she'd gone from the joy of the Lord to anxiety—a combination of fear and despair. She didn't like the attention. It was never the good kind either. The woods were her sanctuary. Being alone, her and God, and the forest animals. But because of this, the people who knew sneered, 'Snow White,' making comments about dwarfs and witches. Wasn't Snow White the good girl? If they were going to compare her to a Disney character, especially a happy, singing one, then she should benefit from it. No luck for Rose. She set a cupcake next to her steaming mug. A little sweet to counteract her bitterness. She preferred it without frosting.

She hopped onto a bar stool and dangled her legs, stirring the coffee she made earlier. The morning light made an appearance. The shop wasn't open yet. Patrick would be meeting with Howard today, and the thought made her antsy. There wouldn't be any news of Stephen, otherwise she'd have been invited. It was probably about golf. The pleasure of putting a ball into a tiny hole was a mystery, but hey, it brought joy to hard working men, somehow.

Tilly burst in. Her real name was Atilda, and she threatened death to anyone who dared call her that, so this made her a one name wonder in Filbert Ridge. Not Atilda Stewart, but Tilly the Pie Lady. She spied the half-eaten cupcake. "Oh. That bad, huh?"

Rose shrugged taking in the energy of the slightly plump woman. Tilly's golden locks swirled in curls with a sprig of silver here and there. Her dark brown eyes flashed with more energy than all Rose's children put together. Alone was good and hard to come by. The Tillys of the world chased away obsessive introspection. "Good morning." Rose stood, reaching for a cup. "Do you want some coffee?"

Tilly waved in impatience. "Nope." She poured herself a glass of ice water, her expression glum as she went to turn the sign. She pointed toward the door. "We got company early."

Claudia stood outside the window, staring at the display case with a frown and marched inside the instant Tilly unlocked the door. Rose had the uncharitable thought that letting her in was equal to substituting arsenic for sugar.

Claudia paced in front of the glass case of goodies. "This is the reason why we have become known as Fat Filbert Ridge," her disdain dripping like caramel. "Do you have anything diet? Or sugar-free?"

"People who come to bakeries aren't asking for either, Claude," Tilly said.

Rose noted the cringe on the older woman's face at the shortening of her name.

"Perhaps a baguette?" Rose offered, forever the peacemaker.

Claudia gazed at the long, skinny loaf as though the bread soothed her. "Hmm, sounds almost appealing, sure I'll take that. I'm sorry dear, I suppose I'm a little tense."

"You suppose?" Tilly *hmphed*.

"Sugar-free is all the rage. You might want to consider it. Lots of diabetes around here. I personally love Tab. Of course, Rose, if you serve these baked goods, you will give the church more opportunities to raise the dead. The board is saying a monthly event would bring in better crowds. People are more apt to attend for some spectacular show."

"I don't understand. There isn't a death once a month, and I'm pretty sure we haven't stooped to murder in order to construct a resurrection," Rose said.

Claudia dug through her purse for change. "You are the funny one, aren't you? Obviously, murder is not on the agenda. You know—healings and..." She pulled out the money.

Tilly clucked. "That's why I attend church at the Community Center. None of that hocus pocus going on."

"Claudia, it's not a show, where we use the power of God as entertainment. And Tilly! Hocus pocus?" Rose's role as peacemaker thrown out like burnt cookies.

"Oh, Rose, I wasn't meaning anything by it. It's just, you know—I need a church service I can predict. You sing, you take the offering, have a sermon and promptly at noon you go have lunch with some of the members." Tilly nodded. "Like clockwork. Makes me feel secure."

Secure? "We want to take time to be with God. We like to be open to possibilities." She turned to Claudia. "And we don't schedule them to happen."

"Yeah, well, you know. God can do stuff anywhere, and I can take time at home." Tilly tapped the counter as though timing Claudia's visit.

"Martin is hoping the board will consider—" Claudia eyed the cinnamon rolls.

"Martin?" Rose's voice went up, and she scrunched a cupcake wrapper. "Martin has a track record of causing trouble. Tilly, would it hurt you to open your spirit so God can break the wall you put in front of yourself? Let Him find your heart?"

"No offense, Rose, God doesn't need to find my heart. He put it there, didn't He? And Claudia, you tell the board what they think of less sugar. Because even if you believe everything they say is gospel, I'll be baking the same as I always do."

Claudia paid for her baguette, her lips tight. "Good day, ladies. I pray you are able to have peace despite selling fattening sweets."

Tilly huffed, punching and kneading the dough as though she

was killing something. "Mark my words, Rose, that sugar-free stuff is going to send people to their graves."

Patrick opened the door to his office to find coffee brewing and a baguette from Tilly's lying on his desk next to an apple and a granola bar. His work area constantly sprouted food, and he never knew where it came from, which made him leery. He thought of the book of Isaiah where it claimed you'd have food you didn't harvest. That was him. Before he could break off a piece of bread, more newsprint, this time from the neighboring town of Dockerbog, landed on his desk.

Revival or an attempt to re-invent church? Are the dead only in Dockerbog?

"What is this?" Patrick asked Zach, who did the janitorial work at the church.

"The only news Dockerbog ever had, I believe."

"This isn't even their news."

"Neither is this." Zach turned the page and pointed to a headline.

Stephen McMillan—is he the next miracle?

"And there's more."

"Seen it," Patrick gestured toward the stack next to him.

Zach put on his reading glasses and peered over the stories. He chuckled. "We gonna have everyone in the parking lot gazing at the clouds after service on Sunday? Or the church will be filled with the dying and near dead?"

Patrick grimaced. "It already is."

"Lots of opportunity then." Zach grinned, then turned, whistling his way to the storage room.

Rose left the bakery early. Tilly insisted she take time for herself. Robert often watched Susan and Alex when both she and Patrick were gone. She heard them in the spare room playing Monopoly. Her thoughts, like they did every day, drifted to Stephen. Stephen was the firecracker. At six weeks old his eyes lit up with life and his personality could be seen. Stephen had been into everything. He would have been the *pizzazz* in the family recipe, but she had been denied the experience. The family functioned around the hole in the puzzle. Someday the picture would be complete, but they'd never regain what they could've had. Every one of them missed out, and sometimes this thought made Rose ill.

Patrick came in and stopped short at seeing her. "You're home early."

"So are you." She eyed the baguette.

"Everyone is trying to make sure I eat."

"Doesn't make sense. Don't they think I feed you?"

"Perhaps they are trying to poison me."

"I can tell you where the bread came from."

Patrick raised his eyebrows. "Tilly's, I'm sure."

"Yes. Delivered by Claudia, most likely since she came to the shop."

"Ah, well, that explains my hesitation to eat it."

Rose pointed to the bag. "Patrick, darling, it's half gone."

"Guilty. With every bite, I prayed it wasn't coated with cyanide." He came closer, his eyes crinkling as he grinned.

"We've watched too many British mysteries," Rose said. "How'd the meeting with Howard go? Anything new?"

His flirty, teasing expression changed, and an invisible wall went up. He moved away from her to the kitchen. "I'm going to put this in here. You can use some of it for dinner if you dare."

He avoided the question. Why? Something bad? Had to be something bad. "Patrick?" How many times had people whispered that those prophetic utterances regarding Stephen coming back were ridiculous? She blocked out the naysayers and put her heart into what she wanted to hear. Never would she let herself consider the possibility the prophecy had no merit. Her spirit knew, didn't it? Then why did fear grip her stomach? Every time a body of a toddler was found, her faith mocked her. *See you don't believe.* She'd walk around not functioning or sleeping until the results came. Not Stephen. And then the relief mixed with guilt because that meant someone else's child was dead. Patrick hadn't emerged from the kitchen. She went in to find him staring out the window.

"Patrick, what is it?" Her voice shook, and tears formed.

He turned and looked at her. "As far as the case goes, don't you think I'd tell you if something definite came to light?" He sounded impatient. She bit her lip.

He sighed. "I gotta preach a sermon to a bunch of people who are expecting a miracle in the parking lot later. You want to know what's going on, besides Claudia bringing me food?" He went to the kitchen table and flipped the latches of his briefcase. The stack of newspapers filled the space. With a wave of his hand he said, "There you go. This is what we're dealing with. A big mess. Sometimes—God forgive me—but sometimes I wish the dead-raising hadn't happened at all."

A moment later the front door slammed, and Rose hurried to the window that looked out into the yard, to see Alex flying toward the woods.

✝✝✝

The wind in Alex's ears pounded with the thumping of her feet. If only it could drown out the words her dad had spoken in the kitchen. The blackberry bushes scratched her bare legs and snagged at her shorts. A vine flew at her cheek.

Her dad hadn't known she was about to go in and get a glass of milk. Her steps had slowed, hearing the tone of her parents' voices. Unhappy. And then, as though a haze cleared around her, she heard the topic of discussion. Alex raced out the door and dashed across the yard into the woods.

Did she wish the same thing as her dad? She didn't like to believe it, but right now she searched her heart and found she was running from herself. It was like seeing your reflection and finding chocolate on your face after you visited a fussy aunt.

Her mind untangled what it had denied. The wish that she hadn't been in the parking lot with Daddy—and hadn't rushed toward the screams. Why hadn't she stayed with Susan or Robert? Or Mom? Three other choices! But then, what would the alternative be? Winston in hell? She remembered shouting at Winston, and holding Jesus' hand, but now could no longer feel it. She stopped and closed her eyes, trying to picture Him looking at her. She wiped her cheeks with the back of her hand, seeing blood from where the blackberry thorn pricked her skin. Her legs burned, and she leaned down, plucking out a sliver. The treehouse was only a few steps away.

"Allie?" A voice called to her from above. Jesus didn't call her Allie, but Jimmy did. She looked in the distance toward the sky. Part of her hoped the treehouse would be vacant, and part of her wished for her cousin Jimmy to be there. It marked his yard from the woods that connected with their house. Feet dangled over the edge. Adam Langley. Great. Her friend Breely's brother, who liked to tease.

Jimmy stuck his head out of the opening. "Come up, Allie cat!"

She climbed the wooden ladder, and when she got to the top, Adam reached out and helped her inside. He grinned and started to say something stupid. She could tell by the smirk on his face, but then his expression changed. "Hey, what's wrong Lexie?" He was the only one who called her that, and for some reason it made her face scrunch up, and she looked away sobbing.

The last few weeks, filling her with one tear at a time, bubbled over. The dam inside her soul weakened. It contained the mean things people said and the disdain she'd caught in their expressions when she hadn't quite turned away. This barrier broke, and the tears spilled down her face. Frantic, she put the wall back, sniffling, while Jimmy handed her an embroidered handkerchief from a box in the corner of the treehouse.

"Where'd you get this?"

"Mom's."

"Oh." She glanced at the box, tucked out of the way, holding various items Jimmy treasured.

Jimmy's mom had passed away when he was too young to remember her. "Dad cleared some stuff out." Alex always heard that Uncle Peter smiled more and laughed out loud when Emily was alive, but returned to his sullen, isolated ways after she died. Oddness and Peter clung together like a dog and bad breath.

"I'm all right." She turned away, clutching the hankie.

"Sure, Allie," Jimmy's green eyes squinted at her like a cat. Leaning back, he clasped his hands behind his head, and stared at the ceiling. "It doesn't take a genius like me," he grinned, "to tell that you are not okay."

Jimmy was ten, and because of his use of big words and penchant for causing disruptions at school, he'd been subjected to IQ tests. It was determined that he was brilliant. Alex wished for that excuse. She was just a weirdo.

"And then there is me, of average intelligence, that can tell you are upset," Adam said, offering her some Pop Rocks. "Grape."

"Thanks." She poured some in her hand and they all sat in the silence, listening to the candy pop and fizz inside their mouths. She sat by Adam, dangling her feet next to his. He was eleven, a million years away from seven.

"I wish I were normal. That I didn't raise the dead. That I couldn't see stuff. Maybe there *is* something wrong with me. Claudia says there is. Then I wonder if Jesus would be mad at me for caring what people think because if Winston didn't come back to life he'd be in hell. Maybe I am selfish like Vivian says." She quit breathing to stop the tears, and her fists clenched as she dug her nails in her palm, now sticky and smelling of grape.

Adam took her fist and pried her fingers loose, rubbing her palm. "You're not selfish." His family attended church as often as hers, but when Alex watched Breely, she didn't think Bree had many thoughts toward heaven, while Alex contemplated eternity all the time. Despite teasing Alex and Bree, Adam seemed in tune with God, albeit in a more practical way, like reading his Bible and memorizing verses.

Alex knew all the big words and spiritual meanings from attending "big church"—a phrase used to describe a room without children. In children's church, she got antsy with all the stories she'd heard a zillion times, and constantly feared they were going to play games. Alex would cling to Adam's sister because she was uncomfortable with the other girls, but she and Breely were not compatible—like library versus amusement park. Adam on the other hand was calm. They had a baby sister, Laura, who, from what Alex had seen, would give Bree a run for her money.

"Ah, Allie, those old ladies are jealous that they don't have connections with God like you do," Jimmy said. Unlike the Langley's, Jimmy rarely went to church, especially since Uncle Peter only darkened the foyer on Christmas and Easter.

"And Jesus is not mad at you," Adam said.

Easy to say, Alex sniffled, even though Adam's brown eyes looked like they spoke the truth.

"C'mon, Allie. You know better. Deep inside you know," Jimmy chimed in, and she gave him a glare that said his opinion wasn't reassuring. He sat up. "Can't you ask Him? I heard about a lady that had coffee with Jesus every day, and He told her stuff."

"I don't drink coffee."

"Not the point, goofus. I bet He prefers cocoa, anyway."

A rustling was heard below. "Alex?"

Everyone peeked over the edge and found her dad peering up into the treehouse at them. "Sweetie, come home."

"Here, take these," Adam handed her another package of Pop Rocks. These were red.

"Thanks." She stepped onto the ladder's top rung.

"See ya, Allie cat," Jimmy said.

Her dad grasped her hand, and they walked back home. "Alex, I'm sorry. I didn't mean what I said. You know, sometimes the human part of me wishes we weren't in this situation, but I know it is right. You did the right thing, and I wouldn't have it any other way."

Her body relaxed. "Sometimes I wish I was like everybody else."

"Ah, Pumpkin. I've never wished for that. You are perfect just the way you are."

Cocoa had been made for her return, whipped cream overflowing the mug. She sat at the table, wondering if Jesus really liked chocolate, and then she was overcome with exhaustion from the emotional evening and went to bed. As she lay there, her thoughts pictured the day's events, seeing Jimmy's red hair go straight upside down when he hung his head through the treehouse entrance, hearing Adam call her 'Lexie' as his brown eyes warmed over hers, the sound and taste of Pop Rocks, both sour and sweet, then fizzy, and the smell of rain that hadn't yet come, as her dad took her hand and guided her back home.

VI

Henry stopped short at the crack of the open door when he heard his mother's voice. A peek told him she was on the phone, and he turned to go back into the kitchen for a snack when he heard her say, "A dead-raising?" This made him pause and listen. Her curly hair was tied in a sloppy ponytail, and when she glanced at the door, he stepped away from the opening, and she whirled toward the window. Her freckles stood out against her skin and he wondered if she was sick. The cord stretched too far, and the phone went crashing to the floor.

"Oh, man, just a minute." She picked it up, setting it back. "Are you still there? Sorry." Despite the phone cord inhibiting her movement, she paced back and forth like a wild cat in the zoo. "Oregon barely knows New Jersey exists. Heck, Oregon barely knows Filbert Ridge exists. I'm keeping my end of the bargain. I hope you are keeping yours."

She didn't say anything for a few minutes. "You told me you had this all under control. You can't go back after all these years, none of us can, inheritance gone or not."

Henry leaned in closer, darting behind the door when his mother made another abrupt turn.

"You know what I think? You want to have your cake and eat it too. You don't have any bargaining chips because you're in too deep. Listen, the kid is on his last day of school, and he can be home alone with Minnie, here, watching out for him. I'm coming out there, let's say early June, to remind you of what you're missing

41

and to knock some sense into you." She gave a little laugh. "Who'd have thought I'd have to be the voice of reason?"

Henry's stomach growled. Oregon, capitol—Salem. He knew exactly where it was because he remembered everything he studied. Right now, he didn't care and had no clue why his mom would. She didn't make a whole lot of sense anymore. He'd been at a friend's house for an hour already after school and had hoped to find some sort of snack or dinner preparations happening, but it appeared unlikely. He and his friend planned a big party for the end of sixth grade. Next year, junior high. But he should be thinking of what he'd make for dinner. He knew his mom's moods. She often went into fits of irritability, taking Valium all day long, and by the looks of her, *she* needed to be raised from the dead. He left the door ajar and went into the kitchen. Guess it would be mac and cheese for him tonight.

VII

Patrick was rifling through paperwork when the phone rang. Today he sat alone in the office, but Zach, the janitor, could be heard, here and there, throughout the building. "The Lord is My Shepherd church," he answered, leaning back in the office chair.

The voice on the line was soft and defeated. It took him a moment to understand between the sobs. Lilian Langley. Her husband, George, had been as reliable as a midlife crisis, and now succumbed to one. Laura cried in the background. "Lilian, why don't you come by while Adam and Bree are in school? Bring the baby. I'll have Rose join us." Lilian would appreciate her presence, not to mention the extra help with Laura might be needed.

Lilian agreed in a monotone 'yes' and a sniffle.

After calling Rose, Patrick went back to sorting papers. The name Caroline Randall jumped out at him. This was more than paperwork; this was sweeping up the past. Caroline had been a fiery redhead who left the church. When was that? He found the date of their last appointment. October 3, 1967. Ten years. She'd been unhappy, acting like he owed her more than a counseling session. Said he led her on. He didn't understand how she justified her conclusion. At the time, he was a married man with two sons and a baby on the way. Stephen disappeared, and Patrick's life became a blur. Caroline was pretty much forgotten, until her husband Gary came to him and explained she'd gone to New Jersey. "Far as she could get, I guess," he'd said with a shrug.

Patrick wondered how many hours overall he'd spent on marriage counseling. Did good results ever happen? Many couples came as though they were filling a requirement—check off the box—*yeah, we even went to counseling*. Put in a good effort. All along in their hearts they had already quit.

Hearing Lilian and knowing her husband George acted like a teenager with zits, distressed Patrick, as though he'd put his trust in a blow-up raft with a slow leak. The Langleys were good friends. But George changed, or had hidden his true self. To have George leave his family for a waitress at the Pirate Pub in Dockerbog was a shock. He'd told George not to be stupid. Told him the grass always looked greener, and in the end, you were stuck with a whole new set of problems. George complained that Lilian wasn't any fun. She didn't like dancing or hanging out at bars. Her choice of drink was iced tea. George had shifted his life from faithful husband, father, and friend, to a needy partygoer in search of free love—a late sixties bloomer embracing flower power at a pot-belly age. He was headed toward regret because he would someday wish for the front porch swing and a jug of sweet tea, while holding his wife's hand. But by the time he did, the past would be out of his grasp. He was settling for a few minutes, months, or maybe years of pirate booty.

Patrick had seen the pattern a few zillion times. In 1967, the song was Gary and Caroline. Different couple, same story. Except both of them were pieces of work.

✝✝✝

Evening at home came way too late. Rose left the girls' room and settled next to Patrick on the sofa. He held her hand for a moment, "How about I get the pie and ice cream tonight? You made it, right?"

"Yes." She wondered why he asked. And why he offered. She generally served the evening dessert after the children had theirs. She must look as exhausted as she felt.

"Just making sure in case I was poisoned earlier. I don't want to take the chance of the toxins accumulating and be dead by morning."

"Don't get your hopes up, dear. We all want to go, but you aren't leaving me here yet." She giggled, and he kissed her.

"But you still say I'm going first. That's what I heard," he said.

She rolled her eyes. "Focus, Patrick. Dessert."

He grinned. "Right."

A few minutes later, he came back with the strawberry pie and ice cream. "I cleaned out some files in the office today."

"When did you find the time?"

"Before and after."

"Poor Lily."

"I could throttle George," Patrick said. He stabbed at his dessert, sounding ungracious. "I found Caroline's file today."

Rose's stomach twirled, and her heart accelerated. After all these years that woman's name still stirred a queasy emotion. A sign she hadn't forgiven. She tried, and sometimes succeeded, but unforgiveness had a way of popping back like a pain from a cavity.

"Then Lilian called, and I thought, *Here we go again*." Patrick glanced at her. "What?"

"Lilian is nothing like Caroline."

"Of course not. It was just the timing."

"You know Caroline tried all her tricks on Joe at the bar, too." Rose took a big bite of strawberry.

"I don't know if I'd consider Joe an innocent in that scenario."

"When it comes to Caroline, *everyone* is innocent. I didn't believe that you'd been out with her like she said. Nor did I believe the phone calls I got telling me you were at her house."

"Phone calls?" Patrick paused mid-forkful.

"Yes, Patrick. And I'm sorry to say once I checked, only to find that you were not at her house as the caller claimed. I couldn't help it."

"Why on earth didn't you tell me?"

"I was afraid of saying any of it out loud, as though that might plant ideas that weren't there, I—then Stephen disappeared and everything—well, nothing else mattered." She whispered his name, as though if the children heard, nightmares would be induced.

"And the calls?"

"Stopped." Rose set her dish on the coffee table in front of her. "The last day I saw her is such a blur. You'd taken the boys out and she came by, trying to tell me how you were going through the motions with our marriage. Said you found her captivating."

"Captivating?" Patrick almost snorted. "Has the word captive in it, which I was held in my office while listening to her complaints about Gary. She was here? At the house?" He stared at her. "On that day?" He popped up from the couch, putting his dessert next to hers.

Rose bit her lip.

"You ever mention this to Howard?" Patrick paced.

"Only in passing." Their life divided into two parts—before and after. "It didn't stand out because she was here, with me, so despite all her antics, she couldn't stoop that far. I can't imagine, Patrick."

"When did she leave?"

"I don't remember." Should she? Her mind scrambled, sifting through archives. Painful ones.

"And we never really considered her?" Patrick's voice raised a notch.

Rose stared at him. "I don't think so, I mean, Patrick. She. Was. With. Me." She enunciated every word. "What is wrong? Why are you...?" She watched him bolt from the room and then he came back and tossed a newspaper on the coffee table.

Stephen McMillan: Will he come back from the dead?

She covered her mouth. "What is this?"

"I didn't show you all the newspapers, Rose. Howard's having updated sketches done. The dead-raising has brought it all back." He said it too loud. Rose gave him a warning look.

"Okay, wait, I remember." She pictured it in desperation, his tone giving away its importance. "The phone rang. She left after I answered," Rose said. "I remember her standing there for a second, and then signaling that she had to leave, but I barely paid attention."

That brief expression on Patrick's face—what had it been? Hope? Whatever it was, Rose saw it leave—so fleeting—like it hadn't been there at all.

VIII

October 7, 1967

It was a piece of heaven, having the house to herself. Rose puttered about, stepping outside once in a while to breathe in the autumn air—her favorite time of year. Soon the maples would be turning yellow, and their leaves would drop like a slow rain. Her kitchen sparkled, her bathtub gleamed—if only this moment could last longer. She lucked out, having these few hours. Festivals made her a nervous wreck, and she managed to get out of going every year.

Rose turned back into the house, pausing when a red van came flying into her driveway. Caroline emerged, leaving the car door open as she walked with purpose toward the McMillan home.

Rose wondered briefly if the woman was on something. Drugs were a common problem throughout these parts because of the isolation, and Caroline had been having major marriage upheavals with Gary. Not only that, Rose had been receiving phone calls saying Caroline and Patrick had been seen together for more than counseling. And Rose had not missed the subtle body language Caroline displayed near him. Patrick, on the other hand, was oblivious, and Rose was ninety-nine percent sure—depending on Rose's own insecurities—that nothing went on between them. Today, Caroline Randall resembled anything but credibility. Her red curly hair stuck out in disheveled strands, and mascara leaked down her face.

Going into Pastor's Wife mode, Rose tried for the sympathetic approach. "Caroline, are you okay?"

"Do I look okay? That dope of a husband of mine just sealed our divorce. Patrick is a fool to think I'd try to work it out and stay with him. Gary is a Neanderthal. It's in his genes! Did you know he's a true Viking? He's from Minnesota. I should have known better."

"Well, Minnesota is hardly a red flag, is it?" Rose soothed. "Come in for some tea."

"Tea?" Caroline walked in and sat at the small table in the breakfast nook. "You have any vodka to go with it? I wanted a normal marriage, kids, picket fence, a dog, and a cat. I have nothing. Oh, I take that back. I have a ton of jewelry. Gary gives me rings, necklaces, brooches, every time I suggest we have children. Now instead of the simple life I want, I can console myself with diamonds, emeralds, and sapphires." She twirled the gigantic rock that decorated her finger as she sat at the kitchen table. Rose set on the kettle for tea, despite the lack of hard alcohol in the house. Grabbing the scones from breakfast, she placed them in a decorative bowl.

"I have unfiltered honey from Meredith's." Rose put it on the table as if it were a consolation prize.

Caroline paid no attention. "You're lucky, you know. You have this home, set in this beautiful scenery, and two boys, not to mention a baby on the way. Maybe it will be a girl this time." Her eyes swept about the kitchen and the window that displayed the woods.

"Wouldn't it be nice? I always wanted a girl I could sew dresses for."

"That Stephen keeps you so busy I don't know how you are going to fare with another, let alone have time to sew," Caroline's voice turned into doom. "Guess some of us have more than enough while others have nothing."

"We will manage, I'm sure."

"You don't sound too sure. Is there something wrong with your youngest?" Caroline asked.

Irritation made Rose stand and clean one of her already wiped down countertops. "God gives each child his own personality. Stephen is smart. I personally believe he is absorbing his world with so much intensity he hasn't quite had time for us. Perhaps he still has one foot in heaven. We all start there, you know, in the hand of the Father."

Caroline snorted. "You have to believe what you want, I guess, to make it through. I know I do the same with Gary, making constant excuses for him. Being heavenly minded isn't one of them though, for sure. I just think your life would be a lot simpler if both of that boy's feet were planted firmly on earth. I mean, *one* boy is a lot of work. I have a nephew—I know." She nibbled at a scone, and her eyes slid toward Rose. "And then with Patrick, he may not be as dedicated to you with so many kids. We have spent many hours talking about our lives. He finds me captivating."

Rose thought how three children weren't that many, and it was lucky her impatience was startled away by the ringing of the telephone. "Excuse me for a moment." She might have let it go, being she had company and all, but Caroline had overstepped guest boundaries by criticizing one of her children. And to go on about Patrick!

She picked up the black receiver that sat on a table at the end of the hallway. The news on the other end sent coldness throughout her body. Her ears buzzed, and her vision tipped as she sank to the floor, the teakettle whistling in the distance.

IX

Patrick was stuck in time. The past sat at the McMillan's door-step daring them to move forward—one step too far and Stephen would be gone forever. Having the case back in the limelight was a positive turn, but Patrick feared Rose wouldn't survive the hopes that came with it. He'd lost faith and prepared his heart to watch hers be shattered.

Dim lights from the overcast day fingered in through the slats of the blinds. In his melancholy, he hadn't bothered with the light switch of the church sanctuary, but sat for awhile and closed his eyes, trying to form a prayer. Sunday was coming, and he wasn't looking forward to dealing with the media fiasco.

And then he heard it. Music. His adrenaline shot up for a second, before reality crashed with dread. He had not been whisked to the clouds. It wasn't a trumpet.

Patrick opened his eyes and Stella, the pianist for Sunday mornings must have slipped in. She stopped playing.

"Good morning, Stella," he said, falling back to earth like a roller coaster going downhill. "Hello, pastor." She fidgeted with some music, avoiding his eyes, but grabbing the sheets and smoothing them. "I've come to tell you I won't be playing anymore." She gave him a quick glance, then focused on the window.

"Oh, are you all right?" He walked to the back of the room and flicked on the lights. Maybe her hands were giving her trouble.

"I'm fine. I just can't be a part of this church anymore. I tried, since the . . ." she cleared her throat and gazed into the distance and then back at him, "the incident, but I prefer a church that is a little more grounded. You know what I mean?"

Grounded. Like a plane that couldn't take off. Like not seeing shapes in the clouds, or hearing angels sing in the wind, or seeing the dead rise from the cement. Yeah, he knew what she meant. "I'm sorry to hear that."

"I'm afraid others are doing the same."

He nodded, not needing the bigger picture she painted for him. "Looking for stable ground."

She stared at her hands. "I wanted to warn, or, uh . . . tell you . . . so you wouldn't be unprepared. I've been talking to Martin, and he suggested that I find a different place to worship, you know? Since you are moving into a new building in August, the timing is convenient. At first, I thought I'd stay, but the news articles . . . Martin suggested the Community Church, and many are considering going there. They don't believe in . . ." Here she faltered and gathered her purse and music. "I'm sorry." And darted through the nearby door, the outside exit banging shut.

✝✝✝

Rose needed privacy. To get away. To forget for an hour or so. She wandered the bookshelves of Brooks' Books. Maybe a bit of poetry would soothe her. She randomly selected T.S. Eliot.

"This is not how things are done." The statement came from the sci-fi section, a room off to the left. "It will cause chaos."

"There is always chaos, Claudia." Vivian's voice carried across the shelves.

"But to have Stella go to him? Acting as though she's starting a coup? She even mentioned Martin."

"She had to tell him something, or there'd be no piano player on Sunday."

Rose tuned into the conversation, staring down at the words of John Keats, instead of Eliot. She'd grabbed the wrong book. She regarded the open page, reading with her eyes, but listening with her ears. Their voices dimmed, and she flipped through the poems, no longer seeing the words. Another voice piped up, louder than the first two.

"Like a giant oak, split, not in half, but a branch as big as a normal tree, blocking the path," Meredith was saying. "I don't have dreams often, and when I do, they make about as much sense as that lady in the hardware store."

"Your problem, Meredith dear, is dealing with any tool. The dream, however, can only mean one thing." Vivian said, "The smaller branch is blocking the road. The path God has set before us, perhaps? We'll find out which side the pastor lands, but I'd be careful to put too much stock in a dream."

They were coming. Rose moved to the end of the aisle and around the other side so they wouldn't see her. She lifted her eyes to the section she stood in. Memoirs. Pablo Neruda. How had she come to this point? Hiding among poets and Nobel prize winners—hearing pieces of her life discussed in science fiction.

She turned to flee before they saw her, and ran smack into Joe Brooks.

"Whoa, going somewhere in a hurry?"

He held onto her arms a little too long. She found herself speechless as she stared into his blue eyes, brighter than the ones in her family. The stubble on his face showed a day of skipped shaving, only adding to his good looks by giving him a rugged edge, spelling danger in many ways. *Be aware of appearances,* Patrick always said. She backed away, but not soon enough.

The women came from around the corner, discussing their new fitness class and stopped short, just as Joe let go of Rose's arm. The silence surrounded all five of them. Rose recovered with the grace she'd trained herself all the years of being a pastor's wife.

"Hello, Vivian, Meredith, and Claudia." And then her brain let her down, and she couldn't think of anything intelligent, witty, or serious to say.

"Rose; Joe." Vivian tapped the book she was holding. "You two browsing the shelves?"

"Well, not together," Rose stammered.

Joe let out a hearty laugh. "But Rose, seriously, and I'm sure you ladies will agree, the papers are talking about us again, so we need to display the new sketch. I see you have the recent one here at the store. Of Stephen. Drop one by at the Dockerbogger." His gaze brushed hers. "We tend to get busy when there is any unusual news."

"I will have Patrick bring one by," she moved farther away from him. He smiled at her, and with a nod to the ladies, he went off to another part of the bookstore, leaving her standing with shaking legs, still holding a book of love poems.

X

Alex knew her mother started fixing supper every day at 4:30 regardless of what she made, "because otherwise, I'll be too tired to cook at all," she'd say, but would still wander the hallways on some nights, as though she had energy to spare. Tonight, Patrick sat with her on the sofa, while she paced.

Alex couldn't sleep and around midnight left her bed for a small glass of milk, but stopped short at the sight of both her parents up at the late hour. Usually her mother would help her because of the dark shadows between the door and outside. It was always at night when Alex imagined someone stepping in and snatching her, never to appear again, and no one could ever say it didn't happen, because she knew it did and had. Oh sure, no one came into the house, but still. Then in the light of day, all her fears abandoned her, and she freely wandered about without a second thought to kidnappings and stories of little girls taken by white vehicles while riding their bikes. These girls were always found dead. That was the difference between them and Stephen. She sometimes wondered if Stephen was dead too. If he wasn't, who took care of him? Her mom believed he was alive. Every so often, Alex overheard her parents talking about Stephen when they thought no one could hear. She wasn't sure what Dad believed, but now, seeing a glimpse of him on the couch, he looked sad. Like the mole in *The Wind in the Willows* when he wandered the woods alone and would have died if it weren't for the badger saving him.

Who could save her dad from despair? Would there be a go-between that would stay with him until he was found? Like Rat? *We river-bankers, we hardly ever come here by ourselves. If we have to come, we come in couples at least; and then we are generally all right.* But Stephen hadn't been. A brother, only a mere ghost to her, bounced back in her thoughts, and she wondered if he found a rat to guide him, or a badger to take him in.

Alex crept away, leaving her curiosity of why her dad sat on the sofa in the middle of the night. She no longer wanted milk and sensed how her parents were close together, but something rested between them—an invisible chasm. On the wall, across from where Patrick sat, a picture of Jesus watched the room with concern. If circumstances were different, it could be perceived as peace. Loving comfort. She went back to her bed and hid under the covers, picturing Jesus holding her as she fell asleep.

✝✝✝

"Good morning." Patrick tried to sound cheery at the sight of Alex, while Rose cooked a Mexican omelet. Berries graced the table in a crystal bowl, and the smell of coffee offered hope for a new day. Should he be worried that the church might collapse from the inside out? Last night he fell asleep, telling God it was His church, so if He wanted to fragment it into various pieces like a bomb, then that was His gig. Patrick was done. Washed his hands of the whole mess. Here you go, God. Unpackaged. Not pretty. Burnt on the edges.

Rose put his plate of food in front of him. She hadn't spoken much and her eyes were puffy. Patrick wondered why if he had given God the gift of a disintegrating church, his stomach persisted to roll at the sight of the melted cheese.

"Tabasco," Rose said, putting it in front of him without eye contact.

Sure. Add a little fire to his gut, like a match striking dry wood. He paused, seeing the flames kick up at the edges of the church, surrounding the old building, turning it into ashes. Isaiah

61:3 popped in his memory. "Festive praise instead of despair." A crown of beauty for ashes. His life resembled a fire pit. Bring on the s'mores.

"Cocoa." Rose brought Alex a cup, piled with whipped cream.

"Thanks!" Alex dipped her spoon into the white waves.

Susan showed up and was treated to the same beverage.

"Yum!"

Patrick poured some coffee.

"You've gone all out this morning."

Rose smiled, but it wasn't happy. Years of being married and he could read the smallest gesture, right to the shift of the eyes. And all this food cooked trouble. To Rose, cooking and baking equaled a night at the bar drinking all the woes away. He was a lucky man, indeed, except these bouts of Betty Crocker made his waist expand, and the grocery bill soar. Psychological stability slipped. He watched her take out a sharp knife and slice an onion. Drinking his coffee, he managed a bite of the omelet, then added the Tabasco.

"Rose, sit and eat," Patrick said. Her flitting around made him more nauseated.

"I'm not sure I'm hungry," she said as Robert came in, glanced around with a lift of his eyebrow, and headed for the cocoa on the stovetop, pouring his own cup. He leaned against the counter and stared at Patrick as though to telecommunicate. At that moment, Patrick realized Robert, having just turned sixteen a few days ago, appeared older. A veil lifted, and Patrick knew Robert could see all was not right with his mother. Patrick nodded toward the table, and Robert came and sat by Alex.

"You seriously gonna eat all that?" Robert studied Alex's plate filled with a Mexican-style breakfast and a bigger than normal bowl of berries, to which she had added whipped cream.

"I'm starving."

Robert grunted and then his plate came, complete with toast.

"We'll need to find a new piano player," Patrick said, as though Rose didn't already know this.

"It gives an opportunity for some of the young people. Eva, for example?"

"Perhaps you can give me a list. We might need more than one option," he said. She finally met his eyes. The understanding between them settled. It wasn't known how many would be leaving. Patrick wondered if anybody would be left to play for, but then remembered the papers advertising the church as though it was an event. He put down his fork.

"You okay, Patrick?" Rose asked as she eyed him.

"Just a bit queasy, I guess."

"Oh, well, don't worry about the food. We've plenty of children that can eat your portion." She smiled as he noticed the heaping plates and saw it was true. They were all hungry this morning.

"I'm going to head to the church. Call me later about the music."

"Sure. Would you'd consider a guitar as well? Many churches have guitars. It goes with the newer songs."

Patrick paused. "At this point, I'll take what I can get."

"What happened to Stella?" Robert asked.

The three of them looked at him expectantly. Patrick sighed. He'd almost made it out the door. Why'd he bring it up at breakfast anyway? Why didn't he just go and announce that they would be on the evening news once the new composite sketch made it past Filbert Ridge and Dockerbog? Why not voice his every thought, and drive to the edge of the state, letting the ocean consume him, or stage his own death and live in the mountains like Grizzly Adams? But a Mad Jack always appeared on the scene, didn't he? No matter where you were, crazy followed.

"Patrick?" Rose had finally sat, her eyes lifted over her coffee cup at him.

"I, uh . . ." he stumbled, trying to make his way back from the ocean beach.

"Stella wants to go to the Community Church," Rose said in a matter of fact way. She picked up her fork and took a bite of food.

"What for?" asked Susan, her tone suggesting nobody would choose it over, The Lord is My Shepherd.

Alex stared at him, and he could see the wheels turning. Not much got past her, even at seven, but she said nothing. Robert shrugged. "Lots of people play piano."

Patrick got up. "That's right. Nothing to worry about." For Robert to end the conversation on a positive note manifested as a miracle in itself. He took this grace from God as his cue to bolt while the bolting was good. And it wouldn't be to the edge of the world, but just to his desk where he'd resume his identity and put the mountain man idea aside. For now.

Big mistake. Patrick stood in front of more strangers than familiar parishioners that Fifth Sunday of June, and mountains rose in his vision. He should have run while given the chance.

Eva, the seventeen-year-old, put on a good show of not being nervous, but Patrick noticed a few too many young men eyeing the Swedish girl. Winston sat, front and center, his wife beaming. Guess all those times she came to the prayer line had paid off. Big time. He resolved to listen more closely to people's prayers so he'd know what to expect and be better prepared.

Rose settled in the front, next to Alex and Robert, smiling as though it was an ordinary Sunday. Oh yeah, he knew the drill. Ordinary isn't what you want—well, perhaps the board wanted normal, but he wasn't sure what they expected. *Expectation. Come with expectation!*

He opened his mouth, but only a choking sound came forth. He drank some of the water in front of him, nearly knocking it over. Rose's eyebrow went up, and Robert appeared irritated. Nothing new there. He glanced away from them and out into the sanctuary. Martin stood in the back, and Patrick imagined a magnetic energy propelling anything Patrick spoke to boomerang. *Null and Void. Never heard. Like talking in a wind storm.* His face went hot and a flush rose from his neck. Joe Brooks came and sat in the last pew, looking odd in a suit, as though playing dress-up made one closer to God. Patrick prayed a silent prayer, not trusting himself to speak his true thoughts, lest he called the demons out from the back of the sanctuary.

"Welcome to The Lord Is My Shepherd church," Patrick managed and then as though opening his mouth was the ticket, he delivered, without further trouble, a sermon on being thankful. How many times had they focused on what they didn't have? Stephen. He had so much. Three other children, a wife, a home ...

✝✝✝

"Pastor?"

Patrick having finished the service, had just stepped off the platform. He then realized he had forgotten about his security hat. A couple of unknown young men flocked to Eva at the piano. Rose headed that way.

"Yes?" he addressed the woman in front of him.

"Is it true you have advertised miracles following the service?"

"Uh, no ... I mean we didn't write—" Patrick noticed Joe and Martin moving closer.

"But I saw it in the *Washington County Nickel ads.* Free miracles—"

"The nickel ads?"

"Yes, under the freebie section?"

He glanced toward the front pew to find Alex surrounded by adults he didn't recognize. There were more newcomers than he realized. Where was Robert? His glance swept the sanctuary, landing on his son standing in a doorway, smiling and laughing with other boys his age. Of all the times Robert picked to be social. Terrific. His gaze pulled back to the woman standing in front of him. "Excuse me." He headed for the front pew, bumping through people to get to his daughter.

"Hey," one of them said, as he managed to get to her side. He took her hand and led her out of the crowd. He couldn't set her by Rose, or Robert. No one picked up Susan yet. She was safer downstairs with the teachers. "Stay with me, Sweetie." He noticed her pale, shell-shocked skin. Crowds and Alex had never mixed.

The woman came back to him. He thought she'd given up. "What about my miracle?"

"We don't charge for miracles; we also don't schedule them. I'm not sure who wrote all those articles . . ." he hesitated, trying to think of something to say, but he needn't worry because she turned on her heel and stormed away. "But if you need prayer, we'd be happy . . ." She continued, as though she hadn't heard.

"Got yourself in a pickle, huh?" Joe stood in front of Patrick, and Martin edged closer, with beefy, crossed arms, doing his bodyguard impression.

"A few news stories got out of hand, is all."

Martin stepped near Joe, taking over the conversation. "The way I see it is this is a stunt. You wanted more publicity for your kid. Well, you've done it. I don't appreciate your methods, Pastor. We have been discussing it in meeting after meeting. You can't be a hundred percent on task with these personal family matters going on. Oh sure, a couple of the board guys think this is a new kind of church service, and it will bring in the masses and promote this dead town."

Patrick was hungry. He wondered if he'd be greeted by an English tea, or buffet or just an ordinary egg salad. He'd take ordinary for sure. Martin droned on, "Be something wouldn't it? They talked of a miracle once a month."

"But you don't schedule a miracle like a manicure," Patrick tried to explain. Alex had smashed herself closer into him to avoid Martin. "And leave my daughter out of this." Patrick thought how he once again made a wrong decision. Alex would have been better off next to Rose, but there was just a bunch of guys hanging about Eva, and where Robert was, more guys. Where were the sweet elderly women he could trust his child to? His glance took in Vivian, Claudia, and Meredith. Right. Not happening.

"You get this town's population to grow with this dead-raising business and they might sit up and let you do whatever you Pentecostals do." Martin continued, "But hey, I ain't the mayor. Just watch your step. We are split on how to deal with this disaster." And Martin plowed himself through a group of people chatting, as though a red carpet lay out ahead of him.

"Daddy, can we go home?" Alex pleaded with her eyes.

"Yep. I'll have someone lock up for us." And he put his arm around her, and they went downstairs to find Susan. He couldn't wait to get home where there were no performances expected, just a lot of food in the fridge.

Once they were in the car, they had to wait for Robert, of all things. Another parking lot miracle.

XI

June 1977

The raising the dead incident followed Alex around like a puppy who refused to be forgotten. Calls to pray for Grandma Lincoln, Uncle Sinclair, and Georgie, a yappy pet poodle to whom the rest of the neighborhood had bid good riddance, tempted her parents to disconnect the black phone at the end of the hallway.

On the last day of school, after everyone else had left, Alex lingered near her bicycle. One of her papers fell. It floated across the field and after a couple of unsuccessful attempts, her fingers latched hold of the edge. An old spelling test. All of them correct. A good memory came in handy for some subjects, and spelling didn't cause anxiety. She stuffed the test back in the folder and turned when she heard her name.

The grasses revealed nothing beyond the stump, and the dip in the ground she and Nikki referred to as *the grave*. Darkness stretched across the sky, and the hairs on her arms tingled in the stillness. Alex took in the field. Not a soul in sight. Her mind played tricks on her. She went to grab her bike when a stirring of wind sighed along the ground, bending the long weeds flat, kicking up debris by the bicycle rack. The *ping* of small gravel hitting the metal of the bike preluded an enormous gust, shoving her with such a force she lost her balance and fell. A roaring filled her ears and pounding hooves approached. Color streaked across her vision as the wind blew through her hair. She rode a horse, flying fast, not alone but clinging to Jesus, and then a moment later walking along a river of turquoise and sapphire highlighted with the most incredible green. The sound of the wind dimmed, and bird songs blended with the moving water.

Children. She could hear them laughing. Had she died? But how could one die while unlocking a bicycle? Peace fluttered with every movement made, notes coming from the flowers, grass, trees, and the river. She smelled a hint of coffee and chocolate followed by a vision of Willie Wonka. But they never mentioned candy in the Bible—only cake. She made a face. Raisin cake.

Jesus laughed as though she had made a joke. She laughed too, and they ran together along the edge of a wood, the river disappearing miles away. Birds chattered. The landscape changed with each thought, and a whoosh of the crystal sea thundered in her ears just as Jesus said, "He's not here." And then without warning, neither was she.

"Alex." Someone shook her. She opened her eyes. Robert?

"He's not here," she said, sitting up.

"Who's not here?" he asked, while inspecting her forehead. "Something hit you. That branch over there."

"What happened?" Now that he mentioned it, her head did hurt. And where'd he come from?

"Everyone is home, except you. I borrowed the truck." Robert got his driver's license the day he turned sixteen. "You can put your bike in it." He helped her up, grabbing the bicycle himself, tossing it in the back. "You'll have a doozy of a bruise, but it could have been a lot worse. Don't know how you managed to be alone in this field and get hit. The branch could've gone anywhere." Robert opened the door for her. He made it sound like it was her fault. "A freak windstorm tore through town. Gone as fast as it came. Blew out a window by the theater. Mom's crazy with worry, so we gotta go. When we get home, put some ice on it. You okay? How many fingers?" He held up two.

"Eleven."

"Yep, you're fine." He gave her a small smile, put the truck into gear, and took off with a sudden lurch.

She stared out the window. To be with Jesus in heaven one moment and then back here was like culture shock, something she hadn't experienced before. The closest thing was when she prayed for Winston, and the Holy Spirit engulfed both of them, while Jesus held her hand in His. But this was more visual—more intense. From what Robert said, she'd been knocked out, could have imagined all of it. One thing was certain—she heard the voice of God, but she didn't know what it meant.

Alex, Jimmy, Bree, and Adam stood at the edge of the woods on the McMillan property. A day of seventy-degree weather was promised—a rarity for the first day of summer vacation.

"We're going to climb over the sticker bushes? She can't do that with her shorts." Jimmy glanced at Bree's long legs. She stood a whole foot taller than Alex.

The blackberry vines before them tangled around each other. "There's a better way over here." Alex walked along the grassy edge. She and Bree could manage this part. Less stickers to avoid. The boys would have to follow.

Jimmy, she knew, gave no thought to the beauty of the trees or the sound of the birds and frogs. She and Breely took a step, and in a flash, he passed them, dodging branches, and leaping over brush, shouting, "Another year finished! No more pencils, no more books, no more teacher's dirty looks!" Climbing onto a log, he slowed to walk across it, arms out to balance. "And did I get a lot of those this year!"

Adam caught up to him and sat on the other end, making Jimmy jump off and into the ferns with a declaration of, "Let's find the trail!"

Alex strained her eyes, and Bree squinted through the trees. "There is no trail," Alex said. "It's all overgrown."

"No, I see it!" He pointed to a tree. "The yellow ribbon. And there's another one. C'mon!" Jimmy darted among patches of thick woods, ferns, logs, and bramble.

"Those ribbons are still there? I remember Alex and I marking our way with them," Bree said, following the others with caution.

Alex strained to see and walked on with reluctance, stepping over thorns. Bree, a few paces behind, took precaution to protect her bare legs. The fat vines snagged their clothes, scratching at their skin. Jimmy had to slow down, taking to lifting each one that blocked the way, then bending his body through the brush. Adam and Alex trailed after him in the same fashion. A cold drop from an overhanging branch fell on Alex's head, dripping down her back. She shivered, wishing for the open expanse and the warm sunshine.

"Jimmy, we're going to get stuck in all this!" She glanced back at Breely.

"There's no way I can get through," Bree came to a stop in the midst of the overgrown woods. The firs stood tall, the shadows deepening in their thickness, only catching momentary glimpses of sunlight.

"The key is to not panic," Jimmy looked over at Alex with a grin. She stuck her tongue out at him. He pointed a few feet ahead. "The indentation of the path is right there."

Ferns, logs, dirt, and vines all jumbled together. He sprinted further, like a startled deer, leaving Alex and Adam behind in the thorn prison. They pulled the vines from their jeans, stomping them down. The scent of soil from a recent rain, mixed with a teasing hint of blackberries that wouldn't be ready for another whole month, gave Alex a new wave of happiness; the kind only known by children being released after nine months of a dreary school building.

Encouraged, Alex put more gusto in her step, then found clearance. "Thorn free . . ." she sang, spreading out her arms with a twirl, then caught up to Adam. But then Jimmy tripped.

Alex rushed toward him, stopping short.

A hand stuck out of the brush and into the clearing. Blackberry vines bordered the trail they made last summer, but one section lay flattened by the body of Joe Brooks.

†††

Alex's eyes flitted over the stretched out form of Joe while Jimmy scrambled from the ground. Adam edged closer. The maples fluttered, light bouncing off the moving branches, and the birds twittered, hopping from one tree to the other. Every wood-like sound jolted Alex's senses, and colored spots danced in front of her eyes.

She covered her ears and whispered, "Is he . . ." *dead*. She couldn't say the word.

Adam looked from her to Joe, and then Jimmy bolted, taking the path he'd flattened out at the highest speed possible. Alex took off after him, but something grabbed ahold of her ankle, and she fell. Joe's eyes opened. "What's d'matter, you don't wanna pray for me?" His speech slurred, his eyes bloodshot.

Alex screamed. A flash of light, as though an explosion filled the space between the two of them. She jerked her ankle free, scrambling from the dirt. "Jimmy," she shrieked, running after him, following his red hair bobbing in and out among the brown and green that blurred together. Joe's voice chased her with its high pitch. "I'll make you sorry for the day you prayed him back to life! You don't scare me with your tricks!"

She kept her eyes on Jimmy, catching glimpses of Adam, and almost tripping in her hurry to get away.

"What's happening?" Breely's eyes widened as they all came rushing at her, the brush slapping at their legs, arms, and faces.

"Just go!" Jimmy said, and she took off. He passed her in her uncertainty of the way. Near the clearing, the tangled thicket stopped them like a barbed wire fence. Alex climbed over thorns, slowly. They grabbed at her hair. She screamed in panic.

"Alex, stop! I got it." Adam came from behind her to untangle the ends of her ponytail. Once free, she hurried toward the open sky, between magic and reality, a few steps away. She looked back.

67

Adam followed Alex's glance to where Breely stood amidst the overgrown blackberry vines, helpless, like prey caught in a web.

He made his way back to her. "Calm down. He's not following us," Adam said, his voice, a tone of reassurance. He lifted Bree over the tall sticker bushes and placed her on shallow ground.

They all emerged from the clearing, Alex yanking her pant leg free from the relentless thorns and dragging out weeds that clung to her.

"Oh, Breely, your legs," Alex winced, seeing the scratches and blood.

"The sun was warm, and I forgot how the woods are." She shivered regarding the sticker bushes they had escaped, then gingerly sat on the weedy grass, hugging her knees, her black hair hanging in messy strands. "What exactly were we running from?"

"Joe. I tripped right over him," Jimmy said.

Alex's legs shook, and she sank to the ground with Jimmy and Adam, all of them trying to catch their breath. The sunlight sent immediate relief to her body, and she fought to keep from throwing up.

The contrast between the bright sun and the dim woods made the frightening moment an imaginary drop in time. A spirited Irish tune drifted from the house. Rose called them home.

They all sat still. "She has something to do with this," Jimmy glanced toward the house.

"What? My mom? No way."

"He is in *your* woods," Jimmy said, as though that provided all the proof needed.

"And she ran out here and thumped him on the head? Didn't quite kill him?"

"She's always in the woods." Jimmy stretched back, gazing at the cloudless sky, then glanced at Alex. "Plus, there are rumors . . ." His voice trailed off when Alex narrowed her eyes at him, mentally sending the one word message: *Traitor*.

"Uncle Peter," Alex said pointedly, "is the one who hangs out at the Dockerbogger." The tavern sat in the middle of the border of Dockerbog and Filbert Ridge. "Mom went there to get help finding Stephen. Lots of people hang out at bars—people that know things, so it would make sense for her to talk to Joe. She gave him a poster to tack on the wall. Big deal."

"Yeah, and checked in everyday and brought brownies, muffins, stew and home-baked bread," Jimmy added.

"Like you know! That was for Mr. Brooks' bookstore."

"Just wondering why he's out here, by your house." Jimmy picked at the grass, putting it in a pile.

"Mom always has said somebody knows what happened to that boy," Bree straightened out her legs and picked at her hand. "Sliver."

Everyone went silent. Adam and Bree's mom, Lilian, had taken to pacing and staying at home since her husband ran off with the Pirate Pub waitress.

Alex was still irritated at Jimmy, who stretched out on the grass with his eyes closed. "If we found Stephen, everything would be okay. I know it," she said. "That's all Mom was doing. Trying to make everything right."

"Find him? He's probably . . ." Jimmy stopped when she stared over at him.

She'd overheard her parents talking plenty of times when they didn't think she was awake or nearby. "Mom says he's alive, and I believe her."

There was a pause—the kind when no one knows what to say— and when no one believes what you've said. Something niggled at her memory—heaven, and the river. Was she forgetting already? What was the point of a trip to heaven if she was going to forget? Had it been a dream? "Anyway, did you hear what Joe screamed at me when I ran away?"

"No, what?" Jimmy sat up and plucked at the weeds. "Heard him yell."

"Said I'd be sorry for praying for Winston."

Jimmy snorted. "A little late." Picking up a wide blade of grass, he put it between his lips and made a musical sound.

Alex leaned back on her hands and stretched her legs. That's when she noticed a tear in her jeans.

"Why did he come to the woods? To scare you?" Adam asked.

"I don't know." She brushed off the dirt from her pants, still feeling where Joe's hand had been.

The Irish music rose in volume, dancing across the fields.

With some difficulty, they got back on their feet. Alex's legs still shook, and her ankle hurt.

They entered the house, and Rose, seeing them, turned the volume down. Her pale blue eyes had no make-up today, and her hair stuck out of her hairband, but she didn't look like she'd been frolicking out in the woods, attempting murder. Alex stared at her mom's nails, just to be sure.

"It's stew, darling," Rose said. "You boys and Bree staying for dinner? Pete should come on over; Lilian too," she spoke, giving Adam and Jimmy a glance. She stopped peeling the potato and turned from the counter, staring at them. "What on earth have you children been doing?"

Alex then realized how they looked. Snagged, scratched, hair disheveled, and Jimmy had a gash on his cheek where a trickle of blood ran down his face.

XII

For Alex, the horror of the event diminished after dessert. She hung tightly to Patrick's hand in the approaching twilight. Uncle Peter, Robert, and Jimmy joined them. Lilian had taken Adam and Bree home.

They ducked under overhanging branches and stomped down blackberry vines, tripping along in the dim light before arriving at the spot where Joe had been, now a flattened area in the bushes. The breeze turned gusty, and a beam of the flashlight reflected off something on the ground. Patrick picked it up. An empty vodka bottle.

Uncle Peter lifted an eyebrow. "Guess that explains why he'd be making his bed in the sticker bushes."

Patrick scanned the area. "You kids must be awfully desperate, climbing over all this stuff to get back in here."

"We had a fort." Jimmy dodged a log. "This year we will make it better. Right, Allie?"

She nodded, biting her lip.

Peter frowned. "So, what'd he say to you, Allie?"

"That I'd be sorry for raising Winston from the dead. Why wouldn't he want his dad to be alive, anyway? He should be happy."

Robert slapped at a mosquito. "Dad, you should report him for grabbing Alex's foot and charge him with trespassing. He shouldn't be threatening little girls."

Alex frowned. "I'm almost eight."

"You shouldn't be out here anymore, Alex," Patrick said.

The flashlight wavered as the night turned shades darker, and Alex saw summer boredom stretch out farther than the illuminated beam could shine. Daddy hated the woods, and she'd been lucky to have as much freedom as she did.

"Please, this is the only weird thing that has happened. I'm as safe here as anywhere."

"It's not the only . . ." Patrick stopped. "Just for awhile, let's be cautious."

"I'll talk to him," Peter offered. "Still go to the bar at least once a week. Joe's always working."

"What if someone's with her?" Jimmy asked. "I mean, most of the time we're together."

Patrick took in their surroundings, flashing the light here and there. He sighed. "Keeping you kids out of the woods is impossible. Just be careful."

Alex breathed a prayer of relief. The summer without the wooded playground would be like a small child without his favorite toy.

"You know, he probably doesn't remember doing anything," Peter added. "He's out here, spouting off stuff, stumbling his way home." They all hiked back to the house, pulling vines away as they passed through so the branches and stickers wouldn't snap into the person behind them.

"Maybe he came to see Rose?" Peter asked.

"What on earth for?" Patrick asked, stopping. "And why not come the normal way instead of being like Robin Hood and hiding in the forest?"

No one said anything, and they all concentrated on heading for the opening where the house lights glowed in the distance—a welcome presence beckoned, promising warmth and refuge.

"You kids run on in," Peter said. "Wait in the house, Jimmy. We'll go home in a bit."

Robert led the group toward the door and Alex glanced back, watching as Uncle Peter lit a cigarette, a small ember dividing the open expanse from the dark veil where they had just emerged.

†††

Patrick watched them go, then eyed Peter, "Thought you quit."

"I tried. That brief stint of bronchitis nearly convinced me, but . . ." he tapped the cigarette and the embers scattered, "guess I'm more hooked than I thought."

"So, you know what this is about?" Patrick waved his hand toward the woods.

"I've heard things."

Patrick contemplated the possibilities of what *things* were heard. He'd dealt with *things* being said for so long. He longed to whisk Rose and the kids to a new town, near the ocean, somewhere they could be anonymous, and the waves would drown out rumors.

"So, what do you make of that?" Peter asked, flicking his ashes on the ground.

Patrick's thoughts returned to where he stood. He had missed something Pete had said. No ocean, no escape, just stuck here, trying not to breathe cigarette smoke.

Peter stared at him and then grinned. "Try to stay with me. This is where Allie gets it, you know, all the mind wandering. Pay attention. I'm getting cold out here."

"Sorry," Patrick muttered.

"Okay, Winston Brooks is eventually going to retire."

"From Brook's Books. So?"

"You haven't heard?"

"No." Patrick shifted his feet. "You know I try to block out town gossip."

"Yes, of course, it's how you preserve your sanity, but this you might want to pay attention to." The light streaked across the yard from the porch, and the small burn of the cigarette, mixed with the swirling smoke, emphasized Peter's face, craggy from too much smoking, too much drinking, and not enough happiness. He turned forty soon after the New Year, but right now, Patrick thought he looked a lot older.

"He's thinking of the future of Brooks' Books."

"And?" pressed Patrick. He agreed with Peter; it was getting chilly standing on the lawn in the dark.

"I guess," Peter said at last, "Winston has decided when the time comes, in about five to ten years, he's leaving it in care of the McMillans."

Patrick stared at him. "To us? Why? I still have my church, you know, however small it may be, but—"

"He is talking of leaving it to Alex, in care of Rose, and then Alex can have the business once she is old enough. If she wants, of course."

"Isn't that premature? He should wait before making these kinds of decisions."

"He knows her love for books, and he already died once. He's trying to be ready." In the silence, the crickets and frogs sang as though the road Patrick traveled didn't make a sudden spin toward an unknown destination. Peter fidgeted. "Of course, anything could happen in the meantime. I mean, you all could leave, or she might have other plans. She's his first choice. This better not interfere with my patronage of the bar. Joe bans me when you McMillans cause trouble."

"Cause trouble? We didn't do anything—we—"

"Yes, you did." Peter finished the cigarette and waved it around. "You raised Winston from the dead."

"Jesus raised him from the dead. Let's back up here," Patrick said.

"I backed it up as far as it will go." Peter paced, kicking at the taller grasses here and there.

"Where'd you hear this?" Patrick asked.

"Hank's Hardware."

"I guess that's reliable, about as good as The Grocery."

"It's better than The Grocery, and you know it. What is spoken among tools is true."

"I'll wait for an official statement from Winston." Patrick fingered the item in his pocket. As a McMillan he'd had first-hand experience in how *the truth* wasn't anything but a twisted lie.

"Yep," Peter said, as though this wasn't a problem. "Brooks' Books. It'd be something, wouldn't it?"

"Yeah." And Joe wouldn't be happy. The bookstore, unique enough to bring a selected flavor of tourists to Filbert Ridge—the intellects, the hippies, the Portlanders going for a country drive, held its own. The attached garden in the back gave it a small town charm.

"The problem is, Joe and Winston had plans together for the building. Joe had the idea of making it into a restaurant bar. Kind of fancy for out here. With Winston leaving hell behind, and turning into a good guy—" Peter stopped. "Winston is considering his wife and her love for books and the garden. She never wanted him to change what it was, even after retirement. His plans with Joe are now dust."

"Why don't they update and expand the Dockerbogger? It'd be much easier to improve an establishment that already serves food and drinks, wouldn't it?"

"Sure, but you've dashed Joe's dreams on the piece of property he wanted. The tavern is a dive, plus the creek runs too close. Place needs more repairs than anyone has time or money for. You've waged war on Joe Brooks. Perhaps he came here to strike a deal and drank too much liquid courage."

"It's not the first time I've been at odds with Joe." Patrick turned to go back in the house, stopping when Peter chuckled. "Guess you'll think twice before raising the dead next time. A lot of trouble comes to life with it."

"More trouble if you don't listen to what God tells you to do."

Peter grinned. "That's why me and Him, we don't talk." He walked toward the house.

Patrick stood in the dark, and took from his pocket the hair ribbon he had picked up from the ground by the vodka bottle. In the moonlight he studied it—turquoise gems dangled, held by a leather tie.

Peter turned. "You coming?"

"Yeah." He stuffed it back in his jacket and followed.

XIII

Patrick couldn't deny that the day Joe drank himself horizontally onto the McMillan property marked a separation of opinion, dividing a town.

The shift in the church carried a subtle air at first, then the whispering—an invisible vapor of poison, gained strength. The rumor symbolized trouble leaping back to life again, like kindling on a dwindling fire—Joe, Rose, Alex—the talk continued all summer and followed them right into the new church building the Sunday after Elvis died.

The air, heavy with mugginess, promised a sweltering day, extending to the week ahead. The McMillans piled out of the station wagon, Patrick staying close to Alex. Lately he had created reasons for her to be near him, as though he dreaded the possibility of another parking lot miracle. He told himself it was for her protection, but guilt layered the top of this reasoning like extra calories added to a dessert. Here he was, a pastor, afraid of the work of God.

"Rose, how nice to see you. This weather is downright humid, isn't it?" Vivian appeared out of thin air. So much for being alerted to approaching darkness.

"Hello, Vivian."

"I heard how Joe paid you a visit but never made it to the front door, or should I say back door." Vivian's step fell into theirs. "I've been gone most the summer, but the stories circulating around are astounding."

Rose dropped a pen, and her foot gave it a kick, making it skitter across the lot. "Oh dear, excuse me a moment," she chased after it, while herding the children into the building. "It's too warm for us today, I'm afraid," she called back with a wave.

Patrick wished for something he could drop and then have it roll him right to the pulpit.

"Pastor, I'm afraid the attention of the people is once again on the Brooks' situation. The rumors can be ugly. The fact that Joe was three sheets to the wind in your woods, seemingly coming in the back way to your house, leaves people's imaginations to roam too freely."

"God gave us an imagination. Should be used properly though. People need to . . ." How could he say *mind their own business* in a polite way? "No reason to worry. I mean, it's not like I have a still in my woods. Plus, it's been a couple of months—"

"A still? Oh, goodness, no, I don't believe that is where people are going with this—this *problem*."

"I don't see how it's a problem, except Joe might consider not going out when he is indulging in vodka."

"Patrick . . . Pastor, as a person who cares after the welfare of the church, you need to realize it's not Joe's indiscretion we are worried about."

He walked faster, taking longer strides, needing the coolness of the building.

"He said your daughter Alex is involved in things we don't find appropriate."

What else was new? "Is she drinking vodka?" he asked. "I'm pretty sure whatever it is, it doesn't involve the church."

"I would suggest you take this more seriously. Vodka is not what is being discussed." Vivian's voice became impatient.

"She's seven. She's not much of a threat to anyone."

"She has raised the dead, and now Joe claims she called forth a light that threw his arm back."

Light force? "Like *Star Wars*? You know the kids have been fascinated—"

"Not *Star Wars*."

"I'm sorry, Vivian, but we are going to have to continue this conversation later," he said with a check of his watch. "But Joe grabbing my little girl's ankle in the woods would be more worrisome than some drunk claiming light came down. Saying it out loud makes it sound ridiculous, doesn't it? In his drunken state, he was probably hallucinating. My guess is the sun flashed on the vodka bottle he had with him. No need to spiritualize everything." He paused. "But if you must make it a supernatural occurrence, then I suggest that angels were protecting my daughter from Joe. Or perhaps Joe needed the protection?"

Vivian's lips went into a thin line. "Regardless of what really happened, I'm saying it doesn't bode well for your daughter to be getting a reputation. I mean dead-raisings, mysterious lights, you don't know what will be interpreted, especially Rose being home while Joe is trying to sneak into the back way of your house. I trust I have clarified the concerns we are addressing." And with those final accusations, Vivian turned on her heel and nearly collided with Claudia who lingered close enough to catch the final bomb.

Patrick shut himself in the office, even though worship started without him. He could get through this morning. His family would be in the front row. Alex hadn't told him about any light or whatever Vivian had been rattling on about, but what would be next? Healing the sick? Surely the church could move forward and practice doing what Jesus did. He didn't understand Vivian's opposition to the supernatural, which to Patrick was a natural part of the Christian life, yet lately there was an air of secrecy—to take the miracles of God underground. Sure, it had been a little wild, and he had been warned in the beginning. He sank in his chair and leaned back, staring at the ceiling. As far as Rose being home, where was she supposed to be? Joe wandered to the wrong place at the wrong time, but hadn't tried to get through the McMillan's backdoor. He wasn't even close to the house. They moved Joe around like a chess piece.

Patrick chose the evils of the tongue as his topic—perfect for the occasion and not accidental. The sideways approach to the issue—a warning to those that understood, landed with a dull thud, rather than piercing the heart. The faint whisper in his ear told him he needed to be bold and defend his family, but he didn't know how.

Afterward Martin came to him. "Good sermon. Nice and practical and to the point. I get tired of revelation and glory stuff. You get too out there, and I start thinking about football. Speaking for a lot of us too, so take note."

Patrick wished to say, *hope you take it to heart*, but refrained and smiled while his soul feared his spirit might go into hibernation. He didn't want to deliver an ordinary, calculated, safe sermon, and Martin proved he had done just that.

"Oh, and Pastor, I trust everything is going well for you at home. I was near your side of the woods that day everyone keeps talking about, and I heard the row between Joe and Rose. Since your sermon, I wondered if I should tell you, rather than someone else, you know?"

Way to turn a new leaf, Patrick thought, then admonished himself for the sarcastic thought. "Did you see them?" The ribbon played in his memory, and his imagination always gave different scenarios, none of them inviting.

"No. I stopped within earshot." Martin shrugged. "Better fighting in the woods than kissing, I suppose."

"Rose has not been kissing Joe in the woods," Patrick said, just as Claudia emerged from a far pew. Those ladies were as stealthy as ninjas. She lifted an eyebrow as she passed. So here he preached about gossip only to be causing stories to fly later. Terrific. He doubted that even his optimistic wife would find a bright side to this conversation.

Patrick watched Rose for any indication her heart was divided. He could prevent her from snapping if he stayed alert—keep her from wandering like a ghost looking for the living-presumed-dead by everyone else.

He heard her that night, walking in her stocking feet across the living room. The front door opened and shut. His heart raced as he sat up too quickly, then he fumbled for his slippers and hurried outside. Relief flowed through his body to find her standing at the far end of the porch.

"This is the time of year for falling stars," she said, not turning toward him. The night air simmered with warmth, the kind where you could sleep outside without a blanket. He stood close, almost afraid to touch her, lest she jerk away or melt into sobs, so he leaned into the porch railing, gazing at the sky as though they were doing a normal, enjoyable thing.

"I should do something different, a tea party, perhaps?"

He wondered why she didn't weigh three hundred pounds. She still managed to keep her petite frame, but to her the world's problems were solved with food. He grimaced at the idea of a tea party as he swept over the possibilities of what could go wrong. Then he realized he would not be expected to attend. Men didn't do tea parties. Enduring another dinner gathering was out of the question. "I think," he said, "you should relax, let it die. The excitement will wear off." Yeah, right—about as likely as Elvis making an appearance from the grave. Had his life become a bucketful of lies and half-truths?

She met his eyes, as if to see if he believed what he said, and shook her head. "What do you make of it? The bookstore? The funny thing is, I can picture myself there, helping Alex when she's older, more so than where I'm at right now. This is God working in our lives, right? But it has this cloud, making me uncomfortable, as though we've stolen a business from Winston's family."

"Joe doesn't care about books." Rose didn't need to worry more than she already did. Martin's story echoed in Patrick's head.

"No, but it is real estate, you know?"

"Right, he could turn it into a liquor store. Need more alcohol in this town." He opened his mouth to mention the argument that had been heard, his curiosity almost overriding his judgment, but just in time, shut it again. The conversation would lead to places he didn't want to go.

Rose's attention went back to the sky.

"Think, sweetheart. Would Winston want his bookstore turned into a river of martinis and piña coladas?" Patrick edged closer to her.

Rose laughed. "Putting it that way makes it sound like we are saving Filbert Ridge. We could make the garden into a miracle cafe. Imagine it. Free miracles."

"There you go with a forward plan, except the newspapers have beat you to it. The parking lot of the church is already advertised for such events." Patrick put his arm around her. Despite the muggy air, her skin felt cold. "We should go in."

"He'd be in junior high."

His gut seized. He'd been so close to getting her in the house, back to bed without mentioning *this*.

"He'd be getting his growth spurt, and getting all gangly, and liking girls."

"Rose," he wished she'd stop. He wanted to shake her, make her forget and move forward. Weaken the pull of the past.

"He would have been handsome, you know? He resembled you."

Patrick's agony froze. She spoke in the past tense. Did she realize it? Had she grasped the reality? This could be good—a turn for the better.

The posters had gotten them nowhere. Patrick's heart dragged as though being pulled from a truck that wouldn't slow down. He needed closure. Ten years passed. Couldn't he ask? "I was thinking, Rose. We should have a memorial. Have a service dedicated to Stephen. I believe—"

"What? That he's dead? You're giving up? You wonder why I go elsewhere for help? Because you never believed he was still alive. He is. I know he is, and I will never have a memorial." The glare she gave him said he was an idiot. As a pastor he took advantage of the pulpit to say what he thought and believed. The sermon covered him. Whenever he tried to intervene elsewhere the results went south, but often the sermons didn't bode well, either. He imagined being shipwrecked on a deserted island . . .

"Patrick." Her eyes flickered in the moonlight. "I get it, you don't believe, and if you do, you are judged by the rest of the *rational* people in our lives. I wish for once, you could be on my side. Not make excuses for me, not *tolerate my obsession*, but truly stand by me and know our son will come home."

He hesitated, looking at the ground, then into her eyes. "I'm sorry. Your faith exceeds mine." So much for reality and the dream he had of closure. "Please, come to bed." His inner voice spoke, *take charge, don't let her dissolve into a puddle that becomes murky stretching the past into the present—like watercolors running together.*

He waited for her to answer or move, bracing himself for barbed words as she paused, staring in the night.

"Choose me, Patrick. Choose me over rationality and common sense and probabilities and over the church and their opinions. Never over God, but over all those people who stand against us or speak curses on our family." She turned toward him, and a tear glinted in the moonlight. His finger caught it running down her cheek, which he caressed, taking in the blue eyes, paler than his own, wishing he could be everything she needed—then he leaned in, kissing her.

His voice mingled with the breeze, low and unwavering. "You and me, crazy or sane." The words tumbled out, and as he spoke them, he still couldn't let go of doubt. They stood side by side again, staring at the sky. Finally, she withdrew from the railing, and he took her hand to keep her connected to him—at least to the bedroom, if nowhere else.

XIV

October, 1977

A *memorial!* Rose kneaded the dough at the bakery with extra zeal, then shaped it into perfect loaves. She took advantage of being alone for a few minutes before Tilly wandered in, loud and making thoughts impossible to process. When Patrick looked at her, she saw the emptiness in his eyes. To forget that summer night when he mentioned closure wasn't possible, and the coming anniversary date brought the pain all back to her again. He tuned out the past like it was a bad flu and mentioning their son's name would spread disease somehow. Burying reality deep inside was how he moved forward in life. She punished herself daily for the disappearance of Stephen. If people spoke ill of her, then so be it. She deserved it, didn't she? Tears formed, and she made her thoughts go elsewhere.

"It will be a good day for the bakery, I'm thinking." Tilly burst in with her enthusiasm available without caffeine. Rose envied her.

"How are you, Rose? You've been busy making extra bread, I see. Good. I feel the need for comfort food." She took in the overcast sky. "It's a bit cooler. If we don't sell it, I'll sit and eat it myself." She put the ready ones into the oven.

"If this shop ran on optimism, Tilly, you'd be a millionaire."

"Don't you know it, girl."

They chatted for a few minutes while Rose gulped more coffee to match Tilly's upbeat attitude. The woman's energy dried Rose's tears.

Helen Scott, Alex's third grade teacher, arrived when the door opened. "Good morning, ladies," she said.

"Good morning, Mrs. Scott." Rose smiled at her and received in return an expression that tried to be pleasant, yet only managed to look constipated.

Helen's gaze shifted to Tilly. "I'd like a dozen sweets, please. Donuts, I suppose. I thought I'd try something else, but you can't go wrong with the usual."

"Nope. It's what people expect. If they want different, they'd rather choose it themselves. That's what I say." Tilly put on her glove, grabbed a box, and went to the case to fill the order.

"Mrs. McMillan," Helen said, "I've wanted to talk to you about Alex."

Rose had an urge to stuff a donut in her own mouth. Sedative sugar would be needed for whatever came next.

"She has quite an imagination."

Rose didn't respond but waited, meeting Helen's eyes, pretending to not know there would be a *but* coming.

Helen blinked and fiddled with her wallet then rummaged through her purse, and Rose waited, wondering if the perfect speech for this moment was filed inside. Helen fluffed it back in shape and glanced at Rose again. "I am concerned that she has some sort of—" She hesitated, pursing her lips.

An urge to slap the woman and tell her to spit it out made Rose clench her hands into closed fists.

"She can't focus, always staring into space, drawing outstanding though rather intense pictures. The stories she writes, well, it's worrisome."

"I'm not sure what the problem is exactly?" Rose had no idea what the woman was talking about. "Imagination is a good thing."

"She's always talking about animals. If someone's pet dies she says it's in heaven. It's not appropriate since some of our children believe her. She says animals talk up there. The fact they are there at all, well—"

"Isn't that what parents tell their children when pets die? Brutus went to doggie heaven? I don't see the harm. Lucy was taunted about Narnia being real. And we all know the story."

"Narnia? It isn't real, so I'm not following your train of thought."

Rose smiled, ringing up Helen's order. "But maybe it is. Can't prove it's not, can you? And all the animals talked. You've known Alex all of three weeks. I think you'll discover she is perfectly fine."

Helen pushed her glasses higher on her nose, taking her change. "I see, Mrs. McMillan. At conference time your husband can join you. It's always good to involve both parents." She flashed the same clogged smile and with a swift motion, took the donuts, her heels clicking across the floor, accenting her exit.

Tilly burst out laughing. "That was priceless."

Rose giggled. "I hope I haven't made things worse for poor Allie."

"I'm sure the teacher will be more understanding because now she sees that the apple didn't fall far from the tree, as I like to say," Tilly huffed.

Rose sat with Tilly for a break. "Look." Tilly pointed toward the sky. "There's a smiley face cloud up there. Enjoying our bakery jokes, no doubt."

Rose peered through the window. "Yes. You know, I think I see that cloud often, and there," she pointed, "right next to it. It's a cat."

Tilly stared for a bit. "I don't see a cat. You are messing with me. Next thing I know you'll be telling me you can get to Narnia through the freezer door."

XV

Alex witnessed the cracking of her mother's façade—dinner—picture-perfect with multiple courses. The definition of mania at the McMillans. Alex would lie awake, listening to the footfalls walking back and forth through the hallway and the living room. She saw her dad's eyes go dim, yet he remained silent, watching family and church fall apart, his only voice being in a sermon. Sometimes, she wished he would scream. Sometimes, she wished he would rescue them all.

Like a familiar spirit returning, the McMillans fell into a routine, a déjà vu, and behaved in a way they were accustomed to—everyone take your roles, act your part—when the rumor mill turned cruel and partnered itself against the family of a lost boy. The anniversary date haunted them, flashing the month and day on the calendar, demanding action.

Robert's anger increased, and Susan smiled bigger. Everyone around Alex disintegrated, and sometimes when she stood in front of the mirror accusations reflected back to her soul. She shut the reality out like her dad did. Life had been hard enough when things were about Stephen, but she had helped bring the pain to the forefront. Why couldn't God have used someone else to raise Winston from the dead? Anyone but a McMillan. Her role became escaping into the woods and hanging out with Jimmy in his treehouse.

Summers in Oregon often lasted well into the fall, and today's crisp, early October breezes and apple-scented air cut through the cloudless sky. Uncle Peter, in a fit of autumn energy that coincided with the beginning of each school year, spent hours, every chance he could get, writing pages and pages of a novel he couldn't describe from the loft of his house.

Robert was a junior at Creekside High. He studied long hours, as though already in pre-med. His plan was in motion. He had one step out of the house, and once both feet left, Alex wondered if he'd come back. When he wasn't studying, he worked part-time at the Burger Barn, hanging out with guys who drove cars, saving for his own vehicle. Alex knew he'd be gone in a couple of years. He was her ally—without him she'd blow away, carried by the words appearing uninvited in her vision and the music singing through the maples. The whispers traveled across the yards, through living rooms, kitchens, and back out again, like the scent of a cartoon pie in the window, only not as sweet.

Alex and Jimmy dangled their feet from the treehouse. Creaking branches swayed and shook plate-sized leaves downward in tiny whirlwinds, covering the length of Peter's yard. Rose had taken to playing the piccolo in the woods, having grown weary of baking, and wandering.

"We should make a town paper," Jimmy said when a particularly loud note reached the top of the tree house, drifting back in a swirl of twittering music.

Alex frowned. "How?"

"I don't know, but think of the stuff we could put in it, not to mention, we could tell good stories about Aunt Rose and Uncle Patrick—try to change the way people talk about them."

"The only thing that would make them normal again is if Stephen came home," Alex said.

Jimmy made a snorting sound. "And what are the chances?"

If they found Stephen, everything would be all right. And the dead-raising forgotten. "Wish I could make it up to them, for causing more problems." She swung her feet harder against the treehouse.

"You got it all wrong, Allie cat. You are a celebrity. If anything, you've brought the case from cold storage. People are taking notice again."

She swallowed the lump in her throat, and her burning eyes threatened to spill over. "Molly's mom won't let her near me and is glad I don't go to children's church. Most of them are." She sighed. "Don't want to be with all those kids, anyway."

"Ah, Allie, they just want to talk about something," Jimmy continued.

"I wish Adam would still hang out with us." Breely's brother was a big tease, but he always had the right thing to say when she was upset.

Jimmy leaned back, looking at the treehouse ceiling. "He's spending half his time with his dad and the other half helping around the house and watching his annoying sisters. And face it, Allie, no one wants to hang with you and me. After all they might end up like us."

"Like us?"

"Yeah, you know, freaks."

Nothing more needed to be said. All hope of normal gone. And Stephen coming back, despite her mom's pining, wasn't much of a reality either.

Alex sat next to Jimmy, contemplating this information. Did Adam think she was a freak? They smoked their candy cigarettes and watched the squirrels run through the trees. A loud bang, followed by cursing, startled them and they both stared over at the house. White papers came flying from Peter's loft—hundreds of sheets, swirling in the wind.

XVI

Eva grew comfortable with her role of piano playing, and the music shifted from the solemn "In the Garden" to a more upbeat chorus of, "I Am the Resurrection and the Life." The worship progressed for better or worse, depending on how old you were. Patrick did manage to find a couple of guitar players to accompany Eva on stage. Complaints came in the prayer box, in the rolling of the eyes, and in folks stepping out when the song wasn't what they wanted in either tune or beat. No way to please everybody, and Patrick treated any positive feedback like gold.

The sun still held the warmth of summer in the middle of the day, if only for an hour or two—perfect weather for raking leaves. Patrick had his coffee in relative peace, as though all problems still slept, and managed time alone in his office before anyone arrived. The morning mapped out into a beautiful routine. He found it reassuring. The miracle news had died down, and this slight piece of predictability made him ready for whatever the Spirit decided to bring to the service. Let heaven meet earth. These kinds of days Patrick loved being a pastor.

Everything went well, until the announcements. Holidays were approaching, and Patrick delivered a list of what he thought to be lighthearted events coming, like pot-lucks and gifts for children in need, but then Dana, the mother of a baby who recently passed away, stood near the back row.

"So, I have a question."

A shifting of everyone in front of her, as they turned to stare, rustled through the pews, and a few people bolted out the doors for their cup of water or bathroom break.

Her tone didn't suggest asking if people preferred pumpkin pie to apple, or to define a date, or volunteer. Patrick's pulse raced and he tried to remind himself of his carefree morning. Peace fled as he waited for a supernatural occurrence or conflict to cause another half of the congregation to leave.

She looked around at everyone before speaking, and then zeroed in on Martin. "Do children go to hell?"

Sounds of horror swept through the pews, and Martin spoke. "We are all born in sin." Silence descended and then a "shut up, Marty," and a shout from the opposite side told Martin where he could stuff his opinions.

Options arose, as though Patrick's thoughts had a habit of entering a panic room and gathering arsenal. Passing out would possibly be perceived as being slain in the Spirit—one step short of rolling down the aisles. This Pentecostal act would, however, provide a welcome distraction from a question deemed more unpleasant than political debates. Patrick attempted to recall his inspiration from barely an hour ago—*being ready* for whatever came dimmed into a dream-like idea, and he wondered if there would be a brawl in the sanctuary.

Rose sat in the front, watching Patrick, waiting, he supposed, for him to put out the fire. He held up a hand as a large study bible rose too close to Martin's head from the pew behind him.

"Children do not go to hell. There is a certain age of accountability, and I believe it is different for everyone. Once one understands—" He paused as they all stared at him.

"But how do you know for sure?" Tears ran down Dana's face.

Patrick failed this congregation. They had no clue of the nature of God. "If you'd all take time, spend every day seeking to get to know God better, you would realize He doesn't send children to hell. He's a God of mercy and is a good father."

"What if that's just what we want to believe?" Martin went on.

"Sentimental hope. Your family is practiced in this, and I understand, but it is nonsense believing your kid is alive out there, somewhere."

And then it happened. Patrick shouldn't have been surprised. He hadn't liked Dana's question, at least not the timing, and detested Martin for bringing up Stephen in the middle of church. But when Alex stood, a trickle of sweat and slight tremor of his hand betrayed his anxiety. Her voice, clear with conviction announced, "Children go to heaven. I was there, and I heard them."

Patrick contemplated a way out of this one. His hand fingered the pulpit, wishing for an eject button. He imagined himself falling off the end of the earth. It wasn't round at all, just an edge, and he would plummet toward the dark abyss . . .

"A perfect example of unbelievable optimism. As you all can see, this child is influenced by her mother," Martin continued.

A brief thought of why anyone would consider taking the time to prove that children went to hell stumbled across Patrick's conscience, making him take a step back from the impending darkness as he stared at Martin. Why did Martin continue coming here? Why hadn't he run off to the Community Church where many of them were fleeing? He sent others there, yet remained to be Patrick's splinter.

"What do you mean?" Dana's voice came out in a choking sound.

"I mean what I said, you can deny—"

"Not you! Her." Dana stared at Alex.

What Patrick witnessed next reminded him of himself when someone asked him a question, and he responded without consideration of the outcome, the reason many dinner parties went south.

"Jesus took me on a horse. I could hear children in the background. I just knew they were there," Alex said. Patrick's stomach tightened.

"Were you dead? You can't go to heaven unless you die," a woman said.

"No, I wasn't dead, but I was in the schoolyard, and then I wasn't."

A few giggles played out here and there. Patrick glanced at Rose, hoping for a telepathic message. She gave a small smile as though she enjoyed the whole thing. No help at all.

"Fanciful imagination," Vivian spoke. "But even though, I must say, Martin, I am shocked at your belief."

"Obviously, Alex was hit on the head during recess, and Martin hates children. We all know he can't stand them," Claudia said.

"So there are horses in heaven?" Meredith asked Alex.

"Jesus and I were on one—a beautiful, huge white horse."

A groan came from next to her. Robert.

"I take it you haven't taken the child to the doctor yet, Patrick?" Claudia asked.

"There is nothing wrong with Alex," Patrick said before he could stop himself. A white hot anger made him take a deep breath. Of all the nerve to use the middle of church to discuss his daughter's mental health, his missing son, or how his family coped. He tried to veer everyone in a more biblical path, anything to avoid scrutiny of their personal life. "These are all good questions, and I can lead you to a verse. It should shed light on the subject."

Back in control, Patrick put his finger on his Bible. After all, it wasn't the first time he'd addressed the issue of, *Is my child in heaven?* Just not with so much animosity and in the middle of a service. "Second Samuel 12:23. Where David had lost the son that was born to him and Bathsheba, and says, 'Why should I continue fasting? I will go to him, but the child will not come back to me.'" Patrick paused. "David, a man of God, knew he'd see the child again, and we can all agree David didn't go to hell." He looked at Martin, daring him to rebut his statement.

"I had a pet horse once," Meredith said. "Do pets go to heaven too?" She addressed her question to Alex. Patrick inwardly gave up. He didn't know whether to thank Meredith for continuing to focus on the horse instead of the matter at hand, or throw his hands in the air in frustration.

"Jesus' horse would be awfully lonely if he was the only horse around."

Was it getting hot in here? Patrick pulled at his tie, loosening it.

He couldn't recall any verses regarding pets in heaven. What had he planned to talk about today? His mind went blank. A sermon. Perfect in preparation. Gone, like dust.

"We can also turn to Psalm 139." He cleared his throat in one last attempt to answer the question at hand. "God knows us and has knitted us in our mother's womb." Patrick eyed the congregation for any hope of understanding. Faces stared out at him. "Let's pray." Yes. God help him.

When he opened his eyes, Martin was gone, and Dana leaned on her husband, Nathan's, arm. Nathan was the silent type, and Patrick was certain he had only heard the man speak twice in the whole five years he knew him. Must be a wise man. Patrick wished more of the people who attended The Lord is My Shepherd church would practice silence. Instead, they just blurted out whatever came to them, not having any regard for what he had planned to say or do. Shouldn't he be more assertive? Speak truth and say, "children go to heaven, and if you don't want to believe that then you have a problem, but I have a planned sermon to deliver, thank you very much." Everything resolved in a couple of sentences, no stories about horses and people visiting heaven when they aren't dead. Only in a perfect world.

And after that rant Patrick delivered silently, he decided to let people say how they imagined life in heaven. The ladies disapproved because some of the ideas included food and actual fun, which they thought irreverent. Patrick reminded them of the banquet, but they were convinced after the marriage supper of the lamb, heaven became a convent where people only spoke telepathically and spent quiet hours walking along a street of gold.

"It has to be more exciting than that because children are there," Alex said.

And back to square one, but at least the voice of doom left during prayer.

"Well, that was fun," Robert grumbled as they walked to the car, barely dodging more debate.

"Why do I miss everything?" Susan dragged her feet. "Nothing exciting ever happens in children's church."

"You get snacks," Alex said.

"Yes, and prizes for memory verses. See what I got today." Susan held up a plastic horse.

Patrick stared at it and then unlocked the car. God had a sense of humor at least. "That's great, sweetie."

"Believe me, you're better off where you are," Robert told her. "Alex, you should go back there."

"No." She smiled at Patrick. "I like to hear Daddy preach."

"Ha, that didn't happen today, did it?" Robert climbed into the car.

"Robert, behave yourself," Rose's voice finally joined them. Patrick watched as she appeared lost in thought. He wasn't sure if she had disagreed with something he'd said, or maybe he handled everything wrong. "It's the kind of service that makes people come back."

"That's a scary idea. This is church, not town hall," he started the car.

"Have a little optimism, Patrick."

"Right. I think that's your department." The instant he said it, he regretted the words.

She turned away from him and stared out the window, and they rode the rest of the way in silence.

†††

Irritated and tired, Patrick went into the bedroom, tossing his keys, with Rose at his heels. The kids were always ravenous after church and rummaged through the fridge, finding leftovers from previous meals. Robert, the only one who perceived the tension, sounded extra cheerful about eating lunch. Patrick found that a distraction in itself. Robert and happiness were rarely found together these days.

Patrick leaned against the dresser and stared at Rose. He wasn't in the mood to play nice. He wished he could take back his comment, and now he'd be paying for it. He saw her shaking hands and knew they were cold. She wore a silky material—church clothes. The remainder of his day could have gone a lot better, but chances of that resembled a looter in the snow, peeking in the window, hoping for some warmth.

"Would it hurt you to try, just a little, Patrick?"

Yeah, this wasn't going well.

"Try? You mean pretend everything is going to be all right? That a teenage boy is going to walk into our lives and say, *Here I am, I got lost is all.* C'mon Rose. Some realism wouldn't hurt, would it?"

Everything always went back to what they lost. Stephen.

Her eyes widened as he blatantly threw aside the expectation they were supposed to share. "Your reality is blocking out our possibility. You can't see the light in anything. You focus on the negative—everything being the ruin of your life!" She threw up her hands. "If I can't have hope, what can I have?"

"Closure? A life beyond that day?" He bit out the words quick—a lightning bolt, aimed for the heart.

She came inches from him, her finger touching his chest. If it were a dagger, it'd slice him through. "*You* want that. Guess what, Patrick, you quit a long time ago and don't think I don't know it, so do us a favor and quit pretending. Take your closure. Have your memorial, but don't expect me to attend." She turned around and threw open the bedroom door, revealing Alex standing on the other side with a peanut butter sandwich in hand.

Patrick and Rose froze, staring at the blonde girl who appeared to have no idea what she interrupted. Well, thank God for that mercy.

Rose focused on the sandwich. "Sweetie, we had leftover roast."

"I wanted peanut butter."

"Oh, okay." Rose faltered. Her lips closed, and she backed from the door.

"What do you need, Pumpkin?" Patrick asked, sitting on the bed, taking his shoes off. Slippers, a warm blanket, and a decade to disappear . . .

"I remembered something. Something I forgot."

"At church?" Rose asked. "We can go get it."

"No. I, uh, it's about when I saw heaven."

"Yes? Why didn't you ever mention seeing heaven?" Patrick asked. He could have been more prepared.

"It sort of faded from my memory, almost right away. I remembered Jesus and the horse, but the rest of it was like a dream, as though it didn't happen, but today . . ." She drifted and stared at her shoes. "When Dana asked that question, I remembered. I could hear them. Laughing."

"You aren't worried, are you honey, about saying anything in church? Because it's totally all right. We don't have any problem with what you said," Rose tried.

Patrick thought she could tone down how okay the whole thing was. He didn't want a repeat.

The blonde curls bounced as Alex shook her head. "There is something He said. I forgot about it. I didn't know what He meant."

"Who?" Patrick had a hard time following.

"Jesus."

"What'd He say?" Rose asked, her voice gentle, soothing even Patrick's frazzled nerves.

"He's not here," Alex took a bite of her sandwich and continued talking while chewing, "and when Martin said what he did about Stephen . . ." Her eyes darted at Patrick. "I remembered."

Patrick's eyes flicked to Rose's face, a variety of emotions played there. Expectation once again renewed. He didn't have it in him to believe. A wall blocked his spirit, preventing him from taking on her glass half-full outlook. He gripped onto self-preservation because at this point in the game, he couldn't hide his lack of ability to pretend.

XVII

October 7, 1967

The house buzzed with people. Those awful ladies were there. Rose usually found a way to tolerate them, but this time she couldn't find the grace. Claudia's trademark tone hit the hardest, saying kind things in a way that made acid bubble to the surface. Howard hovered near Patrick and constantly spoke on the phone with the search team.

"Make sure you check the woods. That crazy man ate everything in sight at the festival, hung out at the Halloween display, and watched people. I betcha anything he is living in the trees somewhere."

Rose's stomach turned, and she bolted to the bathroom and threw up. The coolness of the porcelain held her like a magnet. She begged God for it to be a bad dream, while she clung to the toilet bowl as though it were a life preserver. Reality remained. If only she could die right now. She finally forced herself to stand and then opened the door. A sea of faces and voices speaking all at once made her take a step back. The room tipped.

"We have a team searching the woods, Claudia." Howard turned to Rose when she came out of the bathroom. "Sit," he ordered gesturing to get Patrick by her side. "We are searching the whole festival grounds and beyond. We've talked to some of the children, and that kid Jacob thought he saw Stephen near the parking area."

Near the parking area? Where cars were? "What if he's hurt

somewhere?" She had to go. She had to do something. She grabbed her purse and keys.

"Rose, what are you doing?" Howard stepped into her path. Patrick appeared right behind him.

"I'm looking for my son," she jerked past them, ran for the car, and stepped on the gas before they reached her. Leaves blew across the road, falling like snow. The vehicle went off the edge of the pavement, and a cloud of dirt whooshed up behind her. She couldn't stand waiting around anymore, listening to one-way phone conversations. Patrick ran after her, shouting protests about leaving, his words turning into the sound of water in her ears.

It only took her a few minutes to get to the remains of the festival. A few people were cleaning up. She got out of the car and checked around the parking area and off into the brush. What if a car hit him and left? Every rustling noise made by a bird in the bushes gave her hope. A deer jumped out into the open, jarring her into thinking her little boy found his way through the woods after wandering too far. She realized as a new weakness rumbled through her that she'd forgotten to eat something. The baby demanded food.

"Rose?" The voice behind her made her jump.

"Joe." She didn't want to see him here, didn't want to see anyone. She couldn't hold herself together—the second reason for escaping the house. All those people took the air she needed to breathe.

"You should be home." He paced himself next to her. "I'm sorry about Stephen. Have you had any word yet?"

She shook her head, willing not to cry. "I can't just sit around waiting. I heard someone saw him near the parking area. I had to make sure he wasn't in a ditch." Tears fell, and she turned away from him, gazing across the empty orchard. Maybe he climbed a tree. She squinted into the branches.

Joe followed her gaze. "They've been walking the orchard. And the woods beyond."

"Everyone is searching. You need to go home. The first person Stephen will want is you, when he gets there."

The sobs came despite her trying to hold them back. "I can't stand being there. People everywhere, watching me, and talking about possibilities of what happened, and whispering awful things as though I don't know what they are saying." Her body tingled. She alone could be the answer to the energy crisis if they hooked her up somewhere. She'd have a heart attack right here and now. What good would that do for Stephen?

Joe took her arm and guided her to a park bench left over from the festival. "Rose, everyone wants to help. They don't know what to say, and some don't know what to do. Heck, some of them say and do all the wrong things."

Rain fell, slowly at first, then the drops came bigger and faster, but she barely noticed. "He's not here. I had to see for myself." Water dripped down her hair, and her clothes became drenched. A piece of her went numb, like a mindful anesthetic to dull the pain. She and Joe sat side by side, neither one saying anything. Howard and Patrick drove up behind Rose's car. When she finally acknowledged them in the distance, Patrick strode toward her, his steps long and slow, as Howard drove away.

XVIII

October 1977

Patrick couldn't focus. Sunday after Sunday came and went. In reality, he could deliver the sermon he had prepared last week. He sat in his office, his head in his hands. Things at home were tense and work tedious with misplaced mops and talk of not allowing children in the adult services, along with more serious doctrinal issues.

The dead-raising, speaking in tongues, and trips to heaven were more than enough to generate talk about a new pastor. God had already made it clear that The Lord is My Shepherd church hadn't built their faith with the easy stuff. Rose declared the miracle to be a prelude to their son coming back. Just once, Patrick thought, he wished he could believe in Rose's predictions. Crumpling a piece of paper on his desk, he tossed it in the wastebasket. He was often accused of being too far out there; heavenly-minded—but Rose was on another planet.

He leaned back in his chair, taking in the view from the window; the leaves of the nearby maple tree hung in soggy colors, and a thick rain fell. High winds were expected later. Maybe he'd blow away. He should take a vacation. Picturing a scenic destination cheered him a little. Rose might welcome a little trip. They could use the break. While they were gone, he'd probably be replaced by a more sedate pastor.

Patrick recalled Rose pointing out his negative attitude. He needed a paradigm shift. A good third of the church had left, but on the positive side, he still had a church. There had been no call for his resignation, though he waited day after day, and it was the usual ones who complained. Why change their role in this church scenario? There may be more fall-out from last Sunday's odd series of events, but why buy trouble? His wish could come true. Maybe they'd be chased out of town. He should succumb to the ordinary for awhile. I'm okay, you're okay; no surprises to ruffle feathers. Just for a few Sundays.

His hand went to a pile of papers and ran into the coffee cup, spilling steaming liquid all over the desk. Terrific. He grabbed at some towels nearby and mopped at the paperwork scattered on his desk.

"You might need another cup?"

He startled, almost dropping the pencil holder. Rose. Bearing cinnamon rolls. He looked at them. Upcoming baking mania, or just a token of love? He chose to believe the latter.

"Peace offering?" She lifted a heart dish out of her food bag, placing a warm pastry in the center. "I couldn't think of anything else to offer."

He glanced at the cinnamon roll and then took in her body with a slow smile. "I can think of other things."

"Now, Patrick. Obviously, we can't do anything like that here." She fiddled with her hair and took a step back.

He went around her and shut the door. He took her bag and put it in a chair and then kissed her.

"Well," she said. "I guess there's that."

He sighed. "It will have to do for now, unless we want to give them something to talk about." He grinned.

"Which happens no matter what, but I don't think we need to go overboard." She leaned in and kissed him again.

They broke apart, and he put a stray hair behind her ear. "Thanks for the cinnamon roll. It will go perfect with my second cup of coffee. Stay and have some."

She smiled, appearing younger, vulnerable. He vowed to try harder, to be more what she needed. She was a mother after all, and the fact that Stephen disappeared was his fault—something he always tried to forget.

XIX

April 1978 ~ New Jersey

It was the week of spring recess in Edison, New Jersey. Henry sat on the bed listening to sappy love songs on his transistor radio. He was only thirteen, but some of his friends acted all grown up—smoking, going out with girls—even though their dads had to drive them on dates. Older siblings helped them gain access to beer, cigarettes, and parties they were too young for—none of these things were part of Henry's life. He knew his mom had prescription drugs and vodka in the house, but she kept the alcohol hidden, while the other sat tucked deep in the kitchen cupboard. He didn't have interest in scavenging for either one.

Sometimes Ricky would come over, and they would walk around the neighborhood out of sheer boredom and get Big Gulps at the nearby 7-Eleven. For something different, however, they often begged their mothers to drop them off at the roller rink or they'd ride their bikes to Menlo Park Mall. A theater sat across the street, and every now and then they'd catch an afternoon show.

Ricky's mom tried to fit in with the younger set—not mom-like at all, which sealed the deal for him and Rick to become friends. Neither one of their moms would get the mother of the year award. Mrs. Younger dressed the part, wearing stuff the sixteen-year-olds wore, still clinging to the 1960s. Her signature clothing—orange instead of black with bright red lipstick and a yellow head-band for her sleek platinum blonde hair, made her easy to spot. Wherever she went, heads turned. Henry's mom faded into the background around Nina Younger, who traipsed around in her knee-high white boots.

On this particular Wednesday, she dropped Ricky off, and the instant the car door closed, her brown Javelin lit up the gravel with its tires spraying rocks against the fence.

"Where's she going in such a hurry?" Henry asked.

Ricky made a divot in the tiny rocks. "Probably shopping. She's been all about some fancy handbag, like there is a race to be the first one to get it or something. She's got all her tennis friends from the club to impress."

"Huh." Henry's mom bought her purses at a dull department store, or sometimes she'd snag a designer bag at a thrift shop. And the only club they belonged to was the gun club. But that was Beckett's gig, and Beckett left them five months ago. Just another string of his mom's boyfriends. This one, however, appeared sad to go, and he'd outlasted any of the others. Henry's mom hit her prescriptions hard afterward, and Henry never knew what mood she'd be in. Beck leaving made her spiral in a strange assortment of sadness and paranoia with intermittent spurts of euphoria. Henry thought she was unhappy being alone, but that didn't seem to be the problem. He'd watch her when he couldn't sleep, following the light, a dim glow coming from her desk. She'd be leaning over a rectangle of paper, tapping her pen, pushing the little button on the end over and over, as though she was composing something of incredible importance—letters that she'd shred afterward. An attempt to read the scraps she left in the trash didn't bring anything to light except an occasional, 'see?' and a mention about hiking. He went through each bit of paper in search of a salutation, but only found one addressed to 'Dear,' and then dot, dot, dot, as though the recipient was undecided. She never signed them because she always quit before the end.

Moving away was mentioned at times, but in reality, they had a good thing in Edison, New Jersey—a lucky break when coming here—a house renting at a decade old price. Edison had lots of

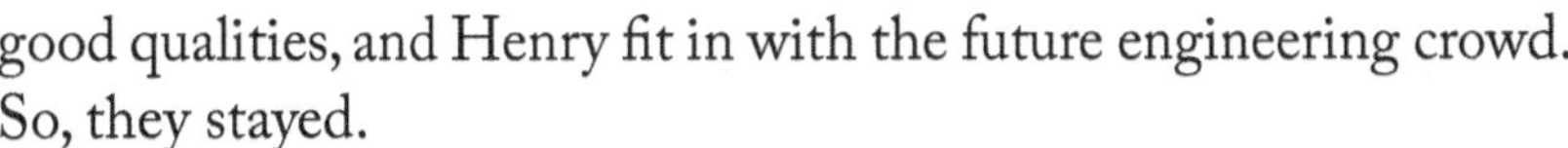

good qualities, and Henry fit in with the future engineering crowd. So, they stayed.

"Heard from your dad?" Ricky asked.

"Beck? He's not my dad. Nah. He said he wouldn't be contacting us. Acted all Kojak when he left."

"Dude, what if he's a spy on a secret mission?" Rick unwrapped a chocolate lollipop, sticking it in his mouth.

"What? No, he's just—you know, Beckett."

"He has a gun."

"So? Half of Jersey has guns."

"He didn't say where he was going?"

Henry got annoyed with the conversation. Like he hadn't thought about where Beck took off to no more than a million times. When Beckett left he had tears in his eyes and kept staring at Henry as though he saw him for the first time—the hesitation of something unsaid hovered in the air, and then Beck deflated as though he'd been outwitted, or the world gut punched him. Henry couldn't find sympathy, however. If Beckett cared about Henry, he woulda stayed.

"Of course not. He doesn't want to be found." He'd heard his mom saying Beckett left for Europe. He wasn't about to tell Ricky, whose imagination twisted simple happenings into something worthy of a full blown movie.

"I know! His life was in danger, and he had to leave to keep you and your mom safe from his big dark secret."

"Ah, shut up."

"Or he is an alien," Ricky did some ridiculous movement with his hands and mouth, the universal code for Martian. Henry shoved him onto the pile of pillows on the bed. "Come on, let's have ice cream and play Monopoly." He went to the kitchen, ending the conversation about the closest person to a dad he ever knew.

After Beckett disappeared, Henry found himself staring out the window more often while he imagined his real dad. What if he could get to know him? Or Beckett could come back. Henry gazed at the only photo his mother had ever given him of his real father. It sat on his dresser by the window—a man with light hair, surrounded by autumn leaves, laughing like someone told a joke. Henry needed to get out of this funk because his thoughts and those stupid love songs were sending him down a dark road. He pictured the pit yawning, waiting for him to fall in. He backed up a few steps, away from the despair and focused on gathering the money earned from Miss Minnie, his elderly next door neighbor, who paid him to mow her lawn and pull weeds. It was Friday, and soon school would be back in session. He and Ricky made plans to spend their last weekday afternoon at the mall.

The magical swoosh of doors opened into the coolness of Woolworth's—the smell of newness, inviting colors, displays of candy under squares of ceiling lights gave Henry a longing for things that moments ago didn't have any importance in his life. Then the whiff of fries and grilled cheese from the lunch counter on the left made his stomach growl. The life of the mall awoke a part of Henry's brain to a subculture he never allowed himself to dwell on—this place represented fantasy. Ricky, who grew up with the mall being his second babysitter, went charging toward one of the bar stools. "I'm starving," he announced, leaving Henry no choice but to follow him.

They sat on the bolted seats, frozen Coke's beside their plates, and split a bacon and tomato sandwich, dividing the perfect squares while nibbling on fries.

"I want to check out the records," Ricky was saying, breaking into Henry's thoughts.

"Yeah, sure."

"Where'd you wanna go?" Ricky asked.

Henry wiped some ketchup off his fingers. "I'm just glad to get away from the house. We could see the birds."

"Yeah. Someday I want to get a parakeet. A nice blue one," Ricky said.

They cleaned their plates, throwing away napkins and straws. The cobbler sang from his shoe repair corner, the song covering a portion of the store. When they got closer to the pets, Henry stopped short, the tune of the shoe man and the birds blending together as he froze in front of a display of pictures. A blur of orange, yellow, brown, and red caught his eye. A laughing man in each frame—small, medium, large—an array of autumn.

"Wow." Ricky stopped and stared at all the pictures. "Your real dad is famous?" he asked. "Or your mom has sold you a big fat lie."

If Henry hadn't any doubts to his mom's story of his father in the first place, he'd have defended her, but in a matter of seconds, the truth settled in.

"You think?" Henry said, his sarcasm brushed with anger. How stupid he'd been to believe the picture was of his dad. All the times he stared in the mirror, pretending he saw a likeness. He'd been an idiot. His throat burned with emotion he had to hold in. What he would give to grab a bat and bash every metal frame sending glass shattering across the store.

"Hey. Don't worry about it. My old man comes around once a year. It ain't so great, believe me. I was always jealous you had Beck." Ricky shuffled his feet. "Come on. Let's check out the pets. You should talk your mom into letting you get something. A cat, dog, parakeet? Should be easy now because she owes you after this."

Henry followed Ricky. The birds in their cages hopped around—a bundle of color, and the big gray parrot sat on the wire perch squawking out "hello" with random wolf whistles. The sounds and colors of the store dulled together—hazy and dreamlike. Henry listened to Ricky rattle on about his favorite bands and nodded at intervals, following him out of the pet area and to the record department, passing the girls hovering over the albums: Prince, Kiss, Aretha Franklin, and Johnny Cash, front and center for the *New in April* display. They gave him and Ricky sidelong glances, giggling, as they passed by leaving an aroma of flowery shampoo and strawberry lip gloss in their wake. Ricky smiled, elbowing him, and Henry made his lips turn up slightly in an attempt to be present, but inside a piece of him fell away.

†††

She lied. Lied! He would go to his room and take the picture and throw it in the trash. Stepping into the house a whiff of Pine Sol gave him pause and then the smell of a roast. There it sat with mashed potatoes and gravy along with a small pan of canned green beans. He glanced out at the backyard. The wheelbarrow overflowed with weeds his mom had pulled.

"Did you have a good time?" she asked, setting the table for the two of them.

"Sure, yeah." His plan of confronting her faltered, and his hunger pushed it aside into a *for-later* file. The half sandwich he had at Woolworth's hadn't filled his earlier hunger. He sat, taking in the feast, glad he didn't have to come up with something to eat, but also knowing what all this energy spent meant. He'd seen the prescription the other day—oxycodone. She left the room for a second, and he walked to the cupboard, grabbing the bottle that sat on the shelf. Half full. He calculated how long before she'd be non-functional again. The side had a sticker—may cause drowsiness, but for his mom, she would have the energy and happiness of a toddler. Everything depended on whether she had refills. He read the label. Zero. A pill a day. A couple of weeks maybe? He heard her coming and shut the cupboard, hurrying back to his chair.

Henry wanted to tell her he knew about the picture, but everything he wanted to say stopped like a lump in his throat. She was fresh and tan from spending the majority of her day outside, the house was clean, and he didn't want to ruin his chance to enjoy the homemade dinner. Usually he only got these kinds of meals from Miss Minnie next door. He took a bite of mashed potatoes as his mother laughed and appeared years younger. She told him stories of her childhood and teased him about his hair getting too long. Guilt stabbed at him; he enjoyed his mom at times like this, but the reality of why darkened the happiness, like something poking you that shouldn't be there. He knew she wanted to be like this—have the extra energy and feel accomplished. Maybe the pills made her what she used to be—happy and carefree.

†††

The pseudo idyllic days Henry enjoyed came to an abrupt end sooner than he anticipated. Two days later he found his mother curled up on the bed sobbing. He backed away and went to the kitchen, grabbed the bottle, and found it empty.

He ran into the bedroom. "Where are all the pills?"

Her expression made him step back. "What are you? The pill police? I take what I need. Don't go acting all high and mighty." Her tears smeared her make-up and her mouth twisted in rage. She wailed so loud that Henry wanted to cover his ears.

Her arms twitched, moving in odd random jerks. He threw the bottle at her. "How many? How many did you take?"

She flinched as it landed on the bed in front of her. Her swollen eyes narrowed, and she pointed at him, her voice raised. "You took some, didn't you? Is that why you're here demanding to know why it's empty? You and your bratty friend coming in here. Look I lost track. I took ten—or twelve—a couple every two hours or so. I'd still have some if it weren't for you." Her arms continued jerking about in strange motions.

Henry stared at her. "You're crazy. I don't take your stupid drugs!"

"Get out!" She flung a nearby book at him. "Get out!" He dodged the paperback and ran out the door to Miss Minnie's.

†††

Cherry blossoms glowed under the cloudy sky, soaking in the rain, and then twinkled in the sunshine as the weather changed back and forth. Henry sat on Minnie's front porch eating crybaby cookies, guilt coating each bite. Guilt because he didn't want to go back home and take care of his mom. He wanted her to take care of

109

him. An emergency hospital visit had followed his departure the day he found the empty bottle. Within twenty-four hours she had taken thirteen pain pills. Miss Minnie insisted that Henry stay for the two weeks that his mother would be in rehab. He missed Beckett, but Beckett had gone, just like his own mysterious father. Henry saw now how his mom drove away the men in her life. He wondered if she wished him gone as well. The sun sank from the horizon, and clouds blew across the sky. Dipping his hand in the tin can for another cookie he contemplated the dark house next to Minnie's and made a decision. He would make himself as scarce as possible and stay out of his mom's way.

XX

July 1990 ~ Filbert Ridge

Thirteen years had passed since Winston got a second chance at life. Children graduated into adulthood, and some adults still behaved like children. Filbert Ridge remained the same, yet wasn't, like a song on a different stanza. The treehouse, a symbol of Alex's childhood, now faded: a few loose boards, the bottom rung of the ladder crooked, rope ends tattered. Her cousin, Jimmy had traded candy cigarettes for an occasional scotch and taught literature at Creekside High. He'd left Filbert Ridge for four years of college, vowing at the time to not come back, but there wasn't a better fishing spot in all of Oregon. Alex suspected he missed Breely, Adam's sister, but Bree never gave herself a minute to miss anybody. It appeared, however, that Jimmy was content with his job and schedule. He couldn't beat having the extra free time in the summer to fish.

Robert lived in Portland while attending his Internal Medicine Residency Program at the Oregon Health and Science University, and Susan married right after high school. She and Stan had been together for five years already, and were now expecting a baby in November. Alex didn't feel much different at twenty than she did when she was eight. Even moving into the apartment that sat above Brooks' Books didn't make her feel grown up. Perhaps when she was the official owner of the bookstore in a little over a month, she'd feel like a validated adult.

Her latest faux pas at church hadn't even registered in her mind. She took this particular morning off to meet Jimmy at her parents, only to find Vivian, Claudia, and Meredith at the McMillans unannounced.

"As though they are trying to catch dust on the stairway rail," Rose muttered when she spotted Vivian's car. The family home sat as a time capsule, floating, unchanging, its heartbeat speaking the name of the one that remained missing. Alex's parents did the same dance, trying to remain neutral in their difference of opinions. Her mother's hope laid dormant, and her dad's unbelief roamed about the hallways, doorways, and empty rooms like a silent houseguest.

The chattering chipmunks with an occasional buzz of a cicada followed Alex inside as she went to say hello to her mother. Summertime was the Pacific Northwest's best kept secret with its clear blue skies crowning the evergreens below, serenaded by a refreshing breeze. Alex frowned, watching the car park under the apple tree. Her timing to meet Jimmy couldn't have been worse. Her happiness dimmed at the sight of the ladies, for just as sure as thorny vines brought juicy blackberries in July and August, these three brought trouble in the form of ripe gossip. One coated in sweetness and pleasure, the other turning bitter after being swallowed. It was a mistake coming here. She had plenty of work to do at the bookstore and gladly would have worked it to avoid these three clouds. Alex had never been lifted from the microscope the ladies held over her, always looking and waiting for her to do something wrong.

"Escape while you can," Rose told her. "You can pick up the mail for me from the post office box on your way back." Alex slipped through the back door to where Jimmy waited with his fishing pole, renewing her hope to pick enough berries for a cobbler. The season was short.

"Saw the blue beast," Jimmy said, referring to Vivian's newest car. "Something go down at church again?"

"Not that I know of." Had she done anything? Her steps matched his as they walked. "Oh, I did tell Katie she could pray for her cat to get well." Alex helped Lily with the handful of five to seven year-olds in children's church.

Jimmy squinted his green eyes at her. "And did it?"

"I don't know. That was Sunday, it's not like I got a report." She glanced back at the house.

"I can paint a scenario for you."

"Can't wait to hear." There was no sense stopping him. Just like his dad, he'd taken to writing novels at night, horror stories to be exact, while living in a tiny home tucked in the woods.

Turning toward the gravel drive, a soft breeze shivered through the willow tree.

"So," Jimmy began, "Katie prays for her cat, and it is full of life and vitality, unfortunately Katie's parents hated snowball, and you are to blame for their continuing suffering." He said this as though it were fact.

"Snowball?"

"A basic cat name."

"That doesn't sound very likely."

"Or, Katie prayed for the cat, and it died, and she is in distress."

"I told her the cat would be in heaven if it died."

"Haven't you gotten in trouble for that before?"

"Yes. But it's true."

Jimmy smirked. "Probably why they are here."

"I don't see why they'd care."

"Because that's what they do. They are very caring," Jimmy grinned.

Alex rolled her eyes. He had a point, but a visit about a cat would be ridiculous. "I hardly think they'd waste their time."

Jimmy laughed. "You've always been optimistic."

"Oh, wait, I forgot the post box key. I'm getting the mail while we are there." The country grocery doubled as the post office and sat across from the bridge that went over the creek. "I'll run in and grab it and hopefully slip out before anyone knows the difference." Alex took off back the way they had come and opened the front door slow and quiet, grabbing the tiny key from the hook on the wall, but before she could wedge herself back outside, her mother appeared in the hallway with Vivian behind her.

"You best be careful out there, Alexandria. We aren't as safe as we used to be." Vivian's voice announced the danger.

Alex froze. Then Claudia appeared. "Oh yes. It's a sad time we live in when missing children grace the covers of papers and magazines on a regular basis, and now break-ins happening in our own town. Imagine! Not sure you should be living alone in that bookstore apartment."

"I'm perfectly fine. And right now, Jimmy is with me, see?" She pointed toward the open door.

"Oh well then, you will be safe. I won't even go out alone any-more," Claudia said with an air of importance. "But still, how is business, dear? I'd think it'd be a bit lonely."

"Really, Claudia. You must know that it is every young person's dream to move out." Rose winked at Alex.

"No need to worry, Miss Claudia. I am not lonely at all." She took a step to leave, but the next comment stopped her. "There have been rumors that children believe they can pray for miracles to happen. Healings and who knows what else is meant to be left in God's hands."

"Matter of fact," Vivian interrupted Claudia, "I heard Jessica was praying for Grandma Burky to come back to life. Grandma Burky has been sitting on top of the family piano for at least five years."

Alex glanced at her mother who looked like she was about to choke.

"An urn, you know cremation. It isn't the most popular burial method amongst church folks, making God put all those ashes back together when you could have just left the body intact in the first place, but the Burkys always went against the norm."

"I'm sure Jessica's grandmother would not want to come back here after being in heaven." Alex gave the most practical expla-nation she could.

"Can you imagine? What would she do about her social security number?" Meredith piped in from the other room. "What a paperwork mess that would be."

Rose let out a snort and with a few quick steps went somewhere into the kitchen. Alex longed to disappear as well.

"But this is all because of your help in the Sunday school classroom. You shouldn't suggest prayer for pets." Vivian peered over her glasses at Alex. "Adam is in charge of the children's ministry, is he not, Rose? I think we should bring this problem to his attention. Alex here should teach a less impressionable age. These children will believe anything she tells them."

"Oh, I hardly think—" Rose started.

"I don't recall telling them lies. How is Katie's cat?" Alex jumped in, to save her mother from comment.

"The way I understand it is she prayed, and the cat was eating its food the next morning, all better. Raises people's expectations. And now we have this Burky problem."

Alex looked out the door, taking a step back toward the sunshine and the willow tree as she caught a glimpse of Jimmy pacing where she'd left him. "I need to get going. I will consider your advice which if I'm understanding would be to not encourage prayer because prayers may be answered exactly as you ask." She hurried out the door with a backward glance at Vivian who clamped her lips shut in a straight line and Claudia whose mouth hung open in a response left unsaid.

"That took long enough," Jimmy said, scuffling his feet along the gravel.

"You would not believe those women."

"Didn't I tell you?"

"I just need to get out of here. I may be barred from helping with the children."

"It was about the cat, wasn't it?"

"Yes," and she burst out laughing. "You should have heard their reasoning."

"So, what happened?"

She stopped walking. "It's not worth rehashing but in the end I'm afraid I sounded just like my dad."

"I mean the cat. Did it live?"

"Yes," she said with a grin.

After a morning of sunshine and watching her cousin throw his fishing line in, again and again, only catching twigs, Alex felt refreshed for work mode.

"Heard you've caused a catamount of trouble," a voice above her said.

Startled Alex dropped the romances she held.

"Sorry," Adam bent down, gathering the paperbacks, then handed them to her.

"You are too funny, as usual," she pushed the books onto the shelf in their proper series order. "It is quite the catastrophe." She giggled.

"You know what this means, right?"

"I'll be banned somewhere, maybe to the dungeon of the church library. A place where no one goes." She turned and leaned her back against the shelf of romances, looking at him. "Oh, I see. You've come to deliver the bad news. I am being fired from children's church." Alex didn't understand why he'd chosen the ministry after witnessing what went on at The Lord is My Shepherd.

"You really think your father is going to send me to tell you that you can't help with the kids? Plus, it's not like volunteers are lining up. Can't fire someone who isn't being paid, can we?"

"Claudia and Vivian came by to speak to my mother, making sure to tell her that you should fix the problem—as in me. Babies could be my new assignment. I mean, I wouldn't corrupt them since they don't know what I am saying."

"I only came to ask you if you'd like to have dinner with me. And it has nothing to do with church." His smile was smug, evidently happy to catch her off guard with a non-church event. "I've only heard the story, but no one has come to me to suggest your removal. Why would they? Your dad is the one in charge. My mom loves having your help."

"Okay. They just sounded so determined." She looked at her watch. "I have a break at 5:30."

"Sounds great. I thought we'd go to Harry's, since you probably don't have long."

"Hamburgers are my favorite."

He grinned. "I'll be back in a bit," he turned toward the exit then glanced back at her. "Oh, and by the way, if I see Grandma Burky bowling at Creekside Lanes, I'll let you know."

"You heard about that, too?"

"People tend to talk too loud in the church hallways forgetting they can be heard by those of us on the other side of the closed doors," he said with a wave as he went outside, and she wondered why he'd dare to be seen with her.

XXI

August 1990 ~ Manhattan, New York

Summer's sun grew weary, and the crispness of fall edged in, giving Henry a new found energy as he took the elevator to his Manhattan apartment. Life had fallen into place just as he planned. He graduated from New Jersey Institute of Technology. The college sat a mere half hour or so from his home in Edison. Part of him had longed to get away and go across the country, but he decided to be practical and save money with the in-state tuition. After an internship with an architecture firm, he had a real job and enough money to live on his own.

Twelve years ago—that night he sat on Miss Minnie's porch—marked a new beginning for Henry. He worked at the lunch counter at Woolworth's as soon as he was old enough, then the grocery store, saving every dime for college, getting straight A's, and receiving as many scholarships as he could. Sometimes his mom had clarity, but she struggled to enjoy her life leading her to succumb to two more overdoses. By the time he was sixteen, gone all day at school and working all evening, he realized he wasn't the problem. Nothing changed by making himself scarce. She was still either overly productive or did nothing, and Henry no longer cared for the pill-induced mom that had to do everything fast, as though there was a timer waiting to go off. He didn't need her attention because, like perfect weather, it always came to an end. Leaving after college cut the cord. Setting up his apartment brought a sigh of relief, and the sky cleared offering new promise. A dark curtain lifted, and he blinked in the brightness.

He could eventually buy a place in upper state New York. He sat on his sofa and pictured a sprawling home with acreage of trees and a garden. Maybe by then enough time would have passed for both his mother and him to heal from the past—to come together without narcotics standing between them like a needy friend. She wouldn't have to self-medicate because he'd make her life stress-free. She loved gardening and could live near him. He imagined her happy, relaxed. He realized these thoughts were a contradiction to finding his own way and breaking free, but sometimes—

The phone rang interrupting his daydream.

"Henry?"

"Miss Minnie?"

"Listen, honey, I need to tell you something . . ."

He closed his eyes. No. Not again.

"It's your mother . . ."

"Minnie, there's nothing I can do. The same thing . . ." He stopped, realizing his good intentions came with stipulations, possibly ones that steeped through a filter of unreality. His daydream vanished.

"It's cancer, Henry. I'm sorry, I didn't want to blurt it out—" Silence fluttered over the line. "She's known for awhile—the prognosis is bad, I'm afraid. There's not much time left."

He clutched the phone, leaned against the wall, closing his eyes to the view of the city, his throat too dry to speak.

"She's in the hospital. I told her I'd tell you. She couldn't bring herself to call you. She'd pick up the phone and then hang up. "Henry, I've tried to tell her to call you sooner, thought you deserved to know."

His mother wouldn't want to come to him for anything. Despite his big ideas of making her life wonderful, he'd left her, just like everybody else. This time of day the traffic would take him over an hour to get to her.

"I'll come. I'm leaving now."

"Oh, honey. That's perfect. She'll be glad to see you."

Henry hung up the phone, his earlier happiness deflating like a pop of a balloon.

XXII

Winston died for real on September 23 in 1990. Evidently, he took to dying on Sundays, but this time he waited until after church. The weather took an odd turn after being excessively hot for the past week. The day of the service marked a break in the heat, and maple leaves twirled in the air, dancing to the sound of the heavy wind; collars turned up, and ladies dodged through the parking lot, holding down their skirts.

Patrick spent extra time preparing what he had to say, not sure how to approach the death of someone who had already died in the parking lot thirteen years ago. The extra rattling of the windows made him jumpy, but it was just the wind. He spotted women in hats peering over the pews as if waiting for Winston to rise for a second time, but much to Patrick's relief the dead remained quiet, and the service indicated all would go as planned. Joe stood as far away from the casket as he could get, perhaps also worrying about a repeated event.

This time, Winston slipped from earth to heaven while taking his Sunday nap. No shouting, no fanfare, just stepped into eternity with Jesus. He had remained faithful the whole thirteen years since he'd been dragged out of hell. The only mess he hadn't cleaned up was with his son, Joe. He tried, but stubbornness had a streak in that family, getting stronger with each generation.

The song started up, sang by Betsy with her crackly, aged voice, "And He walks with me and He talks with me . . ." and Patrick's eyes caught Alex, sitting near the back, and Winston's nephew,

121

Paul Brooks, almost directly across, glaring her way. She, however, seemed oblivious.

During the third stanza, his mind wandered, taking in the attendees—some he hadn't seen in years. Gary, Caroline's ex-husband had come and sat near the middle pew, his expression filled with accusations. Robert who hadn't darkened a church door since stepping foot in a dorm, had shown up. Sitting behind Alex, he shifted in his seat, noticed Paul, and frowned.

A loud silence announced the end of the song, interrupting Patrick's thoughts. He took a moment, finding where he left off in his notes and continued with the service, until at the end, Winston could have been named a saint.

"Sometimes people have strong faith and love for God, but they turn away never acknowledging Him again. Others follow a rocky road, and it may get rockier before they hit good soil, but in the end, they find Jesus. Ending the race well is important. And Winston did just that."

The piano music jumped in with a more upbeat tune, of "I'll Fly Away."

Stifled hiccups from the middle of the church punctuated the song, and what Patrick thought would turn into a wail came out as laughter. "Sorry." Her whisper echoed throughout the building, bouncing off each pew. "It's the song. I see Winston flying around—"

Much to Patrick's dismay, others joined in, and Winston's funeral ended with everyone making too joyful of a noise. He shouted above the outburst. "Graveside services will immediately follow at the Filbert Ridge Cemetery." A new wave of giggling rolled through the sanctuary as he escaped the building, catching out of the corner of his eye the only one not laughing—Joe.

His glance swept to Gary—two people not laughing.

The service, once again, spun things out of control.

The cemetery sat on the Filbert Ridge side of town, across the road from the Dockerbogger. Joe's tavern had the prime location for both Dockerbog and Filbert Ridge which gave him business from both towns, but the building itself lacked structural care. The cemetery also got the double business due to location. Clouds rolled in, and Patrick held onto Winston's widow as she staggered against the increasing wind.

"Goodness, what odd weather. I'm afraid you'll need to be brief, Pastor. I mean, I'm not telling you how to do the service, but it is chilly."

"You are the boss, Mrs. Brooks. I'm sorry the conditions are not ideal."

"You don't control the weather. Can't say I know what God is thinking making Winston's going home service so blusterous. Wonder if He's trying to tell us something?" she shouted above the gale.

Patrick stood under the blackening sky. The crowd thinned for this event, so he did a quick introduction with John 3:16. "For God so loved the world that he gave his only begotten son that whosoever believes in him shall not perish but have eternal life.' Winston is with the Lord now and in a better place, for as it says in Second Corinthians 5:1 'for we know if the earthly tent we live in is destroyed, we have a building from God, an eternal house in heaven not built by human hands.'"

A stillness settled as the wind stopped. Everyone looked around, and hair was patted back into place and postures relaxed. Patrick gave a glance at Mrs. Brooks, then continued speaking of the virtues of heaven, but when he opened his mouth, a gust of wind with more force than before, ripped through the cemetery, twigs and leaves blowing across the ground. The Brooks family stood in a row, and Mrs. Brooks teetered right into what must have been Winston's brother.

A horrendous roar and the sound of a building ripping had the mourners checking out the sky, while some kept their eyes on the casket that sat waiting to be lowered into the earth. A voice shouted from across the street, "It's the tavern! Half the roof blew off!" Attention turned to the building, and a piece of siding blew into a window. The sound of shattering glass and Joe's swear words were muffled by howling and furious gusts as he took off toward the bar. One of his relatives stopped him. "You'll get killed by debris if you go over there. Can't stop the wind."

Joe turned from the destruction of his tavern and came at Patrick. "You did this! I don't know how you did it, but this is your fault! Lucky me that this is the last time my father dies, because every time he does, more of my life is ruined!" Joe's shouting faded into the wind as another crash came from the Dockerbogger.

✝✝✝

For Patrick, the next few days blurred into phone calls and office visits from both those who loved and hated Winston Brooks, wanting to discuss the way the funeral went, and how relieved they were that the bookstore would remain. Or, if they were from the other camp, how the business should be returned to Joe immediately. Especially now that the tavern needed extensive repairs.

"An act of revenge, Patrick. His own son should be the one to inherit the business. I can't get Winston's wife to see reason. You'd think she'd be on Joe's side!" Vivian sat, uninvited, in the chair opposite of him.

Adjusting his reading glasses, he looked over his schedule, weighing his response. "I can assure you, Vivian, it wasn't revenge, but was only about what Winston wanted the store to become, or in this case—not to become. And what is your interest in this matter? You don't like bookstores? If Joe had the building, it would be rezoned for a restaurant."

"We could use a nice eatery in this town." Her voice had a spark as though just the idea lifted her spirits. "A great German cuisine, perhaps fondue? Wouldn't that be fabulous?"

Patrick's thoughts drifted to war criminals, and the strange man who claimed to be searching for Nazis that had made their way to the United States through the Canadian border. A picture of Vivian burning books came to mind next. Not to mention he couldn't picture Filbert Ridge residents dipping into something as foofaraw as fondue.

"Winston made his decision about the bookstore years ago, and it is all legal. Frankly, since Mrs. Brooks is okay with it, I fail to see what your interest is."

She leaned forward. "I wanted to bring your attention to the talk in the town. If Winston would have stayed dead the first time, the property would be Joe's, but your daughter interfered with the natural course of life. It's possible the whole thing was a hoax, like all this UFO talk we keep hearing about. Lots of stuff not true anymore."

The pounding in Patrick's head felt like Satan had set up camp and took to banging at his skull, but it was just Vivian. Sometimes when people found out he was a pastor, they'd say, "Oh, isn't that nice." Right.

XXIII

The Lord is My Shepherd formed a small choir in the past year, and Rose decided to be a part, for something to do—an attempt to move forward. But when she sang, her voice carried across an orchard of trees, through the woods and along a highway—reaching, forever stretching toward her lost son. In her dreams she'd take his hand, and bring him home, then waken to the crash of reality, losing him all over again. Yet, with slippers on her feet, she'd pad across the floor, not breathing, the knob of the bedroom door turning, as though she expected to find something different than the empty bed. It mocked her, covered with its cheerful primary colored quilt. She hadn't had the dream for years—until last night. This time there was no child's bed to curl up on and sob, washing away the cruel lie of the dream, but more importantly, Stephen appeared as a grown man, and that had never happened. He'd never aged in the dreams. She always held the small hand of a child.

Alone in her bed because Patrick had already left for church, she stared at the ceiling, not wanting the picture to fade away. She'd nearly given up and tried to pretend she'd moved on—for Patrick's sake, for the peace of her marriage, but now she could barely breathe with this new possibility blooming large, dormant, and real. Sometimes she convinced herself that Stephen couldn't possibly be alive, but the rest of the time, she clung to a hope that everyone else whispered was delusional.

Rose arrived at church, her heart leaping with expectation. God had given her a vision that she declared as truth. Her spirit saw him alive. Then the realistic side of her would admonish such thoughts. *Why can't you let it go? Give up. Let Patrick have his closure.* The devil sat on her shoulder giving advice.

She hurried along the hallway, ducking into the ladies' room to check her make-up before coming on the platform with the choir. Faces passed her in a blur, and their emotions were displayed like words being thrown into the air, polluting the atmosphere. Explaining this—experiencing people's feelings just by being near them—usually resulted in eyes darting away and tiny steps, backing up from her, as though she had the most recent illness promised to kill any that got close. "A spiritual gift," an elderly woman, brave enough to listen, told Rose, with a nod of understanding. "But a burden. Take care you don't go down with the downers."

Down with the downers. The phrase had stuck with Rose, and the older she got, the more she understood. But today, emerging from the bathroom, the crowded passageway cleared as did her head. She put in an effort to lighten her step. Autumn. Leaves floating to the ground letting the sky peek through the bare branches made way for a sunny spot, shedding doubt.

"Good morning, Joe," she said with the kind of brightness one used when attempting to slip quickly by. She didn't expect him here. Maybe his father's death had him contemplating eternity.

"Funny you should say that." Joe stepped into her path. "For you, it obviously is a good morning, but for me, not so much. After my business was one step from being destroyed, good is hard to come by."

Rose backed up a step to create space between them in the narrow hallway. A streak of sun splashed onto the carpet from a nearby classroom window. "I'm sorry for your loss. It must be difficult."

"Difficult? A mild word for it." Joe moved into her space and she leaned into the wall. "I need the bookstore. The building is on prime land. My dad gave you what was mine, and now from the grave, he took what I already had. Oh sure, in a short time I'll be able to open while renovating, but it takes money to fix a place. How do you justify all of it? I've been quiet about Brooks' Books, assuming Alex would get bored with it, or get married and move away." He smiled. "You could talk to her for me. You and I have spent a lot of time trying to find your boy and all." His hand went to touch her shoulder but she side-stepped him.

"I'm sorry, Joe. It's out of my hands." She hurried around a corner and ran into Vivian.

"For goodness sakes, Rose. Where's the fire?" Her glance went to Joe. "Oh, I see. Yes, at least you are using the biblical principle, flee from the devil."

"Vivian, I'm not fleeing, I'm just nearly late."

Joe let out a laugh, "And I'm not the devil."

Rose clamped her mouth shut, *if the shoe fits*, she turned, brushing too close to Vivian, then slipped into Patrick's office, shutting the door. The encounter had left her hands unsteady, and her voice would follow suit. Singing could only be faked at this point. She'd stay in here. After all, one never knew when a pastor's wife needed to counsel someone, and in this moment, she needed counseling from God Himself. Her absence wouldn't be thought of twice.

✝✝✝

Patrick noticed Rose missed the service and wondered if she had fallen ill and had gone home, or maybe someone needed to talk to her in private. He went over the morning and didn't find anything amiss. He delivered the sermon while still apprehensive about his wife and finished with an announcement.

"Now, everyone is invited tonight for ice cream at Martin's home." The silence boomed louder than the chatter that had stopped. Patrick struggled to bring normality to this strange offering of hospitality from Martin. "Meredith is making apple pie, I hear." Sighs of relief followed. Of course, the invite had been all Meredith's doing. Martin lived in a fancy mansion in the part of Dockerbog people weren't afraid to visit. The area on the hill could be considered one of the state's best kept secrets for beautiful housing at a lower price. "Directions to his home are available out in the foyer. We won't be having a sermon or study, just be armed with your favorite Bible verse to share. See you tonight."

Patrick left the podium and made quick steps to find Rose, but was apprehended, front and center by Claudia.

"Pastor."

"Yes, Claudia. How are you?"

"It's unusual for you to ditch preaching on Sunday night for pie and ice cream."

"Well, getting together once in awhile for a more casual meeting is pleasant for everyone. Can be restful for the soul."

Claudia took his arm, steering him to a quieter part of the sanctuary. "Claudia," he pulled away from her, "it is a social—like old school—a gathering among friends."

"It's not that."

"Then what?"

"It's Martin."

Yeah, Martin. Not exactly his prime pick to have church in his home, but—

"And Meredith."

Oh.

"They seem to have hit it off, lately." He stumbled in his response.

"Half the time they go golfing instead of coming to church." Claudia gripped her Bible tighter.

Patrick pictured each Sunday—nope, he saw Martin every week. Faithful and usually furious about something. "I'm not sure that's correct—"

"You didn't notice they weren't here on Meredith's birthday? They both missed September second, the first Sunday of the month. Martin missed communion. He always helps set it in order."

"Of course. Sometimes people are gone—"

"To golf? It is inexcusable." Claudia frowned. "Surely you call people when they miss a Sunday. Isn't that part of your job?"

"I, well, I wouldn't hound anyone. It, of course, depends on the circumstances. Always good to check if someone is all right if they haven't been seen for a while."

"Oh, fiddle! A while? You need more help keeping people in line. They need to know they have obligations, responsibilities."

"You should do it, call when you notice."

"Me? I'm hardly the type to make small talk and yak on the phone."

"Of course not. Will you be coming tonight?" Patrick asked, giving up on appeasing her while he scanned the room for Rose.

"You bet I am. I tell you, Meredith is getting herself into a bad situation. I plan on keeping things under control."

"I see." Meredith and Martin must be more serious than he thought. Merry Weather would cheer the man up. He'd have to pay closer attention. "I need to find Rose. You haven't seen her have you?" He took the chance to disengage from the conversation.

Claudia's eyes turned to blue daggers. "I should know better than to expect you to keep a congregation on the straight and narrow. You can't even keep tabs on your wife. And by the way, I am pretty sure I saw Alex speaking in tongues during prayer." She turned on her heel and went toward the middle of the sanctuary. *Most likely,* Patrick thought watching her, *to save someone else from a bad relationship choice.* He turned, and before he could take a step, Vivian came at him.

"Patrick, where has Rose gone? I haven't seen her since I saw her in the hallway with Joe."

"I am looking for her myself."

"She missed the whole service," Vivian said. "People come up with all sorts of scenarios when that happens."

Of course they do. "Rose has never done anything to deserve people thinking anything but the best of her. If they do otherwise, then they need to check their own motives and hearts. See Vivian, if everyone worried about their own relationship with God the Father, we'd all be better people. It makes life much simpler, also."

Vivian's attention already drifted, and she stepped away to cross the room. "Yes, Pastor, you can use that for a sermon in the future," she patted him and walked away.

Patrick, relieved to be done answering questions, headed to the foyer, hoping to escape to his office. He managed his way down the hall and unlocked the door. Rose rested on the sofa.

"Ah, there you are," he said, coming in. "The inquisition has been searching for you. You're not sick are you?"

"No, it's nothing. I needed a break, so I came in here."

"I should try that next Sunday," Patrick grinned. He sat next to her. "So, what do you know about Martin and Meredith dating?"

She shook her head. "It's possible Meredith can turn his heart around—find his soft side."

"I happened to think the same thing."

"Really, Patrick? You aren't such a realist after all," Rose said, laughing.

"Claudia is concerned."

"I'm sure. Although I can't say I blame her."

"And she watches people during prayer."

Rose leaned on his shoulder and giggled. "Claudia or Meredith?"

"Claudia. Said Alex was speaking in tongues, not out loud, of course. Technically most people would have their eyes closed. My prayers aren't long."

"If you're going to catch someone doing something, it is best to keep your eyes open."

"Vivian mentioned you were with Joe earlier." Patrick nearly added that he hadn't seen him in the service neither, but bit his tongue. He would not add to Vivian's subtle accusations.

"With Joe? The man practically assaulted me on the way to the platform, which, if you must know, is why I am in here."

Patrick listened to her account of Joe's lamentations. "What does he expect you to do, exactly?"

"How am I to know? Convince Allie to marry and move away, evidently. The man doesn't think straight. Half the time he's drinking his profits."

"I don't want him coming near you again." Patrick'd had enough of Joe and his mentioning of the past and sneaking comments to Rose here and there, as though she owed him something.

"It's never a planned meeting, you know."

"No, I don't know. I wouldn't put it past Joe to *plan* finding you alone. You should stay closer to me on Sundays." He smiled then. "I need a little background beauty around here."

Rose laughed. "I can try, but you are always very busy. Following you around could prove exhausting."

Patrick offered her his hand and pulled her from the couch. He kissed her and whispered in her ear, "I love how all the children are grown and gone—just you and me." He saw her flinch, which she covered with a smile. So quick, so delicate in its passing that he backed up with the realization of how practiced she was at hiding her feelings.

"You have never let it go," his voice hoarse with accusation.

"What are you talking about?"

"Stephen. You're going through the motions every day. I am never enough. The kids you already have, are never enough."

"Patrick, stop it! What do you want me to do? Forget?"

"Move on. Let us have all of you. Let me have all of you." The desperation in his voice clanged in its selfishness. But couldn't he have his wife without his mistake between them—forever cursing his marriage, his family, his church. A black pit of dread opened. He gulped for air. Panic. He looked at her—fire in her eyes, her arms crossed—and then her expression changed.

"Patrick, I know you don't forget. There is no way you can really let it go." She sat and stared at the floor. "I do the best I can. I try to carry on, but last night—last night I had the dream."

That blasted dream. Patrick remembered all those times she cried on Stephen's bed—it'd been years. He stood there, fighting to let go of what he wanted and be what she needed.

"He was all grown up. Looking just like you," she glanced at him, a shyness in her expression. "It was so real," she whispered, tears falling. "I suppose it is because today is the seventh of October. They say your body remembers . . ."

He came and sat beside her, holding her in his arms, his own tears flowing. He hadn't forgotten or let it go. He'd placed the hurt in a box labeled, *Don't Open,* because acknowledging his missing son on a regular basis would make him die inside.

XXIV

Martin's house displayed a show of white pillars gracing the front porch and a water fountain centered in the middle of perfect green grass. Rose couldn't imagine the man doing his own landscaping. The lawn was too beautiful, too manicured, like hair that just left the salon. A line of white roses, petals littering the ground, perfection bending in whimsical relief. Glancing over her shoulder, she saw Meredith coming up the steps, a pot of purple pansies in one hand and a pie in the other.

"Here, let me help you," Patrick, who stood beside Rose, took the plant from Meredith.

"Thank you, I've told Martin he needs some color around here. This decor reminds me of a mortuary."

The door jerked open, and Meredith's mouth shut as though the two controlled each other. Martin smiled at Merry, and Rose caught herself staring. Had she ever seen Martin's teeth or his face stretched out in a pleasant expression? A quick glance at Meredith softened Rose's heart. The woman blushed. "Looks good, Merry." Martin took the dish from her.

"You can't even see it. Foil is covering the whole thing."

"Doesn't matter, anything you make is fabulous."

Rose smiled. Yes. Meredith brought out the softer side of—

"What the heck is that?" Martin frowned.

Rose redirected her thoughts of Martin as Patrick studied the flowers as though trying to guess what offense they had caused.

"Better not be for here."

"Don't be such a wet rag, Marty, and quit glaring at the pastor. I brought you this lovely purple flower because your yard is a total bore." Like a cymbal cracking on the wrong beat, the attraction a moment ago took flight.

"I pay good money to keep up this yard." Martin stood straighter.

"Yes. I work hard in my yard, and the only money spent is on beautiful flowers such as these. Be a love and set it on the porch." She nodded toward Patrick who handed the offensive plant to Martin. He took it with a frown.

"Where do I put this exactly?"

Meredith eyeballed the covered entryway with its bench. "Right here, by the door and the sitting area. Yes, much better. I think some bright yellow or orange would do next time."

Martin set it by the door with a thud and stalked back inside, Rose and Patrick followed while Meredith straightened the pot to perfection.

The group represented a handful of the church, perfect for a home gathering. Claudia, Vivian, Lily, and Adam who sat beside Alex, along with a few others. Rose went to help Meredith in the kitchen.

"Oh, Merry, you've outdone yourself." Rose attempted to smooth over any hurt feelings Martin's lack of kindness caused, but found Meredith unaffected.

"There is nothing as comforting as a good ol' apple pie. Reminds me of my grandmother. It's my favorite, I must admit."

"You're right." Rose pulled the vanilla ice cream from the freezer. She leaned toward the older woman, "Have you and Martin been dating?" Curiosity won over minding her own business.

"Stubborn as a mule, that man." Meredith found a sharp knife to slice the dessert. "I know he is an awful crank at times, but deep down he is a pussycat."

Rose smiled. In her wildest imagination, Martin couldn't be anything close to a pussycat.

"So, you two are serious?" Rose asked, adding ice cream to the dish Meredith had set for her.

"Serious?" Meredith spooned the next piece on a plate. "At my age there are two trains of thought. You ain't got much time left to waste dating and carrying on. If you like the fellow and he likes you, marry him. Then there is the other side. I have been alone too long and am set in my ways, and it'd be best to have a buddy kind of relationship. Someone to hang out with, take away the loneliness."

"And which train of thought are you?"

"I don't reckon I know yet. When Marty gets his crab face on, I'm not inclined to spend the rest of my life with him, regardless of how short it may be."

"Makes perfect sense."

"But when he talks to me and listens, I don't want to go home. Just want to stay here with him, despite his interior and yard needing some warmth."

"Would you miss your home? It has your lovely garden. I mean if you decided to take the serious route."

"I'd sell it in a heartbeat. Of course, many of my plants would come with me. This place would be transformed with color." She beamed. "I don't have many things. I like to garden, and I have shelves of yarn. Martin would have to accept that part of my life. None of this hiring some fancy landscaper to do the work."

"He seems attached to his theme of white and green."

Meredith added forks to each dish. "I can make him see the error of his ways. If not, we may be destined to the buddy system."

Rose giggled, putting the ice cream back into the freezer. All the dishes were ready to pass to the guests. Just as she sat with her own dessert, a hard rapping sounded at door.

Martin got up. "Joe. Nice of you to join us. You're just in time for apple pie."

"I heard you were having a get together, so I decided to drop by and see if I could persuade the offering to go to one of your valuable church members, as in me. And guess who I found standing by the door. Gary, like a cat that was kicked outside." Joe pointed him to a chair. "Sit there, you need more than a little dessert. So, anyone want to contribute to the *Save Joe* fund?"

Rose slid Patrick a glance. He stopped the forkful of dessert halfway into the air, then put it down. "Salvation is free," he said with a grin.

Joe laughed. "Righto, Pastor, however, this here saving is more an immediate need. Not of eternity. I'm trying to keep the Dockerbogger from closing. The repairs are extensive. Right now we resemble a tent more than a building."

Meredith passed him, handing a plate of pie to Lily. She patted Joe's arm. "Why don't you sit and have some dessert, Joe. I'm a firm believer food can fix a bucketful of woes."

"And prayer," Vivian chimed in.

"Food and prayer. You all are saints. Well, sure, I'll sit over here and try both." Joe grinned as he chose the sofa, a little too close to Claudia who abruptly shifted a foot away from him.

Rose popped back into the kitchen and leaned against the counter. Her eyes rested with longing on the back door. Why not? A reprieve wouldn't hurt. Must have been the pattern of the day. Ditch the crowd. She opened the door and stepped out onto the lush green lawn, the scent of the white roses letting go of their last blooms of the season floated across with the soft breeze. A water fountain bubbled—faint in the distance. She understood Meredith's point, but at the same time, looking across the expanse of the yard, a comfort soothed her, as though waiting for something magical to happen. She absorbed the unearthly quality; the flowers, little blips of white here and there, the smell of sweet grass—like stepping into an in-between place, where everything was forgotten. Rose recalled her grandmother reading *The Magician's Nephew*, by C.S. Lewis—right before bed, propped on her pillow, her grandma's voice a lulling cadence. Like *the wood between the worlds*, Martin's yard bubbled around her, wrapping her in a peace—a contradiction, because there was nothing peaceful about Martin. She had wandered away from the house, edging closer to the fence and near the woods, when the brush crashed, making her jump. A deer appeared, followed by two smaller ones. A door slammed and they bolted back into the woods.

"You are insufferable, Martin." Meredith's voice carried across the breeze.

"And you are a meddling woman. I like my place the way it is. You can take your purple, pink, orange, and whatever back to your own cluttered yard."

"Cluttered? At least mine has some life to it. This place is downright hoity toity!"

"It's peaceful. Your place is good for all the woodland critters. Chaotic."

Rose ducked out of sight as apple pie flew from Meredith's fork, hitting Martin in the chest, splattering onto his chin. Meredith set her dish down on the bench, turned on her heel and marched away, her pansies left on the porch like an exclamation point.

Joe emerged from the house. "Ha! Looky at you, Marty! Need some whip cream with that?"

"Blasted tarnation!" Martin stomped, flinging a dripping apple from his shirt.

"No funds to save the Dockerbogger tonight, but this almost made it worth coming," Joe said as he walked to the road.

Rose held her breath. *Don't let Joe catch you alone, again.* She and Patrick managed to pass through the afternoon being pleasant despite their pain being reopened. She berated herself for letting it slip about the dream. Time had proven her thoughts regarding Stephen needed to be kept to herself. But she saw him falter this time. He had buried everything deep. How could that be healthy? A glance at her watch said the get together would be over in a few minutes.

As soon as Joe made a greater distance between Martin's house and her, she'd slip back inside, but movement in the trees made her pause. Probably the deer again. She turned dismissing the sound, but then caught sight of Joe. Hadn't he gone the other way? Backing behind one of the larger bushes, she waited. Another man appeared. Familiar in a way. She studied them both, trying to put the pieces together. Then she knew. It was the man from the woods. She hadn't seen him in years, and from Joe's body language, and tone of voice, he wasn't a welcome sight. Joe always claimed no one knew the guy who roamed the woods, but watching them now told a different story.

XXV

Alex arrived at the bookstore and brewed a fresh pot of coffee. Probably not the best choice, considering the anxiety that settled over her whenever she pictured pieces of Joe's tavern blowing away in the wind. She had turned from the casket when the sky darkened and the heavy gale swept over the Dockerbogger. There had to be some sort of spiritual symbolic meaning for the storm to come and rip up part of Joe's roof. Not like she had ever been accused of over spiritualizing things—especially from Robert.

Unfortunately, the volatile weather and damage it caused didn't help her situation. Joe only wanted the bookstore more than before. Alex sometimes caught the way he stared at her mother—the unfinished emotions, as though they never were able to let the past go, each one of them holding a different piece. Without the middle the equation didn't fit and couldn't be fixed. From what Alex saw, now that she was older and had a different perception, they remained to be a jumble of awkward sentences, glances from Joe that shouldn't be there, her mother avoiding all contact while attempting to act natural; a song playing out of tune and in the wrong time.

Alex took a mug from the shelf and poured her coffee. One thing that gave her peace about her decision to accept ownership of the bookstore was the joy that Mrs. Brooks had when working on the garden that connected to the building. Even in these upcoming dreary months the woman had a knack in giving the outside spark, and was a master at inside décor as well.

After a few sips of coffee, Alex set to straightening the magazines. She removed a stack of outdated home decorating periodicals when a movement out the window caught her eye. A white sign seemingly floated across and then turned around and went the other way. Then another and another. She walked over to get a closer look. Shouting split the air, "Save Joe! Save Joe! Save Joe!" A stream of people walked back and forth in front of the store.

Meredith and Vivian emerged from the mystery room with a handful of the latest crime novels. "What's happening?" Meredith gripped her stack tighter.

"I'm not sure," Alex watched out the window. "A protest, I guess." Not what she needed.

"Can you ring me up? I hope it is safe to get to my car." Meredith set her books on the counter.

"Can never trust mobs like these, you know. Very unpredictable." Vivian frowned at the crowd.

"To be extra safe, I'll have Barry walk you out. See, he's coming in now."

Barry Spencer was the steadfast bookstore employee who had come from England a decade ago and had worked for Mr. Brooks upon arrival. He dodged the crowd when he found an opening and came inside the store, taking off his hat he shook his hair. "What have you done, Alexandria?"

"What makes you think I've done something?"

"This has raising the dead, healing sick animals, heavenly encounters, and whatnot, all over it."

"No it doesn't. This is about the bar."

"And a bookstore. Can't they just be friends?"

"Barry has a point, Alexandria. If you'd let things be that day, none of this trouble would be upon us now," Vivian stated.

"Can't change the past, now can we?" Alex narrowed her eyes at Barry. *Really?* He had to bring up all her deeds in front of the ladies? She put the stack of books in the bag. He mouthed an *oops* with a shrug, and she rolled her eyes.

A crash sounded from the romance section.

"I'm on it," Barry made his escape to check out the damage, but right before he got there, a big, fluffy dog ran toward him, then changed direction to greet the ladies.

"Oh, my!" Vivian scooted closer to Alex. Meredith set her books down and patted the dog. "Aren't you a sweetie, now."

"Toby!" A woman rushed in, and the dog charged at her. "What are you doing in here? I thought Paul was watching you." She looked at Alex. "I'm so sorry." Her attention went back to the dog. 'C'mon boy, let's get you some treats at home. It's going to rain any minute."

Vivian stepped back to the other side of the counter once the girl and dog left. "Sorry, Alex. I'm jumpy around wild animals."

"I understand. He was sorta cute, though," Alex said.

"Cute matters little once you see the romance room. The Harlequin display has been slobbered and chewed thoroughly," Barry said.

"How'd he get in? I would have noticed a big dog coming through the front door."

"Back door was wide open. Don't worry, I closed and locked it—considering . . ." he nodded toward the crowd.

Alex turned her attention back to Meredith who was double checking titles. "I'm hoping Martin will like these. What do you think?"

"Perfect. Clive Cussler is a winner for sure, and the others, well you can't go wrong with a good mystery."

"Merry is just trying to butter the man up so she can move her plants into his space before the rest of her follows."

"That is not true, Vivian. I would never shack up with a man I'm not married to, and we are not even close to discussing ever after. It's his birthday, and that's all."

"Excellent choices, then," Alex said, as the voices outside rose in volume.

"Save Joe! Save Joe! Save Joe!"

Vivian gave a jolt when the bullhorn came out. "Oh, for land's sakes! I declare Alexandria, you'll have to pray me back to life if they continue that ruckus outside." Vivian stared out the window. "How are we supposed to get to our cars?"

"I will escort you," Barry said, sounding like English royalty.

"It makes you think, doesn't it, Alex? All this nonsense. Is it worth it for you to hang onto this place?" Vivian asked.

"It is worth it to both me and Mrs. Brooks. She has wonderful plans for the garden and would be horribly upset if this bookstore weren't here. Really, Vivian, wouldn't you miss it? You are here quite frequently. And how would Meredith have found the perfect gift for Martin?"

"That is true," Meredith nodded her head. "I mean I can hardly find something for the man at the Yarn and Yak."

"Now there's an idea. You could knit him a nice sweater."

"Surely you know about the boyfriend curse? Knit him a sweater and *poof*, he disappears from your life. Nope, Marty is not getting any knitted items from me, however, if we can walk farther down business row, I'd like to pop in and grab some knitting needles."

"I could use some yarn myself," Vivian said. "Perhaps Mr. Spencer can just make sure we get out the door, and then we'll be on our way."

"Absolutely," Barry nodded toward the window. "But it is getting dark out. I'll give these people five seconds in a downpour and they'll disperse. You may want to put your purchases in your car first, or Martin will have some soggy reading."

"Agreed. Goodbye, Alex. Hopefully, you'll really think about all the trouble you are causing to these poor people." Vivian followed Meredith and Barry as they opened the door.

"Let's get this straight, Prohibition this ain't. Save our tavern!" The shouting filtered through the store.

"Save Joe! Save Joe! Save Joe!" Alex caught a glimpse of a sign displaying the bold letters, complete with a halo over the J. Another sign read, "Make Brooks' Books, Brooks' Bar."

Barry reappeared a couple minutes later.

"What on earth were you thinking bringing up how this is my fault?" Alex asked him. "You do know how those women torture me all the time?"

"I'm sorry. You're right. It was just a joke. Bad timing on my part."

"At least you got them safely on their way."

Barry grinned. "And I felt the first raindrop. Look out, here it comes, and it will be a doozy."

Alex watched large spatters start to fall. The picketers continued, not seeming to be detoured. Then the steady drops turned to waterfall proportions. Signs began to waver, the shouting weakened, and the bullhorn dropped down. The door opened, and a deluge of wet people emerged inside the store.

Water dripped into puddles, and Alex cringed, her gaze drifting upward, stopping on Paul Brooks. He stood front and center, the leader of the protest group. Of course. Her mind drifted to the woman with the dog. "You let that dog in the store."

"He got away from me," Paul said. "This rain is your doing, I'm sure, so we're even."

"I am not in charge of the weather."

"Really? I've heard it said you can do anything if you believe."

"I'm not currently trying to believe in weather control." *Not a bad idea, though.*

"You should have it in your heart to help a man whose business was destroyed by a windstorm. Especially when you are responsible for taking part of his inheritance."

Soggy picket signs went back in the air. SAVE JOE's halo bled in streaks of black ink.

"I have an obligation to Winston and Edith. Mrs. Brooks loves the garden, and she loves books. I plan on making it the best bookstore I can. I've left the name the same to acknowledge that they started this business."

"Edith does a beautiful job on the garden," someone said.

"I love your mystery section," another woman piped up. "And the sci-fi room is amazing!"

Paul's face reddened, and he turned toward the group. "We don't want this bookstore here. We are against it. If you're not with me on this then get out!"

No one moved or said anything, then someone dropped their sign on the floor. "Hey, let's go over to Harry's and get a burger."

Murmurs of *starving* and *famished* were heard as they left, one by one, leaving signs in a puddle of paper and ink.

Paul now stood alone. "I'm sure you'll be hearing from Joe. We had plans, you know." He glanced around the store, looking a little lost without his support group, then ducked back outside, blending with the rain, the low clouds, and the gray road. Alex watched him fade away.

XXVI

After his mother's death, Henry went through her things, giving away sofas, dressers, clothing, kitchen appliances, shelves that held small bird statues, and bathroom towels, then sat on her bed, physically and emotionally worn to the core. This was the last room to clean out, and all that remained was an old sewing machine. The closet was empty, and the bare walls accused him of sucking the life from them. He'd kept a few things for himself, even though he wasn't especially sentimental, but because that's what people were supposed to do when a loved one passed. He set aside an antique, oddly-shaped cookie jar, and an old cuckoo clock that she never parted with. Cuckoo clocks were long past their prime for acceptable décor, but Henry planned on hanging this one in his kitchen, just above the cookie jar, except he wasn't sure where *home* was right now.

Henry stooped to investigate under the bed, then reached, grasping a cardboard box and lots of dust. Pulling it out, he blew a few cobwebs out of the way. It was full of pictures and a large manila envelope. Setting it on the bed, he rummaged through the rest of the box. Many of the faces were of his mom, cousins, aunts, and uncles. His gaze went back to his mother, healthy and smiling. It'd been so long since she looked like that. They only had each other, and besides the few friends of Henry's, they lived in isolation. His own life was filled with going to school events—dances, football games, and the local pizza parlor, but his mom was pretty much a loner never making friends beyond a superficial acquaintance.

When Henry was in grade school, his mother would do things with him—make cookies, play board games, gaze at him as though he was a window to happier times and say, "I love you Henry; it was totally God how you came to my life." But as he grew older she became more agitated, and he felt in the way, especially after Beckett left.

He flipped through handfuls of pictures of himself—ages three, four, five, six and on and on—multiple photos of Henry—kindergarten graduation, fishing, camping trips, boat rides, swimming competitions, trophies, and his first car. Everything except baby pictures. Nothing before three. *A fire,* his mother had said. *Lost them all.*

He tossed a black and white Polaroid photo of himself with his dog Sandy into the box and picked up the manila envelope. He undid the clasp and brought out a fragile newspaper article, yellowed with age. The room grew hot, the atmosphere fragmenting. Henry wiped sweat from his brow, letting the paper fall on the bed, sensing a need to stop time, as though a glass bowl in the spirit realm dropped and now hovered in slow motion, waiting to land and shatter into hundreds of shards.

He got up and opened the window. The breeze blew in, picking up a corner of the faded newsprint, lifting it across the bed. His hand trembled as he held the paper again. He unfolded it, the creases cracked. The headline, thick and black, demanding notice: Stephen McMillan, missing October 7, 1967. The date gripped Henry—his own birthday, except the year. Henry was born in 1964. According to the reports, the boy had been a bit peculiar and didn't answer to his name, or talk at all for the most part.

His face sweltered with the heat, and he realized that he was holding his breath. Another date caught his eye—March 10, 1965. Stephen's birth date, five months after Henry's. The paper's corners crumpled with age, and Henry leaned closer to look at the picture of the missing boy. *Blond hair and dimples—could be any kid. Okay, enough with similarities.* He forced himself to find differences. Well, here was one. Henry was only familiar with New Jersey and New York—very different from Oregon. Second, had he ever suspected anything growing up? His mother often mentioned Oregon in passing, usually on the phone. Wouldn't there be some indication, internal knowledge, intuition, or whatever they might call it?

He picked up an old photo cover. Opening it, he found himself staring at his prom picture. He stood next to a beautiful girl—auburn hair and green eyes. His mind traveled back in time, searching for something—anything that might indicate that he had an inkling that something wasn't right. It stopped at a moment when Henry was thirteen years old. A sensation of liquid pictures—he couldn't quite make out or grasp them. At the time, it left him with a vague uneasiness.

He was at a skating rink in New Jersey. The DJ announced the Hokey Pokey and images—flashes of memory—flooded Henry's senses. At the time, he waved it off as a dream he'd forgotten, and it didn't hold him for long. The main reason the day held importance was because he had been with Paulina, roller skating to Peter Frampton singing, "Baby I love Your Way." Her auburn hair fell down her back and those green eyes looking at him—he remembered her face inches from his when they fell in a tangled heap, right before she had clamored off of him. Henry had been in love. The kind of instant love that happened when one was thirteen. He closed his eyes; the images seared inside his brain—blurred around the edges. A sinking sensation hit his gut. An orchard. The woods. *No.*

"Paint me a picture, Henry." Her voice sang in his head as he indulged the moment from the past to escape the newspaper article in front of him. It was the day they graduated from high school in 1982. They had been sitting under the tulip tree in a nearby park. He and Polly had attended winter balls and proms together between serious relationships, but always came back to each other. She tried to do one of those pacts. "If we're not married by the time we are thirty, let's marry each other."

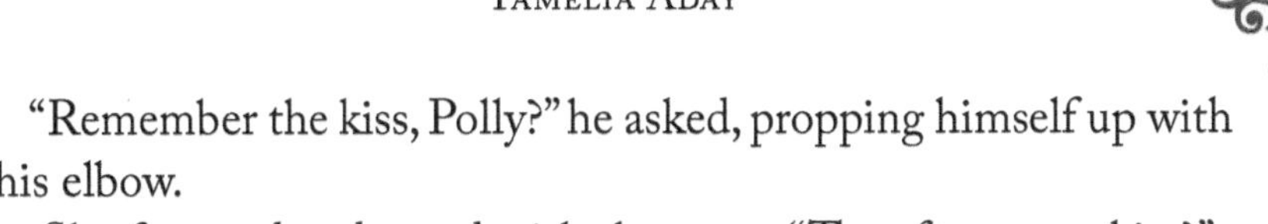

"Remember the kiss, Polly?" he asked, propping himself up with his elbow.

She frowned and toyed with the grass. "The after prom kiss?"

"Uh, yeah. The one and only."

"It felt like you were my brother, or something," she shuddered.

"Right. Maybe we're related. That makes marriage not an option."

"Let's try again," Polly said, moving closer. "Maybe it will be different."

Henry laughed. "I'm not sure kissing on demand is really going to tell us anything."

"I'll spend the rest of my life wondering."

He gazed at her. She was killing him here. Despite all her strange theories of UFOs, out of body experiences, and ghosts, he was drawn to her, but deep down he knew they wouldn't work—not like that.

"Kiss me, Henry. Let me be sure. Or I may be hunting you down when your thirty."

"Polly, there's no way you'll remain single. You're too beautiful and full of life." Sadness wedged inside his soul. "If anyone needs the pact it would be me, but I know you can do better than Henry James."

She reached for a dandelion and fingered its petals. "You told me that you were going to succeed in life—take care of your mom. Remember that? You're not giving up, are you?"

He swallowed. "Of course not, but right now I am at the bottom. It will take awhile to get to that place. Others have a much better start than I do."

"I believe in you Henry James." Her face was inches from him. "A goodbye for now kiss then?"

Before he could respond, her lips were touching his, gently, her flowered scent making his head feel light. His hand went through her long auburn hair. For him, this kiss had no sisterly feel to it.

He opened his eyes, and she pulled away. He stretched out flat on the grass, looking at the sky. "Well, what's the verdict?" He tried to keep his voice light.

She flashed him a grin. "Maybe I'll see you in ten plus years." Her laughter filled the space between them as she laid beside him pointing out all the things she saw in the clouds, leaving Henry to wonder where they'd both be later in life. He'd bet his last dollar that Paulina would find true love before the age of thirty. He on the other hand would most likely be thinking of this kiss for the next decade.

Henry pulled his mind back to what was in front of him. Why would his mom have this newspaper article? And another question: how'd she get it? Living in Jersey, why have a copy of this story from *The Oregon Journal?* Why even care? Another hand-written note slipped out of the folded article. *We need to talk.* And there he was, right back to the evidence going the other direction. The more he looked at the picture, the more he saw himself. But then everyone had a twin, right? And everyone had a mom who tucked away old news stories about missing children with their family photos. His whole life from three onward, in a box. The story she told about the house fire now had the flavor of a lie. His biological father also seemed to go up in smoke. He stuffed the pictures from the box into the envelope. Henry took off his sweatshirt and tossed it on the bed. *Was there any air coming from that window?* His heart raced, and he struggled to breathe. Once again he was surrounded by lies.

XXVII

"It's been twenty-three years," Howard Trent walked over to the coffee pot and poured the dark liquid in his cup, dumping in sugar.

"I think you made that into dessert," Patrick leaned back, staring at the ceiling, glad to have a distraction. Once a year they tried for a serious meeting to discuss the case which grew colder without a thaw in sight. His eyes took in the office. "I know a cleaning lady . . ."

Howard moved from his chair and threw some wrappers, plastic ware, and stray papers away before his next sip of coffee. "Better?" He went back to a comfortable pose, but the lines of his face and the streaks of gray in his hair told a different story.

"How's the wife?" Patrick asked. "You two doing all right?"

"We're adjusting. Delores is going through that empty nest thing. Now she's stuck with only me and no children to keep her happy."

"She'll come around. She knows she's the apple of your eye."

Howard sighed. "She is beautiful. Don't worry, we'll get all settled again. Frankly, I don't know what the big deal is. We have more room to ourselves. How's Rose holding up? Is the anniversary date causing chaos?"

"My clothes are getting tight."

"Thought you looked a little pudgy."

"Thank you."

Howard glanced out the window, and the silence stretched because Howard's life moved forward, and Patrick's always had to look back.

"There isn't much to say, right? What leads could we possibly have?"

"I know it appears bleak, but it's what we do, right? We never give up. You've seen many miracles, maybe someday you'll get yours. I'm here for you," Howard said. "Heard Winston Brooks died."

"Yes, just did the services for him."

"And another recent development," Howard put on his glasses, "Caroline Randall, who took on her maiden name after divorcing Gary—what was it?" He scanned the paper. "James. Died of cancer, real recent. Survived by a son."

"She always wanted children. I think that's why she left Gary."

"She was never a primary interest since she was with Rose when the phone call came that Stephen had gone missing."

"Rose and I recently discussed Caroline." Just another piece that looked significant but didn't fit.

"I try to keep tabs on everyone we considered back then. Joe puzzles me. Why was he on your property after that resurrection?" Howard tapped his pen. "It still rings like a bad note, for some reason."

"Just drunk, I guess."

"Yes, but my question is why? He spent time helping Rose search for Stephen, he had a close relationship to Caroline," Howard said and waved a hand. "This town should be too small for secrets. My question is, what's Joe's interest in your family? Seems like there is more there than what's apparent."

Patrick kept his face neutral, but his eyes shot away from Howard's intense dark ones. Some people thought prophets came to church and read their minds, but Howard was scarier than any prophet, even if it wasn't God he listened to. He could guess what you were hiding, from a flick of an eye or a twitch of a finger. "Joe had an interest in Rose at one time. She dated him before she dated me."

"That's hard for me to picture."

"Joe wasn't as rough back then."

"So, you stole her away?"

"It was my charm. She couldn't help it," Patrick grinned. "And I didn't steal her. They had already broken it off."

"So that's his beef with you."

Patrick tilted back in his chair. "Things were never the same between the three of us. As far as him being in the woods, we thought it had to do with the bookstore. Winston considered his retirement, and my daughter is obsessed with books. He wanted to give her something."

"A whole bookstore." Howard sipped his coffee. "Which made Joe mad. So, his being in the woods didn't have anything to do with Stephen. I wanted to make sure, because the time he spent with Rose always had to do with Stephen, but Joe may have had other motives."

"The rumors are out there."

"I don't put a lot of stock in rumors, do you?" Howard asked, taking a donut.

"No, of course not." Patrick avoided meeting Howard's eyes. He had never asked Rose about the hair band he found, always afraid of what it meant. Other people's stories were bad enough, but couldn't compete with his own thoughts that sometimes went rogue.

XXVIII

Rose threw back the covers and put on her slippers, then padded toward the door and into the living room. Alone in the dark. Just her and Patrick here now. She remembered when it was the five of them. *Should have been six*, the voice said. *You should have been thankful that you still had a family. You should have moved on. All that looking got you nowhere.* But there was the prophecy, and God's words do not return void.

She quit pacing and sat in her chair. A strip of moonlight lit a spot on the floor. She could barely make out Patrick's snoring from down the hall. Thank goodness, she hadn't wakened him, since he appeared preoccupied lately. The sky rumbled outside, and a crackle of lightning flashed. She stared out the window, wondering if that's why she had awakened, if that's why she felt so unstable. Maybe she was just responding to the weather.

Considering everything, it was an amazing feat that she and Patrick had managed to stay married through all this. Where would she be if she weren't a pastor's wife? Maybe the loony bin or a lone wanderer in Europe. Being alone in a foreign country, where no one knew her, seemed appealing right now.

Louder rumbling, like surround sound at the theater, followed by the sky lighting up, made Rose forget about roaming a mental ward or wandering another continent. She waited, hoping for the voice of God, but instead heard a faint meowing and clawing at the screen door with a constant thudding. Making her way across the living room, Rose opened the door to the cat, Tiny, who pushed his fat body through the opening. "Oh, poor thing." Before she could reach down and pet the wet creature, a gust of wind tore the screen from her grasp, blowing it against the house with a *bang!*

She stepped out on the patio, grabbing the screen, and noticed a movement that looked like a man out near the woods. Leaning farther, she tried to make out what it was exactly, but another howling of the wind almost tore the door out of her hands and she was forced back inside. It slammed her in with another *bang*. Turning, she saw Patrick standing in the hall entrance, and she jumped in fright.

"I let the cat in," she said, in hopes of recovering smoothly, as though it was a normal thing to do in the middle of the night.

He looked at Tiny, and then Rose. "Quite a storm. We could go on the porch and watch."

"It's pretty windy. About blew the door off its hinges."

Patrick smiled. "Well, then. Maybe not." He came closer. "Are you alright?"

"Yeah. Just got a bit spooked." No sense in going on about the possibility that she saw someone. It would result in Patrick getting soaked, possibly catching a horrible cold, when in reality, it could have just been a deer.

"I wish I had better news about the meeting today," Patrick said, his glance shifting from the storm to her.

She shrugged. "Twenty-three years. Should be some sort of milestone, but it's like being on a journey and getting farther from home." She wrapped her arms around herself, as though that would shield the pain. She didn't want him to hug her. She didn't want to cry, and if he took one step closer she'd be a mess.

They both stood there, as though they had just started dating instead of having been married for over thirty years, the awkwardness unsettling. "I should be getting back to bed," Rose said, edging past him. Patrick turned and followed her. They eased under the covers and lay next to each other, listening as the storm raged outside. Rose didn't move a muscle until she heard Patrick's soft snoring, and then she turned on her side and went to sleep. She'd been wrong. His arms around her would have been comforting after all.

XXIX

October 1990 ~ Filbert Ridge, Oregon

The blackness of the night was about as clear as what Henry James was supposed to do next. He longed to talk to Minnie again, his next-door neighbor growing up. Heck, he'd even sit on the porch and eat ravioli or mac and cheese like he'd done as a school boy. Comfort food for Henry consisted of familiarity.

He'd come full circle, but any romantic notions of déjà vu upon arriving in Filbert Ridge disappeared long ago when the sun set. Moonbeams flickered, wavering with rainfall, appearing as unsteady as his life these days—like a flash fragmenting downward with interspersed darkness. *Coming here was a mistake.*

Easels stood among the unpacked boxes, waiting for inspiration to claim them, but they hadn't been touched since he uprooted his life.

Painting used to be his solace. Now, even the peace of this pastime was stolen from him. In an instant, everything Henry had known about himself, as in the most basic of things, down to his very name, wasn't true. It was another joke on him that he held the name of a fictional writer, only to find himself in an alternate universe, playing a character through life.

The unrest started with the dreams. His paintings became the same thing, over and over again, his mind trying to tell him something, like a constant knocking without an answer, as though trapped in a snow globe. His art narrowed into tunnel vision with misty borders—trees in the background, blue eyes, and coal black hair, mingling with the dim green and brown surroundings. Nothing like he'd ever painted before. Henry didn't paint people, but now he saw her in his sleep and on his canvas. And that was before he discovered the box under his mom's bed.

He paced the length of the living room, his shoes clicking onto the hardwood floor of the rented farmhouse. Nice plan moving right into the reality of his nightmare.

Answers—that was what drove him here. His mother, dying of cancer, had turned into a human skeleton. In her last breath, she clutched his hand with more strength than he thought possible and whispered through parched lips, "I'm sorry, I shouldn't have, didn't mean for it to be . . ."

Henry had no idea what she was talking about and figured the morphine muddled her mind. Isn't that what the hospice nurse told him in that quiet, slow voice used around the deathbed? Why'd they have to be so quiet all the time? He wanted to slam doors, throw things and scream—not talk in whispers, as though hearing actual life around her might lead to leaving the world that much faster. Personally, if Henry were dying, he thought he'd rather have noise, lots of it, to block out the approaching death squad. He didn't think a whole lot about heaven or hell; one scared him, and the other made him feel highly uncomfortable, but now life itself wasn't so pleasant either.

He stopped pacing, letting the truth sink in. He heard God was creative, and if that were true, couldn't God have used a little more creativity with someone else's life? *Guess one can't argue with the sense of humor of the Almighty.* Was that why Henry thought about God and found himself complaining to Him so often? Was it a genetic strain in his DNA? He wasn't even sure he believed in God.

At any rate, the lack of sleep and watching his mother suffer for months, made him short with coworkers. He'd spent all his life learning to control rages, so at work he became withdrawn, and soon they were all whispering, "Look, it's the dreamer."

Now here in Filbert Ridge, Oregon, he had arrived with his Jersey accent and a leave of absence from his Manhattan job. His coworkers nicknamed his journey Operation Egypt as the nightmares led him across the states.

Henry glanced at the table where the phone sat. He could call Polly. They spoke about once a year. He should tell her that he moved—that his mom died—that he was alone in some small town of Oregon.

He only had designer clothing which, with one look at his new residence would make him stand out like a pumpkin in July. His bank account was padded because of his frugalness. He may have nice things, but he found them all on sale, and once his mom's house sold, he'd live in comfort for awhile. Heck, it looked like his money would go a lot farther in this hole in the wall town. In the Big Apple, the mantra was *money, money, money,* and Henry had done what any career-oriented, ambitious business man would do. He followed the rules and hoped for the end result, by the time he hit fifty—a long way off.

He pondered his mother's statement, how she "didn't mean to." That brought up the possibility of a number of things. Was she referring to the drugs she used to flounder through each day? Or did she mean Beckett? Those two things caused a shift, and he saw her as weak and fragile. Minnie filled in the gap, having him over often. She became his anchor while his mother floated on colored clouds.

But now there was this. He picked up the manila envelope, never far from him, and tossed it onto the sofa. There was no one to ask—no one except the family of the missing Stephen McMillan, and at this point in his life, what did it matter? He grew up normal, had career goals. Everything was hunky dory.

New York held his future. He studied the way of life, planning to be more of a participant in the excitement at some point. But in Filbert Ridge, it was like turning on the radio and finding dead air.

An old piano sat abandoned in the farmhouse, and when he sat to play it, the echo throughout the walls made his insides empty. His soul kept scanning his new surroundings on this opposite coast, looking for something that said he'd be okay. Even if he was only a watcher, New York reflected his style—like constant background music. A flicker of hope burned in him. He wasn't Stephen McMillan. Wouldn't he detest the night life and all the city lights? Wouldn't a knowing deep down inside cause a longing for the landscape that now surrounded him?

Henry's recent microfiche search on the McMillans led him to think they were all kooky. The dad was a pastor, and Henry had immediate discomfort at that revelation, and then to make them more freakish, the youngest daughter was responsible for a dead-raising. What had he gotten himself into? Not only parents, but three possible siblings to deal with as well?

He'd just turned twenty-six years old. His foot was in the door doing the grunt work of his chosen occupation, so he could be at the top later, but now here he stood, thousands of miles in the opposite direction, trying to find out who he was? Who he was! A literal step backward in time. Now that he thought about it, if he *was* this Stephen McMillan, his birthday was five months away. What was his next achievement? Oprah? His life sounded like something straight out of one of those talk shows—*Twenty-six-year old man searches his past to discover the roots of his nightmares.*

"Filbert Ridge," he said the name out loud to connect to it—to feel more like he hadn't been crazy to come here. Did it sound like home? A small town where seemingly nothing happened—well, nothing except a kidnapping and a parking lot resurrection. But small towns, just like quiet neighbors, had their secrets.

He looked out the window, into the night—the lights behind him dim. A flash of lightning illuminated the nearest row of trees on the other side of the road. That's when he saw her, in the sprinkling reflection. He blinked. She was out there, the woman he couldn't stop painting. He pressed his face closer to the window.

Her black hair dripped water down her body. He squinted, imagining the icy blue color of her eyes as another streak of light flashed.

Henry ran to the door and opened it, dashing out in the rain, his Italian shoes hit a puddle and water seeped through a tiny opening that he didn't realize existed. Relentless sheets of water played tricks on his vision as he looked to the right, and then to the left. She vanished. *Or,* he corrected himself, *was never there.* Looking up to the sky, he let the downpour drench his face, willing it to wash away this insanity.

Here he was, his new temporary home in the middle of nowhere. His suit jacket still managed to whip around him in the wind, even though it was soaking wet. Water dripped from his eyelashes. Yeah, he was nuts, probably should seek therapy first thing in the morning—but he knew he wouldn't. Therapy required talking to someone and talking scared him. He was chasing ghosts. Rather embarrassing for a man his age.

XXX

Rose decided some cleaning might distract her. She'd been sorting out her thoughts for days—taking walks, trying to pray but not finding answers. Now, at home, she decided to take on a major project of throwing out as many items as possible. Minimalism—declutter the house, declutter the soul. All the clothes they owned were piled in a heap on the bed, spilling out onto the carpet. Time to make a run to the thrift store. Half this stuff she'd worn when the kids were babies.

She tossed old dresses onto the growing mountain of clothes, not having much attachment to any of them. She should go shopping and get new things. One of Patrick's jackets fell to the floor. She picked it up and checked the pockets for spare change before piling it with the giveaways. He was just as bad as her. This jacket reeked of the seventies. A lump could be felt in the pocket. Digging her hand inside, expecting loose coin, she pulled out a leather ponytail holder with turquoise beads dangling from the ends.

Patrick came home for lunch, but instead of the dining table set like British Tea, it was wiped clean. The edginess from the night before shone like a faint prelude to what he feared was coming. Traveling down the hall, following the noise of drawers and footsteps, he turned into the bedroom to the sight of clothing strung about everywhere. Okay, evidently the cooking mania had taken a break, and the cleaning mania took its place, as though Rose might find Stephen buried amidst the clutter. Patrick had gotten spoiled with the lavish meals, and his stomach growled.

"Patrick, you're home." Rose stopped for a moment, but then turned her back on him and grabbed another garbage bag, opening it with more force than needed.

"I came for lunch," he said and grinned. "Looks like I'm on my own today. Not sure I remember how to use a butter knife."

"I really don't think you've ever been alone, darling." She threw some jeans on the bed and went to a dresser drawer, dumping the contents on top of the pile.

Patrick noticed the tone Rose used with the word 'darling,' and it wasn't filled with love. He also noted the lack of care she took when tossing clothing on the bed—her movements clipped, her eyes on everything but him. He knew she'd worked earlier at the bakery, but she didn't speak much about her place of employment. A lot of town gossip went through the rows of cupcakes and loaves of bread, and sometimes he wondered what sort of negative church news came to her work place. Reports against the Lord is My Shepherd may have kept her silent.

His appetite dimmed, and he took one of her hands, as it rested for a microsecond on a nightgown she'd put down.

She pulled it away. "There are leftovers in the fridge."

He knew she avoided looking at him. Instead of heading to the refrigerator, which would prove warmer than Rose's greeting, Patrick sat on the edge of the mattress. Rose's cleaning streaks gave him more discomfort than her cooking frenzies, but this seemed— he took in the clothes tumbling about the bed, and more being added to the pile, still on hangers—excessive. "I hope you aren't giving all my clothes away. I can hardly be naked at the pulpit."

A glare was given for his wit. Okay.

"What is it, Rose?"

He watched as a heap of sweaters were deposited on top of pajamas. Some fell against where he sat. She grabbed something off the dresser. "*It*—is this." Rose held the leather ponytail holder. "In *your* pocket." She threw it at him, and it landed in his lap.

It'd been years since he'd seen it. He'd never forgotten—always the image of the turquoise beads hovering in the background of his mind. "This is yours, I found it—"

"Mine? You have the nerve to not remember that I have never, ever had a leather ponytail holder with beads dangling from it? Really? Maybe I should just walk around naked because *you* wouldn't even notice!"

His eyes went to the calendar. Had he forgotten an important date? The square with the number stared back at him—blank.

He looked at her. "I would definitely notice if you walked around naked. Would prefer it actually . . ."

"Patrick!" No returned flirting, or pretending he was being annoying. "That beaded hair holder—is not mine."

He fingered the leather string. "I'm sorry. Does it belong to one of the girls?" That would make sense. He remembered the angst, the impending darkness descending when he'd found it where Joe had been. Martin's story, all those years ago, of the argument in the woods confirmed that she'd been there, or so he thought. Would have been a great relief to know the hair trinket didn't belong to Rose back then, not so much now.

"Yeah, one of the girls!" Her voice mocked him. "Try Caroline Randall, or James, or whatever her name ended up being! Why was it in your pocket?"

"I found it. A long time ago, I might add. I thought it was yours. C'mon, it's just a hair ribbon. I don't notice hair ribbons."

"Obviously not. There are a lot of things you don't notice. The way people look at us, what they say about us. Do you ever pay attention? Were you thinking of Caroline the day you lost Stephen?" Her blue eyes bore through his, flashing with what she had held inside for years.

The moment Patrick dreaded had arrived, the panic and guilt resounding through his soul and stomach. He stood and stared out the window, then turned back to her. "My mind was never—"

She waved a hand at him. "I know. You can't focus, your attention wanders. That's why part of me blamed myself, letting you take care of them for the afternoon."

"Rose." His voice had an edge. He was losing ground. His heart was being stabbed with a knife. "And what about the present? What about our grown children? Can't we enjoy each other and let this go? No. You are stuck on the past and how things didn't work out the way you have predicted and still are predicting!" He should stop, but he had already crossed a line, and years of grief tumbled out of him. He had been in the eye of the storm too long, bringing him to this category five moment. Her face paled, but he didn't quit.

"You know what I thought when I found this?" He dangled the leather close to her face. "That Joe had come to see you. I found it next to where he was in the woods. And guess what? Martin said you were arguing with Joe. *That day.* My mind wanders, but my heart has always been for you. You, on the other hand, went running to *Joe*, trying to get *his* help to find Stephen."

"Because *you* were doing nothing!"

"That's what you think? I consulted Howard on a daily basis back then. Twenty-three years and no news. I've listened to your *hope*, your *prophetic utterances*, your *Pollyanna-ish outlook*. It's delusional. Let's be truthful here. Just for once, tell me that Stephen might not ever come back, because I *cannot* live this charade anymore. I can't believe I've let it continue this long."

"At least I believed in the possibility. I tried to do something. I didn't bury my head in the sand, and if you consider that deluded, so be it." She paused. "Secondly, your reliable source, Martin, is way off. I did not see Joe. At all. Let me guess. The owner of the hair ribbon? Joe and Caroline together in the woods isn't unheard of. All I did was pass out posters with Joe. We scoured the neighborhood, and we checked around Portland. That's all."

"You hung out at his bar. You brought him stew, muffins, and cookies. You caused rumors to fly around town and through the church. You are right—I did nothing. You know why? Rumors die. I told myself they weren't true, that it would fade. But *I* didn't know where your heart lie, and if you tell me you were only thinking of Stephen in this whole matter, fine. But I'll tell you this—Joe was not. Joe has never thought of anyone but himself, and he set out to take you from me."

"I did not *hang out* at his bar! You want to play this accusation game? People called me and said you were with her!"

Back to Caroline. They argued in tornado-like circles, causing destruction with every word. The tiny hair ribbon had created this disaster. How Patrick wished he would have left it laying there in the indentation of the flattened bushes.

"People spin their lies. She's dead. Did you know that?"

Rose flinched. "I'm not a monster. I never wished her dead. I just wished you hadn't cared for her."

Patrick's jaw clenched. "I *didn't* care for her. She lied. I don't understand it, even now. As far as I know, she'd stopped pursuing me and went for Joe. The ribbon was where Joe had been. I assumed he was on his way to see you. I'm telling you the facts. He has always wanted you, and Alex having Winston's bookstore is another mark against us in his eyes. I need you to stand by me. I need you to partner with me, and that means we need to embrace the truth."

Closure. He needed this to end—for all the years to melt away and a new existence to begin. That's what he wanted in his life. He took a step closer to her.

Rose tossed tops, dresses, and pants, in the garbage bags, unfolded, not looking at him, stuffing the first one so full, the seams nearly erupted. She snapped another one open.

"Okay, Patrick," her voice, smooth and cold, "you lost Stephen at the festival. I got the help I needed at the time. Action, doing something. Not just talking about it. Not dragging false lead number two-thousand and fifty-five into existence between golf and coffee. I'm not responsible for whatever Joe tried to get out of the situation.

I am the mother of a little boy who went missing. That is the truth I accept." She walked to the bedroom door, leaving him in a tomb of clothing—then with her hand on the knob, she said, "but don't ever, *ever* expect me to say he is dead. You don't have to pretend. I know you gave up many years ago—but I won't."

She slammed the door, sealing him with the past—decades of fashion falling off the bed when he sat back down—the mattress sinking as low as his spirit.

XXXI

Rose had put on what she thought was a good front on Sunday. She and Patrick managed to smile at one another, but their most recent words left cracks on their hearts, much like age added wrinkles to skin.

The fight the other day bobbed about with dull jabs of regret. They were on a carousel. *Here we go again. Around and around. Seeing the same faces. Passing the same scenery. When it stops, everything shifts for the next round. The people watching, change, but the story remains the same.* She paused. *No. The people never change. They all play the same game over and over and nobody ever wins.*

She gripped her sweater as the chill of the woods settled on her. When Patrick had mentioned a memorial, a wall wedged itself between them. And that was fifteen years ago. She'd never stop searching for Stephen. Someday he'd come back to them. Someday they would all be vindicated. But then there would be new criticisms. The immediate story would veer in new directions, fading into history, but the fault line had the same beginning. Being pastors of a church where half the congregation wanted to control God didn't make their job rewarding. Sometimes she wished Patrick were an accountant.

She couldn't quit waiting for Stephen's return any more than a drug addict could quit heroin. The *realistic* road never worked for Rose. It would go along for a bit and then crash into a ditch. She was the last believer.

"Rose!" A voice called across the air. Unexpected and male.

Transporting her to another year—when she was younger and could eat things that weren't good for her.

A cracking branch in the distance caused her to squint into the array of greens and browns. Another snap—closer this time. He looked masculine, ghostly, unshaven with a smile not reaching his eyes. Joe.

Her breath caught, and she stopped, taking a step back.

"Rose?" He kept coming toward her. Rugged. Handsome. Where Patrick's good looks were refined and respectable, Joe's held an air of expectancy and danger.

Part of her said *Run*, but the part that didn't want to look like a lunatic stayed planted. He stood in front of her. Up closer his ruggedness crossed the line to unkempt.

Rose didn't want him here but remained silent and took another step backward. His eyes shifted, traveling over her, and the air sharpened, winter chasing away autumn in icy breezes rustling through the maples. Leaves fell around them. She remembered laughing, having picnics . . . She snapped the vision shut. Patrick saved her from Joe. He came along, and she never looked back—until Stephen disappeared.

"We should stop pretending," Joe said. "We have an intuition for each other, deep inside. You wander the woods to find something. Well, here I am." He smiled opening his arms as though he were a welcoming sight.

He had to be joking. "Joe, anyone can love someone for a short time. That's all we had back then. I'm in my marriage for the long haul. With Patrick."

Joe let out a laugh. "Sounds real appealing, put that way,"

"You know what I mean." *Lame, Rose. Real lame.* Her teeth clenched. The past didn't need to revisit her in the form of Joe Brooks. She'd grown up. She had a husband and three kids, for goodness sakes. *No, four.* "How many children do you have?" they'd ask her. "Four." Then the explanations would follow left by an awkwardness. "Three." Sounded like a lie.

Two more steps back and her foot caught on a vine. She lost her balance. His hand went out and pulled her upright. Her past. In desperation, she had turned to him all those years ago. Perhaps she used him. Brushing at her clothes, dirt and dry leaves came loose. A dagger had fallen out of her pocket, and she picked it up.

Joe's eyes widened, and he laughed. "I can guarantee you aren't going to need that thing. I come in peace."

"You shouldn't be here."

"You're awfully jumpy."

"You're trespassing."

"I remember when I was welcome."

"We were looking for Stephen." Her eyes flitted away. Why did she still stand here? She didn't owe Joe an explanation. "What do you want?"

"My store back. I can make you an offer."

"You mean, make Alex an offer."

"Right."

"I wouldn't count on anything. It's not for sale as far as I know."

"Maybe she's tired of it. Has her tied down. She's young. She might want to do something else with her life because I haven't seen her much lately." Joe sat on a nearby log.

"The bookstore is Alex's business, not mine. So, when she is there, or not there, I have no idea." Not totally true, but Alex didn't answer to her. Rose could breathe easier now that he had put distance between them. Patrick's accusations lingered. Why did Joe have to be here now?

"Yeah," Joe shrugged. "It could be a real burden in the end."

A cold drip fell from the sky. "What are you saying?"

"You could put in a good word for me. See if she's still into making it a go. I want the property, and I'd give her a good price."

"You need to talk to her yourself," Rose said. *Of all the arrogant—*.

Joe smiled. "Sure. Probably be in my best interest to do that." He stood and turned back toward the road beyond the woods.

She stared at his back, wondering, *How far would Joe go to get what he wanted? How far had he gone in the past?* Turning to him proved to be a mistake, and yes, in her desperation she thought only of herself and finding Stephen, but not until later did she realize how he had taken advantage—or how being with the tavern owner looked to everyone, including Patrick.

"Joe," she called out to him.

He stopped and turned.

"Stay away from us. Every time you come around, people talk. I value my marriage. There's not anything between us, you know. I don't owe you anything."

He took a few steps closer. "Sure, Rose, whatever you say. But I know as well as you, at one time you liked being with me."

"I just wanted to find Stephen." Tears slipped. "What do you want from me? I'm sorry for the past. I'm sorry for taking advantage of your help, but what can I do?" Fear fingered her spine. Patrick always hated the woods. She couldn't stay away. They called to her like ice cream in the freezer. But Joe wasn't dessert. Joe was poison. Delicious on the outside but would put holes in her spirit—thin and vulnerable. He reached out and lifted her chin. "Please don't," she turned away.

His hand fell to his side, and he picked at a nearby leaf. "I get it. You're a pastor's wife, and it would cause gossip. By the way, there is something I didn't tell you. About Stephen. That prophecy."

He was baiting her. Her spiritual radar had been off while they searched for Stephen. If she hadn't been in such a vulnerable place, she would have seen him as an opportunist. Patrick warned her. Joe's attention might have been flattering, but she only cared about her son and had given little thought to appearances. Now she wanted to tell him to go away. Her memory flitted to everything he told her when they were trying to find Stephen. There had been false leads through Portland, crazy theories had led them deep into the countryside. She cringed at how she'd been with a man out in the middle of nowhere, even though she'd done nothing. God's grace saved her from Joe instigating any physical contact.

Opportunity had presented itself, just like now. Her hands fingered the knife in her pocket.

"You want to hear it?"

"I assume you're dying to tell me," she said, forcing nonchalance.

His expression didn't change much, considering his next few words. "The guy in the woods. Remember him?"

The dope guy, as *the ladies* referred to him. "Of course." Was he going to admit he knew the man all along?

"It was him."

She met his eyes, not understanding. "What do you mean?"

"He delivered the prophecy."

Rose quit breathing. "You're lying. He was a leader from a church in Montana." *It was Montana, right?* She scrambled to remember, trying to picture the man's face again.

"It's amazing what a razor and haircut can accomplish, isn't it? Not to mention a suit and tie. Gives him an *out of town pastor appeal.*" Joe smiled, and she wondered how on earth had she ever thought that he was handsome. "Of course," he went on, "no one ever paid close attention to him, did they?"

Her vision spun. Thou shalt not kill had some sort of loophole, didn't it? "It can't be true. Why would you search with me if you knew the prophecy wasn't real?"

He smiled, his eyes flicking over her. "Aw, c'mon, Rose. You know why. I underestimated your dedication to Patrick. I'm a business man. I see opportunity in all kinds of situations."

A wave of nausea hit her. "Why would he do that?" She had no connection with the guy in the woods. "You said you didn't know him. He didn't know us. Why?"

"Did anyone see him in the woods after that day?"

Rose grasped the tree branch to support her lightheadedness. "He's back. I saw you with him after the pie social—at Martin's." Her legs weakened, and she wanted to sit.

"I didn't realize you kept such a watchful eye on me, but yes, he threatened to come clean to you. But being how things are, I have decided to tell you myself. He thought blackmailing me for more money was a good idea. That's what made him do it in the first place. Needed the cash. He did a good job. I mean, he flubbed up a little—might not have been the sharpest tool in the shed. I asked him to do a simple thing, but I suppose he got freaked out being on stage, pretending to be a preacher and all, but I adjusted my goals and had some fun."

A breeze drifted through the leaves, and she caught a whiff of stale cigarette smoke as the truth settled in. "You put him up to it? How could you do this?"

"Guess we all use each other, don't we? Did you expect Stephen to be alive? I didn't, but it made the perfect opportunity to spend more time with you. And as far as my help, I expected more gratitude."

"There was nothing going on between us. You thought—"

"Exactly. So, for both of us, I guess the moral of the story is to be aware of what the real truth is. See you later, Rose." He strolled back through the woods, whistling to himself, turning back one more time. "Remember, I am creative at getting what I want. I'll be in touch with Allie soon."

The nearby tree became her anchor as the bark pressed into her skin, tears streaming down her cheeks. The surrounding colors deepened as clouds hid the sun, a shiver of cold forced her to turn around and go back. After her fight with Patrick, what would this truth do to them? Not until the white of her home came in sight, did she close the knife with a click.

†††

Rose paused, seeing Patrick's car in the driveway. She had stayed in the woods too long, and now her dinner wouldn't be ready on time.

Taking a deep breath, she entered the door by the kitchen. Fresh coffee scented the air, and the familiarity and relief to be in the warm house overwhelmed her.

Patrick came in and stopped upon seeing her. "Rose." He walked over and took her in his arms. Safe. She was safe with him. "You're trembling." Holding her back at arm's length, he studied her, putting her hair behind her ear.

"It's a bit chilly."

"No jacket?" he asked, and her eyes darted to his face.

"I didn't bring one. I was warm when I left."

"Honey, it's mid-October, starting to get colder out now." He watched her. Her eyes moved to the coffee pot and then to the window that overlooked the woods. He walked over and poured her a cup, then added a dash of cream. "Here. It'll warm you up." He left the room for a second, coming back with a fuzzy bathrobe, draping it over her.

"You hate this thing," she clutched the warmth of the covering around her.

Patrick grinned. "The night is still young."

She rolled her eyes and smiled. Patrick never did hold a grudge. "Guess it's safe to wear, then."

She didn't know if he believed all was well. Patrick played on a lot of silence. He was an expert in body language and what was *not* being said, which made her nervous. She should tell him—but how? *The prophecy, it wasn't true. All these years—I was so sure . . .* Tears threatened to come.

"Promise me you'll take a coat from now on," Patrick interrupted her thoughts. "I don't want you to get sick. It's also hunting season. You need to be extra cautious. I wouldn't want you to fall prey to a stray hunter."

Rose paused, her cup mid-air for a second, before taking another sip of coffee. "Hunters have never come close to the house. I think I'm pretty safe."

His blue eyes rested on hers. "It takes all kinds." He set the cup down. "I have a meeting tonight and should be getting back to the church soon."

She nodded as a barely perceptible tension, like a faint wrong note, played between them.

The doorbell rang, jolting Rose as though a shotgun went off.

"I'll get it. I took the liberty of ordering us a pizza."

"I could have whipped up something." Relief followed, and a weariness came over her. "But I'm glad I don't have to."

"You deserve a night off," Patrick walked toward the door.

She leaned into the sofa, listening to the murmur of him paying. Her eyes strayed to the kitchen window that displayed a view of the woods. She imagined Patrick standing there, looking out …

He took the boxes to the kitchen and a moment later came back to her, grinning. "Dinner is served." He handed her a slice on a plate, sitting beside her with his own. "I'll wolf this down, then I'm out of here. Should be a couple of hours," he took a big bite.

She sat there watching as though the day hadn't just changed everything. Joe showing up like an apparition. Swift, intense, and then gone. Her eyes went over Patrick. He was real. He was her rock, her covering of protection. She smiled as he topped her plate with an extra piece, and he winked. The split in her heart closed, pushing Joe aside.

XXXII

Henry opened his eyes each morning to a free-falling groping silence. It struck him with a panic for those first few seconds upon awakening, then he'd land on steady ground. Instead of impatient car horns, he heard birds and remembered he had come to a weird place where buildings didn't block the sky. In New Jersey and Manhattan, he was anonymous. Here, everyone would know him by the end of the week; and there were still boxes to unpack. Unbelievable.

The farmhouse echoed with excess space, as Henry made his coffee. The sky, vast and unprotected, made him feel small, like an ant. Why hadn't he rented a studio apartment in some high rise in Portland? Because he wasn't thinking. *Good job, Henry.* Here he resided, pursuing his face-on-a-milk-carton mission in the middle of the boonies.

A new problem became clear. An awful realization. He didn't know how to approach the McMillans. Showing himself and saying "Hey, I'm your lost son, Stephen," seemed like a dumb idea. They had lived without him this long. And why did there have to be so many of them? They were even multiplying. Fear knocked at his heart and whispered excuses.

Images of Paulina—what he'd give to hear her Jersey accent right now. Digging in his wallet he found her business card. His hand hovered over the phone, calculating the time difference. She'd still be awake.

"Hello?"

He settled into his sofa, leaning back and closed his eyes. Hearing her voice was like drinking hot chocolate. Soothing comfort. "Polly, how are you?"

Silence filled the line. "Henry? Are you really calling me?"

He frowned. "Yeah."

"I always call you."

"I didn't realize our relationship was so one-sided." He pictured her hair in a messy bun—her eyes lighting up.

She laughed. "I'm always the one chasing you. So, what is so important that you thought of me? I know it's not time to propose yet."

"Who said we had to wait till we're thirty?" He grinned and then sighed. "It's good to hear your voice."

"What's wrong. You're scaring me."

His eyes teared. He should have prepared himself better for this conversation. "It's Mom, Polly. She's passed away. I'm selling the house." So much for easing into the bad news.

"Oh, Henry, I'm sorry. I can come. I'll drive the two hours."

He smiled, wishing only two hours separated them. Polly lived in upstate New York, and she thought he still inhabited his tiny studio apartment in Manhattan.

"Henry?" She said when he didn't answer. "Are you in Jersey? Wherever you are, I'll come. I mean it."

"You may want to take that back."

"No, really."

"Polly, I'm in Oregon."

"Oregon?" There was a pause, and he knew she tried to pin point the location, never having been a geography whiz.

"West Coast. Above California."

"What are you doing all the way out there?"

"Mom had connections. I had to come here to wrap up some things." He gripped the phone tighter. Yeah, sounded like he was visiting an aunt—not finding a whole new family.

"What happened? How did—?"

"Cancer."

"Oh no, I'm sorry."

"Yeah, me too. I never got to, you know, do anything for her." Despite certain truths, Henry still wished he'd made her life better. He couldn't turn off the fact that she wasn't his mother. She was the only mother he remembered.

"I know you, Henry. You were there for her at the end. I don't have to ask you."

"Yes, I was."

"That matters. A lot. When will you be back? We will get together. Get a pizza."

Henry looked at his cardboard boxes still packed, and the easels standing in a row, waiting to enlighten him.

"Henry?"

"I'll be here a while." He stood and paced, glad for the new cordless phone.

"How long?"

He sighed. "I don't know. I—Polly, I rented a farmhouse."

She laughed.

"No really, I did. Here in Oregon."

The pause on the other line, made him question his reasons for disrupting his entire life. "You're *moving* there?"

"I ..." he sighed and sat back down. "It's a long story."

"And a farmhouse? You'd better spill it. It's a woman, isn't it? Have you found true love?" Her voice went whimsical, like a little girl who still believed in happily ever after.

"Nope. Nothing like that."

"Then what? What could make you do something so rash? I know grief can—"

"I was kidnapped."

She didn't say anything, then laughed. Henry closed his eyes, picturing her, wishing she sat here next to him. "I have a hard time believing you were kidnapped. You're a grown man."

"No, I mean, I was kidnapped before I was three. That's what the evidence is pointing to anyway. It's complicated."

There was pause. "Caroline—she isn't your mother? Your real mother, I mean?"

He'd kept all the stuff bottled up inside, and now it spilled from him. Once he said the word, *kidnapped*, nothing could stop the rest of his story from exploding and falling like debris—burnt and in bits that couldn't be fixed.

His soul lightened, freeing itself by getting the words out. Telling Polly released the tension that didn't allow him to relax. He knew this would be the first time he'd be able to sleep well since arriving in Filbert Ridge.

"Oh, Henry. I don't know what to say. That's awful, yet, *wow*, they will be over the moon to have you again. I can't imagine ..."

He couldn't tell her his doubts, how he had purposely held back on unpacking and often contemplated a way out because the Risley family hadn't made him sign a lease.

"Yeah," he said instead. "Let me give you my new number." He rattled off the digits, and the call ended with Polly saying she'd save her money and fly to be with him when she could. "Wouldn't that be fun, Henry? Like old times—you and me, hanging out together. And you can introduce me to the family. Oh, this is so exciting!"

He'd expect nothing less from Polly to luminate the upside of the crazy situation. She always wanted an adventure. "Yep," he said. "Hope I can see you soon."

He hung up the phone, and homesickness fell on him. Henry took his coffee and sank into his designer chair, dreaming of returning to the city life. Polly would flourish here in the country among the trees, but unfortunately, Henry David Thoreau, he was not.

XXXIII

Cookie sheets lined the counters, muffins baked in the oven, and bite-size cakes were cooled and individually wrapped, stacked in the far corner of the McMillan kitchen. Rose breathed in the sweet aromas, but peace escaped her. She could only think of Stephen and her reliance on a false prophecy.

Instead of God, the inner voice condemned.

Covered with flour and spilled vanilla, the cookbook lay open beside her. She scanned the page with her finger. Anything to get her thoughts from skidding in thousands of directions at once. If she focused on baking, she'd be okay. It would keep her from running. And right now she could run and run and run and maybe never come back. At least baking kept her from slipping off the planet—her feet planted on the cool kitchen floor—and if she cooked long enough, perhaps her equilibrium would come back, replacing the torturous demon with a calm spirit. Stirring the dough in the bowl faster, her thoughts popped about like rapid gunfire.

She had yet to talk to Patrick about the prophecy. It was too embarrassing—the least of her worries, however. What a fool she'd been! This new info would seal the deal in his opinion, leaving Stephen in the *gone forever* category. To make it worse, despite the lie, she couldn't put it to rest easily. There were too many years invested of searching, waiting, and claiming that the word came from God. Her thoughts had adapted to this way of life, and spun like a boat in a storm trying to steer them toward what she now knew. So easily deceived!

Patrick, take this hope, it looks good, tastes like there is a future—a promise from God. Her stomach clenched in a panic. He might never want anything to do with her once he knew.

"Sure you haven't used everything in the cupboard already?" Patrick leaned on the doorway of the kitchen.

The cookbook, teetering on the edge of the counter near her elbow, crashed to the floor, and she flushed with irritation at being caught in this baking frenzy, desperately needing to be alone. She was a contradiction—wanting him to listen and hold her, forgive her—but not wanting him to be here right now.

Patrick walked over and picked up the book, placing it safely away from the mixing bowl. He took the nearby spatula, as though this is what he came home to do, and moved the over-sized chocolate chip cookies to the wax paper waiting to be filled with more sweets.

Sensing the upcoming lecture, Rose longed to escape out the open window and into the woods. The fall breeze drifted through the hot kitchen, and the vibrancy of sunlight warmed her face at the same time. Autumn's beauty had been wasted with this anxiety-ridden baking.

"You left the golf course early," she commented, wondering why. This could be the last weekend before the rainy season. Not the kind of day a golfer wanted to waste.

"I thought I'd come home to my beautiful wife." Patrick grabbed a box for the finished cookies. Rose set the bowl aside, pushing a stray hair out of the way that hung in her eye, nearly knocking a muffin tin to the ground.

Why was he here? They had played nice since their fight, being civil and gently sweeping the issue under the rug, but the words spoken still lingered in the air like a blown-out candle. She watched his calm manner as he boxed up the cookies. The lecture hovered in the air between them. Rose flopped the cookbook back open and pretended to read the ingredients.

Patrick stepped behind her, and she tried to focus, but the word *bouillabaisse* swam in front of her eyes.

The oven beeped, startling Rose from her pretense, and she whirled around with lightning speed, grateful for the interruption. Opening the oven door, a wave of heat hit her face, blowing the same wisp of hair against her forehead. She grabbed an oven mitt and pulled out the hot muffin tin and set it behind her, then slammed the door closed with a bit too much gusto. Turning back to Patrick, she nearly knocked over the box of baking soda, but he caught it, walked to the cupboard, and put it away.

"Just baking some treats for the children's center. And stew for the ladies at the shelter," she added, when his eyes drifted to the stove.

"Not fish soup?" he asked with a raised eyebrow.

She made a face at him. He turned and took a cookie he had placed on the wax paper earlier. "I hope there's enough for me to have one without you having to make another whole batch."

She brushed off flour from her apron, avoiding his eyes. "Well, since you're here, I suppose you can help me load these things. I honestly don't know why you'd leave a game on such a beautiful day. Is everything all right?" She leaned against the counter to study him and noticed he looked pale. Was he ill? Or had something happened to a fellow golfer?

"I'm fine. A little tired." His eyes took in the kitchen around him. "But it would seem all is not well."

"There is nothing wrong here. Nothing to concern yourself with." Her jaw clenched, and a headache pounded its punishment, paying her for adding lying to her list of sins.

"Good, then." He lifted the baked sweets and placed them in packages while Rose put the stew in a container. As he headed out, hands full, he abruptly stopped and faced her, his back against the door. She practically ran into him. "Um, this doesn't have anything to do with your restless night, does it? Another dream? Or the time of year?"

Some of the tension left her body, and she almost dropped a bag. "You don't need to bother yourself with my dreams." She meant it kindly, but it didn't sound that way once she said the words.

He searched her face, and she stared back at him, trying to be unaffected. He did know her after all. "But the game? Is that why you left?" she asked.

"One of the many reasons, yes." A silence danced between them—thoughts that could find no voice. She wilted, and the bags she held gained weight. He appeared to notice and opened the door, taking one of them from her while juggling the things he already had, and walked toward the car. Rose's feet refused to follow for a moment as she watched his tall frame and noticed the sandy hair had more silver than she remembered.

Together they packed the goodies into the back seat, and Patrick leaned on the driver's side of the car as though they were going on an outing to enjoy the warmth of the sun. Rose came to him, keys in hand, annoyed that he blocked her door. "Thank you for your help." She gave him a smile she didn't feel and waited for him to move out of the way.

"I'm driving you."

"What? No, I can drive myself. I don't need you tagging along." She chewed her lower lip, sorry for sounding horrible, but longing to be left alone.

His eyes flicked over her face and took in the hands clenched, one knuckled over car keys. Her fingers relaxed slightly, and he reached out and touched them. "Rose, I'll drive you anywhere you want to go."

"Fine." Her voice sharpened like cutting glass in contrast to his gentle offer. She turned, brushing by him and back to the passenger side. She blinked and breathed deep, looking to the sky, trying to stop the tears before getting into the car beside him.

†††

Patrick ventured in new territory here. He'd never caught any of Rose's baking binges but always managed to get there for the aftermath. Pure, divine intervention allowed him to overhear someone mention his wife during the fifth hole. The *ladies* who talked about everyone, were advancing toward the sixth, and though they were a distance away, their voices carried to where Patrick and his friends stood. When he saw they were playing, he hoped they would remain far ahead, but since the women spent more time lifting weights at the gym than on the golf green, his group of men soon caught up and found themselves waiting for them to tee off. Evidently seeing Patrick there reminded Meredith of her early morning grocery shopping.

"Rose McMillan bought a cartful of flour and sugar. I wondered if she was giving Tilly a run for her money." The voice traveled across the green.

"She should consider it. She has a gift for baking sweets. Must be making food for the center again." Claudia's voice came, her tone like a sharp knife slicing through a succulent cake.

The rest of the conversation faded as they disappeared across the fairway. Howard Trent stood staring at Patrick. "You gonna tee off, or what?"

Patrick gazed across the manicured course. Years passed since Rose had done what he referred to as mega baking, but just recently their kitchen had been exploding with all sorts of extraordinary food. He should have paid closer attention. He remembered the fancy breakfasts and lunches, how he had excused the signs as a whim or special meal. Then after their fight—or discussion, disagreement, whatever the proper thing to call words flying like weapons—"I, uh, think I need to go home."

How could he have ignored her distress? He had puttered around in denial. The mania hadn't reared its ugly head to this extent in years. He'd prayed enough times—what, his daughter could raise the dead as a child but a simple healing of his wife's mind eluded them forever? Or better yet, finding an answer to the disappearance of Stephen? Closure—that's all he wanted.

He now considered the prophecy invalid. Twenty-three years must be beyond a statute of limitation for that sort of thing. How long did they believe a man in a suit and tie? Did he really speak words they were supposed to cling to as God's truth? Rose had quit speaking of Stephen's return—for awhile anyway. Patrick knew she still held onto expectation, but until the other night he had imagined it had shrunk to an almost invisible speck in the sky, floating around in the air blending with reality, no longer seen or smelled, just—gone.

Howard leaned on his golf club. "You sick?" He eyed Patrick. "No, it's just ..."

Baking equaled disaster. Howard already knew that. Patrick's spirit stirred. This went beyond a prelude to calamity. He possibly stood at the peak before the explosion. Time had run out, and she would disappear for days, wandering the woods, feeding the homeless, spending time at the shelter. If he didn't get home, she would spiral into a depression once the mania wore off. Patrick didn't know if he could handle the emotions attached this time. A weariness made him question his ability to bounce back—their marriage to survive another episode.

An inner voice told him to calm down. *So what if she went to the store?* After all, pantry items were essential, especially for someone with a cooking ability like Rose. But his spirit sent out a warning, while his mind tried to reassure him with lies because responding to the truth might suck the life out of him.

Howard tipped the end of his driver toward the ladies. "I heard. People don't realize how their voices carry out here. Sounds like you have treats to get home to," he said with a half-smile.

Patrick knew Howard wanted to lighten reality. "I doubt they were concerned about their voices carrying. I'm sorry, Howard, Phil." He nodded at the other man who stood close by, staring at him as well, "I—uh—" Patrick found anymore explaining too exhausting.

Meredith's voice bounced through the expanse, "I saw your ball in the woods somewhere. I really did."

Howard took out a tee as he glanced at Patrick. "Sure man. Hope it's nothing."

"Yeah, thanks," he slapped the two men on the back and left the field, praying he wasn't too late.

They delivered the goods in silence, and he brought her back home and watched one of their favorite shows, hoping to settle her nerves. He tried to be there. He tried to prevent the next step from happening, but in the end, it hadn't mattered, because when he woke in the morning, she was gone.

Patrick searched the house, hoping for a glimpse of her, but silence met his inquiry. He got dressed and walked to the edge of the wood in the cold morning light. A gentle rain fell. He scanned the openings in the trees, imagining he saw her when he caught sight of the color red waving in the branches. A leaf mocking him. He considered all the time spent searching these parts because he'd taken the boys out for some daddy time.

Rose's sanity took a leave of absence, tossing her into a dark place, dodging everyone's opinions. And Patrick had done nothing to stop them. He watched his wife waste away physically, and he froze, like right now, standing at the edge of the woods hoping to find her but unable to take a step. He faced hell, and the shadows were demons. Would she ever come back? The children were all grown, and his stomach clenched whenever he thought she might not return for just him. He'd lost a child too, but he always had to be the stable one. He brushed away the resentment that tried to sit on his shoulder.

His body shook, and perspiration beaded his skin mixing with cool rain falling in a fine shower. He'd ignored the signs of impending illness he felt the day before, but now his throat burned, and his head hurt. The forest spread before him, waiting to devour his soul if he stepped into its brush.

Patrick sank to the ground and wept.

XXXIV

Patrick awoke, his head unclear, stuffy, and throbbing, to find Robert sitting beside him in a chair by the bed. He licked his lips, his mouth the equivalent to cotton. "Is she here? Did she come home yet?" How much time had passed?

Robert shifted, leaning closer and placed his hand on Patrick's head. "Not yet." He reached for the water on the nightstand and stood over the bed to help Patrick take a few sips. Patrick closed his eyes when he was done and leaned against the pillow. "I need to go there, the shelter. I need to bring her home." He wanted to jump out of bed and go search for her. His energy drained, and Robert appeared even more weary. "You look beat, son. Are you okay?"

Robert smiled, and a pang for Rose hit Patrick. "Dad, I'm staying in the guest room. I invited myself over. I may look beat, but you nearly ended up in the hospital. You were incoherent in the woods. There's no way you can find Mom right now."

"In the woods?"

"On the edge," Robert clarified. "You remember being there?"

"Yeah. I hoped that she just went for a hike." Patrick grimaced with the memory. "Couldn't go in."

Robert reached into his bag and gave Patrick water and two pills. "Just pain medication, the over the counter variety. No narcotic police needed. It will help the pain and the slight fever you still have," he explained.

"Not sleeping pills. I don't want any of those."

"Don't worry. I'm sure you are worn out enough without giving you medication to sleep. You were beyond making sense out there."

Patrick took the pills and drank the rest of the water. "Guess Alex was sick for awhile. We are keeping you busy."

Robert crossed his arms and leaned back in the chair. "Churches are full of germs, especially in Alex's case working with small children, and you going around shaking everyone's hand. I believe she made it back to work today, against my advice to rest more."

"And how's Susan? Heard she filled in at the bookstore."

"I am going to see her later to tell her about Mom. If I don't, she'll find it out around town."

"And we go around the mountain again."

"Perhaps medication—" Robert started.

"Your mother won't take anything."

"But I think she's gone to the next level. Medication may keep her out of a hospital. She hates those even more than pills, right?"

"Tell me you're not going to blackmail your mother."

Robert sighed. "I just want her to be okay, and I want you to be okay."

Patrick took his hand. "I know, Son, but you can't fix everything." He closed his eyes for a second, and then opened them again. "I'm tired. You don't need to hang around."

Robert nodded. "I'll let you sleep. I'll be here later to fix us some dinner."

"Won't argue about that, although you should check the fridge for leftovers first. I'm sure there's something."

Patrick listened to the soft click of the door and turning of the lock. After the pills started to work, instead of trying to sleep, he got out of bed. Rose was wandering out there somewhere in the cold, and she needed him. He wasn't going to ignore her this time.

He looked upward and in his mind took his sword to redeem what the locust ate. To make right the past. To rise and save his bride from destruction. To venture to the third heaven and bring the glory down to earth. Rust covered the blade, he bent down, dipping the sharpness into the River of Life, and brought the weapon forth, gleaming. The crystal waters dripped, landing in splotches on a dry barren ground. In his vision, he stood on miles of endless cracked earth, but each splotch of water that hit bounced and green shoots sprouted. Life! It surrounded him, and a dormant hope bloomed, filling his heart. The prophecy from many years ago, the one Rose held onto, spoke once again. Loud. Bold.

He thought he'd forgotten the words.

XXXV

Alex took a week off after the picketers made their appearance. Paul's threats, no matter how weak, raised her stress levels, lowering her immune system, and she succumbed to the flu. Adam had sent flowers, and Robert hovered, buying her groceries and fixing her soup. This morning the timing had been perfect for her sister's phone call saying that she was done with books and the people who read them. Susan, being seven months plus pregnant, shouldn't be there anyway, so once Alex hung up the phone, still slightly under the weather, but glad to get out of the house, she checked the mirror and hopped into her Volvo to go back to work.

"Nice scarf," Alex commented on the knitted forest green that Barry wore over his sweater. Barry's mom was always sending him things that she knitted—blankets, sweaters, gloves. "You must tell her you're freezing all the time, or that we don't use heat."

"Yes, I'm very mistreated," he sounded like C3PO. "Customers will be happy that you're back, and I am especially glad."

"It was only a week."

Footsteps clicked in the distance. A voice carried across the aisles. The door opened with a swoosh as a laughing couple walked out.

Alex started to say more, but then a customer came to the cash wrap with a pile of books, so she went to ring her up. It was a handful of romances, the kind that came out every month. She had an urge to read one to make her forget her own sad attempt at dating and try someone else's formulaic adventure. "I was about to go crazy with boredom. And Robert, well I can't bad mouth him

I guess, since he did help, but I thought I'd have to sneak out of my own house to do anything again. Susan's phone call was just the ticket," she said as she headed to the back room. When she came close to the pink-walled romance section, a large cardboard cutout made her stop. "What is that?" she asked Barry, who stepped right at her heels.

Barry's lips twitched, one side rising slightly. "That, my dear Alexandria, is the latest and greatest in romantic fiction."

"Life-size Fabio?"

"All the rage, it seems."

She went closer to the propped-up figure to get a better look. "Really? I mean, isn't he a bit tacky?"

"A bit? I'll be doing something and then catch that thing out of the corner of my eye and do a double take, thinking it's one of your fan club guys looking for you."

"Is that what they look like?" she laughed.

"Wouldn't you like to know."

"I've never had a fan club, so there is nothing to compare him to, I'm sure."

"You always have me, Alexandria."

"Oh, knock it off, already. Julia would kill me."

"You know how to dash a guy's hope." He sighed, looking up at Fabio who towered above them, flashing all his teeth in a hero's smile. "We had to cheer ourselves up somehow. Susan especially enjoyed him."

"And what would Stan think about Susan's obsession with Fabio?"

"That *he* should grow his hair out?" Barry grinned. "I just had the perfect idea. You could put Fabio here by the door, have his face peering through the window. As good as having a dog."

"I can think of two reasons to not do that. One— 'Oh, look, Alex loves Fabio so much she has a cardboard cutout of him front and center.' Or two—'Have you seen that guy at Alex's, you know, the preacher's daughter? He is obviously living with her.'"

"Such a pessimist you are. Sounds entertaining to me," Barry said.

"Oh, sure, for you," she continued toward the back of the store. "I'm going to check the deliveries, see where we are."

Books spilled out into another aisle next to the mystery room with its footprints leading like a maze. Why were all these books on the floor?

Barry was still at her heels when she reached the wide steel door. It hit something and she pushed it with more gusto, sliding a stack of boxes across the floor. She stood in the doorway, staring at the towers of brown going up beyond her head.

Mixed emotions played through her mind. She came to work, and work greeted her in all its UPS glory. From the doorway, she saw a trail to the bathroom and one to the computer, along with a straight shot to the desk. She stepped in—cautiously, looking up and around. Her entrance demanded one of two actions, and with Barry watching, falling in a heap of despair, letting the boxes bury her alive, wasn't one of them, so she managed a smile. "Well, guess it's good that I'm back. Lots to do. I need the distraction." Barry's expression relaxed a bit.

Once he was gone, she sank into the old wooden chair that sat at the desk and put her head in her hands. Her goal was to operate at one hundred percent, so she needed to look the part, act the part, and do the part. She closed her eyes to say a prayer. "Please, God, help me." You'd think she could come up with something better, being a preacher's daughter and all.

A couple of hours went by, and Alex left the back room to shelve the books that were stacked here and there. She had just repositioned a bottom shelf in the mystery room when Barry peeked in. "Silver Lexus out front," then he whisked out with a flash as quick as he had entered.

Rushing around to talk to Robert wasn't a priority. Let him find her himself. Continuing to work for a bit, she thought it might be a false alarm, but then his shoes appeared from her crouched position. She tried to wedge another book onto a full bottom shelf.

He sat on the floor next to her. "Hey."

She stole a glance and did a double take at his disheveled appearance. Not typical of Robert. "So, what happened to you?" she asked.

He smiled. "That bad, huh?" Leaning back on the bookshelf he closed his eyes for a second. "I'm kinda beat, but nothing some sleep won't cure. I see you are back to work."

"Yep. Can't sit around anymore or I'll go nuts." She prayed he wouldn't pay attention to how much needed done. She reached to the next shelf, shoving books over to make room for Julie Smith. "Have you seen Mom at all?" Alex asked, stepping away to continue shelving—Martha Grimes, Agatha Christie—finding room for the mass paperbacks came easier than expected. This made her job pleasant, almost canceling out her brother's all too serious presence.

"She is making herself scarce," Robert crossed his arms, glancing away.

"It's the time of year." Alex frowned at the books near Robert. They weren't anywhere close to where they were supposed to be. She examined the rows. Shelves of books would have to be taken out to fix it.

"As always," he said.

Alex turned her attention from the alphabetical disaster to Robert. "How about a cup of coffee? I could use a break, and I think you need some."

Robert stood as though the mention of coffee revived him. Alex set her books on the cart and led the way to the main hallway where the tables and chairs were arranged beside the kitchen. "I have new beans from Peru. You want an espresso? Or something sweeter might be in order."

"I'll have what you're having." Robert found a table and sank into the wooden chair.

Alex grinned. "Sweet it is. I made caramel the other day. I could just eat it out of the jar."

"Glad you got your appetite back," he said.

She made their espresso, mixing the milk and syrup, topping it with whipped cream, and came back, taking a chair across from him. Being sick had robbed her of all her stamina.

Robert took a sip. "You've been working too hard."

"I am totally fine. You're the one who looks like you've been up all night."

"Probably because I have. I don't get to sleep normal hours. Not only that, but Dad is sick. I've been with him, dozing off and on in a chair. I have a reason to look this way."

Alex frowned. "Will he be okay? I should go there and be with him."

"I left him sleeping. He'll be fine. I'm going back there this evening."

"How's Susan? I worried she did too much when working here."

"Susan has enough energy to dole out to both you and I."

"Right." She always envied her sister's charismatic ways. But those same qualities had given her a reprieve as a child. Susan could always deflect the negative arrows in midair, making them turn to dust before they hit Alex.

Stirring her coffee, she and Robert sat—silence flitted around them like a bored ghost, and the past crept into her thoughts leaking into the present. The tension grew thick with each passing tick of the clock, and she scrambled for words to say. "So, since it is *that* time of the year, do you ever want to know what happened to Stephen? I mean, do you ever think *we* could find out?" The subject burned in her brain since the lunch she endured after church a couple of weeks ago when the strain between their parents over-shadowed the main course. But once asked, it felt wrong. Out of place. Like a super ball bouncing in a sanctuary.

Robert frowned. "What? You're going to play detective, now? It was a long time ago."

"But if we had some of the answers, our family would be ... I don't know, whole?" Wasn't anything better than tripping on family history or approaching an open door, dark and empty—a place going nowhere? She wanted to find the solid ground.

"Do you ever wonder why we have to live our lives around a tragedy from over twenty years ago?" Robert said. "Who does that? People move on. They get counseling and start to live again. But not us."

"I doubt you can ever get over a missing child." She took a sip of coffee. "What if breaking the silence would turn everything around, instead of pretending we don't know what's going on?"

"*I* can't. You could, Susan could, but not me."

"Why not? You could tell Mom how she's making Dad stressed, and it's not good for his health, right? Like doctorly advice?"

"No."

"Mom is proud of you. You're the oldest and she'd listen—"

Robert stared across the room where the window displayed a large tree, the colors bouncing in the wind. Alex gripped her cup, forcing needed warmth to her hands, waiting for him to say something.

"Every year the change of weather reminds me how this is my fault. If I go to her, I risk seeing it in her eyes. That I'm to blame."

"She doesn't blame you. Why would she?"

"How can she not? It has to be there. I distracted Dad."

"You were six!" The words Alex spoke came out too loud, and she saw Barry glance their way.

"Stephen always got all the attention. Everyone had to be extra careful, or he'd be gone, doing something crazy. I had Dad all to myself. For less than a minute. How could he disappear so fast? I thought he'd be just a few steps away."

"You were just a kid. Kids do things like that all the time. How do you know you are remembering the day correctly? And even so, sheesh, Robert. If you were Dad would you blame you?"

"If you want to run yourself ragged searching for answers, have at it. I'm done. Mom left all of us, including part of herself when Stephen disappeared. You want to do a repeat and let this consume your life—good luck with that."

Robert set his drink on the table, and pushing his chair back, stood. "The thing is, I hate this time of year as much as Mom. I just don't get to fall apart and disappear." A shadow lifted. He wasn't *Robert the judgmental* but Robert—her childhood brother, the one who looked out for her in almost invisible ways. *To make up for the past.* Her insides swirled with dread.

"In the end I have to be realistic. We won't be seeing Stephen again, no matter what Mom thinks." He walked away, and she followed him to the door, watching as he got into his silver Lexus—still human. Talk about body snatching. Right before her eyes she saw a glimpse of what Robert had buried—himself.

XXXVI

Patrick went to the place where the nightmare started. The filberts. Gazing around him, he mustered up the sights and sounds of that day. The apples on the edge of the orchard still gave the air a sweet scent, and today a cool breeze rustled along the branches, the sun breaking up the clouds ever so often. He pictured the wine tasting, the chocolate-covered hazelnuts, and the cotton candy. He remembered the screeching laughter of the kids. If he could only tune his ear to his own son, but he couldn't because his son was silent. Agitation filled him. If Patrick could hear silence in the middle of chaos, he'd find Stephen.

He must think like a two-year-old who took in the world and said nothing. Patrick tried to focus, get a new perspective, despite all the time they'd already put into every avenue of the case. With Howard, he had considered every word spoken, blow of the wind, the slightest shade of hope, you name it; yet, he still tracked the past—like following footsteps buried in a blizzard. Ridiculous.

The Filbert Festival ceased to exist after the disappearance of Stephen. They tried to continue, but suspicion shadowed the event, and soon no one could pretend. Instead, each specialty became its own separate farm stand. The wine tasting didn't venture beyond the vineyard; the filberts and pumpkins all had their own displays. The orchard no longer held parties.

Patrick parked the car in a big dirt area dividing nut trees from firs. He was surprised to see a van there. He rarely came here anymore, maybe visitors had grown more common. Staring into the woods, he envisioned seeing Rose, but only birds and branches swaying in the breeze met his gaze. He walked around to where the vehicle sat with the passenger door wide open. No one inside.

Laughter sounded in the distance, and he saw a woman and child playing between the filbert trees, pausing to take in the Cascade Mountain Range. Patrick walked along the edge of the woods back toward his own car, not sure what he thought he'd accomplish. Out of the corner of his eye, the little boy ran through the orchard, and for a moment the blond hair and the smile became his own son. His heart tore in half. A fresh, unexpected grief mixed with panic, crashed down on him, like someone standing on his windpipe.

The boy climbed into the van.

"Wait up! Jack, slow down." She paused near her vehicle, and a shriek of laughter came from the back seat. Walking to the side, she peeked in. "There you are! You are a tease! Here, have some pretzels, and I got juice in your sippy cup."

The past clicked like a slide show. A thought tried to surface. The woman noticed Patrick staring, and he heard the door shut and locks being pushed down. *Smart lady.* He probably looked like a serial killer.

That's when he remembered the man in the woods. Vivian could have seen something. She claimed the man was a hippie living off the land, *smoking dope* as she put it, but still, he would have had an overall view, watching everyone. This was getting him nowhere. The minivan backed out and took off, making the tires spin and gravel fly—an image, Patrick recalled, much like the day Stephen disappeared.

XXXVII

Turning off DB highway, Alex left the street lights behind and the country road plunged her into darkness. She was picking up a crib that Susan had found for sale. Unfortunately, the item was in Dockerbog, but Alex owed her sister a favor.

The curves came fast, her headlights highlighting the splashing of the pavement with each turn, windshield wipers banging back and forth at high speed, when movement caught her eye. *Deer!* She slammed on the brakes, swerving. Her tire bounced off a chuckhole in the middle of the road, and the car slid. Gravel skittered as she pulled to the side, careful to not land in a ditch. A utility truck roared past, blaring its horn.

The rain continued its drumming on the car roof as though nothing happened. Her hands shook as she flipped open the glovebox. Where was that flashlight? She couldn't remember when she'd last seen it. Another vehicle swooshed by without slowing down, splashing a wall of water over the side of her car. She turned on the hazards and got out. Her feet landed in a rocky puddle and she leaned down, to inspect the damage. She shuddered as the cold water fell down her neck and back. *A flat. Great.*

Another wave of water covered the bottom half of her jeans, and a truck came so close, she had to flatten herself against the vehicle. Another ... but this one stopped and pulled in behind her.

The driver didn't appear to care that he half blocked the road. He slammed his door and came toward her. "You trying to get yourself killed?"

He stood beside her car, a shadow against the lights, but she knew the voice. "Joe?"

He came over to her and inspected the flat. "What in the world did you do?"

She didn't need a lecture. "I dodged a deer. If someone would bother to fix these potholes, I'd still be driving."

"What are you doing out here anyway?" Joe asked.

"I didn't realize I was under house arrest."

"We can't fix this out here unless you have a death wish. Where'd you get these tires?'

"That tire company right before Dockerbog."

He crossed his arms. "Land sakes, girl. Call them. They'll fix this right up."

"You got a magic phone with you?" She swiped at her hair, water ruining her make-up.

"No, but you just passed the Dockerbogger. I'll give you a lift."

"And leave my car right here?"

"Get in your car, and I'll make the call for you. I'll be back in a few," he walked away. She stood staring at him.

He turned around and pointed at her. "Get in the car!" He fired up his engine and did a quick turn around like he owned the entire road.

She sat in the seat, listening to the rain pound on the roof, mortified that Joe, of all people, had to come to her rescue. He did have a point. No room to change the tire, no lights—anyone else would have thought through the situation. In her case, common sense had taken a leave of absence. At least she managed to avoid riding with Joe in his truck.

And he did come back, right away almost, knocking at her window. He held up a thermos with a promising smile. "I brought you something warm."

"Is that cocoa?" she shouted through the window.

"No. Coffee. "I only have adult beverages. No hot chocolate here."

Huh. She unlocked the door. He got in, shaking his hair.

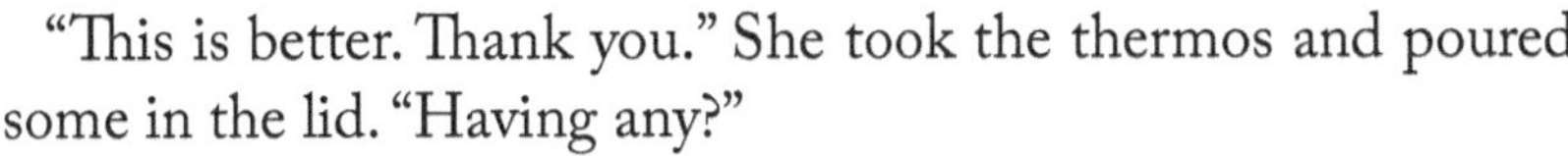

"This is better. Thank you." She took the thermos and poured some in the lid. "Having any?"

"No. It's all yours."

He smelled of pine trees mixed with rain. "This weather is crazy. Ruins my business some nights. At least Gary got the roof and window fixed for me. No one wants to drive in this stuff, but then after awhile, they all get depressed and need to get out. I give it two days, and the bar will be hopping. How's the bookstore, Allie?"

She didn't like him calling her Allie. They weren't buds or anything. "Are the tire people coming?"

"Yeah. They wondered if a patch job would get you to their place. Told them the tire was wasted. They'll be here soon, I reckon, since they close in about thirty minutes. Lucky I came along, huh?" He smiled like he was the big hero.

She took a sip of the coffee, seeing nothing in the dark except when a car's headlights lit the road. "I suppose you can go. You don't have to babysit me." *Way to sound grateful.* "I mean, thanks for calling. I'm good now. And for the coffee." He'd want his thermos back. *Sheesh.* She leaned back closing her eyes to avoid his.

He took out a piece of paper and handed it to her. "I jotted down a number."

What, was his favorite psychiatrist a phone call away? But instead it was digits with a dollar sign.

"For the bookstore. That is what I'm willing to pay."

Ah. Understanding dawned. She imagined Joe standing in the road, directing deer to run into the path of her car—right in front of a hole he made bigger. "I see. I owe you after the coffee and roadside service?"

"I always thought you were sweet and kind. This is a good offer."

"And you think I can be easily bought."

"Not at all," he went on. "This is the chance of a lifetime. You could go to college. Do whatever you want."

College? All she cared about were books—and *not* textbooks.

"Also you may consider. Marriage, babies, the picket fence, instead of the burden that the bookstore will become. The building is going to need repairs, and then what will you do? It could cost a fortune."

"I'm sure I can manage its upkeep. You've done a great job with the Dockerbogger." She cringed inwardly at the insult.

Joe laughed. "You surprise me, Allie. This is a bad time, obviously. I apologize. Very tacky of me to mention this when you are stranded on the side of the road. Think about it. Get back to me. Looks like your rescue service is here." He opened the door.

"Wait, your thermos." She scrambled, splashing coffee.

He waved a hand with a grin. "Keep it. Let me know, okay? Study that number. It's your future, you know."

Why did he have to sound so confident? He closed her car door, and she ripped the paper into tiny shreds, but knew the number would stay imprinted on her brain.

XXXVIII

Patrick contemplated various scenarios, some from many years ago, but now a new perspective came into play. Stephen always liked cars. What if he climbed into one of them? What if he remained unnoticed? Who wouldn't have brought him back right away? Some people came from out of town. A lot of people. Howard and Patrick had relied on news coverage and sketches and phone calls, but the possibilities his mind played out now caused trepidation. Not that he hadn't gone over every imaginative outcome for the past twenty-three years. One small detail could be the key to unlock the story. Who might know something, without realizing it? Vivian. That woman somehow got around without going anywhere.

With the medication Robert had given him still at work, Patrick drove up to what everyone referred to as Vivian's hill. He had been here a handful of times but never unannounced. She made him nervous. Nevertheless, he knocked on her door.

She opened it and stood there, staring. "Pastor Patrick. This is a surprise." Stepping aside, she ushered him in, pointing to a seat, which he gladly sank into. He should have consulted Howard, but his body was charged with the need to know something—anything, as though waiting for another minute might result in an emotional roller coaster and he'd be motion sick.

"Is everything all right? You're a little green. Would you like some tea?" She frowned with what appeared to be concern.

"No, thank you. I wanted to ask you ..." His hands remained still, though they had the urge to twist or tap while trying to put his thoughts and words together in a way that made sense.

"Is it about Rose? I'm worried about her," Vivian said. "The church has made such gains this last year. Your sermons are less lofty. That's all anyone needs. A message they can understand."

Lifeless was the word Patrick would describe his latest sermons. Dusting the ground, never to rise. No gut-wrenching truth prompting people to change. Just like water that didn't flow—stagnant. He wouldn't call it progress.

Her statement of worrying about Rose surprised him, especially since she sounded sincere. This illness might be worse than he thought. What if it made him imagine these possibilities of what happened to Stephen? Too late now. "I've been thinking about the festival." His throat tightened, and he coughed.

"Let me get you some tea, pastor. It's no trouble. Already in the teapot. And some of Meredith's honey."

Patrick forced a smile. "You're right, Vivian, that would be good for me."

"Of course it would." She went into the kitchen.

"I'll give you Frank's old mug," she said coming back. "I don't want a man sitting here drinking out of a petite teacup adorned with flowers."

He took it from her. "Thank you for that."

"Milk?"

"Yes, please."

She poured some into his cup, the swirls blending into a nice caramel color. "It's Earl Grey. I hope that's acceptable."

"Of course."

She took her own cup and sat in a faded red chair. "Are you speaking of the festival when Stephen disappeared, or are you trying to reinstate the event?"

"I'm referring to the disappearance."

"Well, then, it is a benefit to you I'm an old lady now."

"Really?" Patrick reached for a safe reply.

"Yes. Old people recall the past better than they can remember what happened an hour ago, you know. I'm finding it to be true. So, what is your question?"

Patrick took a sip of tea and cleared his throat. "I was at the orchard."

Her look was one of disapproval. "Why aren't you in bed resting?" She waved a hand at him. "Oh, don't be surprised. It doesn't take long for people to find out stuff around here, you know. You are becoming as senseless as Rose. Not meaning to be insulting. She could catch her death out there, and at least one of you should have some sense, but I see that isn't possible. So, you went to the orchard?"

She went back into listening mode, and Patrick wondered if every statement he made would receive a lecture. But overall, the conversation was going better than expected.

"There was a van there, and it got me thinking. Maybe Stephen crawled into one of those vehicles, and what if they drove off not knowing he was there?"

"Obviously, Patrick ... Pastor," she added as though it was improper to call him by his name, "if that were to happen, they'd realize at some point the child was there, and bring him promptly back. Surely they would have heard of a search. Even if they didn't hear or know anything, they would have contacted authorities."

A new idea popped into Patrick's mind, sending chills, a different kind than caused by fever. He set his cup on the end table. "Or he might have been in the car, and then left unseen." Which could put him anywhere in the universe."

"You're as white as a sheet. I'm calling someone. Adam or Robert? I saw your son in town. Rose should be at home taking care of you, for goodness' sakes."

He held up his hand. "I'm fine, really." The ticking of the grandfather clock that stood regal like a butler, grew louder. Vivian's face blurred in and out of focus.

"No, you're not." She leaned back and paused. He didn't want to interrupt her.

"What I remember is that fool Gary made some awful divorce announcement right there at the wine tasting, which I never approved of, and Gary's behavior proves wine should stay with the vineyard. Anyway, Caroline, being upset, took off at a clipped speed, well, to be honest, she tore out of there, which I considered inappropriate and unsafe, no matter what Gary and Joe were spouting off. I'm referring to her because she left early, and had a van, a vehicle you mentioned."

"I remember the upset. Think, Vivian. If someone had a door open, Stephen would have climbed in the car." He blinked, his focus returning.

"But the chances of him not being noticed seem slim," she pointed out. "Wish we knew more about the hooligan in the woods. Wonder what ever became of him?"

"He's never been much of a suspect because how would he vanish with Stephen?"

Unless he parked a car somewhere. Howard and Patrick had discussed the *hooligan theory* many times, but it proved to be an aggravating piece. They had given him all kinds of different names, but nothing pointing to his real identity.

"Lots of families were from out of town. Stephen could have gone in any car, especially if a door were open. If he was in the back—" Patrick said. "I talked to a couple right before he disappeared. Never did see them again, but she had wanted children. They acted irritated at Stephen, and the man practically dismissed his desire at the end of the conversation. Howard tracked them in Forest Grove. Nothing came of that either."

"I do remember them. They said you should have been more pastoral at the festival. That's the rumor I heard, but in your defense, you can hardly be saying prayers hauling around two young sons. As for your theory, wouldn't Stephen have cried or made noise when the car started moving? I honestly think someone would see him, in most vehicles, but a van is more of a possibility."

"I don't know. The kid could ride in a car for hours," Patrick said.

"I guess what I wanted to know is, have you heard from Caroline in all these years?"

Vivian paused, which seemed to be her way of communication—to think before she spoke, which Patrick found surprising because the rumors spread over the years were not pretty. But possibly her friends had spread random thoughts not meant for public ears. "She called me once. As you remember that woman tended to go from one whim to another. Very needy. If she didn't get what she wanted, she'd cause trouble. Her way or the highway. I tried to be a mentor, and you may think you waste your breath in the pulpit—and frankly you often do—I wasted a life force of oxygen on that woman."

Patrick shivered. The pills were wearing off, and he wished she'd get to the point.

"Caroline had panic attacks. For years, I didn't hear from her, and then one day she called. Not meaning to, I'm sure. Doctors had given her Valium, she said. You know, it was a cure-all back then. Meredith took it for a bit and resembled a loopy Dockerbogger patron. I told her people were going to talk if she didn't get off that stuff. So, anyway," she continued—much to Patrick's relief; a weak, achiness grew stronger, his misery compounding by the second—"on the phone, she told me how she needed money," Vivian paused. "I'm a widow on limited means, especially back then. You know, Pastor, I prayed and prayed for Frank to bounce back to life at the hospital when they all went rushing in with their carts. He was a good man. I believed in miracles once, but after that a dose of reality hit me. Then your little girl prayed for Winston to come back to life. Back to a woman who didn't want him. And what happens? All I could think was, why didn't God answer *my* prayer?" She had set her tea on the coffee table and toyed with the rings on her hands. "I gave up relying on miracles or anything out of the ordinary. We need practical teaching. I've seen too many dreams dashed. Healings that don't happen, lives cut short. Even your family. I honestly don't know how Rose manages. I suspect the traumatic event affected her brain."

Patrick had a few questions for God himself. Like why Vivian poured out her heart all of a sudden when Patrick wanted nothing more than to lie in a bed. The woman appeared sharp, yet had taken the conversation to a different time zone. Coming here wasn't the brightest idea he'd ever had. A picture of Frank sat on top of the TV, and a coffee table nearby displayed a dying bouquet of store-bought mums. He blinked. He needed strength, and if Vivian only knew what a miracle it was that he still sat without keeling over, she'd become a full-blown Pentecostal.

"Vivian." He leaned forward, praying for wisdom. "Frank was a good man. He's now doing great things in heaven. No pain. No suffering."

"I needed him!"

"Why haven't you ever shared this with us?" All the hurt could have been spared with a few words, but instead the lack of communication manifested into years of resentment.

She sniffled, her nose turning pink and her eyes red. She grabbed a nearby tissue. "Every time I would say it out loud to myself, it sounded awful and ridiculous."

"It's not ridiculous. These are natural feelings. There isn't anything wrong with being human. Frank is in heaven. Winston, on the other hand would have been in hell, by his own admission. Your husband finished his race, and he did it well."

"Frank always did try to be first at everything." Her tone indicated this was a fault she had endured. "What about me? What good has the power of God done me? I thought you should leave it alone. It gives people expectations followed by devastation."

"You're a strong woman. When Frank was taken to heaven, Jesus didn't desert you, He embraced you. He's waiting for you to embrace him back. He has and always will take care of you. If we don't have the power of God, then what? Let the enemy have all the power? Imagine all the hope I've gained and lost when searching for Stephen." Mostly lost. Okay, not the best example.

At the mention of Stephen, Vivian seemed to muster up her old self with a final sniff. "Of course. I can't imagine how you all do it. It'd be like me hoping Frank was going to walk through the door again, just because I prayed for him to come back to life all those years ago," she settled back in her chair. "So, about Caroline. I told her she wasn't getting any money from me, and needed to take care of herself. Then she said, 'Who is this?' and I said, 'You called me, Caroline.' Then she muttered about meaning to call Joe."

Patrick perked up. "She was in contact with Joe?" He recalled the ribbon. The argument Martin heard in the woods had been Caroline and Joe, just like Rose had concluded.

"I can only go by the story I told you. I assume that's the case. Joe has always had a connection to Caroline. I'm sure he helped her on occasion."

Patrick nodded, contemplating the scenario.

"All I know is that Caroline took her maiden name back—James. There is a Henry James at the Risley place. Did you know that? I guess he's her son, but I don't understand. It's hard for me to imagine Caroline as a mother." She narrowed her eyes at him. "Patrick are you all right? Oh, for land's sake."

He had annoyed her, it seemed. Too much information over-loaded his half-functioning system, and his body ached with fever. The clock chimed announcing the hour, and he barely registered Vivian on the phone, placing a call. Maybe she poisoned him after all.

XXXIX

Rose didn't know where she intended to go—maybe after all this time the way to crazy was a well-lit path. She'd been on the road for a long time, hadn't she? And the idea of checking out welcomed her. The pain crushed her heart and soul, moving her farther from home and Patrick. The temptation to be irresponsible and sink into a heap of rain water, not knowing anything about her life sounded appealing.

Back when Stephen disappeared, time roared as her fear had built up with each tick of the clock. Waiting while others searched the woods. One minute, two minutes, ten, thirty, then an hour. Where were they? Why hadn't she heard anything? She walked back and forth, desperately trying to not make each foot click with the second hand. The woods weren't *that* big; they'd be bringing him in the door any minute. Her body tremored, and more than once she sank onto the floor in the bathroom, ready to throw up, but then a noise would jolt her to her feet. But it'd just be the cat, bumping into the window, making books fall off the desk, or somebody else from the festival coming through the door.

Those first few minutes led to days with news coverage and posters, and she still paced. What if some wild animal had eaten him? Or what if he went to the highway on the other side of the woods? How would it be possible to find him if he'd wandered that direction? What if a car ran him over, and he was lying helpless in a ditch?

Intuition told her he wasn't dead. Even upon imagining the worse, she couldn't shake the niggling at her mind.

She became thin and couldn't remember anything—red-eyed, frizzy hair sticking out everywhere, wearing whatever she found without effort, after spending days in the same clothes she had on when he went missing. To change what she wore claimed distance from the event—one step further from finding him, like admitting defeat. Life shouldn't go on when your two-year-old boy doesn't come home.

Patrick took care of Robert. Patrick forced her to eat. Patrick stuffed his own suffering deep inside himself to make sure she didn't die in grief. He and God kept her from losing the baby. His sacrifice made her not want to drag him down that road again, so she'd bake as a distraction, and wander, like the day Stephen disappeared—when her feet didn't stop walking the floors. She'd take her trays and dishes, laden with baked goods, to the shelters—to the women and their children. It sounded noble, but she always searched for Stephen in those places while trying to make up for what she couldn't give her own child—homemade comfort.

She'd never seen Patrick so astute as he had been the other day, and despite her attempts, she failed to break loose from his sight after the baking. Her methods had grown rusty. This time, an extreme need came over her, resulting in fudged calculations. Should have quit baking much sooner, but he came home two hours early. Afterward, she waited, unmoving, feigning sleep until she heard him snoring, which took longer than usual, and she dropped off, but luckily awakened with the dawn and slipped out.

Now she followed her heart through the trees and the creek bed that flowed this time of the year. Rain spattered, and the drops grew, falling faster. She dodged to a larger fir, taking cover. At last, somewhere she could hear God.

Rose was the only one who waited on the word spoken. She couldn't face any of them. As Patrick had driven her to the shelter, variations of how she'd tell him played over and over in her mind as did his reaction. None of the scenarios were appealing.

She came to the black iron gate of the cemetery and trekked

deeper across the stretch of graves, the water soaking her hair, drenching the long black coat she wore over her faded jeans. She might be mistaken for a ghost in this place. A stone bench under a large oak caught her eye. It was partially dry, not near the covering she'd had under the fir tree earlier, but a bit of rest appealed to her regardless.

From this vantage, the mountains, a focal viewpoint, blended in with the sky and the old stones rising from the grasses. Her eye caught movement in the distance. Probably the wind, or a squirrel, but a drift of air, like floating fog, blurred across a background of green and white. Rose squinted, trying to get a better view. She made out a black jacket over black slacks. A tall gentleman with blondish hair. The way he stood held familiarity. Did she know him? Had there been a funeral? She hadn't noticed any new sites.

The expanse of markers stretched across to the edge of the woods, some flat, some upright, shimmering through a silent gate to find the living. The grass shuddered, and she gripped the cold bench. How many dead separated her from the only other living being nearby? Her thoughts grew morbid. She should leave.

The man turned away from the cemetery. The lines of his face, the lock of hair falling in his eye with the rain dripping from it reminded her of Patrick when he was young.

The first time she knew she liked Patrick, they had been in Ireland for the wedding of mutual family friends. Sneaking away from the reception had been easy enough. Running to the nearby wood filled her with a magical freedom, and despite her beautiful dress she climbed onto a mossy log. Michael, a boy introduced by her family, was her date. She didn't like him and didn't want to dance with him. No way at all. She sat in her hidden spot, breathing hard, partly from exertion and partly from knowing Michael might find her. She jumped at a noise in the brush, then turned, expecting to be discovered by her unwanted date, but instead, was startled to see Patrick. He came into the woods for her. Oh, how she wished he'd come now! A tear escaped as she remembered his sandy colored hair messy from the breeze, the stubble on his face reddish in the outdoor light. The way he gazed at her and smiled.

"Running away?"

She had looked from her perch, and across the woods to the opening where bagpipes and dancing continued. Laughter carried across the sky. "Maybe. What are *you* doing here?" Probably been prompted to drag her back. He'd been eyeing her the whole day. But that snooty Meagan had attached herself to his arm.

"Coming for you." He held out his hand, but she didn't take it. That's when he climbed onto the log, sitting a distance from her.

"You'll ruin your pants," she said.

"You've ruined your stockings," he pointed out.

She looked down and saw the large snag going up her leg, then in a flash, threw her skirt, a swish of lavender, over it. An awkwardness hit her. Patrick—always in the periphery of her life. They'd practically grown up together, so why did she feel … what? Nervous? She wondered if her hair still curled in all the right places. Weddings—they did strange things to people.

He appeared amused. "Come back. Dance with me."

"This is a trick, isn't it? You'll let Michael cut in."

He made a face. "Michael? No way. I'm not letting anyone cut in. We will dance near the edge of the forest. The only thing taking you out of my arms will be the light of the moon, because that means the party is over, until we get to dance again."

She let the image wash over her and laughed. "What about poor Meagan?"

He grinned. "When you ran off, I steered her toward your designated date. Hope you don't mind. It's meant to be, don't you think? Michael, Meagan. Cute, yeah?"

"Perfect."

"Yes." He gazed at her, and her face grew hot with the memory. That moment when the realization someone you always knew became someone you loved, and it had been stuffed deep inside, the truth hit like dawn giving light to a dark sky. The reason she never could make a relationship work, not with Charles, not with Joe, and certainly not with the new family pick, Michael. And now her heart beat—time-traveling to the past—sitting on the log with Patrick adoring her.

They had all changed, or had she blocked Patrick out? She hadn't let him comfort her. If she would have allowed bits of vulnerability, maybe he wouldn't have shut off that part of their life as though it were a leaky water source. He'd been driven to silence. By her. Turning she ran, far from the past—away from tombstones and apparitions.

Now she longed for Patrick and was unable to get to him. A shiver crept up her spine. He was too far away, and she didn't have the strength.

The old abandoned church wouldn't provide much warmth, but it would be dry. She would go home after resting a bit. The sky darkened, and the wind whipped in sporadic gusts. Usually the cemetery made for a peaceful retreat. Today, it betrayed her, and she couldn't wait to escape.

XL

Patrick, half aware of his son's presence, stretched out in the recliner, refusing to go to bed. Robert had camped in the living room to keep an eye on him since the ER visit.

The medication they gave Patrick at the hospital, made his mind travel through foggy places, sometimes dense, and he'd be almost asleep, and then it would lift to a light haze. A face appeared in these moments. The prophet that had visited their church—proclaiming that Stephen would come home again. With his eyes closed, Patrick went over the man's features. They swam in his vision, then Vivian's voice, that *hooligan is out in the woods. You'd better check on Rose.* He opened his eyes almost expecting to see Vivian, but only saw Robert on the sofa reading. The old lady was almost preferable.

"Dad?" Robert closed the book. "I wish you'd lie down in bed. You need rest, and you aren't getting it in a chair."

He didn't answer, trying to will the picture back. He'd seen that guy in the woods before—back when they searched for Stephen.

"It was him." His voice cracked. He got up from the chair. "It was him." He couldn't believe it.

Robert stood. "You know that stuff they gave you is awfully strong. Why don't you—"

"No. Listen. The man who gave the prophecy." Patrick paced. He glanced at Robert. "It was the guy from the woods."

Robert stared at him. "What prophecy?"

Patrick broke out in coughing, then managed to speak, "The one your mother has based her entire hope on."

"I'm telling you they've given you some powerful stuff. You can't trust any revelation you are having right now."

"I know I'm right. It's as clear as a bell. We didn't recognize him, all cleaned up. Someone put him up to it. Who would do that? Who would want us to hold out on a lie?"

"All these years and the prophecy is a lie? C'mon Dad, you are very sick, and this stress isn't good for you." Robert spoke to him as though he were crazy.

Patrick's mind raced. "It's Joe. I bet you anything he did this to get Rose all to himself, searching who knows where, making me be the bad guy. Why didn't I see this before?"

"Do you know where this guy is now? There's an easy way to do this. Ask him," Robert said.

"I haven't seen him, except once, but he had shaved and was all dressed up, and I didn't realize—"

"Please—you are just having a reaction ..."

Patrick sat back down, perched on the edge of the recliner. "I don't think so. I'm telling you, I see it. The drugs cleared my head—it was the same person. All these years." They could have been living their lives. They could have grasped the reality—Stephen wasn't coming back. The closure he always longed for had been possible all along.

"News flash, Dad. Drugs don't clear your head." Robert's voice interrupted Patrick's thoughts that spun in a rapid downward spiral.

"This guy knew all along Stephen was missing. He couldn't have him, could he?" The possibility made Patrick's stomach sick. "How can I tell Rose?"

"Hard to do, isn't it? She's not here to tell. What you should do is sleep. Things will make more sense once you're rested and feel better. Medication gives you a false clarity." Robert's words came out slow and deliberate. Patrick closed his eyes, feeling his son's concern for his sanity.

"I need to find Rose."

"What you need to do is get well. We are talking twenty-three years ago, and now, out of the blue you decide the prophetic voice belongs to the homeless guy in the woods? I'm sorry but that's a stretch."

Patrick's mind fumbled with possibilities. It was Friday, so he had Robert call Howard, who reassured him that he would check the shelters for Rose, ordering Patrick to take it easy. Patrick would sleep tonight, but first thing tomorrow he had a plan, and he knew exactly what he would do on Sunday. His mission was to find her.

His thought wandered into another direction. His sermons. Martin had approached him not long ago, describing them as *Down to earth*—the phrase alone made him queasy. When had he become a people pleaser? He barely registered the slow degenerative condition. Too late to go back. God, family, ministry. God, family, ministry. The three chanted at him. He'd been doing it wrong all these years. Putting God first, perhaps, but stuffing his guilt about Stephen deep inside, while going through the motions as a dad and a husband and pretending to be someone he wasn't at the pulpit. He'd been hiding from them all.

XLI

Alex had never gone to a bar. For her, avoiding Joe was simple, until lately. To waltz in, as though she was a regular patron to get a drink and have a good time, required more than role-playing. Of all the theatrical performances she'd pulled off in her lifetime, this would be the ultimate act. *And the Oscar goes to Alex!* Life was a stage. Disassociation at its finest.

Every persona she pictured—one of confidence and power—couldn't emerge past her posture. Her brain needed to be engaged. She stood straighter, trying to—to what? Alex needed sophistication, power, confidence. She rightly owned the bookstore and had no desire to sell. Joe should be pleased. He didn't like books. It would take him forever to get rid of them all and make the place into his restaurant of happy hours and outdoor barbecues.

She put on her lipstick. Wonder Woman was as close as she could come. With the theme song in her head, she went to her car.

Pulling into the gravel lot, she parked in a spot hidden under the trees, just far enough from the Dockerbogger entrance. Everybody knew her and the car she drove. Gossip would gallop through town if her vehicle were spotted at a seedy bar.

She walked across the scattered pebbles that crunched under her feet, the wind blowing her hair in her eyes. When she reached the blue painted door, she gave it a strong tug, and it scraped across the pavement. She slipped in, it banged shut, announcing her entry. The Wonder Woman theme hit a scratch.

In the dimness and haze of smoke, faces turned her way. *Don't look.* She sat on one of the bar stools, facing all the bottles with her back to the crowd. The place lacked in color, atmosphere, and possibly cleanliness as she noticed a wad of cobwebs gathered on the floor corner. A bare bones bar that wouldn't exist other than in the middle of nowhere. No wonder Joe preferred the bookstore property. The jukebox started, and Snap came on, filling the space with "I've Got the Power." Perfect.

Joe had his back to her, wiping off a nearby counter, but turned upon seeing her. She had to give him credit for remaining expressionless.

"Alex." His eyes glinted. "What's your pleasure?" his voice smooth, with a hint of gravel from smoking too many years.

"Perrier with lime." She omitted the *please* Wonder Woman wouldn't permit.

He turned, tossing the ice and pouring the bubbly soda which splashed on the outside of the glass. He wedged a lime on the corner, setting it before her with an exaggerated thud. To her credit, she didn't jump.

"So, I expect you've come to give me good news?" He shook the ice and poured another drink. "I'm sure you can see the offer I gave you is like a lifesaver."

She toyed with her lime. Taking her time, she squeezed the juice into the bubbles, breathing the citrus scent, and then met Joe's eyes. "I hate to disappoint you, Joe."

He blinked with a hint of uncertainty, but after a hesitation his mouth stretched into a grin, showing a row of perfect teeth, and he broke out in a laugh loud enough to make everyone glance their way. He leaned close. "You didn't come here just to tell me no."

She avoided looking behind her. "The bookstore is not for sale." She handed him back the thermos.

He stood straighter as he took it and stepped aside. "A business can be a messy thing. That house has a lot of upkeep and needs more TLC than you can afford."

She made the mistake of taking another glance behind her, and a bit of Wonder Woman crumbled. She was on borrowed time. The music changed, and despite the haze and the murky lighting, too many faces stared in her direction. One of the guys made a gesture regarding the shape of her body, and she turned her back on the scene, clasping her glass of soda water.

Joe lifted an eyebrow. "You don't belong here, Allie. That offer I gave you can take you places. You could go to college. Do anything you want."

She didn't know why he pretended to be friendly at all, maybe because of his relationship with her mother, but to Alex, what little camaraderie existed between them, vanished like a full moon in a cloudy sky.

Joe puttered around the bar, wiping the counter. "The boys obviously enjoy your presence." His smile lost any warmth it may have been struggling to maintain. He gestured behind her. "You're popular right now. Surely there is more to your life than books."

Alex leaned close to Joe. "I'm not selling the bookstore." Time ticked close to midnight, and soon she'd need to get her Cinderella butt home, because the power of Wonder Woman was on its last lasso.

Silence wavered between them, the jukebox becoming background noise—songs no longer discernible.

"What exactly went on between you and my mom? Why were you in the woods that day you grabbed my ankle?"

Joe took her hand. Caressing it with his thumb, he whispered in her ear, "None of your business, I'd say. You were a snotty-nosed kid back then. If I were you, I'd rethink this line of conversation."

His grip tightened, and she jerked her hand away, sensing a presence behind her. She pretended not to notice and now plotted her exit praying that no one followed her out, especially considering how far away from the building she parked. Fingering the pepper spray, she bit her lip. The possibility of being followed—

"Joe," the voice behind her spoke. Relief and horror smashed into her gut. "Is there a problem?" Adam asked, his hand on her shoulder, and she dropped the pepper spray back in her purse and put her chin in her hands, not turning around.

"What? We gonna have church now?" Joe's eyes simmered with part amusement and part annoyance. "The problem is Ms. McMillan here needs to leave. Meeting over." Yes, the midnight hour had come and gone.

"Are you done here?" Adam asked her, his eyes unreadable in the smoky haze. His hand had grasped her arm, so it looked like even if she wanted to stay, it wasn't an option. She hopped down from the bar stool and walked with him, not daring to glance back at Joe or anyone else.

Pushing on the exit proved ineffective. It didn't budge. Couldn't she leave with some dignity? Adam reached around her and gave it a shove opening the door against the wind, then it slammed them out in the cold.

Adam's truck sat parked in the distance near her car. The light rainfall turned into monsoon sheets of water. Great, her keys were in the bottom of her purse. She grasped various items trying to find them. Adam took her arm, but she pulled away from him.

"What were you doing there?" she asked, taking a step back. It sounded like an accusation. Spots came unwanted into her vision. A weird quirk from childhood when she got overly anxious.

"Me? Why are you here? Most of those guys would have you for dinner. Do you know who comes here?" His voice shouted above the rain banging on the tavern's roof, giving the repair a true test.

"Pastors, evidently," she said.

"I am here because I saw your car."

His gaze took her in—hair drenched, her legging-clad legs and boots. "Well, at least your feet are dry." Water dripped from his hair and down his face as he stared at her. Too close. He was too close.

"I can take care of myself," she said.

He folded his arms. "Yeah. I could see that."

Not her best performance, but she'd had things under control. A chill racked through her as the rain seeped through her clothes.

"I should go home." Alex stepped toward her car.

"Not yet," Adam opened up the passenger side of his truck door. "Get in. At least wait until you can see the road in front of you."

Right. She couldn't even drive at this point. The rain. The colored spots speckled her vision. Not a good combo.

He got in on his side. "You can keep me company till it stops pounding on the roof." He stared out the watery windshield as they both sat there dripping on the seats. After a long silence that made her wonder if he was going to say anything at all, he finally asked, "What *were* you doing exactly?"

She shifted wishing she could drive away and put this night in a box marked forgotten. "I wanted to talk to Joe. He wants me to sell. I don't want to." She wiped the water from her face with her hand. "I had to make it clear."

"So, you confront him at his bar? Alone? I didn't like the way he looked at you."

"That's the way he is to everyone. A grump. I'm surprised he has a business. And I can't think of a safer place to refuse his offer. I wasn't alone. The tavern was filled with men."

"That's right, instead of one bad apple, you have a whole room of them," Adam said. "What I saw is nothing to mess with. It's not just Joe being difficult or his usual grouchy self. You need to stay away from him."

"What's he going to do to me? He helped me when my tire went flat. If he wanted to do harm, that would have been his chance." The rain slowed for only a second, but then continued with renewed determination.

"Any help Joe gives has ulterior motives." Adam gripped his steering wheel. "How'd you get a flat?"

"Potholes. Listen, you shouldn't be here. Everyone knows your day job."

"Probably not everyone. You're the one who shouldn't be here. At all." He reached for her hands, but she sat on them to keep them from shaking. "Why didn't you bring Jimmy with you?"

"He's been banned from customer service. It would have made Joe hostile."

Adam gave her a look. "Wouldn't want that, would we?"

A rolling nausea rumbled through her stomach. It'd been so long since she pretended to be someone else to cope in a situation. Closing her eyes, the rain beat with the songs from the bar. She blinked. Blue, purple, yellow, red, all danced in front of her.

"Lexie," Adam's voice parted through the swimming colors. Her hands were losing circulation from her sitting on them, so she pulled them into her lap. He took one, sending warmth into her aching fingers, and the rain slowed to a soft pitter patter.

He smoothed her dripping hair away from her face, then placed his hands back on the steering wheel as the rain came faster for an encore. "How about I take you to my house? We could have hot chocolate while we dry off and warm up for a bit. My little sister, Laura leaves her pajamas, sweats, you name it, it's there. We could put your things in the dryer. After that, I'll bring you back to your car." The glimpse of the Adam from her childhood made a brief appearance in the quirky smile he gave her.

She sniffed. "It's pathetic how good that sounds." She sulked back into the seat. "I'm sorry. You shouldn't risk your reputation for me. People driving by will recognize your truck."

"If my reputation can't handle the scrutiny of where my truck is parked, then I have a problem." He lifted her chin, "Nothing to worry about, okay?"

Her stomach churned, and her eyes filled and she tried to turn away. And then his arms enfolded her, and she leaned into his wet jacket, letting him hold her as her thoughts drifted from her family and the secrets they kept alongside their bottle of hope.

Exhausted from confronting Joe, she relished the peace of sitting in Adam's truck. Adam was safe. Was the freak factor too high for him to like her as much as she liked him? And that's when she remembered she was a McMillan. That equaled death to any ministry Adam might pursue.

XLII

Henry missed working. He missed the people at the office. What he wouldn't give right now to have someone to chat with about designs, discuss soil and various foundations, pencil some sketches—anything to stimulate his brain cells. Henry learned he needed people more than he thought. He considered himself a loner, but being alone was only satisfying for so long. He parked his Honda outside the Java Jungle, thinking a cup of coffee would set him right, but paused at a piece of paper tucked under his windshield wiper. He scrutinized the parking place. Nope, not a loading zone or anything. He plucked the paper from the car. Just a note.

Meet me at Powell's Bookstore on Burnside in Portland.
6:00 tonight. There's a coffee bar by the calendars. I'll be there.

The message was signed with a scrawl. Henry's heart dropped—

Beck

Under the signature there were directions on how to get there.

Henry scanned the silent street.

Empty.

Even the trees were still. He strained his ears to hear a bird, or anything indicating he hadn't entered a stagnant portal. A swoop of starlings circled the sky, reassuring him. His thoughts strayed to the man he at one time wanted to call Dad. How did he know Henry was here? An uncomfortable shiver made him turn up his collar. Had Beck been lurking around in the periphery of his life since the day he left? That couldn't be because it would be as exciting as watching paint dry. Sure, there were highlights, but not worth

Beckett's time to shadow him and Caroline. He had to know she died. And why did Henry have to go to Portland—an hour and a half drive? Beck probably watched him from across the street, right now, giving Henry an edge of discomfort. He opened his car door and tossed the note on the passenger seat and his keys on top wondering why all the mystery? Why couldn't they have coffee at the Java Jungle? Or a drink at the Dockerbogger? What if it wasn't Beck at all? He picked up the note again. His past tumbled into the present. He'd seen that scrawl many times. The B had a distinct importance that Beck always put into every signature. Not easy to duplicate. What could he want after all these years?

Henry didn't want Beck taking him by surprise, so he left Filbert Ridge a half hour earlier than needed. He didn't have any obligation to the man, whatsoever, but curiosity would have lured anyone under the circumstances. The bookstore was found without problem, except all the one way streets preventing him from turning left. Portland had a seediness air to it—an artist living off the land would fit right in. An odd urban, fend-for-yourself vibe. Once he could turn and backtrack, he parked along a curb with no trouble, not needing the garage offered.

Color-coded maps giving directions to genre's, coffee bar, and restrooms, greeted him as he walked through the double glass doors. The local bookstore in Filbert Ridge boasted an impressive variety of material, but compared to this—his attention went from shelf to shelf—new books mixed with old, a rare book room off to the side, tables of new releases. The place could take hours to explore, and with stairways and aisles, getting lost and avoiding Beck altogether was more than possible, if that is what Henry chose.

Pleasure alluded him, however, because he was too preoccupied with this impromptu visit from the past. Would Henry recognize him? It wasn't fair that Beckett knew exactly what Henry looked like. With reluctance, Henry turned to the left walking through general fiction and through another wide open doorway leading to the coffee bar. His worries that he wouldn't recognize Beck were unfounded. The man hadn't aged in the least, except for extra silver in his hair, which, lucky Beckett still had but longer than Henry remembered. The middle age pouch hadn't found its way to expand Beck's lean form. The man always loved outdoor sports, some of them of the extreme kind, and by the looks of him, he hadn't given up earth's gym. Beckett sipped at a paper cup with its plastic lid. Henry took a step forward. With a quick glance back, he contemplated turning around, but then he caught Beck's eyes trained on him. A smile that probably cost a fortune in dental bills, beckoned Henry forward.

"I can't believe it." Beckett blinked, his eyes watered. "Let me buy you a coffee."

Henry wasn't sure he wanted coffee, but his hands needed something to hold and make him feel less awkward. "Sure, just black is fine."

"You got it. Although you are in coffee heaven out here, you know. You might jazz it up a bit."

"Maybe." Henry wished for a newspaper to duck behind. What could he say after all these years?

They sat, the silence not quite knowing where to land. Beck took a sip of coffee and then set it down. "I saw you graduate. From college."

"You were there? In New Jersey? When I graduated?"

"Yeah. How'd you manage? Caroline get some inheritance?"

"Got a scholarship. Worked as soon as I could. And now I have student loans to pay." After Beckett left and his mom came back from rehab, Henry didn't do much else besides work and school.

"I'm sorry. I didn't know what to do, I ..."

Everything Henry wanted to say froze in his throat, leaving the two of them fidgeting with their cups of coffee, which he sensed made Beck more uncomfortable.

"Didn't know what to do? How about stick around?"

Here was a person that Henry could legitimately unleash his past and present hurts. It wasn't just about Beck leaving anymore. It was a container of *could haves* and *should haves* opening—letting out all the ugliness and blame. His mother—*Caroline,* he corrected, wasn't here to listen to all his frustrations and the questions he had about why she did what she did.

Beck cleared his throat. "I—Henry, why are you here? In Oregon? It's a far cry from New York."

"I'm betting that you already know why I'm here."

"I'm not sure. I have a buddy who has plans for this place—Portland, and what it can become. Especially the River District. He says there is talk of transforming it into some sort of urban paradise." Beck snorted. "Hard to imagine if you've spent any time around this city. I thought you'd landed a job with one of these visionaries. If what he plans comes to pass, there is a lot of work available for someone like you."

"So, maybe I had left Manhattan to get a job here, in Portland, Oregon, to make this some sort of culture hub?"

Beck shrugged. "Well, when you put it that way it doesn't sound very likely."

"You're right. It's not. You know Mom died, right?"

Beck's attention went to his coffee as he swirled the cup. "Yeah."

"Why'd you leave?" Henry asked. The words choked out, as though they'd been held in, locked away, not allowed.

"I didn't want to. I really didn't. It was—" Beck's gaze came back, and he spoke after a hesitation, "Henry, I need to know what you know before I blurt out why I left."

Henry stared at him in disbelief. "You knew." He stood. "You knew all along, and you never said anything?"

"Just sit so I can tell you. I suppose a part of me wished it weren't true. How could I tell you when you were thirteen? Maybe if you'd been three or four—but thirteen? Your whole life would be disrupted, possibly ruined."

"You played God!"

"I saved you from a family that plays God."

"That's what you think?"

"I don't know. I rationalized what I did. I left because my alternative was living with the lie Caroline created and pretending everything was hunky dory."

"So you left, letting her continue to pretend, and me without knowing she wasn't even my mom. Doesn't make much sense."

"This family—in Filbert Ridge. They seemed—I went there, to check it out. I wanted the best for you."

Henry stared at him. "The best for me? I thought of you as a father."

Beckett studied the counter. "It was the hardest thing I've ever done. I took a job overseas. I came to Filbert Ridge and sensed I was being followed. I decided to start a new life. Your biological family ..." he shrugged. "I convinced myself you were better off with Caroline than with them. The things I found out—they act like the Bible is alive—like all that stuff is real."

"He's a pastor. He's supposed to think the Bible is real." A defense rose in Henry.

"Yeah, but—I don't know—raising the dead, talking to God? Life after death?" Beck took a sip of his drink. "When you're dead, your dead, right?"

Henry stared at Beck. "That's what you believe?"

"Sure, I mean, makes more sense than some sort of paradise we are going to live in forever and ever."

"Seems less sensible to believe this is it. I mean, what's the point?"

"The point is, Henry, we do what we can with the time we are given and make the world a better place."

"So, who gives us the time?"

"What?"

"You said, *the time we are given.*" Henry didn't know why he badgered Beckett, as though he were a spiritual expert all of a sudden.

"I feared I'd be a dead man, knowing what I knew."

"How'd you find out?"

"I was here on a business trip. You remember, I'd come to Portland and Seattle, off and on. I saw a sketch."

"A sketch? That's it? Must have been a good likeness."

"It wasn't only that, but yeah, the sketch depicted what you'd look like at the age of twelve, so it was recent. I asked around and found the boy went missing on the same date as your birthday. I remembered how Caroline had no baby pictures of you—not until three. I wondered about her trips she'd taken a couple of times to Oregon. I came home and asked her. I showed her the sketch. She snatched the paper out of my hand and lit a match to it and gave me the ultimatum. I left and tried to find out for myself about this family. You would have grown up with fanatical people. Live to believe fables and possibly be raised by a mentally ill mother."

"Are you kidding me? Did it not occur to you the mother that raised me was mentally ill? Surely, you knew she used prescription drugs like candy? And by the way, it got much worse after you left."

"I'm sorry. I really am, but is a little drug use as bad as being exposed to a lifestyle of unreality?"

"Being on drugs is living in unreality." Henry stood, snatching his coffee cup he crushed it with his hand, chucking it toward the nearby garbage. "It's been nice having this trip down memory lane, Beckett. Thanks for the coffee." He stepped away.

"Henry, wait! What was I supposed to do?"

Henry put up his hand in a wave, then faced Beckett. "Truth. You should have told the truth."

"But it could have destroyed you and Caroline."

Henry walked back a few steps. "Guess what? We were already destroyed because you left. Now she's dead, and I'm trying to figure out what to do with my new identity." Turning the way he came, he walked away.

Beckett called after him, "You're so big on truth, Henry? Why haven't you told them who you are yet?"

Henry paused, but didn't look back.

This chapter of his life was done.

XLIII

Alex sat in her kitchen, contemplating what happened the previous night at Joe's and found no way out of her dilemma. She obviously came out looking like a crazy girl in Adam's eyes. Oh sure, he'd been nice enough, but after she had enjoyed the hot chocolate and the warmth of the fireplace, she feared in the end she'd cause him detrimental damage.

The next Sunday confirmed her worries. The ladies had escalated the cat incident to fantasy proportions. Even though most of the congregation didn't expect to find Grandma Burky haunting the town, Alex sensed when she arrived at church, people either backed away or flashed weird, exaggerated smiles in her direction. The only solution she could think of would be to find a different place of worship. She wasn't sure where. Maybe the next town over. She frowned. She might have to go farther away where people wouldn't know her. The last straw had been hearing Claudia complain to Adam about her teaching the children, and then she caught a glimpse of Vivian marching toward him as well. That's when she knew. Leaving the Lord is My Shepherd would be best for her family and especially for Adam who had decided to make the ministry his career.

Alex baked coffee cake, as though cinnamon and sugar could treat her sadness. There was a church in Forest Grove she could try. Maybe that wouldn't be too far. Picturing herself leaving her family on Sunday to go elsewhere for services made her heart skip a beat, and deep in thought, she pulled out the dessert, setting the hot dish on the stove top.

A familiar rumbling came from outside. Adam's truck. She knew this without looking. She fidgeted with her hair, then dropped her hand. What was he doing here anyway? The earful from Claudia should have scared him away. If not, Vivian would have sealed the deal. "Save yourself." Yep that's what she'd tell Adam Langley.

Hearing him knock, she hesitated, then opened the door, leaning against the frame as a silence swirled around them.

"Hi." She shifted her feet.

"Hi." He looked at her, making her feel ten again.

She closed her eyes. "I'm sorry for causing chaos."

"That's pretty much what I came over for, an apology."

She found him grinning. Typical.

"I heard what Claudia said." She was not going to let him stand there and be all happy like they could ignore reality.

"Can I come inside, Lexie?"

The nickname coming from him wrapped her in warmth. He was Robert's friend, and she was Robert's little sister, nothing more, nothing less.

"You shouldn't be here," she managed to get out, but it sounded unconvincing.

His eyes met hers. "Why not?"

"There is probably something inappropriate about it. We may cause rumors."

"Sure. I mean, I'm already here. Parked in front of your house. In broad daylight."

Her eyes settled on his truck. "Yeah."

"Lexie, we need to talk."

"Fine." She opened the door wider to let him in, directing him toward the sofa. Here came the news. She was being banned from the children, once and for all. "Let me get us some coffee." Coffee cake could be brought out as well, and she disappeared to the kitchen before he said anything. This would give her time to gather her wits. Her eyes glanced at the stove, catching smoke rising from the bottom of the glass dish. Had she had left the burner on? Why had she placed it there? She got the hot pad and moved the pan off the element.

The dish exploded. Glass everywhere. Had to be a sign. She'd let her guard down, and now God confirmed that she was a walking disaster. *It will all blow up in your face. It looks sweet, but it's a bomb waiting go off.* This had to be a prophetic moment.

"Alex, are you all right?" Adam appeared in the entryway, his eyes taking in the glass littered across the floor and counter tops, and she stood right in the middle in stocking feet. A shard had hit her pinky, red now with blood.

"I'm fine." The ruined coffee cake surrounded her with its brown sugar and butter melting together, covered with glass. What a waste. She took a step.

"Wait." He picked up a few big pieces, tossing them in a nearby garbage, then stepped closer to her. "I'll carry you out of the debris."

"Not necessary."

His gaze went to her feet. "You're wearing socks. This is a land mine." Letting him in the house was a mistake after all. Couldn't she do stupid stuff without witnesses? She pointed at the broom.

"Just hand me that, and I'll make a trail."

He snatched the broom and leaned on the handle. "What fun is that?" She glared at him, and he handed it to her. "All right, but my way was better."

She swept until she stood in a glass free zone. "I'm going to grab a band-aid for this," she said, lifting her hand. She went down the hallway to the other room, and Adam followed.

Guess he wants to be sure I don't blow up the rest of the house.

"Here, let me help you," he said when she fumbled with the Band-Aid box. He took out the bandage and then looked at the finger. "You have a piece of glass in there. Here, hold still. It's sticking up. I should be able to grab it." He tried and failed a couple of times. "Tweezers?"

She reached in the medicine cabinet and handed them over. He studied her finger, and she caught a wave of his aftershave.

This couldn't be more torturous. A blend of cinnamon, sugar, and aftershave. Three things she couldn't have. *Sheesh.*

Without looking up, he said, "I didn't get to talk to you before you left church."

"Nothing to say, really. I heard Claudia." She gritted her teeth as the glass shifted.

"But you didn't hear Vivian." He held the small, fine sliver for her to see. "There, got it," and then dropped it in the nearby garbage.

That's why he needed to talk to her? She swallowed. "I don't want to know what Vivian said. It was thoughtful of you to come here to tell me how awful and irresponsible I am with the children."

His gaze took her in as a smile played on his lips. "I don't remember saying any of those things. I mean," he straightened back up, "it would be risky for me to hang out with a person such as yourself—and now I'm thinking I should have parked down the block, away from your house."

She pushed past him and went back to the mess, grabbing the broom.

"I mean, someone like me—an *almost* pastor but not *really* a pastor—has to be careful whom I associate with." He followed her to the botched baking disaster.

"Make fun if you want, the McMillan name alone causes gossip, but then you put me into the mix and you got a big mess, which is apparent today, more than ever." She scooped a big chunk of glass into her dust pan. He took it, dumping it in the garbage. She gestured toward the kitchen. "And this is God talking right here. See? This symbolizes what a relationship with me would cost you. It's stuffed with sugar and cinnamon, but *boom!* you are doomed."

He laughed.

"What?"

"Boom you are doomed?" He leaned on the broom with a smirk. "You've gone to incredible extremes to make your point."

"This is a symbolic warning."

Now he looked at her like she was nuts.

Good. A wake-up call for him.

Then he laughed more.

She glared at him.

"I'm sorry, but destroying coffee cake isn't an act of God. It's an act of Satan. Who destroys good? The cake got as hot as Hades and blew up. Why would God ruin dessert? He likes dessert."

"It is good this happened. Your career would be smithereens. Now that I'm leaving, you'll have a chance."

"Leaving? What do you mean? Where are you going?" His teasing tone gone.

"To a different church, obviously."

"Lexie, you could go on and on with your symbolism how you and I are a danger to all of Filbert Ridge and together we equal death to my career. I mean they might not let us in the church building if we were to go out together. I don't know."

"They don't like me much. You've seen what my dad has gone through. It'd be just as bad if not worse for you. I know you are here to let me down easy, or whatever, so I am saving you from trouble."

"I'm confused as to why you keep telling me the reason I came here. Are you a prophet now?" He scooped more glass into the garbage.

"Fine, tell me why you are here?"

He reached out, putting a loose curl behind her ear, his eyes locking onto hers. Smiling, he handed her the dust pan.

She stared at him, frozen in place as she took it from him. "I'm being realistic. What about Claudia, Vivian, Martin, all of them?" Her voice couldn't sound confident. She had lost her drive to dissuade him.

"Because you raised the dead, hear God, visited heaven, oh, and don't forget, speaking in tongues when no one is looking." He swept another pile. "And now crazy things are afoot; children believe God answers prayers."

"But you heard Claudia."

"Yes." He took the dustpan back. "But you didn't hear Vivian."

"So you keep saying. Fine lay it on me. Whatever it is, it can't help anything, or be anything I haven't heard before."

"I believe you haven't heard this before."

"Really?"

"Like her telling Claudia God does work miracles, and keeps His promises. How she'd been wrong all these years. How she'd blamed God about Frank, and didn't understand miracles still happen. That we should be expectant of what God can do and that miracles should happen in church because a testimony leads people to Jesus."

She leaned on the broom and stared at him. "What?"

"You should have let me tell you why I came. I bring good news."

Her eyes watered, and her nose burned. She blinked the tears away. "She said that?"

"Yep. So you might rethink finding a new church home." He picked up another piece of glass. "You see, Lexie, I want to get to know you—the adult you, I mean. Sometimes, I feel like we are still kids. Even if Vivian would have said torturous things about you, it wouldn't matter to me."

They continued the rotation of sweeping and dumping glass and then they wiped off all the counter tops. "Guess you didn't expect to have to clean my kitchen when you came over," Alex said.

"At your house, Lexie, it's pretty much the last thing I expected. You owe me, you know."

"Owe you what?"

"Coffee cake. One not covering the kitchen floor."

XLIV

Henry was done. He didn't need a mother, father, brother, sister, nieces, nephews, or the neighbor's dog. He could function perfectly on his own.

He tore into his driveway, slammed the car door, and opened the house, vanishing inside as though being chased. *You can't run from who you really are.* Terrific. "Thank you. Not helpful." Talking back to unwanted voices had to be a bad sign. He tossed his keys in a nearby bowl—a cheerful sunny color made from glass that people paid a lot of money for—one of the many from his mother's things.

Henry flopped on the sofa. Did he feel compelled to fix everything? *Fixer upper, fixer upper,* the voice mocked him as he saw his mother—a pillar turned into dust, and now Beckett, a crumbled statue, no longer part of his life—not after deserting them. With Beckett's parting words, Henry couldn't stop the next image of his new-found family as a building. A foundation of rock, with Patrick trying to hold it up, and everyone standing on top of him, instead of the foundation doing the work. Extra stress caused cracks. One column, all but gone, like a vanishing photograph. Each of them fading away—

Henry took off his shoes and hurled them at the wall. He took out the paint and brushes and the easel. He wanted answers. Applying paint to a canvas gave him focus, and his pulse slowed.

The roof had holes. Windows were broken—the concrete base like a face crevassed with age. A lock hanging askew from the gate. He added a cemetery to the side. Blue eyes stared at him.

"I can't fix this! Why are you asking me to fix this?" Henry splashed streaks of paint all over the picture. Who was he talking to? *It's your heritage. Can't run from who you are.* Well, nothing could keep him from trying. Get out of town. He was as crazy as them, and if he weren't, he would be. Self-preservation. That's what he needed to focus on. After all, what man in his life hadn't left him? Patrick McMillan possibly wasn't any different. Henry made a decision. He'd do a load of laundry, pack his important things, send a moving truck out to get the rest.

He paused in front of his painting. The image of the cemetery stared back at him, or more accurately, those insistent blue eyes he couldn't wipe off his easel. The church he painted—where was the location? Picky Lane. He remembered it from the archives. Tapping his foot, a plan emerged. He needed to go where this dead-raising took place. An unexplained desire pulling him. Buildings spoke to Henry, and he understood their language.

✝✝✝

Henry drove to the old, abandoned church building. Brush grew around the faded paint, and what once looked to be a parking lot had weeds growing through the cracks of thin asphalt. This marked the moment. The resurrection. He gave a little laugh. Could he believe someone rose from the dead right here thirteen years ago? Now the building itself needed to be brought back to life. Why would there be a dead-raising in this tiny town anyway? If God wanted to make a big splash, then New York seemed a more likely venue. *God works in mysterious ways.* Words from his past. Going to church with Minnie and hanging at her house when all her friends were there playing cards had been a good excuse to escape his mom when needed.

Henry pulled on the door, surprised that it wasn't locked. Sun slanted through the windows, leaving streaks shining across the floor, showing off the dancing dust. Each step he took creaked, making him question the stability of the boards. A carpet was rolled up and leaning on the left side of the building, as though at some point the place was going to be renovated. He walked across the wooden floor, feeling it give a little with each creaky step, and hoped it was stable. An old wooden cross stood on the podium—empty because it no longer held Jesus. He understood this, but didn't believe modern day resurrections could randomly happen. If he saw a dead person, his response wouldn't be praying them back to life. Insane.

Henry brushed the dust off his pants, then opened a nearby door and stepped down a narrow stairway—typical of older buildings. A bit of sympathy rose in him at a church full of empty pews, with a cross no one contemplated, sitting out in the middle of nowhere, but he wasn't prepared for what he found on the lower level.

Drawings on plain paper posted all along the walls—a family of a mom and dad and two boys. One dark-haired and one blonde. It took only a moment to realize that he was looking at what used to be. Henry touched the picture, trying for a connection with this younger version of himself—Stephen. Then the blond boy vanished, and the mom fragmented in pieces like Picasso. He backed away.

A different piece of paper caught his eye. A magazine article about Saint Patrick. He took a step closer and read the quote highlighted in the story.

"And let those who will, laugh and scorn—I shall not be silent; nor shall I hide the signs and wonders which the Lord has shown me many years before they came to pass, as He knows everything even before the time of the world."

Saint Patrick raised thirty-nine people from the dead—and a horse!

Really? Why a horse? Now it made sense. Alex thought to pray for a dead man because myths of Saint Patrick surrounded her. Surely the story wasn't true. But what did he know of Saint Patrick except celebrating by wearing green and drinking beer?

He turned around, the past chasing him up the stairs. His earlier plan validated itself—do laundry, leave town, have a moving crew get the rest of the stuff later. He didn't care about the extra cost. He couldn't get out of here fast enough.

XLV

It was past the dinner hour, and the temptation to send Peter to the Dockerbogger had Patrick dialing his brother-in-law's number, but he stopped himself before the last zero and slammed the phone down. He was the one that would bring Rose home. Her husband. He needed to act like one, no matter what she thought of him.

Patrick drove to the tavern and sat in the car for a few minutes. He'd been inside plenty of times. Those days of Rose and Joe searching for Stephen sometimes included him. The place, dingy with the need for new paint and just a bit of old-fashioned scrubbing, advertised its deterioration. He got out of the car and pulled on the old door of the tavern, letting his eyes adjust to the dimness while attempting to tune out the music from the jukebox that to Patrick resembled screaming.

Joe froze upon seeing him. "Well, looky here. All of a sudden this is the place for pastors?"

"I'm looking for Rose."

Joe's eyebrows quirked. "And you think she's here?" He turned sideways, grabbing a beer, and sliding the drink across the counter to the corner bar stool. "What would you like to drink, Patrick? It's on the house."

"I don't need anything, just wondering when you last saw Rose?"

"Where is she or when did I last see her?"

Patrick leaned forward. "Don't play games with me."

Joe filled a glass with ice and popping open a club soda. He set this one on a tray, then poured a cola, sloshing the liquid over the top. The waitress plucked the prepared order from the counter. "I last saw Rose in the woods by your house. We had an interesting conversation."

Patrick stopped breathing. His heart rate accelerated with the beat to the new song. He needed to be cool here. Joe was itching for a reaction.

"Would your conversation have any leads to where she'd be now?"

He smiled. "I'm afraid I can't help you. I don't know where she is. Although, she was upset to find out the prophecy wasn't true."

She already knew? Patrick's thoughts went to the last few days he'd been with Rose, trying to land on something specific, any tell-tale sign that she had known what he had just figured out.

"She didn't tell you?" Joe shook his head. "Huh, I wonder why? Rose discovered the prophecy of Stephen being out there was made up. A lie. I tried to—reassure her."

Patrick wanted to deck the guy. "How did she find out?"

"She was horribly devastated."

Devastated? Her mental stability wouldn't be able to handle it, and now his plan to be there to tell her the truth wasn't possible. He was too late. "I need to know exactly when she spoke to you."

Joe glanced at the ceiling, "I'm not sure—"

He didn't get any further. Patrick grabbed Joe by the shirt collar, yanking him close. "I think you can remember when you last saw my wife."

The whole bar had gone quiet behind him. "Okay, good grief, take it easy. I last saw your *wife* three days ago."

Patrick dropped Joe with a shove.

Joe's eyes met his. "She was upset. It'd be in your best interest to figure out why she came to me instead of you."

Patrick's hands clenched into fists, but assault charges would not help him find Rose. He turned and walked out of the bar, letting the door slam behind him. It would have been the most satisfying thing in the world to punch the smug look off Joe's face.

Three days ago. She'd been with Joe the day before Patrick caught her baking. And then he remembered. He'd seen them that day. Through the window of his kitchen.

Despite Robert's warnings, Patrick got ready for church. As he shaved and straightened his tie, he mulled over the conversation he had at Vivian's. *Caroline had a van. That's why I thought of her.* Then Rose. *She was there when I got the call—right with me.*

Scenarios and theories wanted to connect, but the more Patrick tried, the harder it became. During his illness bouts of clarity came after sleeping, and each time he'd awaken, the past filled a blank with a blip of color, and for a second, he knew a bit more.

He adjusted his tie, making it straight, contemplating his reflection in the mirror. The congregation had grown accustomed to Rose not being present. So many things he had let happen. Complacency—a trap he had swallowed hook, line, and sinker.

Walking across the church parking lot, Patrick recalled his first sermon in the new building. That Sunday in August 1977 had been overly hot, both in weather and accusations. He hadn't shielded Rose, and words had spiraled into a storm of negativity. That should have been his first sign—stepping foot in this building thirteen years ago was a mistake. Well, no more. A new career had evidently been waiting for him, but he missed seeing whatever opportunity would have taken him away from the pulpit for good. He stayed and endured years of abuse, with most of the poison aimed toward his wife, and he had done nothing to stop the insanity.

He opened the door, seeking warmth from the October wind and rain. The weather concerned him. He wanted to be done with what he needed to do. His spirit told him if he didn't find her soon she'd succumb to the elements. Each tick of the clock pressed him to hurry. If he dawdled, Rose might be lost to him forever.

"Good morning, Pastor Patrick," Adam smiled as Patrick approached the office.

"Morning. You're awfully chipper today."

Adam grinned. "A day of expectation. It's in the air."

He could say that again. "I like your outlook." The young man was a prophet for sure and at least not a gloomy one.

Patrick caught sight of Alex in the distance and did a double take. *Huh?* She too was glowing. He glanced back at Adam to find him staring at Alex. Revelation dawned. Well, good. At least one thing was going right.

He went into his office, locked the door, and paced, praying in the Spirit. He told himself the next step needed to be done. Long time overdue, in fact. Patrick remembered his vision with the sword.

When he came out, Martin stood in the hallway. "Your daughter is always causing a ruckus. I hope you are considering removing her from the children's church. Maybe she's the reason for the heavenly minded speeches you used to preach, but you know what they say."

Patrick cleared his throat. "Right. Too heavenly minded for earthly good."

"Yep, you got it, Pastor."

The smell of coffee, coming from the open door of the office, combined with a hint of cleaning solution Zach used on the floors wafted between them. Housecleaning applied to more than just buildings. "See Martin, that's a cliché. As you may have forgotten, in Colossians it states that we are to set our minds on things that are above, not on things that are on earth. Chapter three, verse two if you want to check. The problem with many of us is we don't consider heaven enough. Can I do good on earth without the help of heaven? If my thoughts are on heaven then I'm a better person on earth." Patrick walked away as Martin stood frozen in his spot.

Patrick's downfall consisted of speaking his mind, and this time he didn't have Rose making some soothing comment to still ruffled feathers or Susan to change the subject. Now he had an entire congregation to face, and this small confrontation empowered him.

He continued praying. He needed to slay this giant, once and for all.

"Good morning!" He took his place on the platform. Two people answered back, and he plowed onward before losing his nerve. Grasping the podium, he glanced over everyone.

He did some preliminary welcomes. "As a church we have seen miracles. The main one is Winston being raised from the dead." Patrick noticed Alex slouched more in her pew, eyes wide, ready to bolt. He should have warned her.

"My wife Rose declared it as a new beginning when Winston came back to life." Murmurings went through the middle of the pews.

"Our church history includes a resurrection right in the parking lot of the old church." He glanced at Alex, mentally apologizing, "But we all sit here deader than Winston. We've settled for safe, ineffective, and rote Christianity. And I have led the way in that approach to avoid controversy. I thought I deserved a break. I planned to preach a basic sermon for a week or two, but the next thing I know, I'm standing here, years later, just now waking to time passing me by—like Rip Van Winkle."

A voice from the middle somewhere filled the sanctuary, a hiss of a whisper. "Man, I told you we should have gone to the Community Church."

Patrick paused and took a sip of water. "I believe in the Word of God. I believe Jesus Christ is the same yesterday, today, and forever, as it states in Hebrews 13:8. He raised the dead yesterday. He healed the sick yesterday. He loved us yesterday. And today He resurrects, heals, and loves. Has He changed? No. And I will no longer stifle the Spirit to make people comfortable."

"Amen!" Meredith stood and clapped, which made Patrick's world spin. He noticed a couple more exits. He'd better wrap this up before his announcement bounced off empty pews. Claudia gave her companion a frown, and Vivian pulled her back down.

"I believe you need to be equipped with the Holy Spirit, and I've tried to give you the tools to succeed. You don't know how powerful you are, but first you have to know who you are in Christ."

His eyes scanned Vivian, Meredith, and Claudia, all sitting in their row—faithful to the end. Must have been there to shape him. Martin didn't sit next to Merry this morning. He had gone back to the other side by Gary.

"Rose said we would be doing new things, not sitting around listening to some sermon. A sermon's great. A sermon counsels, but what we really desire is to commune with God."

A hand went up. "Are you and Rose getting a divorce?"

Patrick's head pounded. He was doing this all wrong. Too late to stop now. He lifted the mic. "No, we are not."

"Where is she then? Did she leave the church?"

Had this become a press conference? Adam moved a hair closer to the front. Probably thought the service was going to go south in a minute. Patrick should have told him.

"Rose has taken some time to rejuvenate. A little R&R is what we all need at times."

Claudia leaned over to Vivian. "Is that what he calls it?"

"Shh," Vivian said, and it rang down the row, and heads turned their way.

"And before you know who you are in Christ, you have to know who Christ is. And I failed you. I not only have failed *you*, but I have failed my family. I let them be verbally abused while I turned the other cheek. My wife dealt with her pain alone, while I ran from mine or used Band-Aid methods to fix it. I now stand before you and put God first, then my family, and the ministry last. So, with these words, I resign."

An array of voices went through the building, as Patrick stepped from the platform. He wondered if there would be more clapping for his leaving. Alex left her pew and followed him with Vivian a few paces behind them.

"Patrick!"

He turned around. Vivian's voice rose above the music, "Are you out of your mind? What are you doing?"

"I'm bringing my wife home."

XLVI

Susan opened her door and found Robert standing there in the bright morning light. Stan had just left for work, and she wanted to clean house. Desperately. She wasn't like Alex, whose organizational skills exceeded the common folk. Susan's life resembled a chaotic whirlwind as she did mundane chores, then a thought would form, and she'd dash into a room, getting sidetracked with an idea for the nursery. Her scrapbooking spread out on a nearby craft table, needing to be put in a more discreet corner, and the guest room screamed to be fixed, despite her husband's words.

Before Stan had left, she made the mistake of being restless. If she were smart, she would have sat with her feet up, smiling until he shut the door, and then gone into Energizer Bunny mode, but had blundered by mentioning her plan for the day. "I need to wash this quilt. I wanted to use it for the guest room in case Mom comes to stay for a couple days."

He regarded her a moment, and she chewed on her lower lip.

"You realize the possibility of that not happening?" His blue eyes took in hers, his voice kind, and she fought the urge to tear up. Darn hormones. Everything made her cry.

"Maybe I should stay," he said.

She waved a hand at him. "Don't be silly, go." She mustered up a well-practiced smile, all the while itching to get the room into shape, mother, or no mother.

Stan gave her a hug. "Make sure you get some rest."

She inwardly groaned, wondering when to fit that in. Would fifteen minutes count as rest? "Have a good day."

And now, having got one man out the door, here traipsed in another. And he looked about the place and at her like an appraiser. Not what she needed. So, this is what Alex had to deal with all her life.

"Hey, Susan," Robert said. "Sorry to barge in on you, but I wanted to stop by to see how you were doing."

And she'd just started to move that table.

"Baby's grown this past month." Robert grinned as he stepped into the doorway.

She gritted her teeth. Translation. *You're as big as a house.* "Coffee?" She managed to sound nice, and then, on closer inspection, Robert looked pale and rumpled, like he was the one who needed some TLC. "Are you all right?"

He nodded. "Sure. Coffee would be great if you have some already made. You're pale. Stan's right. You need to take it easy. Are you taking your vitamins?"

"Robert, don't start when you come here looking like death warmed over." She pushed him into the nearby chair and gave him a throw she had knitted during the past few months. Being the bossy one was satisfying.

"Yes, ma'am, or should I say Mom? You'll be a wonderful mother, Susan."

She brightened. "You think so?"

"Of course. You're a natural."

She went into the kitchen, poured some coffee and set the cup before him.

"Thank you. Now sit." He took the cup, his eyes taking in the room, landing on the scrapbooking table she'd started to move.

"How's Dad?" she asked. Too quick. He'd noticed her attempt at diversion.

"Tell me you're not moving furniture?" His eyes darted back to hers as though she'd never said anything.

"It's just a table."

He sighed and set his coffee on the nearby stand. "Where do you want it?"

She tried to look sheepish and pointed to the corner. "Over there. You know, more out of sight."

He picked up the table, placing it neat and even—very Alex-like, into the corner. She smiled—her weapon throughout life. Robert didn't buy it.

"You want to go into labor early?"

It sounded almost appealing. "No. Of course not." She settled into the sofa more, trying to appear relaxed.

"Nesting?" he asked, raising a brow. "Suzie, you are wound tight this morning. Can't wait to scrub the walls, rearrange the rooms. I can see it in your eyes."

She swept a hand around the room. "Obviously, things need done." Okay, now she sounded peevish.

"It's all right. It's natural, but still, take it easy."

"Tell me about you. You look awful."

"So you've already pointed out. And thank you. Well, Dad left the other day, about the same time as my car drove from his driveway. He won't rest and insists on searching for Mom. I told him he'd end up in the hospital. But he doesn't listen, so I'm going to work where patients come to me because they value my advice."

"Hmm. Sounds like a good idea. What about Mom? Are you worried? I mean, she has always come back, at night. Where would she go?" *Don't cry. Especially with Robert sitting here.* He needed to leave. Housework surrounded her. The dishes were piled up. And that quilt. She saw the edge sticking out from a far corner. Her mom's first attempt at quilting. Why all the sentimentality?

"Don't worry about Mom. Listen, take care of yourself and the baby and feed Stan. That's all you should be doing, Susan. I mean it. Let me take care of Mom and Dad. You've got enough going on. Worrying won't change anything, right? Except it's not good for the baby if you're stressed. So, I'm going to go to work, and you are going to be careful and take lots of breaks. I know better than to tell you not to do anything. You nesting women are unstoppable."

Relief swept over her. The chores swirled through her mind. But Robert looked too thin. "Have you eaten? I can whip up some eggs."

He put his jacket over his arm and paused at the door. "I'm fine. Thank you, though." He grinned. "Take it easy, Susan." And he left.

She practically danced.

XLVII

Henry approached the side room of the farmhouse and took one of the paintings—blue eyes and forest gracing the canvas, and flung it like an overgrown Frisbee. It landed in a crumpled heap after skittering across the floor and colliding with a nearby easel.

Time to get out of town. Prepare for the long drive back to New York. Throwing a load of wash in the machine, Henry turned on the coffee pot he already had set up.

He would begin again. He had no idea how one just said, *Hey, I'm Stephen McMillan.* Drinking his coffee, several scenarios came to mind, but none of them seemed to be anywhere close to believable.

He remembered praying for a brother. When he was ten. *Well, here you go. Plus you got two sisters too.* "A little late," Henry spoke out loud as rinsed out his cup. "Not to criticize Your methods."

Henry shook himself. Had his genetic connection to a preacher dad and a dead-raising sister seeped into his spirit man, and he dared to communicate with the Almighty? As though Henry would ever pay attention, except when he needed help and there wasn't anyone else to ask. At the age of eleven he had quit speaking to God. Not on purpose. The habit just faded. Like he had outgrown sitting on his bed having conversations with Jesus. For some reason, talking to Jesus had come naturally as a child. For some reason. "Ha." Right.

He went back into the laundry room and put his jeans in the dryer. He turned the switch. Nothing. He checked the outlet, the breaker box. Everything was in order. It just didn't work. Dead.

He wondered if his sister worked with appliances. "Really? Guess I'll learn where the laundromat is." Finding one wouldn't take too much effort. Could only be in one of two places.

After driving about the town, Henry discovered the laundromat near a grocery store and the fire department—not where he'd expected it to be. There wasn't a sign, which didn't help Henry in his search, and neither did the obsolete barber pole beside the building, posing as a hair place instead of an establishment of washers and dryers. Henry dragged in his wet clothes. The room announced its emptiness, each sound he made ricocheting off the metal machines. Good—no one to ignore. Laundromats could be like elevators. People nearby but pretending they are alone.

Henry grabbed the manila envelope with the article and childhood photos. At the last second, he had decided to bring it, in case he'd have a chance to study the pictures more. Sometimes he wondered if he'd imagined himself into this reality. He wasn't Stephen McMillan at all. But there were too many things: the dreams, the paintings, the news articles, the lies his mom told about his real dad—and Beck. If Henry could dismiss everything else, he still couldn't ignore what Beck told him. From what he gathered around town, Stephen McMillan was more than just a cold case. He brought back to life opinions as destructive as a summer storm, leaving sticks and stones in their wake. Stephen wasn't dead or alive. Stephen was a powerful force.

Henry plunked quarters into the machine, tossed his wet clothes inside, then sat and flipped through the photos, which only made him melancholy, and his eyes misted. This had been a dumb idea. He put the pictures back inside and placed the envelope on the counter.

A car door slammed outside, interrupting his thoughts and he glanced toward the windows. A woman with black hair hauled a laundry basket with some difficulty. She was very pregnant, and he took a few steps to open the door for her.

Her gaze met his, the same pale blue eyes the canvas forced him to paint. He froze in the doorway. His mind went from painting to painting.

She stopped, not able to get by. "I'm sorry. I'm a bit wide, you see?"

Henry's voice managed to work. "Oh, pardon me." Opening the door further, he stepped out of the way.

"You look like you've seen a ghost, are you okay? I had to get this quilt done today. I don't know how much time I have, you know?"

"You shouldn't be hauling that thing around. Let me help, I mean, if you don't mind. I can throw it in the wash for you." Henry said as she plopped the basket down on the nearby shelf.

She scrutinized him. "It's amazing how many helpful men there are. No need. You look familiar, but your accent says you're not from here." Her eyes searched him, as though a file existed in her brain, and she flipped through it like a magazine.

"Jersey. New Jersey," he said, nervous at her sudden scrutiny.

"Oh, you must be the guy who is renting the Risley farmhouse. It's lovely there, isn't it? The filberts all standing in neat rows. Wait until you see it in spring. The little purple flowers—Spring Beauties bloom and fill the emptiness. Nothing more welcoming after all the rain."

Henry heard her words, but his mind skittered in a near panic. She took her quilt to a nearby washer. "So, I won't need to alert the fire department or anything, will I?" He gestured toward her belly. It sounded like a joke, but he wasn't comfortable with her being here for more than one reason.

She laughed, closing the washer, and dropping her coins in the slot. A whoosh sound accompanied by swirling water and suds filled the otherwise big and empty space, giving the room purpose, putting Henry more at ease.

Her answer came with a big smile. "November. Day after Thanksgiving. Very soon, but not soon enough, you know?"

He didn't know. He eyed her stomach for a brief second. "That's very close." He hoped his clothes dried quickly so he could skedaddle. "Is it always this wet in October?" Henry tried to switch the conversation to a safe topic—the weather.

She found a bench to sit on, then gazed at him with wonder. "Sometimes. There are some really nice days and then rainy days. We are entering the second half where the temperature drops and tells you summer is officially over. What brings you to the other side of the states? Are you a relative?" She studied him, her curiosity making him uncomfortable.

"What?"

"Of the Risleys."

He fumbled for an answer. *Smart move, Henry. Should've had that one figured out.* Lying wasn't an option. Black and white. That's how he lived. The way she studied him made him nervous. If the youngest sister raised the dead, this one might know his very thoughts. And he painted the future, or the past. The room lost air and became humid like summer in his hometown.

†††

A familiarity tugged at Susan when she watched Henry. His hair neat and almost blond, and he had pale blue eyes—nearly gray. A gesture reminded her of Robert. He hadn't answered her question and appeared ill. Despite the energy surge, she hardly functioned at the top of her game. Her mind processing stuff as though she stared out the window of a speeding passenger train.

Oh, my. She put her head in her hands, the spinning like the Twirl-a-Whirl at the local amusement park. His face went across her vision.

"Susan." His voice in her ear. She made a mistake coming here alone.

"Please, I'll be fine." The bench was hard and uncomfortable, the sun glared in her eyes, and an incredible tightness came over her stomach.

"I'll run over to the fire department, get someone there."

She waved her hand at him in dismissal. "You're a jumpy one, aren't you?"

"There's a payphone out there. I'll call someone for you."

253

The vertigo made her close her eyes. And then it left. "I'm okay," she stayed still, her stomach hard like a rock, but now it calmed to normal. Contractions? Taking deep breaths, she smiled to reassure Henry. He appeared to have paled, and she held back a laugh. "Don't worry, you won't have to deliver a baby." She saw a dimple appear.

"Maybe you should call someone." His eyes flitted to the outside payphone.

She brushed away his worries. "It's okay. Really."

The dryer stopped, and Henry turned to grab his basket. He did this with quick precision, obviously glad for the distraction. She watched him pull open the door and toss his things into it.

If she stood and walked around, maybe he'd be convinced she wouldn't be giving birth or passing out at the laundromat. No need for a stranger to worry about her. Between Stan and, as of late, Robert, she'd had enough coddling.

He took the time to fold his clothes slowly and deliberately. Her own wash done, she opened the door to remove the quilt, weighted with water.

"Let me get that." Henry appeared in two swift steps. She paused. Might as well let him, maybe he'd relax a little. He lifted it out and put it into a dryer for her.

"Thank you. Are you okay?" she asked.

He turned and grinned. "As long as you're standing, or better yet, sitting and steady, I'm fine."

"No need to worry," she put the coins in and the dryer started twirling, then went back to the bench.

Henry finished his folding, and Susan wondered why he dressed up for the laundromat. Maybe all his casual clothes were dirty.

"That's it, I guess, as long as you're okay?" He tapped his basket, as though he wanted to flee. Two more people had come in so they were no longer alone, and some of the anxiety left his features. The newcomers were loud. One pointed to a machine while the other gave orders, their voices bouncing across the metal.

"Maybe I'll see you around again. After the baby," he said.

Susan laughed. "Have a good day, Henry."

"You're sure you're all right?" He grabbed his basket. "I'd hate to leave you if—"

She smiled as a slam echoed from a nearby machine. "Don't worry. It happens, you know, to pregnant women. A bit of dizziness is all."

He smiled, and his dimples deepened. "Well then, best of luck."

"Thanks," and she watched him go.

As his car pulled away, her eyes lighted on a manila envelope. She grabbed it and hurried to the door, but found Henry turning onto the main highway without a chance of seeing her.

She fingered it, curious of the contents. She'd seen him with it, hadn't she?

"Did we bring the soap?" The woman shouted across the room.

"Thought you did. Here, buy some out of that machine." The man gave her quarters.

Susan stared at the envelope. Everything around her became background noise. Her finger rubbed the clasp, and she pictured walking into the laundromat, seeing him. She remembered him opening the door and returning to his spot. He had slid the envelope underneath the basket.

If he hadn't left it, she would never had recalled anything about it. He had taken a conversation up with her, and from there she noticed his features, his slight accent, his clothes. Sure, he'd been friendly, then worried. Because she scared him, he'd forgotten all about the envelope. She'd take her time and possibly he'd be back. He said her name. Had she told him her name? She knew his from the talk of the town.

The couple continued yelling at one another as though they both had a hearing problem, but Susan's thoughts raced. Too much to do—the baby, the nursery—she still needed a crib, since Alex hadn't been able to finish her errand to pick it up that night with the flat tire. It was still on their to do list. After that, baby bottles and clothes. She'd saved money from her bookstore work, which in the end had been a blessing—financially at least.

Upcoming motherhood caused trepidation. Susan didn't like to make mistakes. As a child, she fixed, or hid the faux pas of others. *Such a beautiful girl, not blunderous like her sister, and my goodness, that Robert with a big chip on his shoulder.* The murmurings of the church members played in her memory. Nope. Back then she'd protect Alex by hiding or diminishing her sister's lack of social aptitude and charm her way in front of Robert's grumpiness. This served her well during her life, although there were a few dating horrors, which Robert found in his heart to fix. A big brother did come in handy at times. Her thoughts rambled from here to there until the dryer buzzed. She shook herself. She had almost dozed off.

Susan loaded the quilt in her basket, tossing the manila envelope on top. Henry hadn't returned for it, but she knew where he lived. Walking to her car, she looked up and down the street but only found it deserted.

Opening the back of the vehicle, her stomach protruded out, and the basket became heavy and awkward. The sun finally peeked through the clouds sending an unseasonal warmth. The envelope slid when she tipped the basket, and she had to make a grab for it to keep it from falling to the ground.

"Hey, Susan."

She jumped, banging her head. "Robert, where'd you come from?" She set the envelope in the car. How'd he sneak up on her? She checked her watch. His lunch hour. Most likely he'd been going to the deli, a creature of habit, and he'd found her.

Robert placed his hand on the trunk to close it for her. "So, what are you doing anyway?"

"I needed this quilt done in case Mom can stay in the guest room after the baby is born, you know, for a couple of days. I know what you said, but ..."

The silence between them stretched into a space where words bounced around, but no one knew which one to grasp.

"Suzie, I know how you want her ..."

She glanced away as he faltered, then met his eyes. "She'll be back." An echo, a dark cloud from the past, descended on them. She stumbled to make it right. "This is different. It's not like ..." Years of training to not say the name out loud—she'd always been a stickler for rules.

Her tears built up, and she blinked rapidly to stop them. "Have you heard anything?" she asked, hoping to not sound desperate. "Anything at all?" Okay. Desperate won.

"No. I would have told you at the house if I had any clue." He glanced at his watch. "You want to join me for lunch?"

Food sounded good, only because the baby needed something. A curtain of melancholy fell over her as she wanted Stan, not Robert, for a lunch date.

"I am going home." She tried to sound cheerful.

"Sure." He reached out, giving her a hug. "I'm sorry about Mom. I'll tell you right away when she comes back."

Robert opened the car door for her, shutting it once she settled inside. She rolled down the window. "You gonna be okay?" he asked.

"Yes, of course." But driving away, she could hear the word, *if.* He hadn't said it when he spoke of Mom coming back, but she heard him think it, and she thought it, and between the two of them an angel spoke it through a megaphone. *If.* The dreaded two letter word people of faith weren't supposed to say. A word that could change everything.

†††

Henry flipped through all his clothes. Where was it? He searched through the laundry basket several times, dumping pants, socks, and t-shirts onto his bed as though it would magically appear. He went to his car and searched in every nook and cranny. He'd lost it. The whole envelope of pictures. Leaving town wasn't as easy as he had imagined. Had to be at the laundromat. If he were lucky, it'd be on the counter. He grabbed his keys, hurried to his Honda, and spun out of the driveway.

257

†††

Henry paced every aisle of washers and dryers, scanned all flat surfaces, and peeked into a room with a big glass window purposed as a lost and found. A bright pink sweatshirt, a cream-colored blouse, and a hat, but no envelope. His plans were toast. He knew women, and they didn't find an item without examining it. Nosy and curious. And because of his stupid idea to bring it with him, his secret had the potential to be front page news. He couldn't leave town and disappear as planned. He stood there, contemplating what to do. *Get a passport. Go to a foreign country.* His inner voice mocked him.

Maybe she hadn't looked inside. Even if someone else found the envelope, the McMillan's name appeared all over the news story, and it wouldn't take a rocket scientist to figure it out. Brilliant. Why hadn't he moved to Portland? He'd asked himself that many times.

After his mother's death, he remembered all her good qualities; the bad stuff faded into a more understanding light. But now there was a conflict—the burning question—why take him all those years ago? He tried to remember his past, but the scenes blurred. Red. A parking area with trees everywhere. People and colors all over, extra clarified in the distance, but he didn't know them. His memory had no names or specific faces attached. It was a blur, like that opening day at K-Mart his mom took him to. People's legs were all he could see.

Henry took one last futile attempt to find the envelope as though wishing would make it appear. He peeked in the garbage can. Maybe it was tossed. Nope. He checked the restroom which smelled like it hadn't been cleaned—ever. Nothing. It was time to either go home and pack or wait until someone came knocking on his door. Then he remembered the busted-up paintings all over the floor. If they did find him, they'd think he was a nut. Welcome to the family. He'd fit right in.

XLVIII

Rose entered the church on Picky Lane with caution, her radar set for anything out of place, with an extra cursory glance around what had been the parking lot. She went downstairs, turning on her flashlight. This part of the church already succumbed to the darker hour.

She walked down the hallways that had held classrooms. The abandoned church became her hideaway—a forgotten structure, forlorn in the woods. Rose had inhabited the downstairs and posted her artwork—a picture diary of misery. She remembered drawing them in fragments—herself being the most fragmented of all. Focusing on her family would have been a better use of her time, not the tragedy they all endured. All this artwork. She had given Patrick a bad time about a memorial, yet what was this display of drawing after drawing?

It's not too late. The voice came uninvited. "What do you mean it's not too late? All my children are grown. I don't have anything to give them anymore. I have wasted my life because of a prophecy I thought came from You! Only to find out the guy in the woods pretended to be a prophet. Why would You do this? I could have had closure. I should have listened to Patrick." She sobbed. "All I have is regret. How can I go back and admit I've made a mistake, one all of us paid for? We've lived a charade!" She tore at the pictures on the wall. Ripping them off one by one, tearing them in pieces, littering the floor. Sliding down the wall, she joined the bits of paper, her energy spent.

Her mouth was dry like cotton. Food hadn't been a priority—not that she had an appetite. Nausea accompanied by dread brought on a spinning sensation and she dropped her head into her arms.

The shadows grew long. She'd be in pitch blackness soon. She pushed herself back up to rummage through odds and ends, finding the stash of candles and matches. With a shaking hand, she lit the three wicks, and they burst forth with life, standing at attention, making a glow she used to call hope.

She had clung to, relied on, and trusted in something some man said, instead of God. The realization hit that she never tested the words. Longing for truth, her focus went from God to a prophecy she hadn't bothered to ask Him about.

The candlelight shimmered as a pocket of air brushed its flames. A thud sounded from above, coming from the main floor. She froze. Footsteps approached. No one ever came here. The door had opened easily, as though it hadn't been vacant for years. Maybe others also used the church as a hangout, and her eyes darted about to find somewhere to hide. The floor creaked with weight, the sound coming closer, descending on the stairway. To run would be a good idea if there was somewhere to go. Cigarette smoke floated between them, before she saw his shadow.

XLIX

'What if' played over and over but none of the solutions were that simple. Patrick knew that. If Stephen were really alive he wasn't three anymore and wouldn't remember them, and hadn't grown up in the McMillan family. What values would he have been raised with? What kind of an adult would he be? Patrick's thoughts kept circling to Caroline, Vivian, and the false prophecy. He was too practiced at smashing down hope.

An ache for Rose grew inside him. Didn't he mean anything to her? The day in the kitchen, smelling of cinnamon, stew, and chocolate he had tried to connect with her. She didn't want him there, he knew that, but they hadn't fought. Not since he found her with their entire wardrobes strung out on the bed. That was never resolved either, buried under the surface—just enough to function.

He had no desire for Caroline—not for one second; and Joe's story didn't ring true about Rose. Even though he'd seen them together in the woods that day, in his heart he doubted that she went to Joe about the false prophecy.

How had they managed to live disconnected with an imaginary wall between them? Didn't Patrick always explain the importance of communication? He should pay attention to his own advice, because now, where was his wife? He pictured himself, wandering to all the shelters, asking for Rose, but they wouldn't tell him anything. Shelters were for refuge from the enemy, which in most cases applied. But he wasn't the enemy. *Closer to home.* He dropped the golf tee he had been fingering and grabbed the car keys. He knew where Rose might be.

"P eter?" Rose blinked in the dim light and saw her mistake. Joe.

"Hello, Rose." He walked closer to her. His hair a mess, his eyes bloodshot, and a button hung off his coat. Usually he was a good-looking man, until he opened his mouth, but now old and wasted would be how she'd describe him.

She took a step back. The room spun again. "Leave me alone."

"I thought I'd find you here."

She wondered why he searched for her.

"Patrick came to see me. At the bar. I've been getting lots of your family members in there lately. Might have to put a cross on the roof." He settled on an old bench near her.

"Why would Patrick come to see you?" she asked. Picturing Patrick going to the bar to talk to Joe stalled her thinking, but then the awful truth dawned. He searched for her. And why wouldn't he? No longer did he have children to take care of in her absence. A reason she never stayed hidden long. A new desolation covered her.

"Wanted to know where his wife was and when I last saw her." Joe smirked. "I told him you'd come to me when you found that the prophecy was a lie."

A weariness engulfed her, tears burned at her eyes. Patrick would hate her, and Joe made things worse by lying.

"Yeah, not good is it? I've given up on you, Rose—and Patrick has too."

Her body shook and her pulse accelerated—maybe an impending heart attack came next. This is how her life would end. She deserved the implications. Joe's lies didn't matter. Patrick deserved the truth. The whole evening had gone by—hour after hour, but she had said nothing. He went golfing. She baked. Plenty of opportunity when he found her in the kitchen as well, not to mention another whole night. And now her silence multiplied into lies destroying their marriage. Truth? She hadn't given it a chance.

"Why do you hang out here? Jesus isn't around to come save you. Just me."

"Jesus is always around. And you can hardly save me." She sniffed, trying to hold back silent tears, thankful for the dim lighting. Knowing Jesus never left her, she still struggled with the perception that He was far away. A wall had gone up, and the past attached itself like a chain, making up outcomes she could live with.

Joe laughed. "The thing is, Rose, I know about Stephen. I've known all along."

†††

The pews were arranged in order as though yesterday was 1977, and they hadn't been abandoned. Taking a minute to dust one off, Patrick sat down. It was like a dream—being here again—the church where the dead-raising happened. He preferred not to contemplate the past. Too many painful emotions. He left this behind in the heat of August. No looking back. Walking onto the platform he regarded the emptiness of the sanctuary. Lifeless. Even he seemed to hover, half-spirit, half-man in this strange shadow of time. His ear caught a sound about the same time he sneezed. Dust danced, twirling like a ballet. Sneezing again, he walked to the door that led to the stairway where a faint murmur had come from, and opened it a crack.

The voices—low and high pitches, drifted from the stairway. Joe Brooks. Rose. Together again. She had told him she had no interest in the man. He wanted to believe her, yet the words Joe told him tingled in his memory like food going bad. Each day, the reality whispered she'd gone to him—again. Doubt trickled his thoughts. Maybe he'd been wrong, and she really had gone to Joe about the false prophecy. But was Joe responsible for that whole thing? Patrick wouldn't be surprised. He took a couple of steps down, listening to the conversation.

Rose had to sit. Her legs wobbled as she edged away from Joe. Shivering, her body finally awakened to the coldness of the church. Her stomach hurt, and she doubled over, wrapping the quilt around her, candles nearby flickering.

Her breath came fast and shallow, spots of blackness speckling her vision. If it weren't for her, Joe wouldn't even be here. The demons in the spirit realm laughed. What a predicament to want to get away from something that she herself caused. Who asked Joe for help? She did. In her life story, there shouldn't have been a Joe, but she had let him in and because of that stupidity, Patrick might leave her forever.

Joe spoke lies. Multiple ones. If he could just tell her his point in one sentence before she passed out. The beckoning darkness was welcoming—except something Joe had said—

"I thought I'd bring Stephen home, but by the time I figured the whole truth of what happened, it was too late. The best I could do was steer you away." He eyed her, "Doesn't matter at this point anyway."

Sweat trickled down her face and chest. How could she be cold and hot at the same time? "Why didn't you tell me? Do you hate me that much? You hate *us* that much?" But Joe couldn't tell the truth to save his soul. "I don't believe you anymore."

Dehydration and exhaustion dimmed her optimism and ability to think. This time she wouldn't imagine good outcomes like in the past—expecting rainbows on a cloudless day. Rose didn't believe anymore, but the possibility of what he said jolted her—like coming out of a drugged haze. Then it went out like a bang. Too many times she'd been the fool, and what was always the common denominator? Joe.

He smiled. "This is good information I have." He edged closer and pulled out a bottle taking a swig of clear liquid. "I could be persuaded to share it if you would sell me a certain piece of property?"

Her voice shook. "You are a liar." She longed to beat the truth out of him, like a mother bear poised for attack, except her strength failed. He thought she'd fall for his story? His *I know what happened to Stephen* game so he could get Allie's bookstore, save his crummy old tavern—and then what? Tell her once again that everything was made up? Not happening.

"You could convince Alex to sell. It'd be for her own good. You used me. When you needed me, you sought me out, otherwise I was like an expendable pet. Throw me out when you're done, right? You owe me." His gaze mocked her.

"Owe you? How do you figure? You steered me away from the truth. You gave that guy in the woods money to tell lies instead of telling me what you knew! If anything, you owe me!" He'd twisted the events making himself the victim. "And guess what, Joe? I wasn't thinking about you. Imagine that. My little boy disappears, and you assume I'm trying to have a relationship with you?" Her anger buoyed giving her strength.

"You led me on," he hovered over her. "I have a plan B. I don't get what I want and neither do you." He reached for her, and she jumped backward. The world tipped.

"All I want is the truth!" Her voice filled the downstairs of the church, years bottled inside letting loose—a hurricane waiting on the horizon. *Truth.* Joe was incapable of giving her that, no matter how loud she demanded it.

"Rose." She turned toward the stairs. Patrick? Was she hallucinating? Maybe wishful thinking made him appear—only a mirage.

Joe laughed. "Nice of you to come, Patrick. But you see, I got your wife all to myself—again." He stepped closer to Rose who dodged away from him, but her lack of balance sent her teetering into the candles, knocking them over. A flame touched the edge of the quilt, and fire licked at its edges, latching onto the papers littering the floor.

"We all deserve the hell my dad escaped," Joe appeared unconcerned, taking another drink from his flask. "This is better than I planned. I didn't think to add your corpse to the mix," he said to Patrick. The flame burst to life, and Rose shrieked, throwing the quilt from her, but part of it hit Joe and the bottle of alcohol he held. He sidestepped a flame, and Rose scanned the area with a new panic, seeing the wood light up and the drawings blackening at the edges. Patrick stood between her and the growing fire, but vertigo caused her to trip, followed by the sensation of falling. He called her name as her head hit the floor.

Patrick dodged a new flame, stumbling on Joe's foot that shot out in front of him. Had the man lost his mind? He edged toward Rose, calling out to her, but Joe's hands grabbed his shoulders, pulling him back. Patrick's gaze landed on his wife, but Joe tried for a headlock. "Rose!" No response—not that he expected one. If she came to, she'd have a chance to get out, even if he ended up burning with the building.

He threw Joe off, dodging the multiplying flames. Joe's grasping movements were clumsy, yet he managed to latch onto Patrick's foot, knocking him down, but Patrick kicked free, leaving a shoe behind.

Joe dashed for the stairway running up and through the door leaving Rose and Patrick in the inferno. The vodka, dry wood, and quilts fed the fire. Flames inched closer to Rose, licking their way among the drawings strung across the floor. Now out of Joe's grasp, Patrick crawled to her side.

She shouldn't be here. She should be home, with him. Safe. His body shook from adrenaline, and the smoke burned his eyes, blurring his vision.

He gathered her in his arms, lifting her as he fought to stand, teetering, barely able to manage the first step. She was limp and lighter than he remembered. He stumbled around another burst of fire, his voice staggering over Scripture: *The eternal God is my refuge and dwelling place.* He whispered in her ear. Another flame bounced on the left. Patrick took another step, choking out the words as smoke filled his lungs. *And underneath are His everlasting arms.* His step came lighter, feeling something half push him to the staircase.

He carried her, coughing, the heat burning as though he walked through hell itself. *He drove out the enemy before me.* In this case, the enemy seemed to have done just that, but at least Patrick didn't have to fight Joe while getting Rose out of the building. A whoosh lit in front of the steps, stopping him in his tracks.

He was close. Too close. He finished the verse, "and said, 'Destroy!'"

The flame bounced to the left, giving Patrick the microsecond he needed to get Rose up the stairway, through the haze of the fire and into the sanctuary.

And underneath are His everlasting arms—the presence of God holding him, guiding him toward the outside. With the last of his energy he staggered to the middle of the church parking lot. Sirens blared in the distance. He sank to the ground with Rose still in his arms, among the weeds growing through the cracked pavement, where Winston was raised from the dead many years ago.

LI

Henry arrived home to an empty driveway. He didn't know what to expect. Surely they had found out? Heck, he could have misconceived what they wanted. Maybe it wasn't him—or he was a disappointment? Whatever the reason, His chance to carry out Plan A held promise. Leave. No need to be dramatic and announce to the family he had arrived. Awkward. Take his time, clear his head, then maybe try again. Or not. Without going inside, he did a U-turn and drove toward Dockerbog and the city of Portland.

A few miles past the Dockerbogger, A big banner greeted him—

Pirate Daze

Colors sprinkled the road—mass people everywhere, all adorned in pirate attire. He put on his shades, hiding behind the dark tint, coming to the first red light. They crossed in front of him; some gave his car a pat as they went by, making pirate faces, and swearing at him in pirate lingo accents. Drinking had commenced, and many were sloshed before the dinner hour, if Henry went by the staggering steps that teetered near his vehicle.

He saw a rainbow of balloons near a fenced-in area. Evidently you had to pay to attend the event, and if he went by the crowded streets, the town would make a killing. The smell of sausage filled the air and the Pirate Pub restaurant had a full parking lot. Henry's stomach growled. Where could he get food? Should he throw on an eye patch and walk in? Were pirates violent? He considered turning back toward the Dockerbogger. Joe's cold greetings trumped greasy, one-eyed crowds playing dress-up.

You are running away.

"I know that."

When had he started hearing voices, anyway? Since he arrived in Filbert Ridge. The water must be contaminated.

The voice of God!

The exclamation vibrated from a deep memory. Well, God wouldn't talk to him. Henry wasn't like the rest of them.

An explosion went off, and he swerved, coming close to a group of women in gypsy skirts.

"Hey, watch it, honey," one said.

Another one came too close to his window. "He's kinda cute."

"Looks like a cop," said the other, pulling her away, giving Henry the room to accelerate.

A poof of smoke filled the sky ahead of him. Props. The sooner he got through this weirdness, the better.

Just when he thought all the thematic glory was behind him, flashing blue and red lights filled the whole road blocking the highway to freedom, along with a cop directing traffic to make a U-turn. He couldn't even get out of town? He found himself headed back to Filbert Ridge, his stomach demanding food and his gas tank close to empty. Friday the thirteenth, full moon, some other strange source of nature—he ticked through all the possibilities he could blame this on, but nothing came to mind. Another unlucky day for Henry James, aka Stephen McMillan.

Henry tried to reconcile the fact he had driven through the pirates twice for no reason whatsoever. What did he gain from this experience? Nothing. Waste of time. He hated wasting time. The Dockerbogger came into view but even though Henry really wanted a burger, he refused to go somewhere else that made him uncomfortable. He decided to give up and head home. He hadn't prepared properly, anyway, his stuff thrown together like a toddler packed it. Taking a few extra days to put things in better order would be wise, no matter how fast he wanted to get out of Filbert Ridge.

LII

Patrick had a date. Rose had insisted. The first thing she said, once she had been given oxygen, "I want the memorial."

The words, however, brought no joy to Patrick. Something in his spirit tipped and needed put back in order. The moment he wished for, Rose wanting closure, now fell flat. What he had thought would fix everything gave no relief, but instead brought apprehension. Even his resignation didn't fit right. He couldn't tell her in the hospital, and they had just gotten home after a long check out process. The more time that passed, the more awkward it became. It started to have the feel of deception.

They sat on the couch together, and she interrupted him, right when he opened his mouth to say it. "Where do you suppose he is?" she asked

He looked at her, confused.

"Joe."

"Oh, I wouldn't have a clue." He settled back into the sofa cushion.

"It's not finished yet. I want it to be. Desperately, but something isn't right," she leaned into him.

"I resigned from the church." There. He confessed, not waiting another second or giving a preamble to lighten the news.

She sat upright. "What? Patrick, why?" Her clear blue eyes searched his.

"I don't belong there. We don't belong there. It isn't working, and it hasn't been working for a long time, as you know."

"But to resign? You love to preach."

Do I? He used to. The last years—too many to admit—the podium sucked his words away before they reached the pews. The same question came to him. Had he made a mistake taking the pulpit at The Lord is my Shepherd?

"You can't just quit without telling me."

"I did it for you. For us."

"But what about the dream—for the future. We had a picture of God's plan. He isn't done with the church yet, or with you being their pastor."

"The church needs new blood. Rose, we've been there a long time. They need a fresh start, and so do we. I've been treading water trying to move forward, but my vision has the past in front of it. I need a new slate."

"Patrick, I'm letting it go, don't you see? I'm moving forward," tears streamed down her face, "for your sake."

"And so am I!" His voice sharp, louder than he intended, but he'd given up so much. His resignation shut the door on the gossip, false scandal, and criticism. He did the right thing.

She flinched and moved away from him. "I just . . . I wanted to free you from all the years I wasted."

He took a deep breath. "It's okay. Don't you see? We can move forward together. Take a vacation. Just the two of us." He'd nearly lost her forever, and now he practically picked a fight. He reined in his frustration. "Everything will work out."

Rose took in his eyes. His expression didn't falter. "Okay. I assume you've asked God for direction." She smiled. "To new beginnings."

He smiled back, but couldn't remember asking God anything. God, family, ministry—he chanted the mantra over and over. Had he tried too hard to convince himself? He had reversed roles with Rose. And to top it off, after hearing her recount Joe's story, he wondered if this time Joe told the truth.

# LIII

Patrick paced the floor in Howard's office.

"You're doing the right thing." Howard moved papers around on his desk. "I never wanted to give up, or to let you down, but it's time."

"Beyond time."

"You and Rose are the two most determined people I know. You taught me a lot about perseverance." Howard dragged the waste basket closer to his desk, dumping wrappers and to-go coffee cups.

Patrick fidgeted with his keys. He hung onto them because he considered this visit to be a stop and go, but inside he carried two puzzles he tried to make into one—a missing chunk could connect everything.

"Don't be glum, I'll see you around on the golf course. We will still have our game time." Howard grinned.

"You'll think I'm crazy." Patrick couldn't dismiss the latest unsettled conversations.

A deep laugh from Howard practically shook the room. "Oh, goody. I can't wait to hear what follows that statement. It's hard to imagine what could top some of the scenarios we've already talked about. Lay it on me, Pastor. We have seen crazy before."

"I am not sure I want to have this memorial."

Howard stared at him. "You just said it was beyond time."

"Yeah, but I can't shake my discomfort. And why now? Why not while Rose still thought it possible?"

"Perhaps you never wanted a memorial. It is hard to get rid of stuff sometimes, even bad stuff. You have to figure out what life looks like, not searching for Stephen."

"Rose said Joe told her so many lies she no longer believes anything he says. But where is he? What if he finally told the truth?"

"So, before we call it quits, we should find Joe," Howard said.

"But don't tell Rose. I am still going through with the memorial. I won't get her hopes up again."

"Got it." Howard put his feet on his now clean desk. "Should be a piece of cake compared to what we've been through."

LIV

Patrick opened the glass door and headed toward his office—the office he thought he was done with. Maybe he'd left something that needed taken care of. When Adam called him, he wasn't very forthcoming, and once Patrick opened the door he knew why.

The three women turned in unison when he entered. They faced the empty chair of his desk—waiting, it seemed, for him to take his seat, sipping their coffee with expressions he couldn't read. Or didn't want to. He poured himself a cup, standing until Vivian gestured toward his old office chair.

On the nearby sofa, Adam sat with his leg thrown over the other, leaning back as though he attended a relaxed get-together. Patrick cleared his throat. He appreciated Adam being there, but it made him leerier as to what topic they'd be covering.

"I suppose you thought you were done with this place," Adam said, breaking into the quiet stares that had only been interrupted with the clicking of spoons.

"It feels like I've been called into the principal's office," Patrick remarked with a grin, but the only smile in response came from Adam and a slight giggle from Meredith.

"It's your own office," Vivian's tone may as well have said, *You are an idiot.*

"*Was* my office," Patrick clarified.

"That is what we are here to debate. We are not a hundred percent on board with your *resignation,*" Vivian said as though his decision were a mere whim.

Silence stuffed up the air in the room. Patrick wondered if he should have said he'd stay at The Lord is My Shepherd church forever, since they appeared to operate on reverse psychology. He took a sip of coffee as his stomach twisted in anticipation.

Claudia topped off her drink, and steam rose through the air. Patrick wished the meeting would move along a little quicker, but at the same time, dreaded everything they were likely to say. They always managed to surprise him.

Adam shifted and refilled his own cup. Patrick tapped the desk, then stopped, catching the eye of Claudia. Did she appear amused? The situation was worse than he thought.

All things new. That's what he tried to accomplish here, right? He had faced his congregation and resigned, putting priorities in order, yet here he sat, confronted with the same people that didn't like anything he did or didn't do.

Vivian leaned forward. "Are you all right, Pastor?"

He found them all staring at him. Even Adam.

Vivian tapped her purse. "I prayed you were well. We should have saved this meeting for later, but it couldn't be delayed, could it?" She eyed Claudia and Meredith. "We wanted to say how sorry we are."

"You're—sorry," he repeated in a daze. An alternate universe spread out before him. "I thought you poisoned me at your house the other day."

The three of them cackled. "Pastor, you've always had a vivid imagination. See, like you, we've been operating on a lie. We handled situations in a less than desirable fashion."

Patrick's eyes darted to Adam. "I don't understand the change of heart."

Claudia fiddled with a handkerchief, glancing at Vivian. "We are all sorry." She poked her finger into Meredith's arm, nearly making her spill her coffee. "Oh, yes. We didn't mean any harm." Meredith nodded, her crazy curls going everywhere.

Adam coughed, choking on his coffee. Patrick took another gulp of his own, studying the three ladies. "But I resigned, see."

He simplified the words to explain the situation. Resign. Quit. Moving on to greener pastures.

"We don't accept," Vivian said. "It isn't the solution."

Did these women always get their way?

"After Robert came and took you to the ER, I considered what you said. About Frank. And Jesus. I put up a barrier, and if we let you go .... I want another chance, and you haven't thought this through, have you?" Vivian asked. "You made a decision on the edge of an illness. You couldn't have been in your right mind."

He had done nothing but think, and opened his mouth to say so, but decided it'd be a pointless argument. "I'm not sure what you want me to say here."

"It's simple. You say you will stay," Claudia said.

He wondered if they wished to continue torturing him. There hadn't been any mention of how Rose played into this. Why the sudden apology?

The past wouldn't define the McMillans any longer. He could focus on Rose and do some traveling and not have to consider the needs of a whole congregation which resembled a family with one problem after another. They endured heartaches, ignored counseling, made bad decisions, and then wondered why their lives were a mess, yet his soul ached for them, and he wished he could've served them better all these years. Had he helped any of them?

"We were appalled at Joe's actions. We had no idea of the depths of his deception," Vivian said. "And that is one of the things we are apologizing for."

"He's always been mad at me about Rose. Never got over her, I guess."

Claudia clucked her tongue. "His obsession gave him a lack of sense."

"I can't go back on my resignation without some trepidation, you know. My family suffered too much disapproval."

Adam remained silent. Patrick figured he must be the meeting mediator. A sound voice to rise against bullying Patrick back into the pulpit, although he hadn't heard him take his side yet.

"How did your family take the news? I'm assuming you asked them before doing something so rash," Claudia said.

"I didn't ask, but I did it for them," Patrick said.

Vivian leaned forward. "We understand how you wouldn't want us back, as a congregation, but we are also very sorry for our treatment of Rose and the children. We should not have placed blame on her, or you, for the disappearance of your son. You had the right to handle it however you saw fit." She glanced at her coffee, fiddling with her spoon. "And as far as the dead-raising goes, we are ready to embrace the power of God. We shouldn't have given Alex such a hard time."

Now that was a statement worth its weight in gold. "I want to put my family first. I haven't defended them like I should have." If only Rose could hear this; he wished he had a tape recording. "I appreciate the apology and forgive you. But I have made my decision. It is best for all of us."

"How is Rose?" asked Vivian.

"Much better."

"We were relieved to hear she wasn't hurt in the fire. God protected her," Meredith said.

"Yes, He did." Patrick stood, not sure how to end this meeting. The ladies followed his every move, and Meredith gathered the cups.

"Do you have an answer? Will you give us another chance?" Vivian asked.

"Please?" added Meredith.

Patrick glanced from one to the other. What was he supposed to say? His discussion with Rose had left him unsure, but—

A knock interrupted his thoughts.

"I'll get it." Adam rose from the sofa and peeked out, only to shut the door again, leaning on it and crossing his arms.

"What's the matter?" Patrick asked.

"I believe there is a problem," Adam stepped away.

And they wondered why he wanted to resign. Patrick, breathing a prayer, went to the door and opened it, then froze.

"Rose?" He gave her a hug. "And Alex?" But stopped short at the crowd in the hallway.

"I know why you did it, and the act was noble, but Patrick, this is not the answer."

Half the church stood behind her. "What do they want?"

"They want you back."

He eyed the congregation, awestruck. Did he deserve such devotion? They cared this much about him and his family? He gazed over them in wonder, the appreciation for them hit him in the heart. "I don't see Martin," he said in a low voice.

"Not everybody wanted you back, dear," Rose whispered back to him.

The sea of faces made him almost dizzy with the turn of events. This proved he shouldn't try to direct his own life. Every good idea he had, turned and twisted until it suited The Lord is My Shepherd church. His prophetic radar must have been damaged in the fire, because he didn't know what to do—quit or stay?

Lilian came forward. "You both helped me and my family. You've taken time with the girls, counseling all of us. I've been able to forgive George. I wouldn't want to lose the two of you as pastors."

Others came forward. Many Rose had ministered to while working at the bakery. Women from the shelter with some of their children, who were all grown. Men Patrick had golfed with, and couples he counseled who were still together. Focusing on what didn't happen was always easier than rejoicing over the successes. A major flaw he needed to change.

Patrick turned to Rose. "This is for real? I quit for you. For us. It was the right thing to do."

"And maybe it was, Patrick. Like sacrificing something so God can give it back to you—bigger and better."

Vivian nodded in agreement, "So, Pastor, what do you have to say to all of us?" She made it sound like he should be apologizing.

He paused overwhelmed at all the expectant faces. "Let the holy rolling begin?"

Claudia fanned herself, and Vivian's mouth went into a flat line of disapproval. Patrick grinned. "How about we go back to my original premise? I'll come back if I can be led by the Holy Spirit."

"You're a horrible tease, which I might say is a character flaw, but we will pray for your maturity in this matter, and we very much want you back," Vivian said.

"It's hard to refuse such a heartfelt proposal," Patrick put his arm around Rose. He winked at her.

"And we have a gift for you and Rose," a woman spoke from the middle of the mob of people. Dana. She brought them an envelope. "It's from everyone. And I want to thank you for helping us. We are expecting again. Just when we thought we were getting too old."

"Oh, that's wonderful, Dana!" Rose gave her a hug.

Patrick took the card and gave it to Rose to open. "Oh, Patrick. A vacation. To the beach."

"Some R and R would be appropriate before you take us on again," said Adam. "I can fill in until you return."

"The ocean. I always imagine myself there," Patrick grinned. "Thank you, everyone."

Vivian raised her voice to the crowd. "There is punch and cake downstairs to celebrate the return of the McMillans."

Patrick leaned close to Vivian. "What if I'd said *no*? You were sure we'd come back?"

"If you said no, it'd be a send-off party. Cake is an all-occasion food," Vivian informed him.

LV

Patrick came back to preach on the third Sunday of October, a beautiful and unusually warm day for so late in the year. He and Rose had discussed their beach getaway and decided to enjoy it next summer, especially with their first grandchild due during the holidays.

To accommodate his return, the church decided to put on a skit. Lily Langley performed a monologue of, "The Grass is Always Greener." Patrick wondered if this was aimed at his attempt to leave the pulpit, but tried to relax and let part of the service be filled in, allowing him a shorter sermon. Next week he would dig into the deep stuff, the things his heart longed to speak.

"What if we all left what we had, to explore what we envied?" Lily sat dressed in a pinafore and a wide sun hat. "What if we jumped ship to go somewhere that looked perfect, only to find it was a façade. A world in a fantasy bubble. To leave our own messy lives, our unfashionable clothes and our significant other not looking quite like the day when we married them—"

"Amen!" A shout from the audience, stuttered Lily's monologue.

"—for something forbidden? And we step onto the lush green grass that we dreamed of and enter a house with the more expensive mortgage, only to realize this life isn't any better but has even bigger problems. Sometimes there is no going back. Be thankful for now and what you have. Look to God who wants the best for you. He will move you forward into your own destiny, not what sits on your neighbor's lawn or in their driveway."

"And don't forget desiring your neighbor's wife." Gary sat in the back and now stood. "Interesting performance, Lilian. Holy Spirit inspired? Tell me church, why is he back? Why is Pastor McMillan back at the pulpit?"

Patrick's heart raced. They had sung a few songs, and Lily had gone on the platform. He hadn't even got to say anything more than *hello*. His glance slid to Rose who looked like she'd gone a shade whiter. Gary had missed the welcoming committee, and must have been disappointed to find him still here. More than disappointed. Patrick regarded Gary's red face. Downright angry.

"Gary, this isn't the time for theatrics," Vivian admonished.

"Seems like the perfect time to me. We are smack dab in the middle of a skit!"

A few nervous giggles went throughout the church, and Eva struck up a worship song on the piano as though everyone would be diverted into singing.

"Stop it!" Gary's loud demand startled the poor girl, and she stumbled to a crescendo of wrong notes. "This pastor has committed adultery, yet you let him back. Did you know that, Vivian?"

"What are you talking about?" Vivian asked.

Adultery? The silence screamed accusations, and Patrick glanced at Rose whose eyebrows had lifted to the height of her bangs. Should he defend himself or wait to hear what else Gary wanted to say?

"Gary, I'm not sure I understand." Another sermon gone to dust. No one would be able to pay attention after this outburst.

"That kid is yours, that's what I'm talking about. Pretty smooth move on your part getting Caroline to go to New Jersey, to hide out and have a baby. Nobody would be the wiser. It is your fault that my marriage ended!" Gary's voice had risen again, and two of the ushers walked toward him.

Patrick's mind floundered trying to picture a random child that was his and what it had to do with Caroline. Murmurings and glances darted arrows at him. His earlier resignation mocked him—should have stayed with decision number one.

"Oh, that's right. Kick me out of the service," Gary said to the ushers. "I know what I saw. Caroline's son is your son as well. He looks exactly like you, and I can't believe no one in this town has noticed. I got to thinking about how conveniently she left."

"But that can't be right." Lily piped up from the platform with a glance at Rose. "I was with Rose late the day Stephen went missing, and when I got home in the evening, my husband was gone. I waited around but at two or three in the morning I decided to see if he was at the Dockerbogger. The children were at their grandparents, so I easily could do some spying on George if I wanted. He'd been hanging out at the tavern a lot. When I got there, I saw Caroline's van. Seems more likely she had a thing for Joe, rather than the pastor."

"Doesn't mean anything," Gary said. "We all know that Carly was a flirt. Plus, I tell you, all you have to do is look at this young man and know he is Patrick's. I suggest you accept his resignation."

"We hardly are going to do that because of this story you've conjured up, Gary." Vivian turned in her pew. "We can't send the pastor away because some young man resembles him and we jump to conclusions."

"I'm telling you—"

"For goodness sake, we are in the middle of church," Claudia admonished.

Why change now? Everything always happened in the middle of church. "The young man at the Risley place?" Patrick began, his brain catching up to all the players in Gary's version of what happened.

"That's right."

He glanced at Vivian, recalling the conversation they had at her house awhile back. He remembered the mom and the boy, hiding in the car. He could hear Rose say, "She was with me."

The door to the sanctuary burst open, and Martin appeared. *Yep,* Patrick thought, *my days in the pulpit are over.*

"It's Joe!" Martin's eyes went over the sanctuary. "He's on the church roof, by the bells."

"What in the world is he doing there?" Meredith asked.

"Gonna jump, I'm thinking."

The ushers rushed outside followed by every man in the congregation, then the rest of the crowd followed.

"I'll dial 911," Eva said, going out the doors toward the office.

Patrick took Rose's arm, and they went outside. "It's not true, what Gary said."

"Of course it's not, but what does all of it mean?" She stopped facing him. "I don't know what to do with this information, Patrick. I'm tired of believing. I am telling myself it means nothing, but my stomach is churning because—*what if?*"

They continued outside, and heads turned upward, everyone's gaze landing on Joe who sat on the edge, dangling his feet as though he was going to have lunch and enjoy the rare sunny day, rather than end his life. Sirens sounded in the distance.

"What are you all looking at? Shouldn't you be preaching right now?" Joe directed his last statement to Patrick.

"It's just an ordinary Sunday," Patrick raised his voice to be heard above the emergency vehicles getting closer.

Joe laughed. "I see that. What's with the firetrucks? Somebody didn't die again, did they?"

"You can't jump. Listen Joe, everything will work out, there's no need—" Martin started.

"Jump? I ain't planning on jumping. All this hoopla is for me? I wanted to be here and maybe catch bits of the sermon. The sound floats up here."

"Why didn't you just come to church, for goodness sakes?" Vivian asked.

Joe looked at Rose and shook his head. "I couldn't. Not after ..."

"You should jump. It's all your fault Carly left me," Gary shouted, turning red with rage.

"Oh yeah? You want me to throw myself from the top of a church building, Gary? I could try to take you out on the landing. Oh, but where is the dead-raiser girl?" His gaze swept over them. "Guess she ain't here. A greater chance for dying."

"I'll come up there and push you off myself!"

"Oh, for land's sake!" Claudia interrupted. "You two are acting like Neanderthals!"

"Stop it, both of you!" Patrick interrupted them. "Simmer down. Earlier you said this was all my fault."

"Yeah, but Joe was the beginning."

"Okay, but let's not try to see how many commandments we can break on the Lord's day," Patrick said.

"The only thing I want to break—" Gary's fists balled.

"Gary, let me tell you about Caroline. Let me tell all of you about Caroline. Because of her I've had no peace. Now I can't eat, sleep, or enjoy a shot of whisky without getting sick to my stomach." Joe pulled out a bottle of water and took a sip, then continued. "Caroline came to me twice. The second time, she'd come to town, to straighten me out. I was on my way to tell you the truth." He glanced at Rose. "But she had a point. It had been too long and what would happen to me? I thought I had something to bargain with, you know? Dad was giving the bookstore away, and I drank a little too much and came up with a perfect solution. Info for inheritance, but Caroline followed me." He paused. "We had a fight, but she managed to get me to see her way of thinking. Heck, I guess I passed out after and scared those kids. Bad planning on my part, waiting until school was out. If I would have just spoke up the first time Caroline came around ..."

October 8, 1967—3:00 a.m.

Joe was drunk again, trying to forget about Rose—or more specifically, wishing he could hold Rose. The wish always lingered. The idea. The forbidden. She belonged to Patrick and was a pastor's wife. The rational part of him knew better, but sometimes a weakness pulled at him, and it was a narrow escape today. In the old days, Joe would have thanked God for that, but he lost religion a long time ago. Patrick appeared none too pleased to find them sitting on the bench together, but was it Joe's fault he had let her drive around in her shocked state?

He poured himself another shot when a knock sounded on the tavern door. His thoughts were murky and Rose's Snow White features played in his mind as he opened it, hopeful.

But it wasn't Rose. Caroline Randall stood in the entry, hair disheveled, eyes blood-shot. She shoved past him and closed the door as though she were in a cloak and dagger movie, her glance wild and darting around the room.

"Caroline, what do you want? Need a place to crash?" Her husband, Gary had been jerk-of-the-century at the festival that afternoon, not that Joe would get any medals for his behavior.

"I'm leaving town, Joe. Starting a new life. I wanted to say goodbye."

"Goodbye? Where you gonna go?"

"Far away from here. Things fell in my lap. Meant to be, you know. God's on my side, now."

"You been smokin' again?" Joe eyed her with suspicion. Caroline tended to hear the voice of God when she helped herself to mind-altering drugs. Joe wasn't foreign to a true prophecy, nor was he naive and unable to recognize drug-induced spiritualism. He'd had experience with both, but he'd left the church after seeing his dad swing back and forth like a weathervane. When the forecast was fair, all was good, but bad weather brought the drop in barometric pressure, and Joe's dad, Winston, lost all control and became impossible to be around, yet went to church every week. The only thing that kept him one step from being a hypocrite was his Sunday routine—done out of rote. Never bothered to close his eyes to pray or sing a hymn, just showed up, sat by his wife, and hurried out the door when the service ended.

"I don't do that stuff anymore. I've grown up, unlike some of the bozos we went to school with." She leaned against the counter. "Especially now. I'm turning a new leaf. I don't need Gary, I got something better."

"That's real sweet, Carly, but my eye hasn't quite settled on you yet." She practically stalked him sometimes. Her going out of town would give him some space.

"I ain't talkin' about you, Joe," she laughed, then got squirrelly again. "Look, I gotta go." She came close and gave him a peck on the cheek.

"That's it? A sisterly kiss? You sure know how to hurt a guy's ego." He relaxed, deciding a little flirting was safe, since she was leaving and all.

She smiled, walked to the door with a fluttery wave, and was gone. Joe watched her get in the van, and as she drove away he saw a face peeking out the side window. A child. He rushed to the door and leaned out, peering through the darkness. A gust of wind blew his hair, that had needed a trim for some time, right into his eyes, and he blinked, unable to clarify what he had seen.

If he weren't three sheets to the wind, Joe might've called the McMillans. Maybe it was a mirage, a phantom in the fog. He'd had too much to drink. He thought how he could save the day. Make Patrick look like a loser.

He sat at the bar, knowing he'd be spending the night here. Again. He at least had a comfy sofa for when he overindulged. Joe set his glass on a small stand and grabbed a blanket. A plan simmered—he could be the hero in Rose's life. The world spun, and a moment later, blackness overtook him.

†††

The congregation absorbed the information in silence. The emergency vehicles stayed, and a couple of firemen made their way to the top of the tower.

"I loved you, Rose. And I hated Patrick. Caroline and I were sick at how you two flaunted your perfect life around. She wanted him, and I wanted you, so she thought to take a bit of both of you. She said you were overwhelmed with another baby coming."

Rose leaned into Patrick. "That's what she wished to believe."

286

"I had a plan. I was going to bring him back, but then she skipped town, and when I found her and knew the whole truth, too much time had gone by. What was I supposed to do?"

Rose sobbed, and Patrick put his arm around her.

"I called Caroline. I was going to be the good guy. She said she would turn the tables, and I had no plans to get in trouble with her. I planted the prophecy to say Stephen had died, to make you stop searching."

"You told him to say he died?" Rose looked up.

"Yeah, you'd think he could do that, but no, that goof changed things, forcing me to get more creative. I decided I could be by your side and make sure you never got close to the truth." He smiled. "It ended up being much more enjoyable, spending extra time with you, planning where to plant the next false lead. I thought I could build your trust." Joe stood. The two firemen behind him, took a step closer.

"I wanted to say, I'm sorry."

Everyone stared—the whole congregation silent, waiting. Gary sank to the ground, his rage turning to grief. Rose leaned more on Patrick as he held her. Joe kicked something—a big white sign floated to the ground. He turned away from the opening and out of sight.

Patrick picked up the wooden stick handle and saw the faded words, "Save Joe," its halo streaking down over the J.

LVI

Henry flipped through the tiny newspaper, *Filbert Ridge inFormation*. A larger ad than the rest in the classifieds caught his attention. Memorial for Stephen McMillan. He walked to the window and gazed out over the filbert trees in the near distance. So, this was it. He'd come all this way to be declared dead. A sign from above, right? They didn't need him and were making him a mere memory. Why now? Was this some sort of passive rejection? Did they know and leave a cryptic message in the paper? Maybe that's why the church burned down. They were erasing the past.

It couldn't be all that covert, the reasonable side tried to argue. Was this why he hadn't gone to them and said, *Hey I'm your lost son Stephen?* Because he thought he'd be rejected? And right now, he didn't have the pictures or the newspaper article to help prove his identity.

Henry sank onto the floor, holding the announcement, staring at the paper. He came from a praying family. Did he dare talk to God himself after all this time? His eyes went to the ceiling. The words wouldn't come out, and his life surrounded him in the form of half-packed boxes strewn here and there, as though he never planned on staying. Gripping the announcement for the memorial, a whispery cold breeze sent a shiver through him. He crumpled the paper. Stephen McMillan was dead.

It didn't take long for him to load his car. He'd head back to New York on the day his family said goodbye to Stephen.

But when Henry drove by the church, a quick glance showed him a deserted parking lot. Was the memorial done? Had everybody left within twenty minutes? There should still be people lingering around. Pulling over, he re-read the name of the church in the paper. Yes, he was in the right place. He double checked the date. Maybe they had a quick family gathering and already went home to watch TV and have lunch. An annoying lump in his throat made him swallow. His eyes watered. *No. He didn't need a family,* He laughed to himself, *he had Beckett, right?* Could always come back to his runaway stepfather.

He walked closer to the building and peered into the window. Empty. A piece of paper blew near his feet from the door. He picked it up.

Welcome back, Pastor McMillan! Memorial for Stephen McMillan will be held at one o'clock after today's service.

Huh. The place resembled a ghost town. A large white piece of paper blew across the lot. He walked over and read the faded words. His eyes took in the steeple and bell tower, then the surrounding area. The drive back to New York would be long, and he couldn't wait to blend in with a million other faces. Being lonely in a crowd beat this destitute emptiness. He could at least pretend he had importance and a bright future. But here he couldn't hide behind a made-up reality. He walked to his car, his slow steps crunching on the tiny pieces of gravel littering the lot, and got in the driver's seat, clasping his hands on the steering wheel.

He thought of Beck, and his mom. He'd already tried family.

LVII

Rose stared out the window as Patrick pushed the speed limit toward the Risley farmhouse. She could hardly stand the wait, her plan to not be expectant disappearing like a sun sinking into the ocean. She silently prayed, but proper words, the kind that made coherent sentences, couldn't come. On the radio, a news story began, and she turned it off. Extra noise made her anxiety rise.

"What if it's really him, Patrick? What do we say to him?" She flipped down the mirror and tucked a strand of hair back in its clip. How many times had she imagined this moment but now felt inadequate?

Patrick looked over at her. "You're beautiful."

She smiled, but it wobbled. "I'm nervous. And so are you, the way you're gripping the steering wheel."

He relaxed his hands. "Not many people get to find their lost son after twenty-three years. I'm trying not to expect too much, but Joe's story—"

"He couldn't have been lying this time. I can't imagine sitting there spouting lies. No, it has to be true." She blinked back tears and dabbed at the bottom of her eyes, not wanting to be a mascara mess. What was she doing? Setting herself up for disaster?

Patrick cleared his throat. "Joe looked different. Even being way up by the bell tower."

Rose held her breath when they came around the bend of the country road, filberts on one side and the farmhouse on the other. "There it is." The October sun slanted down in beams across the farmhouse roof. She thought of her dream of Stephen, all grown up. Her whole body shook, just like when he vanished, but this time with anticipation instead of dread.

Patrick pulled into the driveway. Rose twirled her wedding ring around her finger and bit her lower lip. "There's no car."

"He might not be home right now."

She stared out the window, trying to rein in the disappointment—could she take any more? Her hands were clenched and cold despite the warmth of the car. Breathing didn't come naturally at this moment. If she lost him again—she closed her eyes and did not know if she could go on if that were the case, but then her mind flashed with the image of those horrid drawings in the old church, and remembered her resolve to live for those that she had now. She still had a family and wouldn't desert them again.

Patrick glanced at her. "Coming with me to see?"

"Yes." She managed to find strength in her voice. She would step forward and live one minute at a time. They got out of the car. He grasped her hand, sending warmth to it, and they went to the porch and rang the bell. Nothing stirred. They tried knocking and waited.

Patrick peeked into a window.

"What is it?" Rose asked. His posture had drooped and he scanned the road, as if an answer lied along it's gray path.

"Empty. Looks like—" Patrick closed his eyes.

She crowded next to him to peer inside. "He's left? It looks like—like he's moved out." Glancing back at him made her realize how much he had expected and that this wasn't the outcome he'd imagined. Her eyes filled, and she tried to blink the tears away, to recall the strength she had just found a moment ago.

Patrick turned from the house and stared across the road and into the orchard, and she thought how they had come full circle— almost to the exact place Stephen went missing.

She looked in the window again. "We're too late. Why would he leave? If he knew?" He hadn't wanted them. She went back to the porch and pounded on the door. "Maybe he's still here." She

291

rang the doorbell. "Maybe he didn't pack the upstairs, or hasn't fully settled."

"Rose," Patrick took her finger off the bell, and she turned and sank down onto the steps. He edged in beside her, and they sat in silence.

She didn't know what to say. So close. They'd been so close.

LVIII

Henry pressed the accelerator over the speed limit. He couldn't get away fast enough. He wanted to drown out the laughter mocking him. "You want to go forward and you're heading back. Did you think of that?"

Coward. "And just because I am talking to myself doesn't mean I'm crazy—" A deer bolted out in front of him and he slammed on his brakes, swerving to the right just in time for two more to jump to the other side of the road. He slowed down. The familiar orchard came into view. He would salute the farmhouse as he drove by—nice knowing you—then continue on the road leading to Highway 26. But relief didn't come. A vast of emptiness like miles of sand lacking life, settled in his spirit.

You're doing the right thing, he told himself, gripping the steering wheel tighter. He imagined being back in his studio apartment, waking to taxis honking and a clock that ticked faster than the rest of the world.

No mistakes this time. No pirates. No laundromats.

The farmhouse came into view. A car sat in the driveway. He slowed down catching sight of two people sitting on his porch. Patrick and Rose. Doubt tumbled through him. Henry sped up. There was a turnaround in the road just past his house where he could stop and think. He did a U-turn, parking in the pullover meant for people wanting to access the orchard. His heart raced, and he tried to imagine Manhattan again, but the image faltered.

He saw her head on Patrick's shoulder and his arm around her.

Both needed repairs, especially her, but the frame fractured, leaning, and soon would inevitably collapse. No matter how many times he was able to hold someone at arm's length to analyze them as brick, steel, or plaster, it wasn't working this time, and a prick of pain hit his heart. The hurt he buried back when he was thirteen, sitting in the dark on Miss Minnie's steps—a resurrection of feelings that he'd long ago let die.

They had to know. They came to the house. He rested his head on the steering wheel. All the noise in Times Square wouldn't drown out the fact he didn't do what he came here to do. He'd go through life incomplete, partly real, and now that he knew he had a family, he couldn't erase them from his memory and pretend they didn't exist. He'd be no better than Beckett.

Living was about taking chances—wasn't it? If he went back to New York, he'd see Polly, and she would be disappointed to know he was this close and had chosen to drive away. Matter of fact, she'd make him fly all the way back and most likely come with him to make sure he faced the past he didn't remember. Turning off the car he opened the door and stepped out into the sun. He walked—slow with care not to break a creaky branch, or kick loose gravel. He glanced back at his car, each step taking him away from everything he'd ever known and toward an unpredictable future. There'd be no turning back. He froze as though a time portal materialized and entering would make the deed final. Who would he be? Stephen, or Henry? Fear gripped his gut. He hesitated, but then imagined Polly with crossed arms, saying, "Really, Henry? That's the dumbest thing you've ever done." Henry moved forward another few inches, coming closer—he stepped out into the open.

†††

A flutter of chickadees left the lilac bush, making Rose contemplate how life goes on. When something horrific happens, time still doesn't stop. The birds of the air had no care or idea that reality, the one that she only recently accepted and then tried, yet again,

294

had slipped from her fingers. Tears rolled down her face. She told herself that she wouldn't get her hopes up, that truth didn't come from people saying stuff, not until she saw for herself. But here she sat with what seemed to be an equally devastated Patrick holding her. He had finally believed only to be met with emptiness.

"Well find him," Patrick said, staring straight ahead. "It can't be that hard now, can it? Now that we know."

"Or *think* we know," Rose said, her voice edged with something new—unbelief, hopelessness.

Patrick shook his head. "There are too many arrows pointing this way, don't you think?" He laughed, and it held a hint of irony to it. "Here I am trying to convince you. How the tables have turned."

"How much longer can this go on? I think I've finally ran out of steam. Like right now I am sitting here and am just so tired, like there is nothing left in me. What is God's plan for all this anyway? If Henry James is Stephen, why would God make us wait even longer?"

"I'll bring him home," Patrick said. "I'll find him. I should have done more all those years ago."

"You and Howard were doing all you could do. I'm sorry for those awful things I said. They weren't even true, I just wanted to—I don't know—"

He looked down at her face. "I'm sorry too, I didn't handle any of this well. I tried to avoid my mistake, tried to forget—" he dropped his arm and grasped her hand.

Rose lifted her head. Seeing a figure in the distance, like a shadow under the sun, made her squint.

"Patrick," she let go of his hand and stood, her heart pounding.

A tall, thin man emerged from the shade of the trees and stood in the sunlight. Her thoughts flipped to that day in Ireland, seeing Patrick who had come for her—

Her eyes fixed on the man who stopped feet away from them. "Stephen."

Her voice only came out in a cracked almost inaudible sound.

Patrick stood.

Rose took a step, walking, unsure, yet at the same time knowing. Her hopes dashed so many times, her brain had to take a moment to catch up to her heart. The shadows shifted, the glare of the sun moving ever so slightly, and she saw him clear as day. She stopped, drinking in the sight, acknowledging it as truth. The next step she took turned into a run—her feet carrying her across the dry autumn grass, the orchard and highway blurring in her vision, closing the lost decades and redeeming the time. She threw herself in his arms.

"Stephen!"

Henry's arms went around Rose, and something inside of him clicked, like his heart snapped in place. When she pulled away to study him, Patrick, crying and laughing all at once, came and gave him a crazy bear hug, a hug Henry had never experienced in his life, and the rest of him jolted inside. To think he almost went back to his life. They *wanted* him. They hadn't been trying to send him away via news articles about memorials.

A hole had filled Henry's spirit, a long ago memory, just a blur like a scent flooded his senses, and it didn't matter if his whole family was as crazy as a New York night. He needed them, all of them; he shouldn't have waited. He should have ran to their home and said, "I am here. I've come back."

"Welcome home son," Patrick said.

LIX

"Alex, I need you to come." Susan's voice sounded odd, broken and—

"Are you in labor?"

"No, please you have to come. Robert too."

"Why, what's wrong? It's Sunday—"

"I don't care if it's Christmas. Come now. Please. Stan and I are waiting.

Alex hesitated, with a glance at the clock. One minute later and she'd have been on her way to meet Adam at church.

"Please."

"Okay. I'll get Robert if he's home." She heard a click. Susan had already hung up. Had something happened with the baby? Whatever the problem, her sister's voice held an odd panic that Alex couldn't put her finger on.

"I told her not to do too much," Robert rushed around grabbing his keys when she arrived unannounced at his place. "I'm driving."

"No. I'm behind you." This was why Susan called her instead of Robert. "We don't know what's going on. She said she and Stan are waiting. She's not alone."

"Okay." Robert appeared to be dialing down his anxiety with some sort of technique learned in medical school, no doubt. He shook his keys, locking the door on the way out.

Alex drove quicker than normal to appease Robert, soon pulling in the gravel driveway of the ranch-style home.

Susan answered, her hair wild, make-up absent, and had obviously been crying.

"What is it?" Alex asked, closing the door.

"That." She waved her hand over the coffee table where an array of pictures covered the surface.

Robert let out his breath, as though he'd been holding it the whole time. "Pictures? Your emergency is pictures?"

"Not just any pictures," Stan stepped in, leading Susan to her chair nearby. "Susan found this envelope at the laundromat the other day and had forgotten about it until this morning."

"Suzie you need to calm down," Robert said. "The baby."

"The baby is fine. Look! Tell me what you see?"

Alex was already fingering them, her eyes went to the newspaper article. "Wow, I haven't seen the original for awhile. Who—" She looked closer. "This looks like—Henry James?" She held a prom picture.

"He left this at the laundromat. I meant to have Stan take it to him, but forgot. You know, I'm thinking about the baby all the time and ... for some reason, this morning I peeked inside, knowing I should mind my own business, but—"

Robert finally directed his attention at the photos and selected a black and white Polaroid of a young boy and a dog. "Stephen." He scrutinized the picture. "But where is he? What dog is that?" He picked another of a young boy in a boat, this one in color. "Is that Caroline?"

They all flipped through the photos—over and over. Alex made them coffee, and they sat, stunned, shuffling through various parts of a person's life, for well over an hour. Robert held a graduation picture. "It's him. There is no doubt is there?"

"Appears to be pretty clear," Stan said.

"What do we do?" Susan whispered from her chair.

"Where is Dad? I mean, he resigned, right, so ..."

"They asked for him to come back," Alex told him.

"What? I can't keep up with his life anymore," Robert said. "He is at church preaching?" Alex nodded, glancing at her watch. "Well, he's probably done by now."

"Have you eaten?" Robert directed his question at Susan.

"No, I'm too—" she swept her hand over the table.

"Eat, then we will go. We need time to figure this out. After all the next question is why didn't he tell us who he is? We have to remember, even though Henry James is Stephen, we don't know him."

"But today is the memorial," Alex said, and everyone looked up.

"Of course. Finding all this made me forget." Susan stared at the pile.

"We are nearly late. We show up and—I don't know. It could be another resurrection all over again," said Robert.

But when they arrived at the church for the memorial the parking lot was empty, and their parents home was locked.

"Where is everyone?" Robert asked. "The service was supposed to be at our church, right?"

"Yes."

"It's the rapture," Stan said. "We've all been left behind."

"Alex is still here. If anyone wouldn't miss the rapture, it'd be her," Robert checked his watch. "Maybe they had a five-minute service and went to dinner somewhere."

"Doesn't make sense. Memorials often involve food of some sort," Susan said. "If they aren't at church then they should have been here."

"Let's go to the Risley house, and if no one is there we will go home and wait. Who knows? Maybe there is a message on all our phones right now, explaining this," Robert resolved.

They piled back into the car, and a complete silence enveloped them. When they got close to the white farmhouse they craned to look closer.

"They are there," Alex said. "All of them."

"They know." Susan looked like she wanted to leap out of the car. Stan touched her arm.

Alex pulled to the side of the road, a bit behind Henry's car, out of view.

"We can't interrupt this," Robert said from the passenger seat. They watched the reunion

"What I'd give for grandpa's binoculars right now," Alex blinked back tears.

"Okay, Robert. They've done all their hugging and stuff. I think we can make an appearance."

"Suzie, you are so impatient."

"Impatient? Haven't we waited over twenty-three years for this? And did any of us think it would ever happen?"

"Susan has a point." Alex put her car into gear. "I think it's time to introduce ourselves."

Robert looked across the orchard. "We are right where we lost him the first time."

Rows of trees lined up in the bright sunshine, overlooking the valley. The mountains of The Cascade Range twinkled, capped with new snow, glowing under the bright blue sky, as Alex pulled into the Risley Farmhouse driveway to say hello to a brother that she'd only heard about, yet his nonexistence shaped her entire life. All the times she'd slipped into her parent's bedroom when no one would see and stared at the small photo placed on their nightstand and wondered if and when they'd ever see Stephen again.

LX

It was Thanksgiving. A whole month since the family had descended upon Henry and took him back into their fold.

In the McMillan home, Alex leaned into Adam as they danced across the floor. Their relationship had brought an audible sigh of relief throughout the church. Alex shouldn't have ever worried that the parishioners would torment Adam for choosing a McMillan. Matter of fact, they seemed to have gained overly enthusiastic support as the church members constantly hinted at a wedding date.

She closed her eyes as Harry Connick Jr. sang, "It Had to Be You" from the old family record player, the lamps lit for early evening, candlelight flickering on a nearby end table. They swayed, back and forth—words and time and the way they put their lives together orchestrated a song. Harmony to melody, notes falling from heaven, like unseen glitter.

"Lexie." Adam touched her chin and smoothed her hair behind her ear. She lost herself in his brown eyes. They kissed—gentle, like poetry.

Robert walked into the room, making the song in her heart go dim. Adam's sister, Laura bounced in with a shriek of laughter, Breely following. The moment ended. Rose had invited everybody. Peter and Jimmy were shooting their guns at cans into the hillside but would appear soon with demands for more coffee. Stan and Susan had arrived, pies in hand, then ended up leaving for the hospital. Looked like Susan's baby might arrive right on his due date, making Alex wonder if baby Max would be a rule follower like his mama.

Breaking apart from Adam, she glanced over the crowded room. Mom and Lilian must have kicked everyone out of the kitchen. Robert elbowed Henry, who had made a quick dodge from the cooks with a roll in his hand. "I didn't have many home-cooked meals," he explained.

"Sounds very Dickensian," Alex said. "Better milk the special treatment while you can."

"Maybe we should put up some of those pictures Susan found up on the family wall," Robert said.

"Nope. That ship has sailed. Plus, that envelope is tucked in a locked box once I pried it out of all of your hands." Henry sat on the sofa. "I am looking to the future."

"Probably a good idea. How about some chess?" Robert pulled out the board and started setting it up.

"Ha. Robert finally has found someone to reel in for a game," Alex grinned, heading toward the kitchen, as Henry took a chair opposite of his brother.

✝✝✝

When people spoke of the miracle of Filbert Ridge it wasn't only about the return of Stephen, but included a story of love and forgiveness. Once again, Patrick had been wrong about the way things turned out. Stephen, who now went by Henry, had come back. Claudia accused them of being greedy, getting more than their share of personal miracles. "No reason to keep it all to yourselves," she'd say. No one wanted to remind her that not long ago she demanded the miracles stay with Jesus in the New Testament.

Joe, having been given a second chance by the McMillans, turned his heart back to God and was baptized. His tavern regulars filled the front row of the church, waving their *Save Joe* signs as he went down in the water. The Dockerbogger shed its rustic, run-down flair for a new look. Henry drew up some plans and funds came in from friendly town folk along with the McMillans to restore the business, only instead of a drinking establishment it would be a place of fine dining—with a beautiful landscaped garden Mrs. Brooks would create.

Henry tested the waters, coming to church when his spirit grew thirsty. God had called Henry to Filbert Ridge and would call him the rest of the way. Patrick didn't need an out-of-town prophet, or someone pretending to be one, to tell him this truth. He'd wait, trusting that it wouldn't take his missing son another twenty-three years to find his true father—God.

Filbert Ridge saw the dead raised by a child, the lost come back twenty-three years later, and a congregation that once split because of doctrine, now embraced the Holy Spirit. No one rolled down the aisle, but there had been talk of wild laughter at mid-week meetings. Rose wanted to call them mid-week parties, or Holy Raisings, but Patrick told her she ran ahead of herself once again, prophesying the future of the church. They settled for barbeques, small talk, and picnic games. Church had become more than a sermon. Being in communion with God, connecting to Him and each other, just as Rose had predicted. A taste of heaven.

The old building where it all started, and ended, was now a ghost among the trees since the fire—a stray nail, pieces of wood and a half-burnt hymnal scattered over the ground. Anyone who remembered being there back in 1977 could point to the spot where Winston rose from the dead. Green stems pushed through the cracks of pavement among the layers of ash that hadn't blown away. Rose compared it to lighting fire to all their works and seeing what remained.

"Weeds," said Patrick.

"Not weeds, darling. Life. Seeds." Her name fit her more than he thought, because she always had a rose-colored glasses outlook, and no one could say it didn't work for her.

Rose still liked to cook, and right now the kitchen smelled of turkey and the works, and unlike the chaos of the past, all the smells blended together.

Patrick held her in his arms, swaying to the music from the

other room. "Maybe not until you and I are past the pearly gates will the words *party* and *church* go together."

"It will happen. I know you aren't one for parties, Patrick, but don't try to get out of it." She hugged him close. They had moved to an adjoining room where the others sat. "Remember when I hid in the woods from Michael?"

"Of course. I watched you every second, waiting for my opportunity." He smiled at her. "Finding you was well worth it too, those snagged nylons turned me on. A peek of pretty legs, until you threw your skirt over them."

Rose laughed. "Patrick! Sometimes I think it's a pure miracle you became a pastor." She sighed. "Guess we're a lot older now."

"But no less beautiful," he said.

"You're such a sap," she laughed, then fingered his cheek and kissed him. "Together forever."

"Crazy or sane," Patrick said.

Rose glanced toward the sofa where Robert and Henry hovered over the chess board. Patrick followed her gaze. "We got our miracle."

She smiled. "Yes, we did. He is a carbon copy of you."

"We have astounding children. I used to be afraid of them, you know. I'd imagine the future and the mischief they'd cause. They weren't so bad, though."

Rose laughed. "And now you're going to be a grandpa."

He grimaced. "Don't remind me. Baby Max. Yep, sounds like trouble in the making."

"Really, Patrick. Hasn't my optimistic viewpoint rubbed off on you at all?"

He twirled her around and swooped her in a dip with a smile and his face close to hers. "A little," he whispered.

He heard Alex laughing with Henry as the record changed—an Irish tune, scratchy under the needle, blending the past, present, and future—the song Rose played to call them home.

About The Author

Tamelia Aday loves books which led to a life-long desire to write her own. She started writing in grade school and hasn't stopped. She's had various jobs—some disastrous, like banking—but is happiest when at home, putting together stories, and raising her family. When she's not writing or doing things like dishes and laundry, she attempts to knit and crochet. Add some coffee and chocolate to the day, and it's a winner.

She is content making words into sentences and sentences into stories. She likes to weave the power of God into her novels, referring to them as "Miracle Fiction." Also, a fan of mysteries and cats, she is beginning to work on a cozy series.

She has been married to her husband, Jon, for more than thirty-five years, and they have three sons—two adults and the youngest in high school. Their favorite place to visit is the beach. Traveling to some in warmer climes, like Hawaii, is a bonus, but most of the time their getaway is to roam the local coast in Oregon while wearing coats.

Also available from

WordCrafts Press

Angela's Treasures
by Marian Rizzo

Canelands
by Gerry Harlan Brown

Oh to Grace!
by Abby Rosser

The Restless Earth
by Alan Cockrell

End of Summer
by Michael Potts

www.WordCrafts.net